Evolution of an Affair

By Alexandra Adams

Evolution of an Affair

Gabrielle's Awakening

In Honor Bound

Evolution of an Affair

Alexandra Adams

VENUS BOOK CLUB
GARDEN CITY, NEW YORK

This edition published by Venus Book Club of Bookspan,
401 Franklin Avenue, Garden City, New York 11530.

ISBN 0-7394-2857-8

Printed in the United States of America

Acknowledgment

My thanks to Carly Corday, friend and fellow author, for all the help and encouragement she has given me.

Introduction

A self-reliant Westerner chances to meet an intriguing stranger whom she perceives as radiating an aura of danger. Seduced into becoming the mistress of Julian Rakoczy, Mercedes discovers that he intuitively divines her need for the added stimulation which pain inflicted by an expert master confers. Sensing that her lover understands her as no one ever has, cognizant that this sometimes cruel partner reaches depths in her nature hitherto never plumbed, this natural hedonist learns to place an astonishing degree of trust in a man who relentlessly increases the demands he makes while raising her to unprecedented heights of pleasure.

Caught in a dilemma, Julian succumbs to an irresistible urge to bring Mercedes as his guest when he attends the yearly gathering of fellow members of the Order of the Black Lily. Well aware that his cherished companion lacks the training which he knows he ought to have conducted during a rigorous initiation period, he gambles that Mercedes' craving for the pain he inflicts, combined with his conducting an abbreviated introduction to the erotic arts practiced by members of the Order, will suffice to prevent his suffering the disgrace that would ensue should she rebel in the presence of his peers.

Exposed to a culture radically different from her own,

Mercedes adapts with remarkable readiness, even as she battles fears arising from her ignorance of Julian's past. As the week progresses, the woman voluntarily offering herself more and more fully to the master handling a sturdily independent-minded novice with delicate care and surpassing skill, achieves a relationship with her lover that proves to be unique in the annals of the Order.

Chapter One

The gray sky swept the ground, melding with sodden earth to obscure all but what lay an arm's span away. A door opened, and a tall, handsome woman who moved with feline grace stepped onto the porch, and stared into the mist-shrouded environs of her home. Shaking her head in mute negation, she turned, re-entered, and thrust the hardwood barrier back into place, locking herself away from the twelve hundred eighty acres of soggy meadow and rain-drenched sagebrush comprising the outer bailey of her donjon keep. Having doffed her jacket, she hung it on a hook by the entry. Turning, she viewed the kernel of her world: the old, comfortable ranch house she pulled around herself as consciously as she had earlier donned the coat of faded blue denim.

A vivid sense of living apart from humankind struck her. The very solidity of the pleasant interior accentuated the force with which that random thought impinged. Fastening on the idea, Mercedes recalled that she had seen no one, neighbor or relative, for five . . . no, six days now.

That realization in no way equated with loneliness. Well aware that she and her circle of acquaintances possessed few common interests, now that the beloved husband who had lived so completely in the real world of grass, cows, horses and machinery no longer served as the anchor tethering her firmly to the land he had loved, she sighed audibly as his virile, weathered, broad shouldered, larger-than-life image spread itself across her inner vision.

Wondering a trifle uneasily whether her habitual withdrawals into an interior sanctuary—a vantage point from which her physical surroundings seemed to dissolve into a mist as obscuring as that currently crouching outside the door—constituted a danger to her mental stability, the widow pondered that point.

Seconds later, she shrugged. A laugh floated out on the ambient air as she acknowledged that if such were the case, instability ranked as a prime facet of her personality. Adept at fading in and out of an intangible mental realm even while interacting with people she liked, she readily conceded that most if not all of those well-wishers who occasionally dropped in to check on her originally entered her life as friends of her late husband, not of herself.

The mental visualization changed. A well-remembered male figure stood nude, aroused, his eyes raking her every curve, his hands reaching for her. Desire stirred: need as much of the spirit as of the flesh.

Striding into her office, Mercedes yielded to a mental seduction originating deep in her psyche. Seating herself at her computer, she brought up a blank page, and stared unseeing into its flat white opacity. Yearnings never acknowledged except in the privacy of an ardent mind generated new visions.

A whiplash descended forcefully, striking a nude body shivering half in fear, half in perverse anticipation. Writhing in the bonds holding her willing self immobilized, the daydreamer welcomed the primal lust aroused by the thought of the snaking lash. Abdicating all control over mind and flesh alike, she savored her imagined sensations even as her cunt creamed.

Of a sudden, her hands moved. Fingers raced across the keyboard, obedient to an urgent directive issuing from some subliminal command-center in their owner's brain. Words erupted onto the screen, translating into verbal imagery the pictures shimmering in a heightened awareness. The governing intelligence swiftly ordered those most chaotic, ruthlessly paring away excess, slimming, shaping, distilling the essence, purifying it. As the poet's mind achieved a climax fully as satisfying as that produced by sexual intercourse, contractions, pleasurable but minor, made themselves felt at her feminine core.

A soft sigh escaped Mercedes as she read the lines on the screen.

I lie naked on sand,

Face upturned to the leprous moon
Riding the star-branded black vault.

A sheet of hissing surf
Whips away, exposing skin scored with welts.
Salt stings, but scalpels slice the heart bleeding
    from a thousand cuts.

My lover is gone.
Masterless, my flesh shrieks its need,
Its cry ignored by an unfathomable universe.

I remember ecstasy:
Vestigial prick engulfed by voracious mouth,
    flayed by ravening tongue.
His cock completed me.

Amid sea-scoured shells,
I sprawl naked on sand,
Gravid with pain.

A finger touched a switch. The complex sound issuing from the stereo registered on a different plane of the creative faculty concentrating on verbal imagery. That lesser stimulation served at this juncture only to narrow the primary focus.

Again, the woman indulging in unrestrained fantasizing writhed in her bonds as the lash wielded by a lover possessed of her dead husband's body but a stranger's face, targeted bare back, buttocks, thighs, and abdomen. Virtual pain narrowed the dreamer's focus, producing intense, inchoate need.

Changing implements, her master selected a six-thonged whip of thin cords knotted at the ends. Pain racked the defenseless breasts now forming the focus of the tormentor's attention. As agony mounted, the whip-wielder paused to thrust two fingers deep into the cunt awash in its owner's juice. So vividly did the imagination depict the encounter, that moisture oozing from between swollen pussy-lips ran down the thighs the poet unconsciously spread.

No need existed for Mercedes to insert a finger so as to stimulate herself. The scene shimmering in her interior vision accomplished all an invading pseudoprick could have precipitated. A few hard contractions occurred within her feminine depth, but those ceased as the woman longing to experience orgasm failed to achieve physical relief. Seated in her office chair, solitary, still, she fought off a momentary upwelling of despair. A softly uttered sigh of disappointment floated out onto the ambient air.

The tension drained out of the neck and shoulders of the fantasist sturdily resolving to dwell solely on the positive aspect of the experience. Sitting back, she read the lines again, and judged them complete. With the touch of a finger, she saved the creation. The poem etched itself into a creative facility drunk on words, the intoxication subtly enhanced by the flood of melody underscoring the achievement.

Three sharp knocks on the door shattered the intellectual fulfillment almost as sensually satisfying as the physical culmination would have been. Rising, the poet recalled an interruption to another flight of imagination: a distraction that deprived subsequent generations of all but a fragment of a most marvelous vision. Candidly admitting the huge disproportion inherent in the comparison, she yet smiled, glad that her own modest effort escaped annihilation by a well-meaning visitor such as the gentleman from Porlock.

Throwing open the door, Mercedes beheld a total stranger.

Still only half returned to her present time and place, the widow responded to the voice before the face and figure fully registered on her senses. Melodic, full-bodied, the timbre pleased even before the listener grew cognizant of the cultured tone of the words. "I hope I'm not intruding at an inconvenient time," she heard the man courteously aver. "Are you Mercedes Macauley?" The faint emphasis he placed on the word "you" struck her forcibly, generating wry amusement.

"I am," the woman responded, even as she scrutinized the caller. Her habit of withdrawing periodically into an inner sanctuary nowise coincided with any lack of ability to study minutely any phenomenon that intrigued her. Beholding a face more striking than handsome, over which played a smile faintly ironic—as if the owner silently, sardonically chided himself for harboring erroneous expectations—the viewer failed to pinpoint the visitor's age. She nonetheless accurately deduced that this man would never see fifty again.

Intrigued, she studied him. Dark, fine, abundant hair, damp from the mist, swept down over a high forehead to frame a boldly sculpted face penciled at the corners of the eye-sockets and mouth with fine lines. Smooth brows, dark and thick, arched above brown eyes oddly flecked with gold. A thin, wide slash of a mouth drew attention to a strong chin and lean jaw, suggesting toughness to a woman well used to rugged outdoorsmen possessing that attribute in abundance. Yet the smile, which seemed to imply complicity in an amusing facet of their joint experience that went unperceived by others, disarmed her.

"Come in," she invited. "Out of the damp."

The stranger, whose height exceeded her own by only three inches, stepped through the door. Shrewdly judging that the elegantly understated black slacks, black turtleneck, and gray wool sweater gracing his lithe body never saw the interior of any local clothing store, Mercedes sought to place his slight regional accent, but failed to classify him as other than being no native of this or any other western state.

"I'm Julian Rakoczy," the visitor announced, an all but imperceptible hesitation conveying a distinct impression that he identified himself reluctantly. "I bought B. R. Anderson's ranch, a short time ago."

Enlightenment dawned. The name of the out-of-state purchaser had until now failed to surface among the natives disdainfully dismissing the newcomer as one more wealthy sportsman who would undoubtedly look with condescension upon those wresting a living from their land, and would almost certainly prove no neighbor in the local interpretation of that term.

"Rakoczy," the ranchwoman repeated musingly. Smiling with more warmth than she had hitherto displayed, she remarked, "Ancient name, that—aristocratic and honorable. Hungarian, is it not?"

Shock leaped fleetingly into the tawny eyes raking her with

as much interest as she evinced in their owner. "It is," the visitor agreed. "Do you know someone of that name?"

"No. I read history, for pleasure. Francis II Rakoczy, who died almost three hundred years ago, I know to be still revered as a national hero in Hungary. Sit down, Mr. Rakoczy, please. Excuse me, while I turn off my stereo." Waving the guest into a chair, the woman sped into the office, and silenced the riot of sound, unaware that the visitor appreciatively traced the contours of the enticingly round rear rendered the more noticeable by the snug fit of the black knit pants and matching top.

Smiling on the phenomenon she deemed worthy of minute study, the hostess inquired, "Would you care for coffee?"

"If it's no trouble. I far prefer that you call me Julian."

Serenely regarding the purchaser of the neighboring ranch, Mercedes waited for this guest able to pay the exorbitant price demanded by the former owner to state his business. She noted the sinuous grace with which the newcomer moved. The ease with which he settled into the most comfortable of her chairs, and sipped the mug of steaming coffee taken black, devoid of sugar, likewise impinged on her consciousness. No whit insensible to the raw masculine appeal the stranger radiated without seeming to do so knowingly, she waited for him to explain his reason for dropping in at three o'clock on a foggy Friday afternoon.

"I'm told that you hire your sons-in-law to irrigate your land each summer, and harvest your hay," the new resident announced. "Might you arrange for them to do so for me as well, next spring? I'll need only enough hay to feed a pair of saddle horses over the winter. I'll make whatever arrangement you think fair, and pay you for setting it up."

Surprise swiftly metamorphosed into delight at a query that the ranchwoman knew would be welcomed by her family members. "The boys will likely agree to do the work in return for hay and pasture, rather than for cash," came the ready reply. "They'll irrigate, keep your fences in repair, and harvest your hay, for three-quarters of the hay crop and your permission to graze their cows on your meadows from the time they finish stacking the hay until the first deep snowfall. No need exists for you to pay me. I'm happy to oblige both my children and a new neighbor."

"I thank you. I'd willingly agree to the terms in writing, if your sons-in-law demand that I sign a contract."

A slight curl to the lip accompanied by a flash of scorn fleetingly visible in eyes of deep green greeted that offer, but the woman's disapprobation vanished as the import of the qualifier registered. Pushing back an errant strand of long auburn hair untouched as yet by gray, she offered an explanation geared to account for her initial reaction.

"Old-timers in this country routinely clinch deals with each other on nothing more than a handshake and their word," she informed the caller. "They keep that word, even if the market price of hay or calves triples on the day following their making the deal. We realize, however, that outsiders used to modern business practice view that custom as evidence of an incredible naiveté, even though we've grown exceedingly wary of conforming to local custom when dealing with newcomers. I'll draw up a contract on my computer, Mr. Rakoczy."

Well! the visitor silently exclaimed, his admiration for the widow taking a quantum leap. "Julian, Mercedes. You mistook my meaning. I own to being an outsider—expect to be regarded with suspicion until I prove myself trustworthy. I trust *you*, given the regard in which your neighbors hold you. I've no means of proving to you that no man of my lineage ever broke his word, but if you and your family members will take that word, I'll keep it, and gladly dispense with a contract."

Meeting squarely the eyes impaling hers, the woman possessing more than the usual share of feminine intuition judged the claim valid. Even as she wondered whether this man descended from an obscure, illegitimate branch of a family that as far as she knew, had died out, she smiled radiantly.

All trace of that momentary ire erased from face and voice, she held out her hand to the guest shocked to encounter a grip as strong as the average man's. "I've no doubt but that both boys will be delighted, but I'll phone them," she vouchsafed. "Of course, it's my girls who'll move back here in relays to do the irrigating, but I guarantee their competence. Let me pour you another cup."

His intentness unobserved by the woman placing the calls from the adjoining office, Julian studied her aspect minutely. Her voice came clearly through the door she left wide open. While automatically noting that both sets of relatives lived over seventy miles away, the visitor admired the vibrancy of the ageless face visible at this juncture in three-quarters profile. When in repose, that rather elongated oval countenance reminded him forcibly of a painting by Modigliani, but when animated, it mirrored the owner's thoughts with fluid expressiveness.

No less gifted with intuition than the object of his scrutiny, the fascinated beholder divined that appealing verve to constitute evidence of a vitality unquenched by sorrow, loss, or a life lived—by choice? Julian wondered—in isolation. Unerringly judging the widow intelligent, knowing her to possess a sterling reputation for fair dealing and efficient management of her own property, he experienced no qualm at having hired her relatives without ever having met them, despite the variance between her appearance and her reputation.

Sardonically, the man shedding an unwarranted preconception upbraided his alter self for assuming that a middle-aged ranchwoman must of necessity turn out to be a weather-beaten, laconic provincial type notable for a body thickened from child-bearing, and hands roughened by hard labor. Expecting to meet a draft animal, he owned himself most pleasantly surprised to encounter a thoroughbred.

Over new mugs of fragrant coffee the delicate flavor of which further elevated the hostess in the regard of the visitor, the new associates chatted easily, each still taking the measure of the other. Some indefinable aspect of the man's body-language: the tigerish suppleness he displayed with every movement, or the swift but comprehensive survey of his surroundings which the keen observer judged habitual to him, and which perhaps developed as a defense mechanism—against a physical attack? the hostess wondered, intrigued—or the way he sat, only superficially relaxed, seemingly ready to move swiftly if the need arose, set off warning bells. Some subtle quality or combination thereof conferred on the stranger an aura of danger in the mind of the woman whose acquaintance included a number of men who, when direly provoked, were indeed dangerous.

The talk turned to the imminence of Election Day, and touched on a few facets of the national news that Mercedes declared to be given less emphasis by the media than those topics deserved.

Her remark prompted the guest to remark sardonically, "Amazing, how what's reported as news these days blends so seamlessly with the sphere of popular entertainment. Ominous development, I regard that."

"Ahhh . . . you've noticed. The fact that people lead such impoverished mental lives at this point in our history assures that they inevitably turn outwards for stimulation. Too often they strive to experience a vicarious thrill from devouring alarmingly detailed accounts of the tawdry private affairs of celebrities they'd likely loathe if they ever got to know them well."

The musical laugh evoked by that vigorous rejoinder—a response appreciative rather than derisive—warmed the hearer. "I'll agree, a rich mental life's a rarity in this age of gladiator entertainments, slavish devotion to political correctness, and unrelenting promotion of self-esteem as far outweighing academic achievement in social value," the guest drawled, certain now that this woman lived a solitary life by choice rather than necessity.

Fired by conviction, the hostess proceeded to make a solid case for the premise that the United States Government as defined by the Constitution at times seemed doomed to crumble from within, rather than be conquered from without. Two well-read, fiercely independent-minded analysts compared views on what course of events might produce so disastrous a consequence, and what sort of political system might replace that venerable institution the far distant future.

Mercedes regretfully predicted that the Republic would first degenerate into a populist democracy—chaotic rule by the majority, rather than orderly governance by elected representatives—which might well be followed by the imposition of martial law: a step rendered necessary by violence occurring when the gulf yawning between the rich and the poor came to be regarded by the latter as intolerable. "And at that point, a dictatorship would inevitably result," she added glumly.

Julian disagreed. Pointing out that in some important but little-noticed aspects, rule by non-territorial corporation now actually existed world-wide, he contended that a further shift in power to such entities might eventually emasculate territorial governments used to acting as arbiters in international disputes—even the one now classed as the lone superpower.

"Some experts think that a single world government will eventually come into being," he observed thoughtfully. "I doubt that it will, but even if it does, that'll be a passing phase. The bigger an organization gets, the less efficient it becomes. Balkanization will inevitably occur.

"The best that could be hoped for at that juncture would be world-rule by an oligarchy of powerful, intelligent, wealthy individuals bent on preserving a delicate balance between their own interests and the basic needs of the self-disenfranchised hordes they manipulate, rather than with rampant exploitation of human and natural resources by corporate leaders turned world rulers: men whose prime characteristic's greed."

"We Americans seem bent on following an effective prescription for destroying the Republic," the woman agreed bleakly. "We actively deprive many of our youth of a good grounding in world history, familiarity with the classics, scientific literacy, and rigorous training in logical thinking. At the same time, we immerse them unceasingly in a visual wasteland. Those tactics I see as guaranteed to destroy our children's ability to pursue worthy, ambitious, long-term goals with unflagging tenacity," the poet mourned, smiling at this man whose philosophy seemed to parallel hers.

Launched into analyzing in detail the underlying causes of modern educational inadequacy, the conversationalists failed to notice the onset of darkness. Belatedly realizing that four hours just sped away without his noticing their flight, Julian smiled quizzically into the eyes of the woman herself astonished by the lateness of the hour. "Could I persuade you to dine with me?" he coaxed. "At my home? I assure you that my cooking will equal if not surpass that of the chefs in the local restaurants."

A rippling laugh fell on his ears like the upbeat song of the meadowlark. "No great claim to fame, that boast," came the swift retort. "I'll expect better than a mechanically tenderized chicken-fried steak. May I bring something to drink? I've a case of imported lager—a delicious brew. I prefer beer to whisky."

Taken aback, the connoisseur of fine wines nonetheless succeeded in hiding his dismay. "By all means, bring what you enjoy imbibing," he invited, belatedly recalling that on his one and only visit to the local bar in the company of a chance-met neighbor, he had noticed that most of the patrons drank beer. Tartly reminding himself not to hurl accusations of provincialism at people who in some ways struck him as highly sophisticated, he smiled warmly at the woman emerging from her kitchen bearing a basket containing six long-necked bottles separated by the folds of a towel.

"These come in a crate, rather than paper cartons," she informed him blithely.

Good sign, the issuer of the invitation silently conceded.

"If you'd like, I'll also bring exotic greens from my cool greenhouse, and a bottle of my special home-made dressing."

"By all means. But please—let me drive you back with me. I'll bring you home."

Aware that in acceding, she agreed to place herself in a situation that a city-bred woman would likely avoid as potentially dangerous, the self-reliant native shrugged, her faith in her judgment of people far stronger than the momentary doubt assailing her. Having conceived an instant liking for this man, she reminded herself that by purchasing property in the area he placed himself on probation, as it were. He must know that in so small a community his actions will be monitored by a closely knit group of neighborly folk who unfailingly look out for each other, she surmised shrewdly.

Reassured further by her discovery that the cosmopolite clad in designer clothing drove a mud-splattered pickup truck showing signs of hard use despite the lateness of its year, Mercedes banished from mind a momentary pang of fear. Reflecting that the stranger lived only two miles from her home as the crow flies, and that she customarily jogged twice that distance daily simply for exercise, she resolved to walk home if he made threatening advances.

Widow, Julian mused as he drove. Odd coincidence, that. Might this chance meeting with a uniquely appealing woman lead to an outcome as satisfying to me as Michael's union's proving for him? If Fortune recently favored my reclusive brother so lavishly, might that fickle dame heap coals of fire on *my* head, just to keep the scales balanced? My luck ran out early that other time . . . Pain swirled out of a compartment normally kept locked, deep within the man's soul.

Curious to see the house extensively renovated by contractors hired out of the county, the passenger noted when the vehicle drew up before the door that the exterior remained for the most part unchanged. A rather rambling addition conformed to the rustic appearance of the half-century-old, one-storied, steeply roofed house built not of logs, as was customary in this region, but of stone: water-polished rocks which once lay in the bed of the river running through the property. The newer portion blends quite nicely with the old structure, she acknowledged, glad to see the historical integrity of the original preserved.

Discovering the interior to be furnished with an eye for comfort rather than elegance, the guest yet remained half convinced that this cultured, worldly, and perhaps potentially dangerous acquaintance might opt for elaborately formal dining. Relief washed through her when he invited her to sit at the table in the combination dining-kitchen area, and create a salad from the greens picked fresh a short time earlier.

In sprightly fashion, the guest discussed the special challenges posed by gardening at high altitude, while her host set two tender T-bone steaks broiling, and potatoes baking in the microwave. When nothing remained to be done other than keeping a wary eye on the meat, he inquired, "Shall we sample your brew?"

Watching as his guest poured the lager down the side of each tall glass so as to minimize the size of the head, Julian admired her poise. She's so engagingly at ease in the company of a stranger, he reflected contentedly. Raising the glass to his lips, he sipped, delighted to discover the rich, full-bodied taste only achieved through proper aging.

"I'll agree, American beers brewed for mass consumption go from vat to customer in a disgracefully short time, and suffer thereby, taste-wise," Mercedes observed slyly, accurately guessing the man's thought.

Rueful laughter rewarded that sally. "I'm not an habitual beer-drinker," the host admitted. "But this is superb."

Suspecting the stranger's taste in liquor to be as discriminating as was his choice of clothing, Mercedes awarded him points for exhibiting not the slightest hint of condescension. He's a gentleman, she commended him silently as her liking for him deepened.

Buoyed by the brew, delighted by the pleasure deriving from this man's company, Mercedes enjoyed the leisurely dinner, reveling in the flow of talk which continued before a fire newly-built in the handsome, glass-fronted wood stove forming the dominant feature of the living area.

Expounding on certain remarks made by the host regarding the conditions that rendered venturing alone into the local wilderness areas dangerous for those lacking any knowledge of the high country, the guest drew shrewd, insightful, verbal portraits of her great-grandfather, a mountain man who personified the courage, hardiness, and self-reliance of that singular breed; her grandfather, a far-seeing pioneer who was among the first to take up land in the local area; and her father, a stockman/rancher whose generosity, largeness of spirit, and professional competence old-timers still held in reverence twenty years after his death.

Struck by her companion's obvious reluctance to reveal the most fundamental information about himself or his family, Mercedes likewise noted that when the conversation chanced to turn on some point that cried out for an illustration from personal experience, he smoothly evaded offering such.

That observation nowise disturbed her. Entranced at encountering a kindred spirit able and willing to discuss a wealth of topics other than local concerns, the guest deliberately refrained from prying into the host's background. Possessed of an ingrained antipathy to indulging in gossip about friends, relatives, or even figures in the national limelight, she accepted his unaccountable reticence as readily as she did the idiosyncrasies of a few local personalities who most definitely qualified as eccentric.

Driven by need, the visitor excused herself. Upon returning from the small lavatory adjoining the living area, she found that Julian must also have utilized a bathroom. Standing before the fire blazing behind the glass, she basked in the warmth, conscious of the sharp tattoo of wind-driven rain on the roof.

No sound of footstep on plush carpet warned her of her host's reappearance. Two arms slid around her from behind, to draw her against a lithe, hard body. Lips brushed her ear, before deft hands turned her, and strong arms held her in a grip she instinctively resisted. Finding her strength no match for that of the man amusedly assessing her reaction rather than projecting hot lust, she relaxed. Fearlessly prepared to resist with calm, well-reasoned verbal arguments, should that prove necessary, she yet reacted on a subliminal level to close physical contact with a potential lover who projected potent sexual appeal.

Shifting her body slightly, Julian closed his mouth over hers. A questing tongue insinuated itself between lips which opened readily. Held firmly immobile, Mercedes impulsively yielded to the inquisitive organ that teased, rather than intruding aggressively. Without conscious volition, she melted against the man welcoming that sign of surrender.

No swift heightening of his passion resulted. Having freed the lips of the woman regarding him with manifest wariness, he smiled, and drew her against his chest in a gesture more suggestive of protectiveness than any intent to take her by force. "I know," he murmured. "I'm a stranger to you, you're alone with me, and none of your friends know where you are." On beholding the wariness steeply escalate, he added equably, "But you're my guest, Mercedes. I've no wish to worry you, much less to harm you. Will you believe that?"

Unable to pinpoint the subtle cues that prompted her to react as she now did, the woman still held in an embrace from which she knew she could not break loose, frowned in faint perplexity as she replied, "Yes . . . I do."

Shifting his grip, Julian lifted the tall, strong, athletic body of his guest, and carried her to the couch. Settling himself comfortably with his burden still clasped against his chest, the host brushed his lips over the shining fall of ruddy hair spilling in disarray from a part on the left side. Recalling that at no time during the course of the day had this woman projected the slightest hint that she sought or would welcome any sexual advance, he savored relief as he felt her relax against him.

At no time since she opened her door to him, he acknowledged, had any sidelong, arch glance, any drawing close enough to penetrate his personal space, any seductive smile, or words, or touch, conveyed invitation. She had come across until now as purely friendly—wrapped in the armor of a serene self-possession.

Musingly, the guest conceded that neither motherhood nor widowhood had sapped her marvelous vitality, or dulled her intellectual edge. She neither flaunts her shapeliness, nor strives to mute its effect, he commended her silently as his hand idly traced the contour of one round shoulder. She projects not so much innocence, as a pagan attunement with her own sexuality, and mine—an amused, tolerant naturalness on the part of a woman too mature, too appreciative of all the pleasures a man's company offers, to rush with unseemly haste towards the most obvious one.

Even as the man caressing her exulted in his triumph, Mercedes stiffened as a most unsettling possibility rose to smite her. "Julian, are you married?" she inquired evenly.

A light, amused laugh greeted the query. "That's the first personal question you've asked me all day," came the prompt if evasive reply. "Most women, meeting me as you did, would have larded the conversation with probes into my private life, ranging from subtle feelers to frank inquisitions. Any woman except you. But then, a charming ranchwoman who listens to Stravinsky's Rite of Spring as she works at her computer, and shares refreshingly original opinions with a stranger in so beguiling a manner, stands in a class by herself."

No whit sidetracked, Mercedes observed a shade tartly, "You haven't answered my one question."

The amusement fled the striking face. Meeting squarely the almost accusatory glance leveled at him, Julian asserted calmly, "No. I've never been married."

Even as conviction blended with relief in the mind of the observer unable to pinpoint the cues which convinced her that this enigmatic new acquaintance spoke the truth, new fears surfaced. What kind of women taught him what he knows? What sort of life has this man led . . . and where?

As if to prevent utterance of any new protest, Julian shifted both his own body, and that of the guest who now found herself half reclining on the couch, her breast pressed against a chest the muscularity of which grew apparent to her. Grown exquisitely aware of a quickening in her loins, of the faint, musky scent of expensive shaving lotion, of her helplessness against this man's strength, of the darkening of the amber-flecked eyes raking her appraisingly, Mercedes sought to decide how best to react should he attempt to undress her.

To her surprise, no intrusion of a hand impudently sliding beneath her casual knit top occurred. Lips closed once again over hers, teasingly, and then determinedly. The woman responding to the intimate joining of two moist, warm mouths found herself crushed against their owner as he enfolded her tongue, and seemingly sought to ingest it. Swiftly aroused on an elemental level to fierce, hot need, the widow stiffened for a millisecond before flowing against the man holding her, like water pouring over worn, smooth bedrock.

Julian sensed the change. Resolved to take his time, he pulled on the bow of her upper lip with his own, as he freed her tongue. Smiling into green eyes gone soft and unfocused with pleasure, he shifted their owner so that her head rested against his shoulder. His voice an aural caress, he murmured, "I feel as if I've known you for months, instead of hours. We fit each other supremely well, Mercedes. Stay the night, mm? Let me take you to bed?"

Taken sharply aback by that full frontal attack, the recipient of the request struggled against arms that allowed her to sit upright. "Stay the night!" she gasped. "I don't know anything about you—who you are, where you're from, or what you do for a living!" Regaining her aplomb, she moderated her tone, adding as if to clinch her argument, "And I get the distinct feeling that you're as dangerous as you are fascinating!"

A hearty laugh evocative of delight greeted that double-edged assertion. The man's tawny eyes, manifestly amused, watched his guest impatiently thrust an unruly mass of coppery hair back from a flushed face, the better to meet his glance.

"Danger provides spice to any endeavor, wouldn't you agree?" he asked, his tone lightly mocking. Cocking his head, he observed, "I told you who I am. Where I'm from isn't important, and at this point in my life, I don't need to earn a living. But those questions aren't the ones that most concern you, Mercedes. You're weighing the odds of your contracting a sexually transmitted disease, or of my turning brutal—perhaps even murderous. Mm?"

"They're valid concerns," came the level reply.

"I agree. As valid as was your lone personal question. It so happens that I can allay your most fundamental fear, having recently received the results of the physical my need to renew my pilot's license necessitated. I expanded the scope of the exam beyond the requirement, for a reason wholly separate from any anxiety paralleling that nagging right now at you. As for your second worry—you accepted my word once today. I give you my word on this new score: I'll work at giving you pleasure. I'll cause you no bodily harm—now or ever. I keep my word, Mercedes."

That last impassioned assertion carried total conviction. Her mind painfully divided, the woman impulsively thrust her arms around the man who had loosened his grip. "I believe you," she acknowledged bleakly. "But, Julian . . . I . . ."

Grown aware of lips softly caressing her cheek, she heard the man clasping her murmur, "I know. You harbor an intense loyalty to your late husband, even though you're plagued by an equally intense need for the physical intimacy you shared with him. I understand, Mercedes.

"You've handled your loss by filling your days with productive work, and drawn on your ample inner resources to fortify yourself against depression and loneliness. It may be that owing to the richness of your mental life, you've lived too much of each day, lately, out of touch with reality. Why not let me counteract that tendency . . . mmm?"

Shocked to hear that concise statement of the unsettling thought that had impinged on her mind earlier today, the widow marveled at the accuracy of the man's analysis. All at once, her defenses crumbled into the moat. "You need what I can give you," came the melodic, compellingly persuasive voice in her ear. "Say yes, Mercedes." Julian's mouth again closed over hers gently, but insistently. When he freed hers, he urged softly but forcefully, "Say yes."

"Yes," the woman breathed, astonished by the potency of her desire for this stranger. "Yes!"

Borne in strong arms across the spacious expanse of the living room, Mercedes expected to be taken to bed. When her companion set her on her feet in what she saw to be an office, he reached into a cubbyhole in a handsome, old-fashioned desk of light oak, and handed her a folded set of papers.

Jolted out of a befogged state of mental acquiescence to seduction, the guest scanned the page. The line negating her deepest fear leaped out at her. Handing back the document without perusing it further, she whispered regretfully, "I can't prove that I'm no threat to a lover's health."

Lifting her, Julian smiled into distressed green eyes. "You

enjoyed a monogamous relationship for two decades at least, did you not? You were faithful to your husband, eh?"

"Yes! And he to me!"

"Have you taken a lover since his passing?"

"No!"

Intuitively certain that this woman spoke the truth, Julian gained further certainty as he recalled that the neighbor who provided so glowing an account of Mercedes' competence had candidly praised her devotion to her late husband, and her spouse's abiding love for her.

"Infidelity's all too common here," the rancher had commented sadly. "In so small a community, it's almost impossible to keep an affair secret. But then, the opposite is also true: when a couple models a truly happy marriage, their success gets widely noticed. We all felt a dreadful sense of loss that paralleled Mercedes' grief."

The combination of intuitive conclusion and that recollection of the conversation combined to overcome a deeply ingrained sense of self-protection. "I believe you," Julian stated firmly. "I see no cause for worry—or for any need to employ onerous preventative measures . . . mmm?" Even as he spoke, he strode purposefully into the bedroom adjoining the office.

Standing facing him a few seconds later in a warm, spacious chamber featuring a king-sized bed lacking any coverlet—a bed made up only with a creamy silken contoured sheet and an array of pillows—Mercedes observed that the bedframe featured an ornate headboard but no footboard, unless one considered the two handsome matching chests placed with their backs against the mattress, and a two-foot-wide space between them, to function as such. Tearing her eyes from the matching bureau, nightstands and chiffonier, she noted despite the haze of emotion clouding her awareness, the deftness with which her lover undressed her.

Heart hammering, loins quivering with need, the widow experienced a familiar, poignant anxiety: fear she knew this stranger would not sense, as shrewdly discerning as he was. When she stood naked, aroused, her hair thrust back from a face mirroring inner turmoil which Julian intuitively divined nowise arose from embarrassment at finding her nude figure raked by appraising eyes, she set about undressing him, displaying a facility for the chore which matched his.

When he, too, stood naked, his ample endowment erect, hard, Mercedes cast no glance in that direction. Eyes riveted to his torso, she stared wide-eyed at two prominent scars: a long gash disfiguring his left side, and a puckered round indentation in his left forearm which she saw to be matched with a corresponding wider depression on the opposite side of the limb. Gunshot? she conjectured in disbelief. Or just some nasty puncture wound?

Unable to decide, she wrenched her eyes from his arm to his face. She saw that he stood tautly still, head cocked, awaiting her reaction. Disdaining to pry, she silently slipped her arms around him, turning up a countenance on which he read potent desire inextricably blended with trust.

As moved by her reaction as he was aroused, he swept her up, laid her atop the bed, and disposed her body so that she lay with her back arched over his disfigured left forearm. His mouth closed over her right nipple. From that moment, all uneasiness regarding the scars fled her consciousness.

Exquisitely aware now of the rigidity of the cock pressing against her thigh, the woman whose nipples a moist tongue swiftly teased into growing rock-hard, marveled that her patently aroused partner managed to convey so comforting a sense of being in no hurry. Sliding lower, he closed his mouth over her quivering clit even as his fingers explored the cunt dribbling moisture. Held now by an arm thrust under the small of her back, unable to reach the turgid tool she would have caressed if that were possible, she gave herself up to pleasure so intense that it bordered pain.

Circling the tiny tip of her engorged organ of pleasure, her lover's tongue produced indescribably erotic sensations in that exquisitely sensitive site. Closing his mouth over her erect little ornament, he sucked as if to tear the tiny shaft loose from its root. Without conscious volition, Mercedes moaned, even as long fingers probed her slippery inner space, exploring, massaging, stimulating a spot extraordinarily responsive.

Welcoming the quickening, the gathering that she had feared might fail to materialize, she actively sought to yield to it. To her dismay, the mere act of dwelling on her wish aborted her nascent rise towards fulfillment. Frustrated, she ceased arching against the hands and mouth conferring such a wealth of pleasure.

Anger flared: rage at uncaring fate, not so much for denying her relief twice in so short a time, but for rendering her so prone to failure in that regard. Resignedly, she awaited her partner's entry, resolved to offer him what recompense for his efforts that she could.

Lifting his head, Julian withdrew his fingers. In a fluid movement, he changed position so as to lie beside the woman whose chest still heaved. Thrusting an arm under her shoulders, he lifted her, and smiled into eyes striving to project serenity while unable to conceal a flash of disappointment. "Hot and wet, you are," he murmured. "But nervous—a bit ambivalent, still, about consenting to let me take you to bed. You feel obligated to confer pleasure on me, and I've not let you. You're worried that I'll grow impatient, and that's caused a complication."

Closing his mouth over that from which a gasp of astonishment issued, Julian again engaged in intimate, erotic oral stimulation, until the body clasped in his arms congealed against him. When at length he desisted, he commanded, "You're to put everything out of your mind but the pleasure I offer you—hear? Time is of no concern. You're not to think of my need—only of your own. Mine will be satisfied when yours is."

Amazement transmuted into nascent hope. His patience seeming to the woman inexhaustible, the stranger resumed his prior manipulations. Again, he produced the shivers and quivers signifying the onset of culmination. Ceasing his efforts, he lifted his supine partner so that her buttocks reposed on the foot of the bed, and the legs he spread wide each rested on the cushioned top of a chest.

Standing between his partner's outthrust thighs, Julian positioned two plump pillows beneath the ass-cheeks he raised. Standing, he slid his rigid prick deeply within the cunt awash in wetness. His thrusts, slow, rhythmic, sensuous, evoked exquisite sensations in the feminine depth of the woman unflustered by any sense that her lover's climax grew imminent. Bliss mingled with relief as her consciousness narrowed to focus solely on her own pleasure.

At length, her lover desisted. Having withdrawn, he again stimulated his partner's stiff clit with a delicate, evocative touch of a finger. Soft exhalations of breath accompanied little incoherent cries that slid past parted lips to tickle Julian's ears.

Even as desire surged in the object of his attentions, the adept at erotic art conveyed no urgency: no hot, fierce need to ejaculate. Observing his partner's nut-hard nipples, her rapt expression, her rapid respirations, he grew satisfied that she lay close to climax. Driving into her with determined force, he worked her upraised loins by employing subtle variations in the direction in which he thrust within her, delighted to find that she knew how to squeeze her sphincter muscles to confer a most delicious if illusory sense of sucking his tool deeper within her cunt.

Her consciousness bedimmed, Mercedes lost all cognizance of the passage of time. The unwonted posture—uprearing ass and outthrust thighs accompanied by full exposure of her bare breasts to the eyes of the man driving his rock-hard cock into her—produced a voluntary abdication of all control over her body. Mental defenses unconsciously, habitually maintained, suddenly disintegrated.

In a moment of ecstasy surreally stretched into stasis, the woman joyfully surrendering her will to this virile, wondrously skilled lover grew dimly aware of the accelerated pulse-rate manifesting itself in a sustained, hard throbbing deep in her throat. The heat flooding her loins spread as her inner space constricted around the rigid organ relentlessly targeting the nerve centers triggering a shuddering ascent to fulfillment. A wild spate of contractions accompanied by a white heat of release drove a low, gasping cry out of the woman patently astonished by the outcome of the encounter.

That sound coincided with the groan wrenched from the lover relaxing the rigorous control he had maintained over his steadily mounting need to achieve culmination. A final hard thrust, followed by prolonged pressure of a powerful pelvis against that of the woman he penetrated, accompanied the staccato spurting of his juice.

For a few moments he savored his rush, before lifting Mercedes bodily, and disposing her limp body so that her legs now rested on the mattress. Himself in the throes of near-ecstasy, Julian collapsed on her slack frame, and pillowed his cheek on her breast.

Unaware of anything but her own bliss, Mercedes lay still,

half in trance. She remained so when her partner eventually slid off her, stirring no whit when he gathered her into his arms, and held her as she slid into sleep.

Chapter Two

Mercedes woke at six: the hour at which she normally rose. Momentarily confused as to where she lay, she sat up. Glancing down, she beheld the bare back of the other occupant of the bed.

Judging that Julian still slept, she reviewed her ascent to rapturous fulfillment on the prior night. The oval face half hidden beneath the disordered fall of ruddy hair mirrored wonder, gratitude, and more than a trace of sadness. Beneath her, the silken sheet reflected back only a fraction of the warmth of her body, but no chill set her shivering. The air of the room she noted to be considerably above the temperature she maintained in her own home.

Gusty winds lashed the stand of tall pines just beyond Julian's yard-fence, provoking low moans of protest. No rain rode the gale, but opaque gray clouds still veiled the sun.

Driven by need, the guest rose, striving not to disturb her companion. Her bare feet made no sound on the plush carpeting as she strode towards the bathroom, but Julian rolled over, and watched as she soundlessly slid the door shut.

Rearing up, he thrust a hand into the drawer of the nightstand, and withdrew a small object: one of an array of unique devices engineered by his brother, and bestowed on him as gifts. That item he pressed against his upper leg, behind the knee. Upon causing it to adhere by exerting the lightest of touches on its surface, he reclined facing his partner's side of the bed, smiling knowingly to himself as he awaited her return.

Taking pains not to disturb the man she assumed to be asleep, the guest slipped in beside him, only to find herself swiftly drawn against his chest. "Did I wake you?" she inquired apologetically.

"No. You're a passionate woman, Mercedes," he murmured, smiling into eyes that registered a sudden accession of embarrassment.

"You can say that . . . when it took all your amazing skill, and your even more astonishing patience, to make me come?" she breathed, flushing. Unsure for a few painful seconds whether or not he indulged in sarcasm, she unconsciously let her voice take on an edge.

Arms tightened around her; lips brushed her cheek. "When you fail to come, do you customarily blame yourself for lacking passion? Or do you fault your partner for lacking both skill *and* patience?" That query, wholly devoid of any sardonic nuance, instead registered as infinitely gentle.

Her lover's tone breached the woman's guard, annihilating her defensiveness. Unused to subterfuge, she responded with candid honesty. "Before I started dating the man who became my husband, I had two . . . affairs . . . in succession. Neither partner ever made me come. I figured I must lack some essential quality such as . . . sufficient passion.

"When I finally did fall deeply, hopelessly in love . . . I thought, it'll happen now. And it did . . . but only because my late husband's patience equaled yours. Over the years, he worked at increasing his skill. He made me come three times out of four, or perhaps more. Our love grew all the stronger for his needing that patience right up to the end. I learned to give him intense pleasure—worked at that, as he did to give me fulfillment."

Sensing that his question sparked emotional upset in the bereaved widow, Julian gentled her with voice and hands, until he felt the tension drain out of her. Holding her close, he murmured, "Any woman but you, finding herself embarrassed by a difficulty she perceived as posing a trial to my patience, would have put on an act: pretended to come."

"You'd have seen through any attempt of mine to fake orgasm," his partner stated flatly.

"Exactly so," came the ready assent. "And I'd have been sorely disappointed in you. But your honesty's exceeded only by your admirable ability to think for yourself, rather than conform to conventional proprieties."

Thank goodness I didn't pretend! Mercedes silently expostulated, recalling that the insidious notion had crossed her mind.

With sensuous motions of a hand, her bedmate stroked her tousled auburn hair. Tucking the lock obscuring one eye over an ear, he broke the silence into which his partner withdrew. "Your problem doesn't originate in any lack of passion," he observed in a tone almost clinical in its detachment. "You've an abnormally curved vagina. That anatomical aberrance might never have mattered, if your initial lover possessed the least skill.

"However, if an inept first partner mounted you in the missionary position after offering only brief, perfunctory foreplay—if he sought to arouse you solely by thrusting into you—the head of his cock would fail to stimulate your most responsive places. If he'd never learned to control the course of his own passion, he'd shoot his load before you grew even minimally aroused. Very likely he'd compound his offense by stopping at that point—rolling over and falling asleep, leaving you sorely frustrated."

Damned if he didn't! came the bitter but silent assent.

"Climax for a woman occurs as much in her mind as in her body, Mercedes. Making a virgin come tests a man's skill to the utmost. If he succeeds, he does so because his efforts enable her to achieve mental surrender. Each subsequent ascent to bliss reinforces the fragile connections between mind and loins forged on the first occasion, and renders her next ascent to rapture swifter, and more certain.

"Your experience reinforced a negative effect, thereby programming you to expect failure. Cruel twist of fate, that, given that you're hotly passionate. Because your husband loved you, he exercised patience. Instinctively, he paralleled what I did last night—stimulated you so intensely and so relentlessly that your sensory system overrode your faulty mental circuitry."

Astounded by that concise analysis which she intuitively recognized to be the stark truth, the widow sought to order the tumultuous emotions which acceptance of that premise engendered. Gratitude contended with burgeoning fear as she tried to divine how any man who candidly admitted that he had never married, could possibly have learned what this man knew.

Wondering distractedly whether Julian might be some sort of medical therapist, Mercedes recalled the sinister scars, the aura of danger he generated, and the astonishing ease with which he had seduced her. Rejecting that theory, she contemplated other, direly upsetting possibilities, shuddering even as she yielded to the arms crushing her against a muscular chest lightly thatched with fine brown hair. Desire surged through her as a moist mouth closed over hers. Hot lust warred with the uneasiness nagging at her consciousness.

Held pressed to the hard torso of the lover lying slightly on his left side, a scarred, strong arm thrust under her back in such wise as to arch her upper body over its bulk, Mercedes welcomed the teasing touch of a finger on a nipple, despite the sharp misgivings plaguing her, and despite her acute awareness that the man's left hand gripped her upper left arm, effectually immobilizing her.

A light, amused laugh sounded in her ear. "Does it really matter how I learned what I know?" her lover drawled, setting the hair on the nape of her neck stirring.

He reads my mind! his partner marveled even as fear blended with deliciously erotic sensation. The finger vibrated the pink nubbin gone rock-hard, sending waves of quivers radiating outward from loins grown moist.

In the awareness of the woman struggling to regain her inner harmony, the musical voice assumed an hypnotic quality: cajoling, beguiling, irresistibly compelling. "Let me bypass your faulty mental circuitry by employing an unconventional erotic technique," its owner coaxed. "Let me teach you that pain constitutes a stronger stimulus than pleasure. You'll find that pain delivered in close proximity to your clit will enhance and intensify the pleasure I give you, to a degree that will swiftly and surely override your negative programming."

The body clasped in an unbreakable hold stiffened. "You're a sadist?" the woman gasped as her blood chilled. Violent yet satisfying images long cherished by a daydreamer possessed of a vivid imagination clashed forcibly with memories of ghastly assaults given prominence in the national news. Confronted with the possibility that fantasy might at this juncture merge with dangerous reality whether or not she wished for that to occur, she shivered palpably.

The melodic voice soothed even as the hand tightened a grip already viselike. "In a sense," came the lightly stated, profoundly disturbing admission. "As was true of de Sade, I grow deeply, swiftly aroused when inflicting pain on a partner. But unlike the marquis, I obey an even greater compulsion to confer pleasure. When the proper balance occurs between the two sensations, a woman rises to a height of rapture far greater than any achieved through pleasure alone. Let me demonstrate, mmmm?"

Mastering an urge to wage a struggle she knew would prove futile, the guest chided scathingly, fearlessly, "You passed your word that you'd not cause me bodily harm, and I trusted that word!"

"You're making an erroneous judgment at this juncture, Mercedes. I can divorce pain from injury—confer only the former, while totally avoiding the latter consequence. Observe, now." Detaching the object earlier affixed to his leg, Julian held it up for inspection, inwardly commending the admirable self-command of the woman he sought to persuade to submit to a technique he feared she might well regard as too outrageous even to contemplate.

Wary green eyes riveted themselves to a flat, circular golden wafer polished to high brilliance but for two rough spots on the slightly convex surface. The innocuous-seeming object approximated a silver dollar in diameter. "This device clings to skin by electrostatic attraction," the mesmeric voice purred. "It stimulates the nerve-endings below the skin, creating impulses which your mind interprets as pain. It causes no injury, no scarring, no harm whatsoever. Because the nerves thus excited more often transmit pleasurable impulses than painful ones, the sensation includes a most intriguing pleasurable component—an effect less pronounced than the pain, but significant. So. It's designed for a specific site . . . there, now."

A practiced finger touched one of the rough spots before

deftly centering the metallic wafer on the mound of the woman whose body instantly went rigid. The device, warm from contact with the wielder's body, adhered to flesh overlain with ruddy, crisply curling hair, exactly as if it had grown there.

No pain ensued. "It . . . doesn't hurt," the woman gasped as astonishment muted incipient outrage at what she perceived as her partner's intent to force her to comply with his demand.

"Not yet. I haven't activated it. I won't, unless you consent. Now relax; master your fear. I keep my word, and you're still my guest."

Relief at that assertion blended with shame at having leaped to an invalid conclusion. Vivid fantasies shimmered on the fringes of the mind struggling to handle a situation wholly unprecedented in its experience.

Sensing irresolution, Julian pressed his case. "I offer you a potent remedy for a problem you regard as admitting of no remediation," he pointed out. "If you reject my offer, I'll take you home—unharmed, and possessed of my sincere liking. But if your daring combines with your curiosity to outweigh your fear, you'll consent, and thereby achieve a more intense culmination than you believe possible. So. Say yes, Mercedes. Mmm? Say yes."

Mollified, the closet masochist debated fiercely with her alter ego. Why not? He can give you what you've dreamed of experiencing! He swore he'd not cause you bodily harm! Surely he won't. But what if the pain grows unbearable? This man's dangerous! A stranger! But I want . . . So badly . . . Just once . . .

"Say yes." Even as he cajoled, Julian felt the tension seep out of the shapely tall body the trimness of which testified so convincingly to its owner's determination to stay in commendable physical shape. Sensing the onset of surrender, he wondered why capitulation occurred so swiftly. Prepared to spend a wealth of time testing the efficacy of his power of persuasion, he heard a soft expulsion of breath, and felt the body he held immobile go limp.

His lover turned her head, to rest it more comfortably against the hollow of his shoulder. "Yes," she whispered.

Roused to hot lust, Julian touched a finger to one of the rough spots on the wafer. He felt the woman he held stiffen for an ephemeral span of time, and then melt once again into pliancy. Her head still lolled against his shoulder; the body arched over his arm grew slack. The nipples of his companion's outthrust breasts, erect from his teasing, went rock-hard; her breath came in soft, rapid respirations. Relaxing his grip, he shifted his own body slightly, and toyed with the clit that swelled even as he touched it.

Marveling at the swiftness of the novice's acquiescence, he laid her flat, watching in delight as she threw her arms back over her head, and gave herself up to assessment of the dual, intense sensations. Well aware of the potency of the pain generated by the device, he raked her quivering loins with knowing eyes, even as he slid two fingers deep within the cunt he discovered to be awash in moisture. His eyes half-lidded, speculative, hot with passion, he worked her now fully engorged organ of pleasure with moist fingers of his left hand, while thrusting deeply inside her slippery passage with those of his right.

Pain throbbed within the loins thus expertly stimulated, radiating outwards even as an indescribable attendant pleasure combined with that more gripping sensation. A melodic, diabolically hypnotic voice issued commands irresistibly compelling. "Explore the pain, Mercedes. Investigate it; enjoy it. Let it dominate you—force surrender. Ahhh . . . you like that, eh? Spread your legs wider. So. Pain's a potent inducement to surrender. Lavish, your juice. Now then."

Lifted in corded arms, her focus narrowed to exclude all sensory input other than the indescribably erotic sensations centering in her groin, Mercedes grew only vaguely conscious that her lover again disposed her body so that her legs extended out over the foot of the bed, to rest on the two cushioned chests occupying positions at both sides of the foot. Julian now stood between her legs, working her stiff little shaft with the fingers of one hand as he rubbed the head of his rigid cock between the two tender flaps of flesh guarding her dripping orifice. Moans broke from between parted lips. Her voice hoarse with passion, his partner pleaded, "Please . . . fuck me. Shoot me a big, hot load!"

Driving into her moisture-bedewed cunt while consumed by fierce desire, the master of erotic art yet maintained rigorous control over his need to ejaculate. Thrusting both hands beneath his partner's ass-cheeks, he lifted her, and shifted the direction of his thrusts.

Unaware that she cried out, Mercedes welcomed the loosening in her loins. Abdicating all control over her musculature, she entertained no fear whatsoever that this expert lover might grow impatient, much less eject his juice before he gave her fulfillment. The last lingering doubt that she would fail to achieve orgasm vanished as she gave herself up to the pleasure blotting out all other cognizance. Her inner space contracted madly around the invading prick, even as the instigator of her triumph relaxed his perfect hold on himself, to climax simultaneously with her.

At the mere touch of a finger on the golden disc, the pain died away as if it had never been.

Satiated, drained, floating in some nebulous realm of the mind, Mercedes drifted aimlessly, only dimly aware of being lifted, shifted, held against warm, hard flesh.

His pride inflated, his lust quenched, Julian savored the ebbing wash of pleasure even as he weighed the tempting but flagrantly dangerous option opened by this utterly desirable woman's precipitate surrender to an appeal which he half expected to generate icy anger, and an imperious demand to be taken home. Idly, absently, he caressed her, smiling wryly as he acknowledged the seductive appeal of that option to outweigh the danger.

Musingly, he reviewed her reactions. Of a sudden, enlightenment dawned: understanding that further intensified his yearning to run a formidable risk. An upwelling of affection, of admiration, accompanied the flash of insight just gained.

When at last his partner stirred, he cocked his head. Impaling her with a penetrating glance, he spoke, his words couched as a statement rather than a question. "You *knew* that pain in that site would arouse you to primal lust, didn't you?"

Flushing, the woman averted her eyes, and focused on a point beyond the interrogator's head.

"Answer me," her lover demanded.

"Yes." Patently embarrassed, Mercedes felt her cheeks burn.

Drawing her closer, Julian tipped her chin up, forcing her to meet his glance. "Did your husband employ a similar technique?"

"No! Never! No man ever . . ." Scarlet with shame, and annoyed at the inquisition, especially in the light of this man's refusal to reveal the most innocuous information about himself, Mercedes stiffened. Thrusting out her chin, she made no attempt to hide her pique.

"Ahhh . . . I see." Tawny eyes smiled amusedly into hers. "You've indulged in erotic fantasies featuring a demanding master—fantasies the more effective for the vividness of your imagination. Perhaps you've even inflicted pain on yourself . . . eh, little voluptuary?"

That outrageous inference, accompanied by a wicked smile, produced hot anger that swiftly drowned in a floodtide of shame. Drawn against a bare, muscled chest, Mercedes buried her face in her bedmate's shoulder, for lack of any other place in which to hide the evidence that his final shot struck dead on the mark.

Conquering an all but irresistible urge to laugh, Julian instead soothed, caressed, reassured. "No need to wallow in guilt," he asserted gently. "Or shame, or embarrassment. Not with me, Mercedes. Never with me." His hand stroked her back; his lips brushed the top of her head. "My remedy worked to perfection, did it not? Mmmm?"

"Yes," came the muffled admission seemingly wrenched out of the woman still in the throes of acute embarrassment.

Patiently, Julian caressed her, soothing her with hands and voice. "I see that even so resolute a freethinker fears to acknowledge breaking at least one of the many repressive prohibitions ingrained in our national psyche by a puritanical streak in our culture," he observed, smiling into the eyes gamely forcing themselves to meet his. "Rise above those restrictions, Mercedes. I admire your serene acceptance of your sensual nature—your lack of prudish inhibitions."

Sensing that he candidly spoke his thought, the woman slowly regaining her accustomed self-possession nestled against him, comforted by the observation which by rights should have deepened the insidious doubts thrust, for now, beneath the plane of her consciousness. When her lover kissed her, his salute more affectionate than passionate, he reveled in her swift, eager response.

At length, he decreed that they bathe. Rising, he took his

guest's hand, and drew her to her feet. When she reached for the clothing he had laid on a chair on the prior night, he shook his head. Lifting her, he bore her to the bathroom, where he stood her, facing him, in the egregiously oversized tub. Removing the detachable showerhead, he enveloped her in mist. Soaping his hands, he proceeded to offer a most intimate, sensuous scrub.

"Do that for me," he commanded when he finished.

Running lathered hands over his hard, lithe body, Mercedes reflected that no prudish inhibitions troubled this unabashed sensualist who saw so deeply, so accurately, into the darkest, most closely guarded depths of her nature: aspects of her mental life which no one had ever plumbed. Wondering once again how he learned what he knew, she yet found herself ever more deeply fascinated by him. A shade guiltily, she acknowledged that her fear of him lay quiescent at this juncture.

Upon emerging, briskly toweled dry, into the bedroom, Mercedes held the clean sheet and pillowslips her lover thrust into her hands. Briskly, she made the bed he stripped, while he tossed the soiled linen into a hamper in the bathroom. When she again reached for her clothing, he intercepted her. "I'd as leave enjoy the sight of you naked, over breakfast," he informed her provocatively, "but I'll compromise. Here, wear this."

Reaching into a drawer, he withdrew two identical, featherweight robes of black silk. Handing her one, he donned the other. Having tied the sash—the only fastening—he raked the shapely body of his guest with appraising eyes. Wide sleeves fell to her elbows; the collarless neckline bared the column of her throat. The thin, opaque fabric molded itself to the soft, rather elongated contours of breasts no longer as high and firm as a girl's. The robe fell to mid-calf on her, but reached only slightly below the knee on him.

Smiling, he ushered her into the dining area, and proceeded to demonstrate an admirable ability to whip up a tasty omelet.

Gazing out through the starkly non-curtained south-facing window offering the diners a view of sere brown meadows dappled here and there by sunshine struggling to penetrate thinning clouds, Mercedes savored the same comforting awareness of privacy that her own dwelling conferred. A long, gently sloping expanse of meadowland separated the public road from the clumps of pine trees that shielded both houses from viewers driving by.

Turning to regard her host, she sensed in him no urgency, no purposeful haste, preparatory to taking her home. While he brewed fresh coffee, he let her rinse the dinnerware that he stacked in the dishwasher.

That done, he bore the pot and two mugs to the coffee table in the living area, and built a fire in the wood stove. When it blazed comfortingly, he settled himself on the couch. Tapping the cushion next to him, he bade his guest sit. After handing her a steaming mug, he slipped an arm around her.

Reflecting that this enigmatic stranger possessed of sadistic impulses that he indulged with debonair grace seemed to enjoy her company fully as much as he did satisfying his singular tastes, Mercedes acknowledged that she felt amazingly at ease with him. When he commended her for being in shape, she confided forthrightly, "I don't work frantically at staying fit. I ride my mare, take long, brisk walks, swim in the river, ski cross-country in the winter, and do considerable lifting and carrying. But I'm no fitness-fanatic."

"Mm. You don't mind swimming in snow-melt?"

"Invigorating, I find a plunge into my favorite swimming-hole. But I don't stay in for hours!"

The conversation passed to a discussion of the relative merits of counting calories as opposed to vigorous aerobic exercise as a means of shedding unwanted pounds.

An hour sped away. Unhurriedly, the host rose, and pulled his guest to her feet. "Perhaps you'd like to indulge in a brisk swim indoors?" he queried.

"You built an indoor pool?" came the delighted reply. "I would indeed!"

Finding herself guided into the new addition, Mercedes advanced down a hall featuring skylights: a passage that would have been dimly lit otherwise. Intrigued, she entered the door on the south side, which her host opened. The long, narrow chamber, softly illuminated by the sunshine filtering through translucent panels along the south wall, featured a pool approximately ten feet wide and thirty long, obviously deep enough for diving.

"I know. It seems an oversized bathtub," the host remarked, smiling into eyes concealing all but a faint trace of disappointment. "But it possesses a unique feature. When you dive in from this narrow end, your body breaks light-beams of the sort that open supermarket doors. That causes the water to start flowing towards you. The flow-rate adjusts to your swimming speed—matches it, thereby preventing you from reaching the far end.

"You remain held at midpoint, which you can see to be marked by that fluorescent red vertical stripe on the wall. If you slacken your pace, the current readjusts, and if you cease moving, it ceases flowing. You can work out at whatever level of effort you care to expend."

The expressive face of the guest lit with astonishment. "How absolutely marvelous! May I . . . ?"

"Of course—but you'll swim nude, as nature intended." Mischief danced in the tawny eyes of the host.

A rueful laugh greeted that qualifier. Shedding the robe, the woman executed a clean, graceful dive, slicing through the interface between air and water to surface just past the halfway point. Flawlessly, she propelled her body forward in the classic Australian crawl. The water, clear and calm when she plunged in, now flowed with extraordinary force towards her, bearing her backwards until her laboring body maintained a position midway between the narrow ends of the pool.

Intrigued, she increased her speed. Taxing herself to the limit, she turned her head so as to breathe, taking a breath only once for every four forward strokes of her right arm. To her delight, the red stripe moved not one whit. Slackening her pace a trifle, she observed no change in her position. Marveling at the sense of freedom generated by her certainty that she could not smash her head into the wall only two body-lengths ahead of her, she swam with long, powerful, uniform strokes of her arms, and vigorous kicks of her legs, breathing once every two strokes.

Observing the swimmer's unflagging effort and expert style, the host silently applauded her speed, and admired her form. Unconsciously, he furrowed his brow as he wondered whether she had competed at some earlier point in her life, or whether this exhibition merely showcased a natural athleticism.

Seating himself on a long, low, cushioned bench set parallel to the length of the pool, he timed her workout, marveling at her stamina. Well, why would you expect a woman used to strenuous outdoor pursuits to lack muscle tone, or staying power—even if she's in her late forties or early fifties? he chided his alter ego, smiling sardonically. I'll wager she sits a horse with all the supple grace of a painted Sioux warrior.

When at length the guest not so much tired as worried that

she might be perceived as selfishly enjoying herself at the expense of a host gracious enough to wait patiently while she worked out, the athlete ceased doing the crawl. Switching to a slow breaststroke barely sufficient to keep her moving ahead, she caused the current instantly to moderate so as to match her drastically reduced speed.

When she felt for the bottom with her feet, she discovered the water to be over her head. Turning, she employed a slow sidestroke as she proceeded to the end from which she had earlier dived in. The stream-flow ceased when she reached the side of the pool.

Having enjoyed his view of the nude bather as she mounted the ladder, and stepped out, dripping, on the deck, Julian removed an oversized towel from a cabinet next to the bench. With vigorous movements, he dried his lover, and rubbed the long hair darkened in hue by the wetness. Spying no telltale gray roots, he judged the auburn color natural. "Slip into the robe, so you don't take a chill," he urged. "I'll blow your hair dry before the fire."

Seated on the couch, reveling in the warmth of the blaze produced by the host's stirring up the coals and adding two more logs, Mercedes enjoyed the pampering. "Mmmmm . . . what luxury," she purred, as the hot air stimulated her scalp. "Pure hedonism."

Laughing, her lover finished the task. Dropping to one knee, he thrust arms beneath her. Lifting her bodily, he seated himself while holding her against his chest. A hand deftly undid the belt, parted the robe, and cupped a breast.

A trifle fatigued by the strenuous swim, the object of those attentions leaned her head against her companion's shoulder, and congealed against him.

Neither spoke for a time. At length, Julian observed ruminatively, "I should take you home—return you to the retreat so well fitted to allow you to pass your time in productive work. I should then stay away—give you four or five nights in which to sleep alone, remembering the touch of my hands and mouth on your lovely loins. Were I to do so, you'd inevitably build up a backlog of need.

"However, I strongly suspect that no amount of need would cloud your judgment, or weaken your will, Mercedes. I suspect you know right now whether you judge it prudent to end your physical relationship with a lover you consider dangerous—or intensify it."

Roused out of the pleasant lethargy following upon vigorous exercise, the woman glanced quizzically at the man whose purposefulness she intuitively knew did not derive from any desire to dispense with her company. "You offer no middle road?" she queried, accompanying the question with a wistful smile.

"Middle roads tend to be razorback ridges," came the uncompromising answer. "Slippery slopes leading downward in both directions. Do any pressing chores make your going home right suddenly a necessity?"

"No. My two horses graze a pasture offering plenty of grass and access to the river, and my greenhouse features a semi-automatic watering system. It can be left untended for twelve days. Why do you ask?"

Shifting his hold to one better fitted to thwart any convulsive attempt on the part of his companion to break away, Julian smiled into eyes gone patently wary. In a tone half beguiling, half commanding, he replied, "Stay with me twenty-four more hours, Mercedes. Let a master of erotic art introduce you to a mode of sensual pleasure you consciously crave. Submit while I employ techniques of which your experience this morning constituted only a foretaste. I'll inflict pain, but I'll confer exquisite pleasure. I guarantee that the combination will lift you to a height of ecstasy unparalleled in your experience."

Ice seemed to the woman to crystallize in her blood. Shock and fear contended with an inexplicably powerful longing to accede. More frightened by the intensity of that latter reaction than by the sadist holding her immobile, Mercedes sought to picture in a supercharged imagination just what he contemplated doing.

She succeeded only in deepening an overpowering surge of desire. Befogged by lust, she fought to retain her ability to think rationally, even as her dangerous lover's arms tightened around her. Heart hammering, she heard him urge with mesmeric force, "Say yes, Mercedes. You need what I can give you. Say yes."

"Julian," she gasped, her fear drowning out all other emotions, "what if I simply can't muster the courage to say yes?"

"If that happens, I'll take you home," came the equable reply. An amused, faintly mocking smile overspread the boldly sculpted face. "But your courage I judge adequate for any venture. My word still holds, Mercedes. I'll inflict pain, but cause no bodily harm. I'll confer exquisite pleasure while reinforcing your nascent ability to climax with gratifying ease. Say yes, little sensualist. Say yes."

Surprising even herself, Mercedes all at once succumbed to the irresistibly seductive power of the melodic voice, the expert hands, the compelling eyes. "Yes," she breathed.

No change in her seducer's expression apprised her of the fierce exultance generated by that unexpectedly swift capitulation. Sensing her fear, aroused to potent desire by his cognizance of it, Julian merely held her, and stroked her back as the pounding of her heart set up sympathetic vibrations in his own.

At length he smiled into the oval face upturned to his

expectantly, but warily. "You see? Your courage sufficed. But you'll need also to embrace—if only for twenty-four hours—ideas which normally you'd repudiate, little staunch-heart. You'll accept me as your master, submit to whatever technique I employ, and obey any command I give. For the span of time in which you voluntarily remain my guest, you'll exist for my pleasure, Mercedes. So."

With lithe grace, the man outlining those direly unsettling terms rose. Purposefully, he stripped off his companion's robe, and doffed his own. Sweeping her up, he bore the nude woman whose face mirrored her inner turmoil to the hall bisecting the new addition. Bypassing the entry to the pool area on his left, and the closed door directly opposite that portal, he strode on, at length stopping at an entry on his right.

A touch on a concealed switch in the jamb set the panel gliding silently aside. No sooner did he step over the threshold, than the door slid closed behind him.

Borne in strong arms, Mercedes glanced apprehensively about her. She beheld nothing to inspire terror. On the north wall, tall, wide, translucent windows provided non-glare illumination of the spacious chamber half the size of that housing the pool: light that reflected from creamy walls of smooth plaster.

At the midpoint of that expanse stretched a six-foot bar of burnished brass: a cylindrical railing an inch and a half in diameter, mounted on two upright bars of the same metal. In front of that feature for which the puzzled viewer could assign no useful function, stood two sturdy benches of polished hardwood, each four feet in length and cushioned on the top in black leather. A gap of some eighteen inches separated their narrow ends; their long sides paralleled that of the railing.

Against the solid south wall—that separating the room

from the hall—the nervous observer beheld a narrow pedestal table, supported by a sturdy, upright metal pillar. The surface she saw to be divided into an array of rectangular segments, each upholstered in wet-look black fabric. A double bed devoid of both head and foot-boards reposed on the flagging, its long side three feet from the east wall, its mattress upholstered in black leather.

Between the east wall and one of the wooden benches resting beneath the windows, stood a small, round pedestal table fitted with castors, and covered by a black cloth. No other furniture met her swiftly darting glance.

Julian advanced to stand five feet from the west wall devoid of any furnishing. There, he set his palpably nervous burden on her feet, with her back to the vertical expanse. "Remain where you are," he commanded.

Standing tautly erect while striving to dominate burgeoning fear, the woman acutely conscious of her lover's hard erection watched him push the round, covered table nearer to where she stood. Scarcely able to believe that she found herself in a situation eerily paralleling visions conjured out of a hyperactive imagination, she trembled even as moisture gushed into a cunt quivering with need. Shivers raced across bare skin tingling more in anticipation than fear.

Folding the cloth back, her self-styled master lifted two objects off the surface. Turning, he ordered, "Hold out your arms."

When his guest convulsively but promptly obeyed, he snapped around each of her wrists a sturdy metal fetter to which one link of chain attached. As she contemplated those, he reached for what she judged to be a remote of the sort used to activate television sets. A touch on that device set a pair of silvery, flexible cables descending from two vertical brass pipes attached to the ceiling: items which seemed at first glance to be supports for the lighting fixtures attached to their sides.

Raising each of her arms in turn, Julian snapped the link of the fetter confining the woman's wrist, into the end of a cable. A touch on the remote set the cables retracting. Startled, Mercedes let a faint gasp escape her as the bonds pulled her wrists above her head, stopping their ascent before her feet lost contact with the floor.

Standing with her arms upraised, but angled slightly outward in such wise that they failed to touch her head, the novice battled an onslaught of fright. Gamely, she reminded herself that this self-acknowledged sadist had sworn not to harm her. Her fear increased as he attached to each ankle, identical fetters: restraints that she saw to be fitted with elastic tethers. Those he affixed to rings that, at a touch, angled upwards ninety degrees from flat recesses in the stone-flagged floor.

Standing spread-eagled, her hair falling in disarray around her face, the pinioned woman succumbed to fear bordering now on terror.

Consciously employing his melodic voice to soothe that fear, Julian spoke in a tone purely conversational. "During the next twelve hours, you'll learn to submit to pain while unrestrained," he informed her. "But right now, I choose to spare you the need to focus any part of your attention on the necessity to control your urge to writhe, to struggle, to flee. You'll focus only on your sensations. So. Relax, while I lift you."

In response to a touch on the remote, the cables retracted further, lifting the woman's feet a few inches off the floor. The elastic tethers stretched, exerting tension sufficient to prevent all but the most minimal degree of writhing.

Exquisitely conscious of her utter vulnerability, Mercedes mastered the panic assailing her. Palms slid sensuously down flesh rigid with fear, gentling the inexperienced natural submissive. Incipient terror subsided, melting into fierce desire engendered by her very helplessness.

Recklessly, the object of Julian's attentions abdicated all control over her pinioned limbs, achieving a state of acceptance of the pain now imminent. Astonishment gripped her, as she grew cognizant that she craved its infliction.

Slipping an arm around a slim waist, Julian cupped a breast, and vibrated the nipple. "Hard, this little nubbin," he murmured in his lover's ear, his voice pitched to soothe. "Fear constitutes a potent aphrodisiac, if you don't let it escalate into panic," he added equably. "Don't try to struggle, little neophyte. Program your mind to accept the pain—to yield to it. Pain loosens your loins, opens you, and readies you for my entry. So. Observe, now."

Through dilated eyes, Mercedes saw him hold out for her inspection a blunt-tipped shaft about eight inches long and an inch in diameter, which extended from a handle composed of four black glass balls strung on a rigid support. A ring featuring several tiny buttons separated handle from shaft. As she watched, a finger pressed one of those, causing six flexible black thongs about eighteen inches in length to emerge from an orifice which opened in the blunt, rounded tip of the rigid shaft. The thongs, tipped with tiny knots, hung limply.

"Even forceful application of these soft strands would cause you no injury," the demonstrator observed dispassionately even as his prick reared stiffly erect. "The pain arises from a different property." A touch on a second button caused the thongs to assume an aura of blue light. The glowing strands lifted, and sought to distance themselves from the others, in response to the electronic force generating the light.

"The thongs repel each other, but cling to human skin," the user explained. "They excite the nerve-endings, producing impulses similar to those generated by the golden shield, but more powerful. You'll find both the pain and the less pronounced but intriguingly pleasurable component to be intensified equally." Standing facing his immobilized, spread-eagled partner, Julian in a light, quick stroke, brought the six-thonged lash down on the tender flesh of her taut abdomen.

Intense pain blended with an eerie accompaniment of pleasure. Both effects sent waves of pleasure-pain radiating outwards from the patch of skin to which the six strands adhered. The dual stimulus produced a convulsive twitch in the body unable to writhe, unable to avoid the tormenting contact. Seconds later, a touch of a finger on a button deactivated the thongs that had clung to the skin with astonishing force. The pain died away as if it had never been.

Her eyes wide, manifestly fearful, the novice bracing for a new application of the electronic whip beheld her lover reach for a second device identical to the first. When he again stood before her, he activated both. Raking with an intent glance the nude body spread to his view, he commanded, "You're to yield to the pain—let it dominate you. For a woman, there can be no ecstasy without surrender. Control your urge to writhe, to struggle, to cry out. Work at achieving complete suspension of your will. You exist for my pleasure, Mercedes."

Two sets of thongs descended with light force, but indescribably telling effect, on the woman's breasts. Like two sets of black talons, they congealed against tender flesh, generating near-agony during the brief interval elapsing before the man wielding the whips with practiced skill deactivated them, whisked them away, reactivated them, and set them whistling through the air to descend repeatedly on thighs, ass-cheeks, mound. One light but agonizing application hissed upwards between the legs spread wide by the tethers. Glowing strands molded themselves to tender inner thighs, moist pussy-lips, even the hooded clit.

A gasping inhalation of breath shivered the still, warm air of the chamber, but no shriek echoed off the creamy walls reflecting the bulk of the diffuse north light streaming through the windows. The strokes, light, quick, relentlessly repeated, targeted the erogenous zones most receptive to the lesser, pleasurable component of the dual stimuli.

The woman's awareness narrowed. Rendered hyperconscious of the most sensitive parts of her wholly exposed body, she perforce dwelled on her sensations. Desperately, she sought to concentrate solely on the insidiously beguiling pleasurable stimulus accompanying each new application of the lash. Held all but rigidly immobile, she ceased an initial shrinking as the thongs clung. Hanging passively, she yielded to the pain while savoring its pleasurable component.

Her longing for the promised entry of the prick she now saw to be fully engorged lessened no whit, even though she unerringly judged its stiffness to be caused solely by her lover's enjoyment of inflicting the pain enveloping her. Perversely, that conclusion aroused her.

Her mind yielded, even as had her body. Yearning mingled with dread of each whistling descent of the whiplashes, merging with the pleasure/pain riveting her attention on her loins, her breasts, her ass-cheeks, the erect, full clit again cruelly targeted. Her consciousness dimmed; her power of will diminished. Moisture oozed from between the flaps of soft flesh quivering as the thong released them. Fuck me, she pleaded silently. I offer myself fully. Fuck me!

Subtle cues exhibited by the body now passive, pliant, apprised Julian of his lover's mental surrender. Dropping the devices on the table, he slipped his arms around her from behind. The fingers deftly parting her pussy-lips slid into the lushly lubricated orifice they guarded. "Hot and wet, longing for my cock in your love-tunnel, eh?" her master murmured tauntingly in her ear. "Mmmm?"

"Yes," came the breathless answer.

"I'll take you when and how I choose, little innocent—enlarge your experience of penetration, after you demonstrate your willingness both to submit, and to obey."

Cruelly disappointed, her longing intensified by that brief contact with her lover's bare body, Mercedes battled a new onslaught of fear as her tormentor released her from the restraints. Standing, her back to him, she felt him grip her above and behind each knee. Exerting formidable strength, he lifted her, keeping her thighs spread and her back against his chest and abdomen while he bore her to the gap between the two benches ranged below the north-facing windows. Positioning her so that she knelt upright on bent knees, one horizontal lower leg on each bench-end, he commanded, "Clasp your hands in back of your head."

When she bemusedly obeyed, he released his hold on her torso. "Don't move," he ordered. Pausing only long enough to make certain that she remained motionless, he moved the table within easy reach, and picked up one of the inactivated electronic whips.

Having retracted the thongs, Julian again slipped his left arm around the woman kneeling motionless. Parting her nether lips with the fingers of his left hand, he slid the blunt shaft of the inactivated device into her cunt.

A gasp impinged on his ear at the unexpected intrusion of the inanimate object.

"You'll bear the pain I now inflict, without making a sound, and without struggling," her lover rasped into her ear. "Focus on the pleasurable component, which will become proportionately more pronounced, given the sensitivity of the moist flesh to which it will cling. When I bend you forward, you'll grasp the bar and hold on. You'll maintain that position until I permit you to rise."

Even as his intent registered on the woman's horrified mind, a finger activated the shaft, which instantly adhered to the entire internal lining of her cunt. Agony radiated through her loins, accompanied by a surge of indescribably erotic pleasure.

Frequent indulgence in fantasies featuring sadomasochistic practices had created a mindset that served now to blunt both horror and fear, and abort a fleeting impulse to fight this man assuming the role of master. Determined to obey his curt order despite the severity of the pain convulsing her gut, Mercedes experienced a paradoxical thrill at being forced to bear torment so intense.

An arm of iron bent her forward. Hearing an imperious command that she grasp the bar, she obeyed, and held on, her awareness a haze of pain spiced with an attendant, diabolically riveting pleasure.

Focused on the dual stimuli absorbing her full attention, unable to see the man standing behind her upturned rear, lubricating his rigid member, the neophyte failed to anticipate his next move. When he gripped her hips and slid his slick, hard organ slowly, inexorably, into her anus, a cry expressive of profound shock died away into a series of low moans of animal pleasure.

Slick fingers now worked her clit. Himself potently stimulated by the muted but nonetheless sensually arousing combination of pain and pleasure generated by the device separated from his rigid tool by only a thin layer of tissue, Julian thrust rhythmically, languorously, into the tight passage which he accurately guessed to be penetrated thus for the first time in its owner's experience.

Her initial surrender reversed, to a degree, by the onslaught of this new, more severe pain, the woman possessed now in a fashion new to her experience again mounted towards a total suspension of her will. The eerie echo of pleasure she discovered to be proportionately augmented, even as that arising from the penetration deepened. Dominated as never before in her experience, she let go of fear, of shock, of horror, and savored her sensations: all of them.

Her awareness collapsing inward to an incandescent core of savage need for culmination, Mercedes gave herself up to rapture. Her every inhibition vaporized in the white heat of passion. The contractions centering on the whip-shaft exaggerated her agony even as they conferred pleasure so intense as to render her faint. Her tiny shaft erect, wet, throbbing, her loins sensuously worked by the lover sternly forbidding himself to increase the forcefulness of his thrusts, she welcomed the onset of culmination. His groan blended with hers as the two simultaneously achieved orgasm.

The pain died away. Julian caught his partner before her slack fingers lost their grip on the bar. Lifting her back into a kneeling position, he removed the inactivated whip-shaft. Gathering her into his arms, he bore her to the bed, willing himself not to succumb to euphoria before both he and the half-conscious lover in his arms lay entwined thereon. Moments later, two entranced sensualists locked in a close embrace floated weightless in a luminous, featureless, parallel universe.

Chapter Three

Julian came back to reality first. Shifting the woman lying with her face pressed into the hollow of his shoulder, her body molded to his, onto her back, so that her head rested on his upper arm, he studied the oval face gone slack, still. Now that it lacked the vibrancy habitually animating it while its owner interacted with him socially, he noted the fine wrinkles angling out from the corners of the eyes: laugh-creases converted into permanent tracery. Faint, tiny, vertical lines etched into the skin above the rosily bowed upper lip—lines barely visible—testified to the slow but inexorable retreat from youth.

The shrewd observer recalled that before partaking of breakfast, Mercedes had downed medication taken from her purse—a tablet that he accurately judged to represent a hormonal supplement. Silently commending her for refusing to relinquish her sexual potency or risk thinning of her bone-mass, he musingly recalled that when he first laid eyes on her, she wore no makeup. He remembered also that she applied none in the privacy of her bathroom before accepting his invitation to dine. Reflecting that her engaging verve so often sent color flooding into her cheeks, and lent a sparkle to heavily lashed green eyes that needed no artificial enhancement, he decided that he approved that choice as well.

I've never admired heavy use of makeup by any woman, he reminded himself. Maturity becomes Mercedes, he observed contentedly to his alter ego. As does this trance-like state induced by sexual satiety. A chance-found treasure, this partner. Do I dare even contemplate . . . ?

No. She's beginning to comprehend that she could learn to crave the whip—that she yearns to be dominated by a master during a sexual encounter—but she's a strong-willed, fiercely independent-minded woman who'd react first with outrage and then with hot anger, to a demand that she offer herself as that master's slave. She's the descendant of pioneers who valued freedom above anything else life offers. Conditioning her to accept my dominance in her everyday life as well as in bed, will take a wealth of time—if that outcome's even possible. No way could I risk what I so wish to do! If only I'd met her months ago!

Mercedes lifted lids that seemed unnaturally heavy, to find her lover subjecting her to intense scrutiny. An initial bemused wonder died as he watched, transmuting into a fleeting expression that he suspected to mirror guilt. Two furrows deepened across a high, normally only faintly lined brow, patently testifying to the onslaught of some direly troubling notion.

Relieved to detect neither anger nor outrage, Julian smiled into the dismayed eyes riveted to his. Softly, he murmured, "You're a natural sensualist, Mercedes."

Patently upset, his lover whispered, "I . . . I never realized . . . that I possess such strong masochistic tendencies."

An amused laugh, teasing rather than derisive, greeted that confession. "To a degree, you do. But every woman's a bit of a masochist, little innocent, and every man's a bit of a sadist. Those tendencies arise from the differing roles nature assigned us during the act of copulation. I feel strongly compelled to dominate—to force surrender, to impregnate you, to possess you utterly. You harbor a fierce wish to be dominated.

"Consider this. No matter how aroused she grows, no matter how actively a woman seeks to seduce a man, she can't force herself on him. Neither can she achieve ecstasy without surrendering—if not to the man actually possessing her, then at least to some imagined lover born of erotic fantasizing.

"Don't conjure up feelings of shame out of a flawed perception of your sensual nature, Mercedes. I'll agree, utilizing pain as a sexual stimulus poses danger to both partners, but your iron self-control will always prevent your graduating to physically damaging, obsessive excesses, whether consensual or self-inflicted—as will mine."

Upon digesting that justification which she sensed to be part of Julian's philosophy, rather than a clever argument offered simply to alleviate her misgivings, Mercedes conceded that it possessed validity. Reassured, she nestled against the warm, bare body of her partner, who laughed softly, his lips brushing her ear. "At the point in your life you'd reached just prior to our meeting, you needed a demanding master, didn't you?" he queried, smiling the wicked smile.

"No," came the ruminative reply. "I needed . . . you."

Shock rendered the man hearing that calmly stated admission momentarily speechless. Recovering his aplomb before betraying the full magnitude of that shock, he refrained from speech. Instead, he crushed against his chest this woman he unerringly divined to be incapable of coquettishness, even as his mouth closed over hers. His kiss, passionate, erotic, yet managed to convey affectionate warmth to the companion melting against him. Matching his passion, she returned his salute.

At length, Julian held her away, conscious that the tempting notion he had earlier dismissed as too risky now rose to confront him anew, insidiously reinforced by this wholly unforeseen development. Resolving to shelve the idea for future consideration, he queried lightly, "So you've lost your fear of me, eh, Mercedes?"

"No way!" came the instant rebuttal launched with no pause for reflection. "You're twice as dangerous as I originally thought!"

That impulsive avowal evoked hearty laughter in the lover whose admiration for this uniquely honest woman took a quantum leap. "You've given me a wealth of pleasure today, little hedonist," he observed in an amused drawl. "You deserve to be rewarded." Rising off the bed, he lifted his partner in corded arms, and bore her down the hallway to the door opposite that of the pool.

Mercedes now found herself in a spacious bathroom, but in place of the conventional bathtub, she beheld a commodious sunken pool exhibiting a high degree of turbulence. "Relieve yourself," came the casually uttered command she needed to obey. A bit taken aback, she used the toilet, observing to her relief that Julian focused his attention solely on rummaging through a drawer beneath the vanity. From that receptacle, he removed a silken pouch, and a tube of medication.

"Stand over the drain," he now ordered. When his lover stood in the concave depression in the floor occupying a corner of the room—a shower-area fitted with a detachable showerhead—he bathed her torso. Gently, he lathered her groin, and rinsed away the suds.

"I expect you're a bit sore inside," he observed equably. "We'll eliminate that discomfort." Squeezing a ribbon of ointment from the tube onto his middle finger, he inserted the digit deep into his companion's cunt, and gently massaged the inner surface. What soreness existed vanished as if by magic.

Borne into the hot tub by strong arms, Mercedes savored the delicious impact of the roiling water on every square inch of her skin. Seating himself on the lower of two steps encircling the perimeter, Julian immersed the lover seated on his lap with her back to him, to the neck, clasping her beneath her breasts, and letting her lower body extend outwards, lifted on the buoyant force of the surging water.

"Mmmmmmm," she responded, savoring the warmth, the attention, the closeness to this man so utterly unlike any she had known.

Again driven to envision a tempting prospect, Julian once more resolved to postpone considering it.

When at length Mercedes stood naked on the flagging, briskly toweled dry, her hair air-blown to fluffiness, she felt arms encircle her from behind. "Spread your legs," came the brisk command from the self-styled master who dropped to one knee, and inserted into her feminine depth a slippery, flexible black shaft that flared at the base. Startled, she tensed as she felt the flaring edge cling to the flesh surrounding her pussy-lips. To her surprise, no pain assaulted her.

A hand now pressed a cup-like feature attached to the rim of the shaft, over her small organ of pleasure, so that the added feature clung at its edges. A blunt protrusion nestled between the woman's pussy-lips. Soft, flexible nubbins caressed her clit. Moisture seemingly oozed from the device, which at a touch from her lover's finger produced not pain, but indescribably erotic pleasure. The shaft now vibrated, as did the egg-shaped bulge pressed against the base of the hooded flesh that instantly swelled. Each tiny frond shivered endlessly, sending waves of exquisite enjoyment radiating upwards through the wearer's abdomen.

"Nice, eh?" came the amused voice of her lover. "You stand in peril of growing totally dependent on pain as a trigger for surrender, little sensualist. You need reinforcement of an alternate mental route to fulfillment: the normal path of pain-free stimulation. It won't matter how long it takes for that outcome to occur. This charming teaser's infinitely patient, and utterly tireless. You'll submit to its ministrations while we imbibe a glass of wine, cook, dine, and enjoy each other's company. So. I'll carry you, given that you'll find walking a bit awkward while you're stimulated in this fashion."

Flustered, the woman whose awareness now centered on the delicious sensations generated by the device, gamely sought to compose her face as her naked lover bore her to the dining area, where he deposited her nude body in one of the leather-cushioned chairs at the table.

Acutely conscious of the heat flooding her cheeks, Mercedes watched her host expertly remove the cork, and then pour wine from a cobweb-streaked bottle wrapped in a towel. She found that her attention divided between the conversation he initiated, and the unremitting stimulation of her entire genital area. Sipping the mythical nectar of the gods, the guest listened to her companion as he set lamb chops broiling, potatoes baking, and vegetables steaming. By dint of effort, she managed to offer a cogent rebuttal to an argument he advanced.

His preparations complete, the host settled into a chair opposite his nude, patently flustered companion. Smiling at her over the rim of his goblet, he remarked, "So you don't agree that a benevolent dictatorship offers greater stability and prosperity to the citizenry than does a democratic system artificially grafted upon a people with a long history of inspired chieftainship and intricate tribal organization—a people to whom the concept of representative national government comes as wholly foreign?"

"How many dictators down through history ever proved themselves . . . " Breaking off in mid-sentence, Mercedes failed to suppress the soft expulsion of breath that accompanied the accelerated rate of respiration, the parted lips, the little shivers perceptible to the keen observer across the table.

Tawny eyes brimful of mischief read the telltale signs aright, but their owner merely completed the question his guest failed to finish posing. "Benevolent? Not many, I'll readily admit. But the harm wreaked by ill-conceived political experiments in this age defies belief."

Forcing her mind back onto the topic, Mercedes replied spiritedly, "I fully realize that. I'm not defending those experiments; I merely regard the idea of dictatorship—absolute power wielded by one man—as philosophically unsupportable, whether or not the effect's benign. Autocrats tend to fill a vacuum left when an ineffectual political system collapses into anarchy.

"What we ought to be fostering isn't democratic rule, but whatever form of governance might best provide social stability in a specific country—say, one plagued by a concentration of the bulk of the wealth in the hands of small elite, an ominously undisciplined military force, an impoverished, uneducated, landless peasantry, and a lack of skilled administrators able to govern efficiently on a regional level, let alone on a national level."

"You mean, a lack of a middle class. Exactly so, but if you think back, you'll see that authoritarian systems result in the rise of a middle class. Fatally flawed fledgling democracies don't produce that beneficial outcome. Morally indefensible or not, successful dictatorship provides the social and economic basis for the evolution of viable representative systems of governance—no less now than in the past."

Mustering a noble effort of will, Mercedes forced herself to concentrate on the discussion while locking the sensations she found impossible to ignore, into a side compartment of her mind. Twice during the leisurely meal, she failed to conceal the physical evidence that the device again teased her into climax. Well aware that her lover noted her brief, abstracted lapses into incoherence, the disconcerted guest consoled herself that he at least passed no sardonic comment.

The host having rendered the kitchen area spotless while forbidding his companion to do other than relax on the couch, he strolled to where she sat absorbed in the titillation still shattering her aplomb. Concealing potent amusement, he lifted her, and bore her to the bedroom, where he removed the teasers.

"Your mental circuitry's most definitely growing stronger," he observed, smiling at the novice blushing scarlet. "A woman can skim from peak to peak with relative ease, if she's properly stimulated. In that respect, she enjoys a sensual advantage over her male partner, who's done for a time, once he's shot his load. So don't imagine that I've set you up for failure, Mercedes. Well, now. Tonight you'll use all the artistry of which you're capable, to pleasure me."

The melodic voice, cajoling, compelling, sparked naked lust in the woman so relentlessly stimulated for so long a span by the inanimate device that drove her to orgasm, but in a manner she considered unnatural. The twinges of guilt that had plagued her all along—guilt arising from loyalty to the beloved husband so unlike this debonair sadist—fled her consciousness. Subliminally driven by the need not only for carnal pleasure, but also for a cessation of the loneliness the very existence of which she refused to acknowledge, lest she succumb to despair, Mercedes at this juncture consciously cast her inhibitions into the void.

Having disposed himself supine on the bed, Julian relaxed, his tawny eyes aglow with anticipation. Expecting no astounding performance from this eminently respectable, middle-aged widow, he yet savored the thought of watching her strive assiduously to please him, even if her skill turned out to fall far below his standards. Contentedly reflecting that he would enjoy teaching her exotic sensual techniques later on, he prepared to assess just how exacting a task that might turn out to be.

Sitting up, the survivor of a memorable marriage smiled down at the man she suspected to be inwardly amused. Wholly unflustered by his demand, she dropped on his chest, and kissed his brow, his cheeks, his eyes, his lips. Her tongue insinuated itself into his mouth, where it teased, explored, tasted. Its tip thrust between his teeth and his upper lip, which her lips caught, and held. She sucked on the bow, sending shivers of delight down nerves their owner had erroneously concluded to be immune to such teasing.

Drawing away, she moved backwards, kneeling astride him. Provocatively, she nibbled on an earlobe, and kissed her lover's throat. Moving again, she traced the contours of corded arms while letting her pendulous breasts drag along the chest lightly thatched with fine brown hair. A moist tongue licked Julian's nipples, and bit them playfully, as hands and arms he discovered to be strong for a woman's, pressed his arms against the bed.

Backing still further, Mercedes tongued her lover's navel. Her delectable ass rearing upward, her thighs spread wide, her legs astraddle of those of her partner, she licked his abdomen while she retreated far enough to allow her to gaze down at his erect, throbbing shaft.

Dropping to lie prone, she took his stiff cock fully into her hot, moist mouth. Briskly, she moved her head in an inverse of penetration, providing exquisite friction. With long, sweeping strokes, she massaged the turgid manhood of the man astonished by her lack of inhibition. Desisting, she sucked on the head, as her tongue probed the tiny opening in the tip. Savoring the pleasant taste of the drop of juice she teased from the orifice, she sucked harder, provoking groans from the recipient of her wantonly erotic caresses.

Knowing that if her lover ejected the essence of his passion into her mouth, his action, while pleasurable to both partners, would fail to lift her to climax, Mercedes ceased her oral ministrations, and mounted him. Sinking over his engorged member, she took him fully in her now lushly lubricated feminine depth.

Kneeling astride him, her torso erect, she rose and fell with languorous, rhythmic motions, while raising her arms and running her hands through the shining fall of hair half obscuring her vibrantly expressive face. Breasts lacking the high firmness of youth, lifted, swaying enticingly in the fevered vision of the man riveting his eyes to their rosy, tautly erect nipples.

Feeling her partner's pelvis arch upwards, elated at beholding his obvious arousal, Mercedes lifted herself off him. Inserting her right leg between his thighs, she guided his shaft into the cunt from which moisture oozed, as he turned to lie aslant of her loins. When he thrust deeply into her, his head pillowed on her leg, his buttocks within reach of her hands, she slid into his anus a finger moistened with her own abundant essence. Slowly, sensuously, she massaged him there as he drove repeatedly into her slippery hole.

Intuitively sensing that this woman single-mindedly bent on lifting him to climax would not achieve her own fulfillment until she accomplished that goal, Julian relaxed the hold he habitually maintained over the course of his passion. Stimulated dually by the deliciously intrusive finger, and the friction engendered by his rhythmic thrusts, he groaned aloud as deliberate contracting motions of his partner's inner depth forcefully squeezed his cock. Sphincter muscles grown strong by long years of practice tightened on his hard, invading organ. Alternately squeezing and relaxing, the adept at the age-old erotic technique persisted as if seeking to milk her lover dry of juice.

A groan tore from Julian's throat as he welcomed the inexorable, steadily building, delicious onset of culmination. Convulsively, he thrust deeply, crying out as he ejected a voluminous stream of jism into this partner whose earthy sensuality entranced him.

Exulting in her success, Mercedes savored the pleasure arising from intimate coital union, despite her failing to come herself. Satisfied with the outcome of her efforts, she relaxed. As Julian slid off her, she smiled in patent satisfaction. Lying slackly, she waited for him to gather her into a warm embrace. When instead he closed his mouth over her still-swollen clit, and slid a finger deep into the cunt awash in their mingled effusions, she experienced a rush of pleasure that left her breathless.

Relentlessly, expertly, the man demonstrating his mastery of erotic art drove her off the plateau from which she expected to slide slowly into sleep. Only a short span of time elapsed before he lifted her into rapturous, prolonged fulfillment.

Lying in strong arms, awash in euphoria, the woman marveling at the turn her life just took consciously forbade herself to succumb to fear, to shame, to worry about the course this liaison might take. Melting against this man she knew to be cruel and suspected to be dangerous, she slid from bliss directly into oblivion.

Chapter Four

Mercedes drifted slowly out of dream-shot sleep, into the lassitude preceding full wakefulness. Grown aware of warmth, she migrated toward it. Arms enfolded her. Still half asleep, she molded herself against the hard torso of the other occupant of the bed.

Julian, wide awake, devoted a few moments to savoring the special allure this woman held for him, before returning to consideration of the course this unexpected affair might take. Musingly, he reviewed her reactions to his conduct of it, marveling at her acceptance of sensual practices that a middle-aged, personable widow enjoying a comfortably secure lifestyle might be forgiven for regarding as utterly outrageous.

Satisfaction gave way to speculation as he contemplated the course this day could take. Reflecting that if at this moment, he began the time-honored, safe approach to an end greatly to be desired, he would face an enforced interruption bound to be inimical to the success of his venture, he sighed in frustration. I could stay here—send word that I can't attend as I planned, he reminded himself. But that would cause my closest friends problems. Damn my luck!

Enticing visions shimmered on the fringe of Julian's inner awareness. If only I'd met Mercedes months ago! His frustration lessened as he conceded wryly that only sheer luck had enabled him to get to know this reclusive native of a closely knit rural community well enough to divine that she possessed the special allure entrancing him at this moment. Could I possibly . . . take her along? No. The risk's wholly insupportable! She's no initiate—not even a probationer! She'd succumb to shock, rebel, and disgrace me! Damn!

Exert the rigorous control over your emotions habitual to you. What's possessed you, to let that control slacken in the slightest degree? Even as that savage adjuration reverberated in his inner awareness, Julian succumbed to an all-too-enticing vision. Wrenching his mind forcibly onto the present, he fastened his mouth over that of the lover lying slackly in his arms, and kissed her in intimate, erotic fashion, exulting as she congealed against his bare, tingling flesh.

When at length he freed her lips, and regarded her from under half-lidded, speculative eyes, he exulted at beholding the desire mirrored in hers. Controlling an onslaught of fierce need, he gathered her in strong arms. In a single, sinuous movement of his athletic body, he lifted her while turning to drop his feet over the side of the bed. Rising, he bore her to the bath, smiling in manifest amusement at the disappointment overspreading her fluidly mobile face. He found himself well able now to interpret any subtle change in her expression.

Seated opposite the lover who, she wryly surmised, preferred nudity even over casual lounging in a silken robe, the woman herself stark naked experienced no especial qualms at complying with Julian's insistence on their breakfasting in the buff, having grown used to a virile husband who had adamantly refused to wear any sort of clothing to bed.

In sprightly fashion, she chatted over the country sausages, eggs, and fluffy biscuits served by the chef whose culinary skills extended to mixing his own biscuit dough from scratch, and blending real oranges into frothy juice, rather than relying on premixed dough or frozen concentrates.

As she dined, she again wondered what sort of life this man led before settling down in this out-of-the-way spot—if the term settling down really applies, she amended. Ruminatively, she sought to imagine how he learned the unorthodox techniques he employed during a sexual encounter. Desire surged to the forefront of her mind. Denied fulfillment upon waking, she craved it now. Even as she conversed, she gained a sense of living in a surreal stasis: a suspension of the forward flow of time.

No perturbation showed on the face of the man again wrestling with a dilemma he refused, this morning, to regard as insoluble. There's time, he assured himself stoutly. I could subject this natural sensualist to an abbreviated initiation. She'd never guess that I regard it as such. Her courage, allied to that mature self-possession she unfailingly exhibits, will prevent her from disgracing me.

Even as he sought to persuade himself of the truth of that assertion, chills cascaded down his spine. Don't decide now. Put her courage to a rigorous test. If she fails the test, you'll have to live with the galling knowledge that you bungled your handling of this gift the capricious gods tossed into your lap. But if she completes the regimen successfully, you can then weigh the risks, and make an informed decision.

Having launched on a chancy course, Julian bore the woman wholly unconscious of having breached her lover's innermost guard, to the couch. Seating himself while cradling her in his arms, he cocked his head, and regarded her out of eyes gone manifestly calculating.

"Today, I'll either intensify your willingness to accommodate my tastes, or cause you to break off our affair," he declared evenly. "I'm about to put your willingness to bear pain without flinching, to three successive tests, each more rigorous than the last. At no point will I employ restraints. Each phase of your ordeal will be designed to force you to surrender more completely than you've hitherto done. If you submit—offer not the least resistance—new mental circuitry forged by your recent experiences of pain inflicted by a demanding master will steadily strengthen.

"If you pass all three tests of your self-mastery, I'll dispense with pain, and employ every art at my command to lift you to a height of ecstasy exceeding any you've known. But if at any point your self-control proves inadequate—if you writhe, or cry out, or struggle, or even stiffen—I'll take you home. No way will I compel you to endure pain you're unable to bear without flinching.

"You'll either freely submit, so as to take a place among the practitioners of an ancient discipline, or you'll forfeit any inclusion in that fellowship. At this juncture, we stand on the razorback ridge of the middle ground, Mercedes. So choose: opt to intensify our relationship, or to end it."

Faced with that ultimatum couched in an uncompromising tone wholly devoid of cajolery, Mercedes digested her unconventional lover's words even as fierce longing for the ecstasy he promised consumed her. Frowning in puzzlement, she wondered whether he employed the term fellowship in an abstract, metaphorical sense, or a literal one. Rejecting the latter supposition, she weighed how to reply even as fear charged forth from the dim recess in her mind where it had lain quiescent. The fear contended mightily with primal lust.

As if he read her mind, Julian stated levelly, "My word still binds me, Mercedes. You'll take no harm. Muster your admirable courage, and consent. Say yes."

Commanded rather than coaxed, the woman responded to

the hypnotic force of the melodic voice. Yielding to the potent masculine appeal of the man whose arms encircled her, whose lithe body pressed against hers, she nodded. "Yes," she breathed, her assent tremulous but unqualified.

Arms of iron tightened around her. Rising, Julian bore her down the hall illuminated by skylights, and passed into the chamber where he had commenced his introduction to the practices he now intended to render even more difficult for the neophyte to endure without flinching. Deposited on her feet beneath the two cables dangling from above, Mercedes watched as her self-styled master fastened to the cable-ends two stirrup-shaped supports. Obeying a crisp command to grasp those, she complied with another that she spread her legs.

Standing spread-eagled, the cables adjusted so that she could barely keep her soles flat on the flagging, she awaited her master's pleasure. Her heart hammering even as her loins quivered, she beheld him move the cloth-shrouded table nearer to hand. From beneath the cover, he removed two electronic whips seemingly identical to those employed on the prior occasion. When the thongs emerged, and assumed the eerie blue aura, she perceived them to be thicker in diameter and longer than those used earlier.

Facing her, six whiplashes outlined in blue fire extending from the device held in each hand, Julian spoke, his voice now diabolically persuasive. "You'll find that the pain conferred by these implements exceeds that which you bore yesterday," he informed his lover, exactly as if that revelation offered reassurance. "Gear your mind to welcome each application of the lash, not only because by so doing you please me, but also because you know that my inflicting the stimulus will generate arousal fierce enough to enable me eventually to confer exquisite pleasure on you. Narrow your focus, little probationer. Explore the pain, savor the attendant pleasure, and yield to both. So."

Two sets of glowing thongs whistled through the air to adhere with savage force to the outer thighs of the woman whose gut clenched, but whose body twitched no whit. The wielder let them cling for a second before detaching them. Raising the device high, he brought the whiplashes down on the breasts rendered less pendulous owing to the height to which the arms raised.

A gasping exhalation escaped lips that instantly compressed into a grim line. Pain radiated throughout the body forbidden to writhe, or to squirm. The lash descended again and again, targeting breasts, buttocks, hips, abdomen, mound.

Six flesh-seeking tendrils hissed upwards to mold themselves remorselessly upon the tender pussy-lips and the cunt awash now in moisture. After tormenting those delicate sites, they rose off skin feeling flayed, only to land in such wise that one shimmering strand penetrated the cleft of the quivering ass-cheeks. That tendril adhered down the full length of the soft tissue lying within that aperture.

Pain contended for prominence in the woman's awareness with the eerie pleasure integral to the stimulus. Used to achieving a white heat of concentration during intellectual endeavors, well able to block out distracting sights or sounds originating in her environment when she thus engaged her mind, Mercedes now dwelled more fixedly on the pleasure than on the pain. Pain afflicted her, but pleasure absorbed her.

Moisture gushed into her feminine depth, and dribbled from between the peripheral flaps of flesh again pitilessly targeted. Her loins ached for the entry of the fully engorged cock that appeared surreally isolated in the field of vision narrowed to that single focal point. The intermittent nature of the pain, combined with the constant shifting of the sites of application of the stimulus, kept hypersensitive nerves quivering—even those temporarily ignored by the man delivering light, deft strokes that lingered on the skin a shade longer than they did on the prior day.

Reveling in his cognizance that no rebelliousness tempting him to quash it ruthlessly hindered this passionate lover's progress towards surrender, Julian exultingly reflected that this strong-willed woman driven as compulsively by longing for impregnation as by the pain afflicting her, would swiftly achieve total suspension of her will. As he plied the whip, he gauged to perfection her progress towards that goal. When subtle cues met his searching glance, he laid aside the devices. Slipping an arm around the lover hanging passively from the supports, he commanded, "Let go."

Sweeping her up, he bore her to the narrow, oddly formed table mounted on the sturdy metal base. A touch on the remote control that also governed the cables set the disparate padded rectangles forming the top, separating and bending. The tabletop, now convex, rearranged its shape into that of an elongated X. On that altered surface the demanding master laid the supine form of the pliant lover who offered no resistance when he spread her legs to lie along one angle of the X, and drew back her arms along the other.

Mockery tinged the melodic voice of the man smiling down into expectant eyes darkened with passion. "Yearning for my cock in your hot, wet cunt, are you?" he taunted in a drawling tone. Long fingers slid within the orifice awash in juice, and expertly teased the clit hard as their owner's erect prick. "I'll make you come, little sensualist, but only to strengthen mental connections still a trifle tenuous. Ahhh . . . you like that, eh? And this?"

Deftly, knowingly, expertly, Julian massaged exquisitely

sensitive places deep inside the woman arching against his invading fingers. He moistened, and then teased, the tiny shaft protruding from the folds that normally enshrouded it. Nerves still quivering from the intense stimulation delivered by the whips tingled in anticipation. Her will in abeyance, Mercedes yielded to the pleasure as she had to the pain. Moments later she achieved a shuddering climax, even as disappointment at the means employed scalded her consciousness.

Lifted again, she hoped for a surcease from that longing, but found herself draped supine over the lap of the lover seated on the edge of the bed. "Stretch your arms back beyond your head," he commanded. "And spread your legs."

When she lay with her groin arched over his lap, in the attitude he demanded, she felt the familiar touch of metal—cold, this time—on her mound. Deft fingers slipped paper-thin, washer-like metal rings over her erect nipples. The surfaces clung, as did the device adhering to the flesh beneath the crisply curling, reddish-brown pussy-hair.

"From here on, you'll enjoy no relief, even momentarily, from pain," came the ominous warning, the message chilling the hearer all the more for being delivered in a voice forming an aural caress. "This device delivers a stimulus considerably more intense than that which I employed yesterday. The shield governs the rings by remote: a feature that intensifies the overall effect. When I activate it, you'll control your impulse to flinch, to stiffen, to writhe. You'll allow no sound to pass your lips. You'll relax, and accept the pain. I'll monitor your muscular tension closely, little novice. So."

A new, severe onslaught of pain ensued: pain accompanied by an equally enhanced pleasure-echo. A hand spread itself over the abdomen the woman managed to keep relaxed. No muscle convulsively contracted; no limb moved. "Hurts, mmmm?" came the melodic query, light, amused, faintly mocking. "That's right . . . submit to the pain, little neophyte. Let it possess you. Relish the pleasure; let the pain force surrender. Now then."

Rising, Julian carried his passive, limp lover to the gap between the benches. There, he stood her on her feet, with her back to the translucent windows. "Clasp your hands behind your head," he commanded. Having seen that imperious command obeyed, he pushed the table closer before lifting an implement new to the woman riveting wary eyes upon it.

Standing as if carven of stone, Mercedes perceived the object to possess the usual whip-handle, but instead of a shaft, this device featured a long, barely flexible strap four inches wide and eighteen long. The sight of that implement set her pulse racing.

"Turn and face the bar. Kneel with a leg on each bench," came the brisk order.

When the woman tormented by the stimulus already testing her ability to endure pain without flinching obeyed, Julian bent her forward. "Grasp the bar," he instructed. "So. I'll employ the strap on your delectable rear. Your cheeks will grow red, and smart for a time afterward, but won't develop the slightest bruise. The pain arises mainly from the electronic stimulation, which you'll bear without moving a muscle."

Expecting pain, the woman upon whose buttocks the broad strap landed with considerable force found herself unprepared for the resounding thwack jarring hypersensitive nerves. The contact of so large a surface with her shrinking skin produced agony that intensified cruelly during the few seconds elapsing before the wielder switched off the stimulation. Raising his arm, Julian brought the implement down with brisk force. Again and again, he laid the strap parallel to the swath perceptibly affected by the prior blow. His arm fell methodically, rhythmically, each application widening the area now reddened, hot, throbbing. Each span of contact produced agony in the lover whose upraised, unprotected rump offered so tempting a target.

The combination of stimuli affecting mound, breasts, and buttocks produced swift surrender—intense need that blended with an overpowering wish for the pain to cease, for her lover to lift her, and cradle her in his arms.

Judging to perfection when that surrender occurred, Julian laid one last telling blow on the quivering ass-cheeks before switching off the device.

Strong hands raised the woman until she knelt upright, her torso above the gap, her thighs spread, her knees bent, her lower legs resting on the bench-ends. Pain still radiated from her mound and her breasts: pain from which her master allowed her not the most momentary surcease. She felt herself drawn against her lover's abdomen, held by arms encircling her hips.

Fingers again massaged her inner space. The heel of the other hand pressed against her metal-sheathed mound. The middle two digits slid along either side of her wet, erect clit, thrusting back and forth as the heel described a slow, circular motion which forced the soft flesh to which the shield clung, to move in unison with it.

Finding that combination of effects indescribably erotic, the woman yielding to the pain, the intensely sensuous stimulation, and the surrender produced by the whipping, achieved climax—despite her all but unbearable longing to be penetrated by the hard cock stabbing her hot, smarting rear as her lover expertly manipulated her loins.

Lifted anew in strong arms, still gripped by the unrelenting dual stimuli originating with the golden disc adhering to her mound, Mercedes wished desperately for relief from the unremitting pain. She nonetheless succumbed to a fierce craving for the promised pleasure. Never a quitter, she gritted her teeth, gamely reminding herself that this man savoring the infliction of the agonizing impulses coursing down her nerves would cause her no physical injury. When he stood her once again facing him beneath the cables, and commanded her to grasp the stirrups and spread her legs, she obeyed.

"During this third and final ordeal, I'll probe the upper limits of your tolerance for pain," her lover warned. "You now face the final and most rigorous test of your willingness to submit. If you writhe, or scream, or fail to maintain the posture I demand, I'll take you home.

"But if you accept the agony I inflict—prove yourself worthy of inclusion in a select fellowship—I'll dispense with pain, make love to you as you've longed to be taken, and lift you to a height of satiety unprecedented in your experience. The more intensely you focus your mind on surrendering your will to mine, the more quickly that surrender will come, so welcome each new increment to the totality of sensation riveting your full attention. The pain will loosen your loins, open you, set you quivering, shivering, awash in juice—ready you for the penetration I've thus far denied you."

The melodic voice uttering those direly chilling words caressed, seduced, hypnotized. The woman acutely cognizant that her lover's manhood reared even more stiffly erect, conceded distractedly that if he demanded self-control from her, he also displayed astonishing mastery of his own lust. Her eyes patently fearful, she watched him activate two of the less painful electronic whips, and advance to stand raking her nude, shivering, but motionless body with eyes gone cruel.

Employing dual light, quick motions, he simultaneously brought six whistling thongs down on each breast, so that they gripped the soft fullness like talons attached to a stiff, black-glass bird-leg. Instead of deactivating and lifting the devices clinging by electrostatic attraction, he let go, leaving the handles dangling from a point in close proximity to a metal-ringed nipple.

Pain surged into a consciousness unsure whether it could resist the assault. The eerie pleasure-echo, although intensified, failed to compensate for the severity of the new sensation. The sufferer's surroundings blurred, as tears filmed eyes that sought to blink back the telltale moisture. Waves of agony rippled outward from the soft flesh caught in those merciless clutches, but the hands clinging to the supports maintained their grip; the torso remained still as if carven of pale stone.

Fingers inserted themselves into the cunt from which moisture oozed, and assessed the degree of lubrication. "Hot and wet," came the musical comment—amused, provocative, a feline purr. The fingers withdrew. Circling his pain-racked partner, Julian now brought down the twin whips of the more intense variety on two plump cheeks still smarting from the broad lash. Those goads he left clinging, their handles dangling.

New torment enveloped the woman shrieking in the privacy of her mind that she could bear no more. Even as she couched that despairing thought in words, an intransigent stubbornness impelled her to hang on, and resist an overpowering urge to writhe.

Her lover again faced her. Dispassionately, he studied the face from which the rosy color drained. Cocking his head, he observed the lack of tension in the body that neither writhed, nor went taut. Two extended forefingers each targeted a nipple, avoiding contact with the thongs adhering to the flesh in close proximity. The fingers vibrated the nubbins standing erect, causing them to stiffen further.

Reaching for a deactivated whip of the lesser power, Julian retracted the thongs. Deftly, he slid the shaft between the pussy-lips of the partner whose eyes widened in manifest horror as the inanimate object penetrated to a depth of eight inches.

"You're close to surrender, little novice," he reminded her in a tone that beguiled, compelled, mesmerized. "You can bear what I demand that you endure. Let the pain dominate you. Submit, Mercedes. You exist for my pleasure." As the voice died away, a finger activated the device that promptly adhered to the moist inner surfaces of the woman's feminine orifice.

New, diabolically intense stimulation, accompanied by a pleasure-echo equally enhanced, compounded the torment already racking the sufferer who somehow mustered the will to maintain her grip, and resist an all but irresistible urge to scream.

Pain now became Mercedes' universe. Intense sensation momentarily blotted out all coherent thought. Time ceased to exist, as did her surroundings, for the brief span during which body and mind adjusted to the agony enveloping her. The will diminished by the prior stress now thinned to the vanishing point. She hung slackly, wordlessly imploring her tormentor to end her ordeal.

Making no move to heed that silent plea, he queried evenly, "Who is your master, Mercedes?"

"You are," came the whispered, automatic response.

"For what do you exist?"

"For your pleasure."

Fierce satisfaction gripped the man who now relented, and set about detaching the devices adhering to the flesh of the woman whose surrender he judged to be absolute.

Hands reached for the handles dangling from clinging

thongs. The talons released their grip on Mercedes' breasts. Others freed her ass-cheeks from their clutches. The agony suffusing her cunt died away as if it had never been. The lesser pain seeming by now a part of her essential self vanished from breasts and mound.

Bemusedly comprehending that she just managed an astonishing feat of self-control, she hung slackly, her vision narrowed, her awareness diminished. Her fingers needed silent urging by her lethargic brain before they obeyed the command to let go.

Crushed against a bare, muscular chest, Mercedes savored the cessation of the most severe pain ever to grip her. No faintest, lingering trace of that agony remained. Her will in abeyance, her body so pliant as to resemble an effigy molded of warm gel, she melted against the man holding her. Desire flared up from the depths of her being—fierce need which expanded into the vacuum created by the suspension of her will. "Fuck me," she pleaded, her voice a flow of liquid honey warmed by a tropical sun.

The tawny eyes raking her slack form glinted with triumph. Strong arms bore her to the bed, and laid her thereon. Exerting perfect control over raw lust, Julian thrust both hands beneath her back. Sensuously, he tongued nut-hard nipples—licked them, suckled them, bit them playfully, painlessly.

Moaning, Mercedes writhed in the arms that now disposed her so that she lay with her head by her lover's hips. As hands thrust her legs apart, and a warm, moist mouth closed over her swollen clit, a low cry broke from her lips. Laying her head on Julian's thigh, she took his rigid prick in her mouth. Eagerly, she sucked on the shaft, and teased the head with her tongue. Her loins throbbed with pleasure so great as to border pain.

Befogged with lust, she felt him desist. Moving with catlike grace, he laid her supine, and mounted her. Even as his stiff prick unerringly targeted the hole oozing sticky jism, he slid both forearms under her back, arching her so that her outthrust breasts pressed against his chest. His mouth closed over hers as he drove into her cunt with hard, deep thrusts.

Reacting with wanton abandon, Mercedes wrapped her legs around her partner's hips. Arching against him, she gave herself up to sheer, overmastering carnal delight. Her loins loosened, her will inoperative, her mind a haze of hot lust, she welcomed the gathering, the heat, the delicious shivers signifying the imminence of climax. Surrendering utterly, she achieved what had so often eluded her in the past. A joyous cry accompanied her ascent to a giddy height of rapture.

Awash in bliss, congealed against the leather cushioning of the bed, the initiate focused on her sensations. A long sigh wafted through parted lips to impinge on the ear of the man withdrawing his still-rock-hard member from her dripping cunt. Disposing his body next to hers, he clasped her against his chest.

As passion ebbed, the woman thus firmly embraced grew conscious of the insistent pressure of a turgid organ. Taken aback, she stiffened. Drawing away, she queried in dismay, "I failed to make you come?"

For a fleeting half-second, the tawny eyes narrowed; the slash of a mouth tightened. His voice holding an edge, the man controlling an ephemeral flash of anger retorted levelly, "You possess no power to override my will, Mercedes!"

That evanescent ire dying as swiftly as it had appeared, he added lightly, equably, "I'm not finished making love to you. A master of erotic art trains himself to achieve mental ecstasy without ejaculating, so as to prolong both his own and his partner's pleasure. I'll impregnate you when and how I wish, my untutored love-slave." Drawing his astonished partner into his arms, he kissed her—languorously, intimately, possessively.

Flowing against the bare torso of this sadist capable of stirring her to such unprecedented heights of bliss, Mercedes grew once again exquisitely aware of her helplessness against his strength. Her own lust slaked, she yet experienced a renewed stirring in her loins, as he laid her upper body over his forearm, her breasts outthrust, her arm held in a grip she knew she could not break.

A finger toyed with her nipple, which instantly went hard as pink granite, prompting a richly seductive, patently amused voice to murmur a provocative remark directly into her ear. "You'll grow to crave the whip, little sensualist," came the unsettling prediction. "You achieve mental surrender far more swiftly, far more intensely, when subjected to pain, than you do otherwise. But the unreliable mental circuitry that occasionally failed you in the past, I judge to be growing not only stronger, but becoming positively robust. We'll test its efficacy, mmmm? You won a victory earlier today. Lie back now, and focus solely on enjoying the reward due you."

Knowing herself freed by that adjuration from any pressure to confer pleasure on this enigmatic lover equal to that which he gave her, the woman thus adjured relaxed, still caught up in an uncanny sense of existing within a bubble detached from the onward flow of time. Expertly caressed by hands, mouth, tongue, and even the cock remaining so inexplicably rigid, she savored each tantalizing touch, surrendering to the pleasure expertly conferred by a seducer able to dominate her to the point of annihilating her will.

Lying supine, her interior space shivering, awash in wetness; her nipples erect, hard as pink granite; her breath coming in rapid, shallow respirations, Mercedes knew herself lifted, raised off the bed, and carried across the chamber. For a few seconds, she wondered uneasily whether Julian meditated a new infliction of pain, but his action swiftly disabused her of that notion. "Clasp me about the neck," he commanded.

When she obeyed, he moved with effortless grace. Deftly, he shifted her body so that she faced him while held by forearms thrust beneath her thighs so that they forced her legs to spread. Seating himself on the low, three-legged stool, the man supporting the full weight of his lover's body on those corded arms clasped his hands behind her back.

Supported on his forearms rather than on his lap, Mercedes heard him command, "Guide my shaft into your love-tunnel." Bemusedly, she complied. Aware that he could not thrust into her with any degree of facility in this unique posture, she yet savored the closeness—the sensation of being cherished, of cherishing him. Her legs spread, her bent knees resting in the crook of arms clasped behind her, her lover's shaft penetrating her to the fullest extent, she congealed against his chest. Both of her arms remained locked around his neck.

All at once, Julian began to rock, forward and back, forward and back. The woman so direly tormented only a short time earlier, now unconsciously regressed back into her childhood. Awash in euphoria, she savored the sense of being protected, soothed, comforted, treasured.

Back and forth her lover rocked, making no effort to work the cunt awash in juice. He simply let his rigid prick provide an ineffable sense that the two of them now existed as a single entity. When his rapt partner tipped her head back, her face dreamy, her lips parted, he closed his mouth over hers, and sucked on her tongue as if to emphasize the totality of that oneness.

The animal lust generated by her ordeal satiated, Mercedes

now passed to a new plane of sensual experience. Wakened not so much to passion as to affection, aroused not by relentless stimulation of the central focus of her femininity, but by extended contact with the warm, hard body of the lover providing that subtly beguiling motion, she gained a surreal sense of being possessed, body and mind, by this man who in essence remained a stranger.

The loins occupied by the hard shaft embodying his manhood, the mouth joined in so erotic a fashion to his, so that her tongue seemed to be as much his as hers, the flesh molding itself to his torso, combined to send a myriad subtle impulses down nerves rendered hypersensitive by prior stimulation. Her consciousness narrowed to focus solely on that delicious sense of being absorbed into his very being.

Freeing her mouth, Julian maintained his hold on the legs spread wide. In a fluid movement the sinuous grace of which belied the prodigious expenditure of brute strength needed to accomplish it, he rose. Straightening, he stood erect, still bearing the full weight of his partner on those seemingly tireless arms. Penetrated to the full by his turgid member, Mercedes now found herself rocked sideways, her whole body rotated in an arc, left, and then right, left, and right, around her lover's rock-hard organ.

That pivoting around the shaft penetrating her feminine depth created indescribably erotic sensations. Waves of pleasurable impulses radiated upwards from groin to chest, in the woman beginning to experience the gathering, the rippling tremors, the hot-cold shivers preceding the spontaneous, delicious contractions of her cunt around the tool of the man willing himself to eject the essence of his perfectly controlled but now excruciatingly intense passion. The pace of her rise to climax seemed surreally slow: a dream-sequence occurring in an eerie distortion of space-time.

When fulfillment came, it went on and on: a white heat of culmination shared by two lovers fused into ecstatic union. Consciousness fragmented in the woman held by those arms of iron. Awareness vanished, as she entered into full coital trance.

Himself verging on succumbing to that same effect, Julian hung on to his senses long enough to walk to the bed and lower the partner gone limp as wet silk onto the leather-sheathed mattress. Dropping beside her, he crushed her inert body to his, before succumbing to the euphoria wiping all coherent thought from his mind.

Chapter Five

Julian fought his return to reality. Conscious of warm flesh pressed against his, he raised a languid hand. Idly, he stroked the back of the lover lying sprawled prone against him, her face pressed into the hollow between his chest and arm, her shoulder-length hair brushing his chest.

Lethargic, relaxed in body, he yet savored the fierce mental satisfaction engendered by the outcome of a course of action that he knew had posed considerable risk. Contentment wreathed the face more striking than handsome. Musingly, the successful seducer contemplated launching on a new and far riskier course. As he weighed probabilities, he drew ever closer to deciding in the affirmative.

Mercedes stirred. Confusedly, she concluded for a few seconds that she must have passed out from some lingering effect of the electronic stimulation. On assessing her sensations, she rejected that premise as inconsistent with the ebbing wash of carnal pleasure suffusing her entire being. *La petite mort!* she exclaimed silently, stricken with wonder. Reminding herself that she had hitherto believed that term to represent a Gallic exaggeration, she grew aware of where she lay, and of the hand stroking her back. The arm thrown across the chest of her lover tightened around him.

Shifting to lie on his side, Julian proceeded to hold his partner as he so often did: her back arched across his forearm, her breasts outthrust, her upper arm caught in a firm grip. A finger of his free hand absently toyed with a nipple, but his eyes riveted themselves to her still-euphoric face. "Did I deliver what I promised?" he queried with deceptive lightness.

Her head thrown back so that the long column of her throat again reminded her master of a Modigliani painting, Mercedes breathed, "You surely did. I passed into some otherworldly state new to my experience." Raising her head, she whispered, "Hold me close."

Acceding, her companion again pressed her bare torso against his. She melted against him. Lying with her cheek against his chest, she murmured ruminatively, "I think I've ventured beyond the real world I inhabited when I woke this morning. I feel right now as if I've entered some alternative realm where time doesn't operate—a universe defined by the circle of your arms."

Intrigued by her choice of metaphor, Julian intuitively realized that this woman simply voiced a thought which just occurred to her, rather than calculatedly striving to create a theatrical effect. "And do you find that universe confining?" he inquired, raising an eyebrow.

"No," came the murmured but adamant reply. "I find it liberating."

Shock surged through him. The faint but troubling fear that had nagged at him since he made the decision to pursue the course just completed, vanished. Crushing his partner against his muscular chest, he resolved to embark on the risky venture posing so beguiling a temptation.

Rising, Julian bore his lover to the room featuring the hot pool, where he treated her to a bath and a leisurely soak. The pampering deepened Mercedes' sense of living in a dream-distortion of reality. That illusion persisted after she found herself deposited on the couch, still stark naked, and handed a cup of steaming tea.

Sipping the fragrant beverage, she watched her lover build a fire in the wood stove. Sun streamed through the south-facing windows of the room warm enough to render nudity comfortable even without the fire, but brisk gusts of wind lashed the trees groaning as they flinched under its punishment.

Dropping to a seat next to hers, Julian slipped an arm in back of her, and drew her into an attitude permitting him to study her expression. "Have you found your way back from your sojourn in a parallel universe, little innocent?" he inquired, his voice a caress in itself.

"I'm fighting deportation." That candid answer came accompanied by a beguiling smile.

"Mmmm," he drawled, his expression manifestly triumphant. "I gambled that you'd rise to the challenge I set you—that you'd refrain, when I took you home, from calling the County Sheriff and charging me with assault—or even rape."

Shock leaped nakedly into green eyes that perceptibly widened. Stiffening, Mercedes gasped, "You thought I'd . . . Julian, you told me what you intended—asked my consent! I freely gave it! How could I charge you with assault?"

A sardonic smile, punctuated by a raised eyebrow, greeted that patently sincere protest. "A woman who considers herself wronged seldom thinks logically, Mercedes. The chance of your making such a charge, I judged to be slim, but not nil. I'd have handled the legal aspect, but I'd have loathed enduring the notoriety."

"You think I'd bring such wholly insupportable notoriety on myself, even if I did consider myself wronged—which I don't?"

"Ahhh . . . you're a unique woman—as reticent as you are fearless. From the beginning, you sensed my reluctance to discuss my private life, and so you studiously avoided prying. You value your own privacy, respect that of others, and keep your word. My admiration for those qualities prompts me to tender an invitation that I hope you'll accept.

"However, before I explain, I'll ask you to give me your word that you'll keep strictly to yourself the revelations regarding my personal life which I feel compelled to make, so that you'll understand what the invitation entails."

Fear fleetingly afflicted the woman still exquisitely conscious that this stranger generated a palpable aura of danger. Uneasily, she wondered whether such revelations might prove unsettling at the least, and at the worst make her the accomplice of a fugitive from justice.

After a few seconds' reflection, she rejected that latter hypothesis unlikely to prove true. She remembered that the eminently respectable private seller personally told her that he sold this property to a buyer who employed no intermediary—a man who dealt fairly and forthrightly, in person, and paid the entire amount with a personal check. She recalled also that the reclusive newcomer must have openly made the acquaintance of at least one of her neighbors: whoever advised him to contact her regarding the harvesting of his hay. Reassured, she nodded. "You have my word," she averred firmly.

Relaxed, debonair, Julian let no hint fall that he accurately guessed what fear caused that momentary hesitation. "Well, then. I'm a member of an organization unknown to all but those within it, or closely allied with it: an order composed of wealthy and powerful men bound to each other by ties stronger than those of blood. Those men of varying nationalities share a philosophy, a code of ethics, and a culture that differs markedly, in some ways, from that of their native countries. All of us rank as masters of erotic art. All of us practice the techniques to which I today introduced you."

Failing to conceal the shock occasioned by that final admission, Mercedes yet refrained from interrupting. Fascination outweighed the wariness beginning to resurface.

"Were I to mention the names of any of our members, you'd not recognize them. None of us are celebrities from the worlds of entertainment, sports, or politics. None of us qualify as jet setters; none of us are internationally known playboys. On the contrary, to a man, we shun the limelight by eschewing the symbols universally employed to announce wealth or power. We blend into our surroundings—move where and how we please, without attracting attention. Our organization promotes no political, economic, social, or philosophical agenda.

"We may wield power as individuals, in the realm of entrepreneurship, scientific or medical research, investment, or some similar field of endeavor, but our fellowship exists solely because we prefer each other's company and the culture distinguishing the Order, to the benefits conferred by membership in any other organization. We pursue our individual goals singly and privately, but we gather once a year, for a span of five days, to enjoy associations we cherish.

"That annual gathering takes place this coming week—starting tomorrow. I'll be flying to the private estate which doubles as our headquarters. I hope to persuade you to come with me, as my cherished companion. I'll do my best to beguile you into participating in stimulating encounters with fascinating individuals by day, and sharing my bed at night."

Inexplicably tempted to accede, Mercedes castigated the alter ego actually considering the shocking idea of accepting such an invitation tendered by a man still essentially a stranger. I'd be a virtual prisoner within a private retreat of men who indulge sadomasochistic tastes in sensual pleasure! she chided herself savagely. A convention of sadists!

No. Too harsh a criticism, came the instant qualification, as the widow reviewed her lover's description. But how could I run such a risk? Temporizing, she protested, "Julian, I don't own the sort of clothes the wives and girlfriends of wealthy and powerful men would wear to a gathering like that. I'd prove an embarrassment to you."

Inwardly elated to discover that no instant, adamant refusal greeted his proposal, the man now bent on gaining her assent chided reproachfully, "Didn't I just tell you that we eschew the sort of status symbols flaunted by celebrities? We look past clothing to the attributes of the wearer, Mercedes. When we arrive, I'll provide you with a starkly simple black gown identical to those all of the women present will be wearing, from the consort of the Grand Master to the companion of the least influential member. You'll find that the men display equal uniformity of dress."

The will to decline swiftly eroded, in the mind of the woman intrigued by the implications of that revelation. Her reservations weakened, but failed to crumble. "I'd need a plane ticket," she ventured abstractedly, playing for time in which to think up more cogent objections.

"No, you won't. I own a private helicopter that I pilot myself." Drawing her close, sensing her fear, Julian employed every subtle nuance of his melodic, mesmeric voice to batter down her faltering guard. "My word will still hold, Mercedes. You'll suffer no harm of any sort. My friends may espouse philosophical doctrines or cultural values with which you can't fully agree, but no one will pressure you to conform—least of all, me. So put that worry from mind."

Wondering distractedly just why she trusted this dangerous

stranger so completely, so quickly, Mercedes yet let that intuitive certainty that he not only would offer her no harm, but would stand between her and any potential harm-wreaker like an impervious shield, prompt her to agree. Not given to self-delusion, she wryly conceded that she hated the thought of retiring into the semi-seclusion of her home for a week, wondering the while what sort of new, competitive liaisons might spring from Julian's sojourn among his closest friends.

"I accept your invitation," she breathed, searching his face for any ominous, fleeting evidence of fierce exultation all out of proportion to the seeming innocuousness of the proposal. She beheld only a vivid smile evincing genuine pleasure, and affectionate warmth. Hugging her, the member of the mysterious Order murmured, "I'm glad, Mercedes. I'd have missed you damnably."

Warmed to her core, the woman reassured by his reaction wondered anew at the complex personality of a lover who cared for her even as he derived sensual pleasure from causing her pain, but she marveled even more at the intensity of the desire to which that pain unfailingly stirred her. Reflecting that this occasionally cruel partner reached depths in her nature hitherto never plumbed, she shivered, half in fear, and half in anticipation.

Rising, Julian prepared a late lunch. Smiling on the woman who evinced enlightened taste in beer, but drank that rare brew in moderation, he served her a vintage wine while loin pork chops broiled, potatoes baked, and greens steamed.

Struck by a novel supposition, the guest swirled the glass so as to watch the pale amber liquid run down the sides, before inhaling the aroma. Two tentative sips confirmed her suspicion. Smiling at the host watching her intently, she stated forthrightly, "I'm only a middling judge of fine wines—someone ignorant of the merits of particular vintage years—

but this one would set the most exacting connoisseur exclaiming in delight, would it not?"

The mobile face of a premier connoisseur lit with pleasure. "Ahhh . . . you're blessed with a naturally delicate palate," he commended her. "A rare gift of the capricious gods, that quality."

Host and guest smiled at each other over the rims of the goblets as they savored the taste.

An hour later, Julian drove his guest home, so as to allow her to prepare for an absence of a week, and the flight to the destination about which he remained vague.

Grown accepting of his secretiveness, the woman sensed that he nowise wished to provide any details regarding the Order other than those already provided. Accepting his quirk, she launched no delicate queries. Having called her elder daughter, she left a message on her answering machine to the effect that she would be gone for a week, traveling with a friend. That message she pointedly voiced in Julian's hearing.

When she led the way to her greenhouse, and filled the reservoir that would water her plants from beneath for the ensuing twelve days, she smilingly responded to his expressions of admiration for the clever arrangement.

"My husband designed the layout," she informed him wistfully. "Mechanical genius, he was—able to make anything run, even machinery long past its prime, or vehicles so elderly that they ranked as antiques. He could have been an engineer, had he wished, but he loved both the land, and the life of a cattleman. His skill at ranching combined with his neighborliness to earn him universal respect within a closely knit community of rugged individualists like himself."

Mercedes felt an arm slide around her waist, and tighten in wordless sympathy for her loss.

Turning to take one last glance around her home preparatory to leaving for a week, the widow found herself unqualifiedly looking forward to a break in the even tenor of days which slid into one another with little change, and less excitement. The novelty of the trip generated eager anticipation, while her cognizance of being desired by a masterful lover, however dangerous he might be, exhilarated her.

Upon returning to the dwelling as familiar to her now as her own, she willingly indulged in a dual swim against the current responding to the pace set by the man on her right, to whose placement in the pool the sensors responded. Exerting herself, she matched the stiff challenge he set her: kept abreast of him for the span of time the length of which he, rather than she, determined. Tired by her effort, she made no demur when, after a light supper, he announced that they would retire early, given that they would be rising at four.

The trip through the azure blue of a limitless sky on a perfect fall day provided the rapt passenger with a panoramic view far more extensive than that seen through the window of a commercial airplane. She knew that they traveled south, but found it difficult to identify any landmarks. Mountains gave way to rolling hills, which in turn yielded to rugged terrain characterized by desert land forms: buttes, mesas, narrow columns, talus slopes, winding canyons. Unsure whether they flew high over Arizona or New Mexico, she found herself caring no whit. Trusting in her lover, she reveled in the austere beauty visible from the helicopter far larger than the small, bubble-fronted craft occasionally seen flying over her home.

Absorbed by the sight of the earth spread out below her, Mercedes grew aware that the craft now dropped to circle a bowl-shaped depression—a wide place in a steep-walled, narrow canyon featuring a gravelly, boulder-littered riverbed lacking even isolated puddles of moisture. Scanning the ground, she observed that the stream-course bypassed the central portion of the bowl, and yet dense greenery flourished within the roughly circular feature surrounded by steep walls of rock.

She noted that like so much of the arid terrain typical of desert topography, hard horizontal layers interspersed with softer ones that eroded far more easily. Here, she discovered, no talus slopes formed of the products of such erosion fanned outwards from the base of the steep walls. Puzzled, she pondered the reason. Shrewdly, she judged the anomaly to result from human intervention, especially as a heliport could be seen at the edge of the bowl. Rough, hilly desert terrain fractured by canyons and seemingly devoid of roads, stretched away on all sides.

The craft descended onto a paved surface upon which rested a dozen other helicopters. In the view of the woman staring in wonder, the heliport seemed to be the only man-made structure in the vicinity. At the edge closest to the rim of the circular depression, the keen observer beheld a squat stone building.

Upon debarking onto the tarmac, Julian ushered his companion in that direction, a duffel bag slung over one shoulder by a strap, and a hard, flat case too big to be a briefcase borne in his left hand.

Burdened only by a commodious purse equipped with an over-the-shoulder strap, Mercedes reveled in the warmth of sunshine far hotter than that just beginning to dispel the darkness when they departed early that morning. Shrugging out of her down jacket, she laid the garment over an arm as they entered the small building.

A trim, lithe man of uncertain age greeted them warmly. Is he sixty? the guest mused. Or does he only seem that young due to his athleticism?

Having embraced Julian, the man sparking that unsatisfied

curiosity now gripped the hand of the woman noting that he wore a plain, black, short-sleeved shirt and tightly fitting pants fashioned of the same soft knit material. A silver pin of intricate design, worn high on his chest, reminded her of heraldic crests. Returning the pressure, she smiled into piercing eyes of luminous brown. Hair once dark, she saw to be streaked with gray, but Julian's fellow member moved with feline grace.

Retiring behind the counter that formed the only feature of the building other than a circular stairwell, the doorkeeper handed the newly arrived member of the Order a key from which a small wooden square bearing a printed number dangled. "Thirty-six," he announced, smiling conspiratorially on his peer. "I held that room for you, just in case you decided at the last minute against arriving alone. You're anything but predictable, my friend."

"Ahhh . . . I thank you, Alexander." Smiling, Julian introduced Mercedes by her first name only. Surmising that such deliberate omissions would prove a universal custom among these enigmatic members of an Order unknown to anyone but themselves, she marveled at their reclusiveness even as she acknowledged that her own penchant for living in relative seclusion all but matched theirs.

"You've arrived earlier than most of those who signed up to come," she heard Alexander inform her escort. Taking leave of the man evidently on duty at the entry to some hidden retreat, she flashed him a vivid parting smile as Julian tucked her arm into his, and steered her into the stairwell.

Descending a stonewalled, spiral stair reminiscent of melodramatic films featuring castles equipped with dungeons, Mercedes preceded her escort through the door located on a landing from which another flight of stairs led still further downwards. Emerging into a long, dimly lit hallway the floor of which she saw to be a smoothly finished expanse of the hard rock which alternated with that softer and more erosion-prone, she surmised that the facility occupied two such stories at least: levels hollowed from the soft layers, but roofed and floored by the hard layers supported on a vast array of pillars. Those upright columns of mortared stone, visible between smooth, creamy, plaster-finished panels, she observed to function as massive roof-supports, as well as design-elements integral to the walls.

As the couple advanced, their footsteps echoed in the silence. On either side of the long hall illuminated by electric wall-fixtures spaced at wide intervals, doors of heavy, iron-bossed hardwood bearing numbers wrought in the same metal broke the otherwise unvarying expanse of plaster-and-mortared-stone walls. Two side passages led away to both right and left, halfway down the length of the hall.

Those portals Julian bypassed. Thirty-six proved to be the sixth and last doorway set into the right-hand wall. Some twenty feet beyond that point, at the end of the passage, Mercedes beheld a closed door identical to those giving access to what she rightly assumed to be guest-bedrooms.

The chamber into which she stepped seemed quaintly medieval to the woman delighted by the antique aspect of the retreat. An oversized bed, furnished only with a contoured, apricot-colored sheet, and three plump pillows covered by matching slips, stood to her right, its carved wooden headboard set against the outer wall beneath ventilation and heat ducts affixed to the ceiling. Two nightstands flanked that central feature.

On its far side, the guest beheld a circular table of polished hardwood, around which reposed four leather-cushioned wooden chairs. On the near side, to her left as she stood just inside the doorway, a square alcove separated a narrow, open-fronted closet and a counter featuring a sink, from the opened door leading to the bathroom. On the wall to her left, beyond the alcove, a tall, narrow, wood-framed, full-length mirror hung, flanked by a hardwood bench set lengthwise along the wall.

The entire length of wall opposite the head of the bed, the intrigued viewer saw to be bare. Two massive stone pillars divided that broad expanse into three sections. No thick, plastered wall joined the pillars. Behind them, paneling formed of cunningly joined planks of hardwood formed a smooth wall-covering which appeared seamless at a distance. That surface, waxed and buffed to a satiny finish, emphasized the solidity of the masonry roof-supports. The ceiling composed of living rock softened the glow of the long light-fixtures affixed to its russet surface. The stone-flagged chamber forcibly reminding the viewer of cells in a monastery possessed no windows.

Julian laid the case and the duffel bag on the bench. Turning, he regarded the companion gazing around in patent delight.

"I'll wager this hideaway's ancient," the newcomer to the premises breathed, awed by the excellent quality of the workmanship. "And what bliss—no television!"

A hearty laugh greeted that effusion. "The pap delivered via the tube would jar annoyingly on senses soothed by an illusion of traveling back into a less frenetic age, eh, Mercedes?" Slipping his arms around her from behind, he murmured, "That sense I unfailingly gain here, of leaving modern America behind, never fails to relax me. Slip out of your clothes, little adventuress. We need to pay the customary courtesy call on the Grand Master."

Standing nude, uncertain as to whether the uniform would include underwear, Mercedes watched as Julian, as naked now as was she, removed a folded square of cloth, a pair of slippers, and a small drawstring sack from his duffel. Shaking out the fabric, he dropped its tubular length over his lover's head. The soft, flat-black, unbelted gown clung to her torso, and fell in graceful, ample folds to her ankles. The cloth cut so as to narrow continuously as it rose towards her neck, swept slantingly upwards to her right shoulder, covering her breasts, and reaching her shoulder as an inch-wide strap which met an identical strap rising from her back, over that same shoulder.

Those two strips of fabric Julian laid one atop the other, and fastened with a gleaming ornament taken from the sack: a delicate golden ring. The matching pearl-tipped pin he thrust through the two layers of fabric within the circle, allowing the head and tip of the pin to rest on the circumference, thus joining the two ends into a single over-the-shoulder strap. The wearer's left shoulder and neck remained bare.

Thrusting her feet into slippers fashioned of the same material as the dress, Mercedes discovered that the flat-soled footwear stretched to fit.

Standing before the mirror, the woman narrowly inspecting her image grew acutely conscious that the soft knit fabric provided no support for her breasts. "Julian, anyone meeting me will notice that I sag in front," she observed wryly.

"Anyone meeting you will observe your natural shape: one quite pleasing, for a woman your age," came the prompt retort. "We of the Order appreciate natural beauty, Mercedes. We don't judge attractiveness by the standards set by a garish entertainment industry, and we know better than to view youthfulness as the prime element in sexual appeal. You radiate a most beguiling vibrancy when you expound on some topic that intrigues you. That zest animates you—renders you ageless. Your sensuality's subtle but potent, and the more appealing for your never consciously flaunting it."

"What a welcome compliment," the widow breathed, touched. A thought impinged: only four days earlier she had rested certain that she would never again know the joy of sexual intercourse with a skilled, caring partner. Smiling with contagious vivacity at the man now clad in a black, short-sleeved shirt and black trousers identical to those worn by Alexander, she studied the pin worn high on his breast. Julian's silver insignia she saw to be wrought in a different design. The crest of the House of Rakoczy, she surmised accurately.

Intrigued, she wondered whether all of her lover's American peers could trace their ancestry—legitimate or illegitimate—back to European nobility. Shaking her head in an unconscious response to the thought impinging, she dismissed the idea as highly unlikely.

Escorted to the door at the end of the hall, Mercedes passed through the portal, and emerged onto a broad, iron-railed balcony overlooking the roughly circular floor of the canyon. A dense stand of trees sporting feathery green foliage—varieties new to her experience—met her delighted gaze. A vault of cloudless blue arched above; gleams of silvery water visible between breaks in the trees tantalized the eye.

The entranced viewer saw that this balcony, its roof of living rock supported on pillars identical to those within the retreat, extended around three-quarters of the circumference of the bowl which she estimated to be at least one hundred feet in diameter. Gazing across that expanse, she saw that a rock-roofed porch, its floor on a level with the floor of the bowl, occupied the space beneath the upper balcony.

Far away to her right, a waterfall issued from a fissure two-thirds of the way up the steeply rising wall. That eminence she saw to be composed of an outcropping of solid rock: stone obviously different from the hard-and-soft layering of the remainder of the walls. No evidence of human alteration appeared along that one-third of the wall forming the sides of the bowl. Patches of mist hung over the trees, where the waterfall plunged downward.

A stone stairwell led to the lower level. A spacious expanse to the left of the newcomers stepping onto the porch while looking out over the bowl, extended deeply into the canyon's wall at this particular point in its circumference. Pillars joined by wrought-iron railings separated the cavernous space into small, discrete areas furnished with leather-upholstered couches and chairs, and coffee tables of polished hardwood. Those nooks the guest turning to look in that direction saw to be designed to facilitate conversation among those gathered there.

At the rear of the rock-roofed expanse, she caught sight of a curving hardwood counter, evidently a buffet. Some twenty people, men and women garbed exactly as were she and the man retaining his hold on her arm, sat talking in groups of various sizes, or strolled to or from the buffet. A couple emerged from a stone-flagged path leading into the trees. As Mercedes watched, they joined a circle of conversationalists.

Guiding his companion away from the U-shaped, spacious sitting area, Julian turned to his right, and advanced down the porch-like lower level situated beneath the balcony. Having passed several widely spaced, iron-bossed, closed doors, he entered an open-fronted alcove where two people, a man and a woman, sat side-by-side on cushioned, comfortable hardwood chairs. Brilliantly colored flowers contrasted with green shrubs, in plantings occupying a dozen weathered wooden half-barrels: a decor that made the austere alcove seem a pleasant garden.

The pair rose as the newcomers approached, and walked forward to greet them.

The well-proportioned, still-athletic figure garbed exactly as was Julian, exceeded in stature the younger man who himself stood six feet tall. Silvery gray hair, thick, but closely cropped, crowned a head carried with regal authoritativeness. Magnetic eyes of luminous blue-green, deeply set beneath bushy gray brows, generated a palpable electric aura in the space separating their owner from his visitors.

Extending a sinewy hand, the Grand Master gripped that of the member paying his respects. Drawing Julian close, the autocratic figure embraced him for a few seconds before holding him away, and conducting a swift but penetrating appraisal. "You look the better for having enjoyed a span of unaccustomed leisure," he announced ruminatively.

Smiling as he murmured a greeting, Julian nodded. Turning to the silvery-haired, arrow-straight, willowy woman standing at the side of the imposing figure of her companion, the new arrival paying his respects bent with fluid grace over her outstretched hand, and kissed it. That antique gesture seemed oddly fitting in the view of the younger woman now conscious of riveting the attention of the striking personage wielding supreme authority here.

"Mercedes, meet Lorenzo, Grand Master of the Order, and Francesca, his consort." The melodic voice of her lover, grave, cultured, might have been introducing royalty.

A ghost of a smile flitted across the patrician face of the Grand Master as he responded to the introduction. Addressing Julian rather than the woman on whom his eyes rested, he remarked, "Ahhh . . . I see why you lack, today, that habitual tension—that seeming readiness to engage in swift action, my friend. I'll wager that this lady suits you admirably." Speaking now to the woman serenely meeting that raking glance, he observed musingly, "You possess an innate regard for honor, an ardent, sensitive nature, and the soul of a poet, eh, Mercedes?"

Shocked to her depths, the visitor thus accurately categorized by this man meeting her now for the first time, asked herself in disbelief whether this obviously gifted leader might possibly possess psychic powers. Too committed a skeptic to settle for that explanation, she instead credited him with being endowed with a high order of intuition. Concluding that he had grown accustomed to utilizing a wealth of experience at reading people's natures from evidence etched into their faces, she maintained an admirable composure as she responded, "And you see deeply into souls, Lorenzo. A far rarer gift, that, than any I possess."

Smiling broadly now, obviously pleased by her response, Lorenzo turned the full force of his persona on the man savoring fierce pride in the poise exhibited by his companion. "Daring as ever, you are, Julian, but I concede the prize to justify the risk you run," he opined judiciously, his deep voice bearing an unmistakably ironic overtone.

Silently applauding the older man's extraordinary perceptiveness, Julian wryly wondered why he had expected to conceal from this uncannily shrewd observer that his companion did not truly qualify as an initiate. Even as he savored the relief generated by the oblique remark implying that Lorenzo condoned his action, he experienced a tightening of the gut.

Guessing that the cryptic statement embodied some hidden double meaning lost on an outsider, the guest sensed that it nonetheless constituted no reproof. Gratified to discover that the woman now joining in the general conversation projected a vivid individuality which prevented her from being overshadowed, or worse, rendered completely colorless and forgettable in the company of her husband—surely consort equates with wife, the guest assured herself—Mercedes noted the courtly courtesy with which Lorenzo treated both the consort who she judged to be between sixty and seventy, and herself.

Acknowledging that Julian did likewise, the stranger to this company admitted in the privacy of her thoughts to having made the unwarranted assumption that the majority of men possessing singular tastes in sensual pleasure must of necessity prove arrogantly condescending to women in social situations. Judging that she had thus far failed to penetrate a surface veneer concealing the inner workings of a society markedly different from any she had known, she generated a fast-burgeoning wish to delve beneath that veneer.

Strolling on Julian's arm back to the huge sitting area, the guest reviewed her impressions. Her gown she had perceived to be identical to that worn by Francesca, but the golden ornament fastening that of the consort of the Grand Master she had observed to be five-lobed: a design suggesting a stylized, five-petaled flower. A ruby adorned the head of the pin thrust through the delicate figure.

A special designation deriving from her husband's rank, those tokens, the guest surmised. The equivalent of a crown, or a diamond tiara. Amused to discover that she automatically thought in terms of royalty, rather than of honored achievers in a republic, she smiled to herself. They bear themselves like royalty, she conceded admiringly.

Still occupied by her reflections, Mercedes responded to the pressure of the arm guiding her into the company of six people: four men, and two women. The men swiftly rose to greet their peer. Eagerly, they embraced him before turning their full attention boldly and appraisingly on his companion.

No whit flustered, Mercedes smilingly extended a hand to each person, her grip hearty, her manner warm. Julian's melodic voice intoned names which melded in her awareness with faces as striking as his own.

A bear-like hand closed over hers. A swarthy giant, broad of shoulder and massive in bulk, towered over her. Eyes black as polished jet, deeply set beneath thick, black brows, bored into hers. Sable hair, closely cropped, hid nothing of a lined face brown as oiled hardwood. An aquiline nose, a jutting, deeply cleft jaw, a wide, tight-lipped mouth, conferred an overall impression of toughness. The man's stance—erect, shoulders squared, head held high—suggested military training.

Rejecting that latter supposition as inconsistent with the fierce individuality that Julian described as universal among the members of the Order, Mercedes joined the face to the name: Manuel. His ever-so-slight foreign accent she assumed to be Spanish, given the name, and yet it differed in some indefinable degree from that of the local entrepreneur of Mexican descent whom the ranchwoman hired every spring to shoe her horses.

A memory impinged. The face and voice of a close male friend from her years as an undergraduate rose to mind: a foreign student, the scion of a wealthy family in Spain. Castilian, Manuel's accent, I'll wager, she marveled. It's exactly the same as Juan's!

A younger man, tall, wiry, and spare in contrast to Manuel's bulk, now gripped her hand. Jason, the newcomer to the setting silently repeated so as to fix the name in memory. Musingly, she studied a fluidly expressive, vitally animated, but nowise handsome countenance. Returning the wholly engaging smile flashed on her by the man whose accent she readily identified as Bostonian, she clasped the hand of a girl whose hard-muscled body, supple athleticism, and tanned face sporting tiny squint-lines at the corners of the eyes suggested the outdoorswoman to a judge well able to detect the signs. Shirley, she repeated silently, etching another name into capacious mental files. Obviously a Midwesterner.

Jason's arm encircled that of the self-possessed girl whose mane of wavy brown hair, confined in a ponytail, descended below her shoulders. His clasp the keen observer saw to be markedly proprietary. The fastening of Shirley's gown Mercedes observed to be triangular, but secured by a pearl-tipped pin. Wholesome, outgoing, intelligent, she conjectured. Competent at whatever she undertakes, this hardy individualist. Shirley's deeply in love with this overtly possessive associate of older, and I suspect, dangerous members of a formidable fellowship.

Celeste, Manuel's companion, a tall, languid, lissome beauty of perhaps thirty-five, wearing understated, artfully applied makeup which accentuated her air of worldliness, murmured a greeting in a pleasing contralto voice. A mass of straight, shining, superbly ordered dark hair that reminded Mercedes of televised advertisements for costly brands of shampoo, fell well below her shoulders. Her ornament, the woman actively searching for clues observed to be oval, the pin pearl-tipped.

The third man Mercedes guessed to be older than Jason, but younger than Julian. Perhaps, she amended, he only seems so by reason of the Byronic appeal he radiates. Wavy fair hair worn rather long she saw to frame a classic Grecian face. An aristocratic nose, arching brows above eyes of limpid blue, beautifully sculpted planes of cheek and forehead, smooth white skin, a delicately bowed mouth which might have seemed feminine but for the strong cast of the chin and jaw, the forceful set of the handsome features, the deep, wholly masculine voice, and the feline grace of the lithe body broad at the shoulders, but narrowing at the hips, added up to a combination of attributes which the viewer conceded to represent flawless physical beauty.

"Mercedes, this is Nikos," Julian announced blandly.

Eyes bold almost to the point of seeming impudent roved down the shapely figure of the widow certain that their owner undressed her in his imagination. Unsettled by that minute scrutiny, she yet felt the impact of the man's raw sensual appeal—to so forceful an extent that shame scalded her.

Casting upon the handsome peer of the lover she sensed to be observing her reaction, a glance so bland, so casual, as to border total disinterestedness, she pointedly focused her attention on Manuel. Bestowing an approving smile on that no less virile athlete, she silently concluded that he would have looked perfectly at home wielding a cutlass on the blood-drenched deck of a galleon boarded by pirates.

The fourth member, introduced as Albert, proved to be a compactly built man of medium height and uncertain age, notable chiefly for soulful dark eyes and a shining mass of sleek, shoulder-length chestnut hair. Like Nikos, Albert escorted no female companion.

At the start of the ensuing conversation, the woman exquisitely aware of Julian's habitual reluctance to discuss his personal life assumed that the other men would display equal reticence. To her considerable amazement, she listened as Manuel, replying to a question posed by Albert, made no attempt to conceal the fact that he commanded a private mercenary force organized as a corporate business. Fascinated, she learned that his corporation accepted challenging assignments on contract, specializing in bringing order to regions plagued by anarchy, banditry, or infiltrations by terrorist groups.

Mesmerized, she listened as Manuel expertly analyzed the causes and predicted the likely outcome of an incendiary political crisis presently erupting in the Sahara. As he spoke, the listener grew deeply impressed by his lack of arrogance.

She noted that he showed no tendency to swagger, or to boast of his exploits. He's obviously a highly skilled professional, she marveled—detached, businesslike, supremely efficient, and no doubt deadly in combat.

When the mercenary soldier concluded a riveting tale regarding an isolated incident in the Middle East where horses for once proved more useful to a modern fighting force than vehicles, Julian remarked, "Warfare in the desert changed little in method over many centuries. Small wonder that traditional modes of transportation still can prove more effective than armored vehicles. The desert's a formidable terrain to negotiate. Shirley, how far back can the lineages of purebred Arabian horses be traced?"

"Five thousand years," came the prompt reply. "They were a bit smaller in the beginning than they are today, but those ancient steeds looked quite similar to modern examples of the breed. Beautiful beyond belief, and marvelously suited to forays by desert warriors bent on raiding their neighbors and capturing herds and flocks."

That final observation turned the questioner's thoughts down a new track. Turning to Mercedes, Julian asked, "Given that Arabians are famous for their speed, stamina and agility, why do so many American cattlemen prefer to ride quarter horses?"

"Moving cattle seldom calls for speed," the ranchwoman replied equably, smiling at the girl whose obvious love for the breed noted for their arching necks, dished faces, and floating gaits raised her in Mercedes' esteem. "Quarter horses break into a gallop more swiftly, and achieve greater speed over a quarter of a mile than do those of any other breed. That trait assures that if one needs to rope an animal, one's mount can keep abreast until the loop falls. Over greater distances, they can't compete with other breeds in a race.

"However, when you move cattle, you don't run them. That just melts valuable pounds off the cows, needlessly exhausts the horses, and advertises the ineptitude of what we term drugstore cowboys.

"Quarter horses are stout and strong, however. When they plant their feet, they can hold even a bull until the second rider's rope topples and stretches the animal far more massive than either roper's saddle horse. They have 'cow savvy' bred into them.

"A rider has to be skilled to stay atop a highly trained cutting horse when his mount cuts a stray out of a herd. Such an animal will turn on a dime, and leave an inexperienced rider sitting on ten feet of air. A quarter horse can pack a two-hundred-pound man and a heavy stock saddle all day, and still have energy left at the close. Arabian horses exhibit speed and stamina, but they tend to be dainty of foot and more lightly built than horses bred chiefly as mounts that meet the special needs of stockmen, or outfitters who pack dudes into the rugged reaches of the high country."

"Ah, but no horse feels better beneath you than a purebred Arabian," Shirley averred, her eyes alight with combativeness. "Not even a thoroughbred flat-racer. All they can do well is run. Arabians outclass them even at that, unless you're bent on winning the Triple Crown."

During the discussion that ensued, Mercedes learned that Shirley raised and trained Arabians, that Jason openly admired her expertise in that field of endeavor, and that Julian shared her preference. To her private amusement, the ranchwoman discovered that Nikos far preferred the excitement of watching thoroughbreds race on a track, to riding any horse of any breed.

Manuel candidly admitted to mounting a horse only if an exigency arising during some daring strike necessitated switching to that mode of transportation. "I'm spoiled by the availability of modern technology," he vouchsafed readily. "I'll take a Humvee over a horse, any day."

That admission evoked a rippling laugh from the Westerner. "Don't think modern cattlemen don't agree!" she conceded wryly. "Our horses pass an inordinate number of hours being hauled around in horse-trailers, so as to prevent the rider's having to spend more time than is absolutely necessary, moving cows."

After whiling away an hour in spirited conversation, Manuel and Celeste, who only occasionally interjected a languid comment into the discussion, rose and took their leave. A new couple appeared, and joined the group. Some ten minutes later, Julian, professing to be hungry, escorted Mercedes to the counter, where the pair made a selection from an appetizing buffet tended by fresh-faced youths clad as were the members, but in white: lads whom Mercedes guessed to range in age from twenty to twenty-five.

Bearing trays, the pair joined a new group, and engaged in pleasant conversation as they enjoyed the meal. After dining, they circulated about the sitting area, greeting new arrivals. Her ability to etch a myriad names and faces of strangers into mental files from which she could easily retrieve them growing ever more sorely taxed, the widow sought to fix distinguishing characteristics in memory.

To her surprise, two of the women who she saw to be considerably younger than Francesca wore the five-petaled flower on their shoulders. One so distinguished wore the pearl pin, the other, the ruby. That discovery advised her of the erroneousness of her original assumption.

Three hours passed thus. Having greeted all of the members and their female partners, Julian escorted his companion back to their room. Relishing the quiet, and the chance to relax after rising so early, Mercedes shed the slippers, and reclined with a sigh of satisfaction on the bed—a reaction noted by the man emerging from the bathroom.

Smiling down at his supine lover, he doffed his own footwear. Dropping to lie next to her, he thrust an arm under her shoulders, pulled the pin from the ring, and set the fasteners on the nightstand. Thrusting the black fabric downward, he caressed the breast freed from the folds.

Snuggling closer, Mercedes warily ventured a question after reflecting that it involved no prying into his personal life. "What do the shapes of these golden ornaments signify?" she inquired with studied nonchalance.

The probe evoked no sign of displeasure. "The ring identifies you as my cherished companion," he replied readily. "The oval signifies that the woman's either a high-priced, superbly skilled, hired partner—a courtesan able to pick and choose among wealthy patrons, not a common prostitute—or a free soul trained by a variety of masters to be a surpassingly desirable partner. Such women, who value erotic skill in the men with whom they couple, form temporary liaisons with a long succession of masters without forming an emotional attachment to any of them. They aren't considered courtesans, even though the master often supports such a partner while she's with him.

"The triangular shape announces that a master's taken the woman as his consort in a formal ceremony witnessed by other members of the Order. She may also be a legal wife, but the strength of the bond rests on the promise her partner made as a member, far more than on the legal tie. The five-petaled flower signifies that the wearer's master swore to bed no other woman but herself, for as long as she lives. It's an indissoluble bond. She's assured of being consort for life of a man utterly faithful to her alone."

"So Celeste is a courtesan?"

"One revered by our membership for her superb skill at erotic art."

The Westerner familiar with the foibles of cowboys and daredevil riders following the rodeo circuit proved far less shocked by the discovery that men such as Manuel hired courtesans, than a respectable widow from New England or the Midwest might have been. "And the pins?" she asked, relieved to have generated no annoyance at the questioning.

"The pearl denotes your rank as an initiate. The ruby proclaims that the wearer classes as an adept, and therefore commands deep respect from the members. A woman who wears the ruby pin in the five-petaled flower, we honor above any other." A finger teased the nipple gone erect; the arm drew the half-clothed woman closer. Julian's mouth closed over hers, in a kiss more possessive than erotic.

Judging when he freed her lips that he intended only caresses at this juncture, Mercedes slipped a hand beneath his shirt, and massaged his chest. "And who decides that a woman's so skilled at pleasing her lover as to qualify to be ranked as an adept?" she inquired, genuinely intrigued.

Amused, Julian countered, "Do I detect a hint that you possess a competitive spirit?"

"No . . . just curiosity. The better I understand the culture of the Order, the better I'll understand you."

"Mm. The title's a bit misleading, Mercedes. It signifies that the woman underwent the rite of passage separating the two rankings. You came to me skilled enough to qualify for any ranking based solely on skill at conferring sensual pleasure, but I'll never lay the demand on you that would entitle you to wear the ruby pin."

Mystified by that revelation, the guest now consumed with intense curiosity queried, "Why not?"

Appreciative of the innate tactfulness that forbade her blurting out questions of this nature anywhere but in privacy, Julian unbent so far as to tender an explanation. Smiling into long-lashed eyes of emerald green while exquisitely conscious of treading on a thread stretched above a fire-pit, he responded lightly but truthfully.

"Mercedes, you're the only woman here whose master never conducted the rigorous regimen designed to crush any rebelliousness—any tendency, however slight, to disobey—when she underwent initiation. You require delicate handling—a light touch. Your society conditioned you to abhor the idea of willingly offering yourself as a slave to a master used to demanding total control over every aspect of a partner's life—not merely over her behavior during a sexual encounter."

Shocked to her core, Mercedes gasped, "These other women all offered themselves as . . . *slaves* . . . to some master?"

"Yes. Before I invited you to accompany me here, I subjected you to an abbreviated test of your willingness to surrender your will to mine. That test you passed, but I remain exquisitely aware that if I push you beyond the limit set by your lack of the proper conditioning, I'll risk losing a woman who, as Lorenzo so shrewdly pointed out, possesses an ardent and sensitive nature—a woman I'm growing to cherish.

"I also remain exquisitely aware that if you were to rebel in the presence of my peers, I'd suffer disgrace—be regarded with contempt. For that reason, I intend to shield you from certain aspects of our culture which would inevitably cause you acute mental upset."

The shock assailing the hearer intensified as a most troubling implication of that explanation struck her. "Julian . . . if you'd met me earlier . . . long before the week set for this gathering . . .

would you have sought to make me your . . . slave? To persuade me . . . or perhaps even to coerce me . . . into letting you rule every aspect of my life?"

"Most assuredly," came the adamant, deeply troubling admission. "I'd have employed persuasion, not coercion, little innocent. And given my training, I'd likely have succeeded. I may yet succeed, despite the strength of your prior conditioning. Unless you levy a demand right now that I take you home, and henceforth stay out of your life, you'll find that each new surrendering of your will to mine renders you less desirous of living free, but alone. You'll end by craving my dominance—of reveling in the state of euphoria produced by the total abdication of your will."

Will I grow *that* dependent on this dangerous manipulator? Mercedes asked herself, aghast at the thought of losing the sturdy independence she valued so highly. Have I *already* fallen so completely under his sway that I can no longer face living alone? My perishing soul—has he brainwashed me?

Watching shock and fear contend on the striking face so unable to hide the emotions tearing at its owner, Julian winced inwardly as his gut clenched. "Say what you're thinking," he commanded.

"If I asked you to take me home right now . . . would you?"

His gut knotted into spasms, Julian yet unhesitatingly replied, "Of course. We don't abduct women, Mercedes. Neither do we force unwilling women to accommodate our tastes. You may never lose your sturdy independence of mind . . . never find yourself able to offer yourself as my slave. If that happens, I'll accept your decision, and bow out of your life.

"I'll frankly admit, however, to hoping that you don't take so radical a step. If you stay, I'll go on levying the same sort of demands that I have since we met, while shielding you from the aspects of our communal life here that would inevitably shock you. So nothing will have changed. The question of your eventually offering yourself as my slave, we'll address at a much later date. You're my guest here, Mercedes—and Lorenzo's."

Reassured on one score at least, Mercedes sought to determine how she ought to respond. Chilled more by the thought of returning to her solitary life than by the outrageous suggestion that she would eventually offer herself as this man's slave, she reviewed his statements. I *am* his guest, she reminded herself. He's not pushing me to agree, here.

"Julian, no way would I ever knowingly, deliberately, disgrace you," she protested earnestly. "You warned me that the culture of the Order differs radically from mine. I'm not going to rebel, believe me. No way would I cause your peers to regard you with contempt for bringing a woman not fully initiated. Please, rest assured on that score. It's just . . . when you use the term conditioning . . . I think of brainwashing . . . and cults . . ."

The tawny eyes riveted to hers reflected no hint that her halting confession sparked the mercurial anger she suspected this dangerous autocrat could readily generate. "As I once told you, we of the Order live by a code of ethics, but that code differs radically from those generally espoused in this day and age," came the calm reply. "We reserve to ourselves the right to employ subtle psychological means to condition a woman who inspires us with fierce desire. I readily admit that. But let me ask you this, Mercedes. Did any of the women you met today, seem cowed, abjectly placatory, or afraid of the master they accompanied?"

"No," came the swift, honest answer. "None did. But . . ." Determined to judge fairly, the widow refrained from impulsively blurting the objections crowding to the forefront of her mind.

A strong arm tightened around her. "Mercedes," the mesmeric, melodic voice declared, flowing with ease around the mental guard against cajolery which the troubled woman sought to maintain, "had I persuaded you to undergo the rigorous regimen which would have assured that you'd never dare to rebel in the presence of my peers no matter what I demanded of you, you'd have emerged from that initial conditioning harboring no suppressed resentment, no sublimated fear. A master knows his skill to be more than ample for insuring that outcome. The demeanor of all of these women who rank as consorts, stands as proof that each now feels supremely comfortable in her union with the man who dominates her not only during the sexual aspect of their relationship, but in every aspect of their joint lives."

"But . . . they've been . . . brainwashed." Shivers chased each other down the spine of the woman whispering that last word.

"That term doesn't apply," Julian averred flatly. "If we examine its essential, technical meaning, it includes not merely brutality, but physical and psychological torture: a relentless, ongoing, direly punishing ordeal designed to destroy the victim's persona, annihilate his moral scruples, and recast his mindset so as to conform to the ideology of the brainwasher. Nothing a member of our Order does, in any way resembles that sort of diabolically effective but irreparably damaging coercion."

"Brainwashing's too strong a term, perhaps. But . . . even the idea of conditioning scares me."

"Conditioning of itself isn't necessarily harmful. Your society rigorously conditioned *you*: to keep your word, to respect the privacy of neighbors, to accept their idiosyncrasies, to aid them when they're in need of help. That social conditioning's beneficial. It lends order and security to your closely knit rural community.

"Hearing about the regimen our initiates undergo, without having experienced more than a brief introduction to it, may render you dubious at this juncture, but our initiation of a lover lends order and security to *our* culture: one no less cohesive than that of the community of which you're a part."

Frowning, the widow pondering that comparison admitted that her fascination with this strange society outweighed her doubts. "You can out-debate me, Julian, I'll frankly admit. But I don't want you to take me home. I won't rebel, I promise you. I surely don't want you to be sorry you invited me here. I'm perfectly willing to put off any further discussion of my offering myself as your slave, until after we leave here."

"You're amazingly open-minded, Mercedes. I ought never to have brought you here. I ran considerable risk to my standing among my peers, by so doing. I accepted the risk because you proved yourself a partner well suited to adapting to the techniques I employ—a natural sensualist who'll learn to crave the whip. But as I said—you require delicate handling. I passed you my word that no harm will come to you. My word stands."

Passion stirred in the woman hearing that assurance: passion ignited by nuances in the melodic voice making so radical a prediction. Reflecting uneasily that she ought to regard her acceding voluntarily to this man's techniques as more frightening than having succumbed to an expert manipulator's subtle methods of conditioning, she marveled that her appetite for delving more deeply into the secret practices of this society of sadists remained unchanged. No, it's burgeoned, she amended, thrusting all doubt behind her.

"Julian," she breathed, caressing him beneath his shirt, "I

totally lack the tourist mentality. I grew up thirty miles from where I now live. Our rural society differs considerably from that of mainstream America. But whenever I've gone away—to college in New York City, for example, or to take a job in New Orleans during three summers while I was an undergraduate—I embraced new and radically different modes of living. I made friends, and opened my mind to accepting and appreciating their customs. I carved myself a niche in their society.

"I can't promise that the more unorthodox customs here won't shock me, but I can give you my word that I won't let on—won't embarrass you, or worse, disgrace you in the eyes of your peers. You're far more dangerous than I originally suspected, but I trust you. Don't shield me from any aspect of a culture I find fascinating—please. Make me a part of it."

Won to admiration of this woman's daring, stirred on a primal level by the implication inherent in that wholly unexpected appeal, Julian concealed the rabid intensity of his desire to agree. "If you give me that word, little hedonist, I'll hold you to it," he warned, his tone light, but nonetheless uncompromising.

"I don't go back on my word," came the equally adamant response.

"Even to the extent of disregarding some dictate of your culturally inculcated sense of propriety?"

"I've done that already," Mercedes acknowledged candidly, evincing no evidence of being racked by guilt. "I won't balk at any act performed with you, that harms no third person, such as a wife. We're both unmarried, consenting adults. You promised not to harm me. I'll keep my word, Julian."

"Mmmm. I honor your daring. I have your word that you'll submit, and obey, for the span of your stay here?"

"You have my word."

"Will you cut me a bit of slack—allow me to employ a traditional device mechanical rather than electronic—a device universally employed by my peers? It will leave—temporarily—the mark of my favor on tender skin, and will cause lingering pain for an hour or two, but it will neither scar you, nor injure you."

Amber-flecked eyes, dark now with desire, bored into those of the woman feeling as if she had ventured onto dangerous ground from which no avenue of retreat existed. Fear blended with answering desire: a sudden accession of lust. "Yes," she replied in a hoarse whisper. As her lover lifted her off the bed, she melted against him, her volition suspended, her heart thudding erratically, her loins quivering.

Chapter Six

Lifted only to be deposited on her feet, so that the loosened garment slipped to the flagging, Mercedes eagerly thrust her lover's shirt upwards. When he slid his arms out of it, she flung it aside. Grown keenly aware that his erection showed beneath the soft, clinging fabric identical to that of her gown, she ripped opened the Velcro closing of his pants, and slid the cloth downward with feverish haste.

Dropping to the flagstones, she assisted him to step out of the encumbering folds, and straightened so as to kneel erect. One hand pressed his lower body towards her; the other guided his hard member into her mouth. With long, sweeping strokes, she provided exquisite stimulation to the lover the more deeply aroused for witnessing her abandonment.

At length, he bade her rise, controlling to perfection his urge to ejaculate. While she stood naked on the flags, quivering with desire, he withdrew a diminutive velvet drawstring bag from his duffel. That item he set on the nightstand. Lifting his lover in his arms, he laid her supine in the center of the bed.

Reclining beside her, his eyes hot with passion, he commanded, "Throw your arms back over your head, and spread your legs." As the woman resolved to satisfy any demand, however outrageous, obeyed, he reached for the bag resting on the polished surface. A shake caused a small metal object to slide out into his palm.

Deep in the throes of potent desire, Mercedes shivered as her lover's hand smoothed the ruddy hair curling on her mound. "You're used to the shields," he purred, casting a sidelong glance at her flushed, eager face. "The pain they inflict fails to convey any sense of originating in tormented flesh. But this device—the Mastiff—will sink his teeth into the soft center of your mound. He'll bite hard, and deeply. He won't draw blood, but you'll bear the mark of the teeth for an hour or so. The pain will linger equally as long, to remind you that you exist for your master's pleasure. Observe, now."

The woman lying slackly on the bed scrutinized the small sculpture cunningly wrought of copper. A fierce head: ears, eyes, and muzzle, formed one prong of a V-shaped clip. The entire body, compressed and elongated, formed the second prong. Below the juncture where the two spring-loaded prongs hinged, a mouth opened wide when Julian pressed the two arms of the V together. Two rows of interlocking, blunt, triangular teeth sprang apart, and stayed so, as the manipulator maintained the pressure on the two halves.

Having introduced the viewer chilled by the sight, to the device, he spoke, his voice a melodic caress. "You'll neither stiffen, nor flinch, when the Mastiff clamps his jaws on your flesh," he warned. "Welcome the pain, little sensualist. Yield to it; enjoy it." With that, he pinched the skin to form a roll, and let the copper jaws bite deeply into the fold.

Two rows of metallic teeth closed on the tender skin, squeezing rather than piercing. Pain radiated from the site. That sensation intensified as the jaws inexorably tightened their grip, but stabilized as the nerves grew inured to bearing the pain equal in severity to that caused by the shields.

This stimulus the woman experiencing it found to be more frightening than that electronically induced, owing to its resulting from an actual assault on quivering flesh. A hand laid flat on her abdomen detected no tensing, no shrinking. The pain blending in her mind with the desire producing heat and wetness in loins aching for penetration formed a potent prelude to pleasure.

Seating himself alongside the hips of the partner lying slack, unresisting, Julian now slid two middle fingers into her dripping cunt. As that hand massaged sensitive places deep within her, the other toyed with the device, working the upraised head and body of the Mastiff back and forth, sending waves of pain coursing outward from the site of the stimulus.

A thumb dropped between the two extensions, even as two moist fingers settled on either side of the clit rearing stiffly erect. The heel of the hand pressed down on the soft flesh thatched with ruddy hair, and rocked, causing the device to bend back and forth while the fingers stimulated the swollen clit protruding from the folds normally hooding it. "Ahhh . . . you like that, eh, little sensualist?" came the murmured, mesmeric voice. "The Mastiff not only bites. He worries the flesh into which he sinks his teeth. So. Lie still, now."

Both hands withdrew. Moving with fluid grace, Julian turned his partner on her right side, and repositioned himself so that he lay facing her back. His right leg slid between hers. "Lay your left leg over my hip," came the insistent command. His partner obeyed, bending her right leg beneath his, as his cock penetrated her slippery interior space. His right hand gripped her left shoulder; his left again worked the Mastiff while two fingers offered that supremely erotic massage of the small organ of pleasure grown rock-hard.

Slowly, rhythmically, Julian thrust into her, his right leg

between hers, his body scissoring hers, his turgid prick targeting sensitive places deep inside which it stimulated only when it entered from the rear. Mercedes moaned softly, but not from the pain. Consciously, determinedly, she squeezed the invading member, conferring intense pleasure on the lover who now teased her wet clit with expert fingers, even as the heel of his hand pressed cruelly on the device.

The initiate's awareness narrowed to focus on the dual sensations—significant pain coupled with intense pleasure—which in combination never failed to rouse her to primal lust. A low animal cry broke from deep in her throat, as her cunt convulsively contracted around her lover's manhood. Julian instantly released the jaws of the Mastiff. Relaxing the rigorous control that he so well knew how to maintain over himself, he ejected spurt after spurt of his seed, his groan masking his partner's sobbing gasp of pure delight.

Neither hedonist moved. Each lay still, enjoying the ebbing wash of pleasure—self-absorbed even while reveling in a sense of ecstatic oneness. At length, Julian extricated his leg from those of the woman reluctant to stir, and encircled her with a scarred arm. "You come with gratifying ease, now," he murmured, smiling into green eyes soft with remembered bliss. "That lingering soreness, a soak in a mineral spring will soothe, eh, little hedonist?"

"Springs . . . outdoors?"

"Among the trees, in the park."

"Julian, I never packed a bathing suit!"

A laugh, lightly mocking, greeted that protest. "We bathe as nature intended, Mercedes, in company, or alone. As do other cultures—notably, respectable Japanese, who appreciate the benefits of hot baths."

Acutely aware of the amusement dancing in the eyes of this man to whom she had sworn that no dictate of her sense of propriety would she allow to apply in this setting, Mercedes developed a definite visceral tension. She nonetheless nodded gamely in assent. Lifted bodily, and set on her feet, she wondered for a few gut-wrenching seconds whether he intended that they parade nude down the hall, and across the wide porch in front of the dining/sitting area.

Relief surged through her when he pulled from the duffel the two robes of black silk that they had worn at his home. Attired modestly, if casually, while burdened only with a towel snatched from the bathroom, the woman tucked her arm into that of her lover, and held her head high as they emerged into the lower level filled with a goodly number of people garbed exactly as were they.

"Afternoons, by tradition, form the favored hour for a soak," her companion remarked serenely, concealing an upsurge of mirth. "That's the time of day when the air's warmest."

Refusing to appear as flustered as she felt, Mercedes allowed her escort to guide her along a stone-flagged path from which a few other, narrower walks led away, winding among the trees and low growth surrounding their trunks. Puffs of cloud wafted upwards between fronds of greenery, tantalizing the eyes of the viewer drinking in the wild, natural beauty of what Julian called the park.

At length, he turned down a narrow flagged walkway, and stopped at a mist-shrouded pool: one of three separated by ridges of rock. A profusion of robes slung across squat stone benches bordering the path wider here than among the trees, testified to a universal indifference regarding individual ownership of one of the identical items. Through the mist, his companion beheld heads and shoulders rising from the water.

Tossing his garment on the pile, Julian slipped his arms around the woman nervously contemplating striding naked into a none-too-large pool occupied by strangers. Having untied her belt, he slipped the garment off her shoulders, and dropped it next to his own.

Conquering her scruples by sternly reminding herself that she freely passed her word, Mercedes walked in seeming unconcern to the edge. Exhibiting not the least hesitation, she stepped into the clear, pleasantly warm water. She nonetheless grew acutely conscious of the numerous pairs of eyes raking her bare body, notably those of a blonde, Byronic admirer whose intent glance she experienced as a palpable force.

Finding that the rocky bottom dropped away rather steeply, she grasped Julian's arm, and held it as they immersed themselves to the waist. A few more steps forward over level bottom brought them to a drop-off that turned out to be the first of three broad, step-like ledges.

Pulling his companion down as he sat on the middle step, Julian saw that the water reached to her shoulders. Relaxing contentedly against the vertical riser, between two other couples seated on the same horizontal shelf of rock as himself, he slipped an arm around the lover whose inner perturbation he sensed. Pride suffused him: pride generated by her bearing under the stress of violating a social dictum ingrained by her society, so as to keep her word.

Peering through the mist, Mercedes beheld Shirley stretched out supine, her head on Jason's shoulder, her tanned face rapt. Wavy brown hair, unbound, curling at the temples from the dampness, floated on the water. Breasts as tanned as their owner's face drew the eye of the beholder to whom they betrayed the girl's penchant for sunbathing nude.

Across the expanse of water, Manuel's broad shoulders rose above the surface, owing to his height. Conscious that piercing black eyes, which had traced her every curve as she entered the water, still studied her minutely, the newcomer noted that the lissome courtesan reclined languidly in the curve of her patron's corded arm.

Her nudity for the moment veiled by a comforting depth of warm, slightly salty water, Mercedes beamed upon Shirley and Jason. Swiveling her head, she bestowed no less vivid a greeting on the hired companion and the mercenary soldier, prompting the latter to bestow on her one of his rare but singularly engaging smiles. Turning to glance across Julian's chest, she nodded demurely to Nikos. The warmth of the spring-fed bath, added to a lingering sensation of well-being induced by sensual pleasure, combined to drive the assault on her modesty to the back of her mind.

At length, Manuel rose, as did the companion who smiled up at him as she linked her arm in his. Glancing at the shapely body of the courtesan, Mercedes observed that a multitude of red stripes spaced a scant inch apart stood out against the pale skin of her thighs and her abdomen, and even marked her high, firm breasts. When the woman turned, the startled viewer saw that similar wheals adorned her buttocks.

Mindful of her promise, the neophyte lying in the curve of Julian's arm strove to act as if she observed nothing out of the ordinary, but her eyes followed the hired partner being assisted by her brawny patron to step over the ridge of rock separating the pool from which they rose, from the next. The self-possessed courtesan seemed as unconcerned about letting the stripes be seen, as was the virile master who evidently cared no whit who knew that he had inflicted so eye-catching a memento of his passion.

The others now rose, and moved to the second pool, leaving the latecomers alone in the misty environs of the initial bath. Striving to sound casual, Mercedes murmured, "So the devices you employ, that inflict no injury, aren't the norm here?"

That probe prompted a turn of the head, and a penetrating scan of the face managing to appear only mildly quizzical. "No, not the norm, though they're gaining favor. They're an invention of my brother, who willingly makes them for any member of the Order who requests a set. Being far more reclusive than myself, Michael seldom attends these yearly gatherings. He stayed away this year, so I can't introduce you to him.

"Some masters prefer to leave the mark of their favor visible on the body of their companion, but if you noticed, Mercedes, not one of those stripes fell atop another, nor did any raise a welt, let alone break even the most tender skin. Their perfect symmetry testifies to the surpassing skill of the man wielding the whip, and its strokes caused less pain, overall, than do some of the electronic implements—especially when a master employs those in combinations."

Shivering even while submerged in warmth, Mercedes digested that expert, clinically detached appraisal, and shivered again, for a different reason. Unable to explain why she placed such trust in a man who derived keen sensual pleasure from causing her pain, she grew even more puzzled as to why she reacted on so elemental a level to his infliction of that stimulus. Musingly, she wondered whether he had already achieved some sort of conditioning of his voluntarily submissive partner.

Swiftly rejecting that idea, the woman conscious of no radical alteration in her mental life surmised that Julian knew how to reach and excite masochistic impulses deeply embedded in her psyche—impulses which he deftly channeled into fierce passion which he, not herself, controlled.

Intrigued, she debated with herself. When he employs that skill, is his doing so of itself a subtle form of conditioning—of mind-control? she speculated uneasily. Or was I rigidly inhibited on two fronts?

My closely knit rural society condemns wanton cruelty to man or beast, and radical feminist ideas filter down even into a culture where men traditionally offer far more equality to the wives, daughters, and female neighbors who work alongside them at physically taxing and often dangerous tasks requiring strength and skill, than do their urban counterparts.

Ranchers typically consider wives full partners in their business. Men pursuing careers requiring that they work in a sphere almost completely separate from that of home and family, seldom do. Did these primitive emotions exist within me all along, and Julian simply let the genie out of the bottle? Or does he exert some hypnotic power capable of lighting a fire in my blood that he alone can quench?

No eureka flash of enlightenment lanced out of the cloudless blue sky seen through a gauzy umbrella of mist ribbed by delicate fronds of foliage. Jarred out of her reverie by the arrival of two newcomers, Mercedes smiled warmly upon Lorenzo and Francesca, who nodded graciously. As comfortable with nudity as the younger bathers, the pair stepped into the pool, the woman resting her hand on the arm of her husband, as Mercedes herself had done.

Regarding with avid interest the adept held in such high honor by the members, Mercedes noted that she, too, bore an array of red stripes on thighs and buttocks, and seemed as unconcerned that they showed, as was the courtesan. Unabashedly staring, the initiate perceived a design etched into the graying hair thatching Francesca's mound: a small but noticeable imprint wrought of intricate, slim lines formed by a dearth of hair along the length of those lines.

Catching only a tantalizing glimpse, the ranchwoman owned to being eerily reminded of reading brands on cattle. Chilled to the bone by that ominous comparison, she mentally rejected the explanation as the product of a too-active imagination, but the similarity persisted in her memory as she rose with her master to cross into the second, and, she discovered, far hotter pool. Combating the impact of that all but intolerable warmth, she yet assented to a crisp command to submerge to her neck.

Immersed thus between Julian and Nikos, she heard her lover cordially invite his boldly appraising, Byronic, womanless colleague to their room after supper. The lesser conundrum fled her mind as she contemplated spending an evening as the object of the handsome master's almost impudent scrutiny. Shivers again coursed down her spine: an automatic response to the blatantly sexual, potently masculine appeal of the guest-to-be.

Knitting her brow, the widow sought to understand why a man at least ten years her junior found her mature body so attractive. Do the customs here allow a master actively to seek to seduce the cherished companion of a fellow member? she asked herself in puzzlement.

That notion she rejected as soon as it impinged. Julian would never invite for a private visit, a rival he suspected of trying to win me away from him, she asserted to her dubious alter ego. Likely he knows Nikos to possess an inordinately roving eye, but knows as well that his friend merely admires from a distance. Overt attempts at seduction wouldn't jibe with an ordered, secure society steeped in a cohesive culture, now would it?

The dip in the hot, heavily mineral-laden spring ended quickly. "Too long, and we'd grow dehydrated," her lover informed her. "We'll advance to the third pool, and regain our edge in cool, fresh water."

Plunged into what seemed glacier-melt by the unrelenting pressure of a strong hand and an iron grip on her upper arm, Mercedes failed to suppress a hissing exhalation of breath.

"I'm freezing," she gasped to Shirley, who floated with the back of her head touching Jason's chest. His hands clasped her beneath her breasts, lifting them, and thereby showing them to advantage through the transparent veil of clear water. The girl's abundant hair spread out like a dark, glistening fan around her head.

A laugh floated by the ear of the newcomer. "Wakes you right up!" the Midwesterner affirmed gaily. "Exhilarates you!"

Wondering whether the shock had ever stopped anyone's heart, Mercedes emulated the younger woman's strategy: floated, her arms thrown back behind her, her hands clasped, so as to surround her goose-bump-afflicted flesh with the surface water warmer than that of the depths. Bravely, she ignored a feeble qualm induced by her cognizance that her own far less firm breasts now lay bared to the eyes of the men.

Seemingly unbothered by the cold, Julian chatted with Manuel as the courtesan warmed herself by pressing her front to her statuesque patron's back, and wrapping her arms around his massive torso.

Julian rose to leave when his friends did so.

The necessity of stepping onto the path stark naked, in the company of people with whom she had only a passing acquaintance, put Mercedes' resolve to the acid test, but she noted no especially pointed stares at this juncture. The wind-chilled bathers dried themselves with precipitate haste, and reached for robes, caring no whit, evidently, whether or not they donned the one worn on their arrival. The diaphanous folds of sun-warmed black silk protected shivering skin from the breeze stroking the whispering foliage of the exotic flora.

Strolling back among the company, Mercedes saw that subtle cues exhibited by these intriguing near-strangers conveyed heightened acceptance of her presence among them.

Rejoicing that her serene dip in the buff produced that effect, she reveled in a sense of belonging. Reassured, she thrust her self-doubts into a dim recess below the plane of her consciousness.

Again arrayed in the black gown which evidently constituted the customary attire for gathering in the spacious sitting/dining area, Mercedes chatted briskly with the companions—all people new to her—with whom Julian chose to converse over mugs of excellent ale, poured from foaming pitchers filled by a white-clad, youthful server, at one end of the buffet. When a break in the conversation occurred, she observed slyly, "Lorenzo seems to favor malt brews, just as I do . . . mmmm?"

"Albert does. The treat's on him," came the unperturbed explanation. "He owns a famous brewery in Bavaria."

An hour later, when that aggregation broke up, some of the participants moving to new groupings, and others opting to choose from among the delicacies, he guided his companion to the buffet, and joined a company of diners sitting down with heaping plates.

Aware that her escort commanded some indefinably special respect from the men whose groupings he joined, Mercedes musingly sought to ascertain whether that marked deference originated with his seniority in the group, or with his holding some coveted rank within the hierarchy of members, or merely by the force of his personality. Dismissing the first explanation when it became evident that men considerably older than himself accorded the same enhanced respect as did younger men, she conjectured that it might well arise from a combination of the latter two factors.

When Julian offered an opinion regarding any aspect of international affairs, his lover noted that his statement invariably emerged couched in concise, clear, well-chosen words, and betokened expert knowledge of the current conditions in whichever nation or region his comments covered. His familiarity with economic trends she observed to be equally impressive. When the talk turned to theatrical or musical productions, art exhibits, or other cultural offerings such as ballet, modern dance, or opera, he seldom contributed. Instead, he listened, seemingly intently interested, as others offered expert critiques.

Fascinated by the range and depth of the topics discussed, Mercedes yet found herself again baffled by Julian's total silence on the subject of how he gained such wide, deep understanding of world affairs. Nothing he said cast the faintest ray of light on the mystery she most wished to solve: what sort of engrossing career ended with his retiring at a relatively young age, to enjoy what she knew must be ample wealth?

Preceding her lover into their room at the end of that leisurely two hours of social drinking, informal dining, and spirited conversation, Mercedes wistfully acknowledged that she would have preferred to spend the evening alone with her companion—making love perhaps, but most certainly lying relaxed, afterwards, in his arms, and talking solely to him before slipping off to sleep locked in his possessive embrace. The habitually active athlete reflected contentedly that she suffered none of the fatigue that the long day unlike any other in her memory might conceivably have produced.

Pondering that realization, she ascribed her present buoyant mental state to the pleasure generated by novelty spiced with an aura of danger. Retiring to the bathroom, she brushed her hair, which always grew slightly tousled when she engaged in stimulating conversation, owing to her habit of absently running her fingers through the loosely hanging locks when debating.

Her hands, she knew, also traced expansive patterns in the air as she drove home a telling point. Those gestures, punctuations as instinctive as those repeated forays through hair disheveled by ravaging fingers, or the changes in posture or tilt of her head which accompanied them, she acknowledged in retrospect to characterize her behavior, even though they occurred without conscious volition on her part.

Emerging with her hair neatly ordered, her nose lightly powdered, and her teeth brushed, she philosophically accepted the necessity of placing a guest at ease, and conversing with him in sprightly fashion.

Julian gripped her by the shoulders. Cocking his head, he regarded her out of half-lidded eyes, exquisitely aware of treading a sword-edge stretching over an abyss. Employing every subtle nuance of the melodic voice which he consciously wielded as a weapon in his arsenal, he observed, "Earlier today, you passed me your word, little hedonist: begged me not to shield you from any aspects of my culture. I intend to hold you to that word. No need exists for a master to explain his intent ahead of time, but I suspect that you'll require a few minutes in which to gain full control over your expression.

"A year ago, I came to this annual gathering alone, stressed to the limit of endurance by work I'd just completed. Nikos came in the company of a most attractive cherished companion. Sensing my inner tension, he offered to share her with me on the night I arrived. I now consider myself obligated to return the favor."

Shocked all but speechless, the widow spent a few seconds digesting what came across as a flat statement of fact. Struggling to order her stricken face, she gasped, "You . . . you want me . . . to let *Nikos* take me to bed?"

"No. We'll share you, Mercedes—enjoy you simultaneously." His eyes narrowing, he added ironically, "I'm not doing this because I wish to. My honor demands that I let no such debt go unsettled.

"You'll reap the benefit, more so than will Nikos. A woman pleasured simultaneously by two masters of erotic art rises to a height of ecstasy seldom achieved. Your reaction testifies to the tenaciousness of a few lingering tenets of your social conditioning." The hands gripping two bare upper arms tightened; the tawny eyes bored into those in which fear blended with shock.

"I keep my word," the visibly distraught woman retorted with perceptible heat. "But Julian—you offered proof that I'd risk no appalling consequences to my future health by taking you as a lover. But now . . ."

For the first time during this discussion, amusement crept into the eyes exerting compelling force. "Every man here—and every courtesan—sent Lorenzo a copy of a recent complete physical, Mercedes. Mine chanced to serve a dual purpose. Consorts and cherished companions aren't required to do so, but their partners submit a statement that they consider the possibility of an unfortunate effect nil. You'll run no risk whatsoever, but Nikos will be placing perfect trust in my judgment."

"I . . . I see." Relieved on that score at least, Mercedes sought to catalog the emotions evoked by this wholly unforeseen and direly unnerving prospect. The memory of a handsome face framed in hair blonde as the ale served before dinner floated in her inner vision. Eyes blue as the cloudless vault under which she had stood naked in Nikos' sight again appraisingly traced every contour, every curve. Understanding now what prompted that intent scrutiny, she shivered as much in anticipation as in dismay.

Flayed by her consciousness of that dual reaction,

Mercedes experienced an onslaught of guilt: emotion which she knew to be totally irrational, given that her lover, not some suave seducer plying his blandishments behind Julian's back, laid this outrageous demand on her. "I won't embarrass you—or shame you in front of this man who undoubtedly fully expects that you'll share me," she affirmed stoutly, still taken aback at the idea of participating in what the members of her social set would deem an orgy.

A sharp knock on the door sent galvanic impulses coursing down the woman's overwrought nerves. Mercedes gave a visible start, which prompted her lover to crush her briefly, reassuringly, against his black-clad chest. "Guard your expression," came the murmured warning, the timbre of the melodious voice conveying supreme confidence that the order would be obeyed.

Her mind befogged by conflicting emotions, Mercedes riveted her eyes to the guest's strikingly handsome face. Both the cast of his features and the styling of his hair reminded her forcibly of marble sculptures dating from the Golden Age of Athens.

Her perception of the guest advancing to grip Julian's hand, metamorphosed suddenly, in a way she nowise expected. Hot desire surged up from some libidinous depth in her psyche: emotion aroused not so much by the sensual allure of the guest raking her with bold eyes as he offered a conventional greeting, as by fierce longing to experience the enhanced pleasure promised by the lover no less avidly searching her face and body for any sign that she might react in such a way as to disgrace him.

Inhibitions ingrained in her being from early childhood suddenly lost their power to quell raw lust generated by unorthodox stimuli. That circumstance failed to render her brazen: openly provocative. Every fiber of the widow's being, every subtle facet of her personality, forbade overt expression of this urgent, primal yearning to be possessed—simultaneously—by these autocratic, cruel, manifestly dangerous, but unbelievably skilled lovers. Unnerved by the potency of the hunger assailing her, Mercedes yet failed to curb it.

Urged to take a seat, Nikos dropped with sinuous grace into one of the chairs. Leaning back, wholly at ease, a vivid, knowing smile playing over his classic features, he smiled upon the company.

His arm encircling his partner's waist, Julian addressed the guest expecting to hear what the host now announced. "A year ago, you conferred a favor on me which I'm about to reciprocate. I invite you to join with me in raising my cherished companion to an unprecedented height of ecstasy. We'll enjoy her together—take our time, eh?"

"By all means. I welcome your offer, old friend."

Stepping to the rear of the woman gamely striving not to drop her eyes from those scanning her person, Julian reached around her torso. Deftly, he plucked the pin from the ring fastening her gown, and caught the glittering object before it fell. The soft fabric slid swiftly downwards, to fall in a heap around her ankles. Standing nude, flamboyantly exhibited by her lover to this stranger sitting at his ease, examining her every aspect minutely, the recipient of that bold attention grew aware of the heat crimsoning her cheeks.

"Clasp your hands behind your head, and come here, Mercedes," the guest commanded.

Advancing to stand close to the chair in which Nikos sat relaxed, smiling appreciatively, the woman felt as if transported by some mysterious cosmic force into an altered state radically different from the familiar reality suddenly lost to her. The guest's arm encircled her hips. A hand held palm-up slid between her legs from behind. The middle finger insinuated itself with practiced ease into her cunt, as the palm pressed upwards.

A soft, gasping exhalation escaped the neophyte whose loins quivered. Moisture gushed into the orifice so expertly teased.

Turning a quizzical eye on his fellow, the owner of the hand observed judiciously, "Your lady projects an intriguing ingenuousness, old friend—a tremulousness almost virginal. I see why you value her. That illusion of innocence I find potently arousing." Addressing the woman caressed internally by that invading finger, he ordered, "Undress your master, little initiate." When she stood irresolute, reluctant to pull free of the finger invading her moist depths, he laughed in patent amusement even as he withdrew the hand, and waved her away.

Hastening to obey, Mercedes sought to calm her fibrillating heart. Julian's eyes bored intently into hers as she slid off his shirt. Dropping to one knee, she thrust his pants down. Placing a hand on her shoulder so as to maintain his balance, he stepped out of the garments, which his cherished companion deftly folded before placing them on a chair. "Do that for Nikos," came the imperious order.

The guest remained seated in order to facilitate his attendant's drawing his shirt over his head. Rising, he emulated Julian's stance as she removed and folded his pants. She came to her feet, no less graceful for her perturbation. Flushed, indeed tremulous, she faced him as he cupped a breast in a hand, and toyed with the nipple. Intuitively guessing the stance he originally demanded that she take, to be the norm in this sort of situation, she again clasped her hands behind her head.

On observing her response, Julian experienced an upwelling of fierce satisfaction.

Nikos again spoke directly to his fellow, rather than to the woman he caressed. "Not a mark on her lovely body," he remarked almost chidingly. "But of course you favor those implements invented by Michael—share his scruples, eh? Open the panel, friend. I'm minded to reacquaint myself with those clever devices crafted by your brother, while I assess the ability of this doe-eyed, blushing charmer to bear without flinching the pain we'll take pleasure in inflicting."

That ominous statement of the guest's intent set the shivering hearer's heart thudding erratically, even as she experienced relief that he would not insist on employing whatever sort of whip Manuel wielded with such expertise. Leather, she wondered distractedly? A quirt, perhaps?

In her befogged state, she failed to notice that Julian pressed two concealed switches on the wall. Only when the wood-grained panels behind the two masonry pillars slid silently sideways, revealing a well-lighted chamber identical in size to the bedroom, but obviously designed for a single, specialized purpose, did she grasp the import of the initial request.

Startled, she stared about her, even as Nikos gripped her arm and propelled her inside the inner apartment she had not suspected to exist. Chains dangled from cylindrical housings attached to the roof: chains ending in stirrup-like supports. To the far right of that area, she beheld an adjustable table identical to that employed by her lover on an occasion similar to this.

To the far left stood a piece of furniture vaguely resembling a black-leather-upholstered, armless recliner fitted with a divided footrest. A cart occupied a site a short distance from the center. On its surface rested four padded fetters, and a remote control. On the shelf beneath lay a bulging drawstring sack. A short, stout, leather-upholstered wooden bench reposed on the flagged floor next to the cart.

Picking up the hard leather case from the bench in the bedroom, Julian removed the detachable lid, and set the base on the cart. "Ahhh . . . the full collection, eh?" Nikos queried, studying the array of objects occupying numerous compartments built to accommodate their size and shape.

"This is the standard set," came the equable reply. "Michael occasionally develops a spurt of creativity, and invents new additions so as to provide his consort variety. Ingenious, some of them. I've duplicates, but most I've never tested. These I use routinely—know their efficacy." Turning to the partner maintaining an admirable calm, he commanded, "Stand beneath the chains, facing us. Grasp the handholds, and spread your legs wide."

Having obeyed, Mercedes felt the chains rise, stretching her arms until she could barely keep her feet flat on the floor. Trembling as much with anticipation as with fear, she heard her lover issue directions to the guest. "Use these, to start. Narrow our initiate's focus, so that she concentrates on those parts of her shapely body best suited to sensual pleasure."

The woman whose loins stirred even as chills coursed over her bare, utterly vulnerable skin, saw the guest activate a pair of the heavier six-thonged whips. When he stood facing her, his shaft erect, his eyes dark with passion, his unblemished, perfectly proportioned physique embodying every ideal of athletic grace, she felt her own loins grow warm and wet.

Two sets of thongs descended with brisk force, to cling with telling effect around her hips. Whisked away, the glowing tendrils rose before wrapping themselves like talons around her breasts. Employing strokes as light and quick as any Julian ever delivered, Nikos targeted thighs, buttocks, breasts, and abdomen, not omitting to flay the tender flesh between the thighs spread wide.

Used to the dual stimulus now, Mercedes sought to focus solely on the attendant pleasure, but managed only to explore both sensations equally. The guest's openly avowed intent to test her ability to withstand the pain echoed in her fevered consciousness.

Pride merged with fear, with pain, with rabid desire for this modern, cruel reincarnation of a mythical Olympian. Grimly resolved to bear any degree of agony rather than fail the lover for whom she longed with equal fervor, she forbade herself to flinch. Consciously, she willed her flesh not to shrink under the lash-thongs clinging, lifting, and descending to cling again, wielded by a relentless arm.

At length, the whipping ceased. Advancing, Nikos parted the pussy-lips from which moisture dribbled. Having thrust an appraising two fingers deep within the woman's quivering cunt, he again spoke directly to his fellow, smiling conspiratorially. "Unique, this partner," he acknowledged a shade enviously. "That illusive aura of ingenuousness—almost of innocence—provides a powerful incentive to a master to inflict pain. And when he succumbs to the temptation, he finds that pain alone—devoid of any attendant pleasure—deeply arouses her."

Keenly aware that Nikos erred in judging Mercedes' ingenuousness as illusive, Julian experienced a momentary pang of fear, even as he exulted in her ability to grow aroused solely in response to pain.

"Let's see what a combination of the two can do, eh?" his guest suggested. "What item among your clever devices most resembles the Mastiff?"

"Lay her supine, with her back slightly arched," came the reply.

Lifted in arms fully as strong as those of the lover who she saw to have grown as aroused by watching the whipping as he would have been by inflicting the strokes, Mercedes sought to assure herself that Julian would refrain from approaching anywhere near the limit of her tolerance for pain, so as to minimize any chance that he might miscalculate, and breach her self-mastery in the presence of this peer. Finding that line of reasoning unconvincing, she wondered in mounting fear whether he would instead escalate his demand, so as to allay any faint suspicion on the part of this fellow master that his handling of her initiation failed to conform to the norm.

That fear steeply escalated. Nikos laid her on the table as soon as the surface ceased moving in response to Julian's touches on the remote control. Lying with her legs spread along the arms of a V, her arms thrown back along two other such arms, and her back slightly arched, she shivered as her lover pressed over her mound a golden shield fitted in the center with an upright feature which reminded her of the leg-rest integral to a side-saddle. He next slipped two paper-thin, hollow discs, from which a multitude of long, thin, downward-curving talons extended, over her nipples.

The extensions, which fit the curve of the breasts thrust upwards by her arched torso, congealed against the skin, firming that soft flesh, as would the cup of a brassiere. When Julian activated the shield, pain radiated through the sensitive tissue caught in so merciless a grip. Agony coursed in waves through the loins and abdomen enduring the most severe pain of this sort inflicted thus far by the man who styled himself her master.

"Hurts, doesn't it?" Julian observed dispassionately, his tiger-eyes boring into those reflecting the severity of the stimulus. "Accept the pain, little initiate. Let it focus your mind exclusively on the pleasure my fellow master and I will now confer. Yield to both the pleasure, and the pain."

Circling the support on which his lover lay spread-eagled,

Julian stood between her back-flung arms. His own arms encircled her torso; his thumbs vibrated the erect nipples protruding through the holes in the discs. Despite the pain throbbing through the breasts feeling as if caught in claws of fire, the recipient of his touch experienced heady pleasure.

Even as that sensation impinged on the woman's diminishing awareness, Nikos knelt on the cushioned bench that he placed on the flagging beneath her outstretched thighs. His mouth closed over her swollen clit, even as his thumb inserted itself between the two prongs of the extension on the shield. Pressing on the edge of the shield with the heel of his hand, he worked the prongs back and forth while simultaneously producing a rotational motion.

The last shreds of any concern for modesty or for propriety fled the mind of the woman who now knowingly, willingly, consigned her nude, pain-rackcd body to thc ministrations of two masters. She found it no chore to lie slackly. No dangerous urge to stiffen, or to struggle, needed to be conquered.

The conscious act of offering herself as a sacrifice to be used for these men's pleasure produced an ineffably liberating mindset: a mental state formerly achieved only through vivid fantasizing. Those prior, private exercises in virtual submission served now to hasten and facilitate actual surrender to two vitally alive, imperiously demanding lovers.

As her awareness inexorably narrowed to exclude all but the engrossing sensations throbbing through her loins and her breasts, Mercedes moaned, but not from pain. The warm, moist mouth sucking on her clit produced waves of delight: pleasure somehow magnified by the rocking, rotating movements themselves uncannily erotic, though they caused the whip-stimulus generated by the shield to increase twofold. Roused on an elemental level by stimuli so intense, so absorbing to the mind closed to all other sensory input, the novice savored both the pain and the pleasure. Swiftly, she experienced a shuddering climax.

Having achieved that outcome even more swiftly than he expected, Nikos straightened. Meeting the eyes of his fellow, he laughed. "This shy doe so incapable of casting even a mildly provocative glance at any man but her master possesses an insatiable appetite for pain," he observed shrewdly. "She also succumbs with gratifying swiftness to pleasure. She just came, even though she's a long way from absolute surrender of her will to the two lovers rendered rock-hard by the act of inflicting that pain."

I *have* surrendered! Mercedes cried in silent protest. Offered myself absolutely!

"Demonstrate for me how you use these intriguing implements to induce surrender, Julian," the guest urged.

Thus firmly adjured, the man savoring fierce pride in this woman giving him voluntarily what most women only gave after being subjected to a rigorous, diabolically effective regimen designed to subjugate their will without breaking their spirit, meditated on how best to comply. In a swift, intense calculation, he weighed risk against benefit, but chose in favor of the latter. "Set her on her feet, with her legs spread," he instructed his fellow. "Bend her at the waist, so that her rear's well within my reach, and observe."

Held in that ignominious posture by two hands and arms of iron, Mercedes grew convinced that Julian intended once again to probe the limits of her endurance. Bracing herself, she fought burgeoning terror. Stubbornly, valiantly, she mastered her fear, and dominated the pain still tormenting her mound and her breasts.

From the case, the instructor removed a pliable black shaft about six inches in length: a smooth, slender cylinder, rounded on one end, and flanged on the other. On the outside of the flanged end, colored spots indicated controls. This object he lubricated with viscous liquid ejected from a small bottle, before thrusting the shaft into the tight anal orifice of the woman who made no convulsive movement as she felt the implement penetrate until stopped by the flange. A touch of a finger set the device clinging to the flesh beneath the flange, and the inner surfaces of her orifice.

"Observe," the manipulator directed to the man watching intently. "The shaft will expand, when I—there. I've set it to provide mild stretching of this all but virginal back passage. So. It can be reset to expand further—to swell until delicate sensors within the base automatically halt the process before injury can occur—but at this juncture, we'll stop short of full distention. This implement also inflicts the conventional electronic stimulus, the effect of which is enhanced by the lubrication. There, now. Stand her on her feet."

The woman startled, and then frightened by the insidious swelling of the shaft that initially caused no discomfort, now felt pain radiate through flesh unused to either pain or pleasure. The pain dominated, putting her self-mastery to a fearful test.

"Grasp the supports, and spread your legs wide," came the uncompromising order.

Obeying that stern directive, Mercedes watched out of eyes dilated now in fear, as Julian selected the less severe type of whip, and lubricated the inactivated shaft. When he advanced, she all but cringed, succeeding in controlling her quailing flesh only by the sheer power of an indomitable will.

When her pitiless lover slid the lubricated shaft into the cunt that involuntarily contracted, and activated it, the new pain inflicted in concert with that ravaging her anal passage all but vanquished her ability to control her limbs. Yet she stood still as if carven of ice, bearing the agony, yielding before its onslaught, beguiled even while direly tormented, by the enhanced attendant pleasure.

A melodic, mesmeric, irresistibly compelling voice penetrated the haze of pain befogging the woman's diminished consciousness. "You'll bear what I now inflict, little initiate. You'll surrender to the pain that takes you to the limit of your ability to endure it without flinching. When you succeed, we'll confer a lavish reward. So."

As Nikos watched, fascinated, Julian attached by a hook on its narrow end, a small, pear-shaped iron mass to the loop of cord hanging from the whip-handle protruding from between his lover's pussy-lips: an object which the guest saw to be a carpenter's plumb bob. That Julian set swinging back and forth between the thighs gamely held wide apart.

Her mind now a formless embodiment of pain, Mercedes hung slackly, bearing her weight as much on her arms as on her legs. The mass swinging from the end of the loop of cord caused the shaft penetrating her to move in the opposite direction from that taken by the pendulum, while forcing the flesh to which it adhered, to move with it. Waves of heavy sensation flowed outward from the two sites so close in proximity. An ominous faintness prompted an attack of fear, which steadied the woman thus cruelly tested.

Knowing herself at the limit of her ability to bear agony without shrieking, the novice fought not the urge to scream, but rather, an onslaught of bewilderment accompanied by swiftly burgeoning anger. Why is Julian subjecting me to this degree of torment? Why? Even as she phrased that query, the answer lanced out of the blue. Because I surrendered on my terms—not his!

At the instant in which that conclusion registered, Mercedes abandoned all thought but that of remedying her egregious error. Accepting the excruciating pain engulfing her as a sacrifice offered willingly, even eagerly, at this juncture, she achieved a degree of surrender absolute enough to satisfy both of the men minutely examining the subtle cues exhibited by the nude, suffering initiate hanging inertly from the supports.

Of a sudden, the pain died away from every afflicted site. The shield fell inertly into Julian's hand; the claws gripping her breasts dropped into those of his fellow. The swollen shaft distending the sufferer's anal passage collapsed; fingers withdrew the two invasive objects.

Entirely free now of the agony holding her at the limit of her tolerance for pain, the woman yet clung to the supports. "Let go," the guest ordered during the second-long interim during which Julian laid the implements on the cart. Sweeping the initiate for whom he now harbored high respect, into his arms, Nikos bore her to the bed, laid her thereon, and stretched out beside her, having cradled her head in the hollow of his shoulder. "I envy your master," he breathed into her ear, smiling regretfully into green eyes darkened now by fierce desire. "You're worthy to be raised to the rank of adept, little staunch-heart."

Julian heard. His gut contracted into spasms, even as he strode to the bed, and sat, his legs bent, his weight on his rear, his hips pressed against the rib cage of the woman lying slackly still, her face betraying the rabid intensity of her carnal need. Thrusting out of his mind all thought of the complications which he could see looming on the horizon, he smiled upon his guest—a triumphant smile which hid nothing of his pride in his cherished companion. Keenly aware of running an even greater risk at this juncture, he yet unflinchingly instigated the second phase of an encounter that he fervently hoped would not blast the rapport he had so carefully cultivated between this peerless partner and himself.

Chapter Seven

Lying supine, caught up in the throes of raw lust, Mercedes ran her hand down the inner side of Julian's thigh. Her eyes devoured the man sitting beside her, who seemed lost in thought for a few seconds at least.

Nikos slid his arm from under the woman whose head now tipped back, exposing the white column of her throat. In a swift, fluid movement, he turned and lay prone, at an angle to the body of the initiate. Thrusting his arm under her right leg, he insinuated two fingers into her dripping cunt, even as his mouth closed on her erect, full clit. His tongue teased tender folds before he sucked on the quivering organ as if to ingest it whole.

Julian, meanwhile, lay prone on her other side. His tongue tickled two nut-hard nipples—licked them, sucked them, bit them teasingly, painlessly.

The consciousness narrowed to focus on pain contracted further, dwelling solely on the intense pleasure engendered by the dual manipulations. Soft cries of delight impinged on senses attuned to the woman's progress toward climax. Both men desisted. Sitting up, they smiled at each other. "We'll control ourselves as we lift her to fulfillment, this round, eh, friend?" the guest inquired.

"So we will. Carry her to the couch, Nikos."

Borne in strong arms, her whole body aching from need, Mercedes slid hers around the neck of the handsome athlete whose pulse-rate quickened as she made that gesture which he saw to be automatic—unpremeditated. Striding to where Julian now lay supine on the armless recliner, lubricating the male member up-rearing rigidly, he held his burden on two outstretched arms.

"Impale her ass on my cock," Julian directed the man needing no instruction on that score. Nikos lowered the slack form in his arms, so that her anus touched the head of the hard shaft that its owner now guided into the passage still lubricated from the invasive device. His peer thrust the woman's body downwards, so that full penetration occurred as he laid her flat on the body of her master. Julian's arms encircled her; his hands caressed her breasts. He spread his legs outward, resting them upon the divided footrest.

Nikos now stood between the thighs he thrust apart, so that the woman's legs lay outside those of the man beneath her. With the fingers of one hand, her second partner massaged the tiny ornament protruding from its folds, even as he thrust deeply into the cunt quivering with need.

A low, gasping cry tore from the woman as two stiff shafts began a slow, rhythmic, unbelievably erotic dance, the one penetrating as the other withdrew. Her loins worked between two men's fully engorged organs, her breasts cunningly stimulated, her ear tickled by a teasing tongue, she experienced the shivers, the heat, the imminent, unstoppable onset of uncontrollable contractions.

Fulfillment, when it came, persisted, lasting a most astonishing length of time owing to the intensity of her arousal, and the fact that her two partners kept up their thrusting even as they divined that she floated into a rapturous state of half-trance. Each man achieved an ecstatic mental state without ejaculating, being well able to perform so astonishing a feat by reason of long years of rigorous self-training.

Lying once more on the bed, between two hard, lithe, warm bodies, Mercedes drifted in a luminous bubble of euphoria, only dimly aware of which lover pressing against her, was which. Three sensualists relaxed, and savored the lingering glow of carnal pleasure.

Having washed his still-hard shaft before collapsing beside the woman he saw to be no more cognizant of Nikos than of himself at this juncture, Julian reflected contentedly that she seemed not to be growing infatuated with his handsome peer, to the detriment of his own relationship with her.

At length both men stirred simultaneously, exactly as if some telepathic message passed from one to the other. Sitting up, Julian turned eyes brimful of pride on his blissful cherished companion. Smiling at the man idly teasing her nipple, he urged, "Lift her, so that she kneels astride my hips, bent at the waist, and enjoy her delectable tight rear, old friend." As he spoke, he tossed his cohort the bottle of lubricant. "We'll relax our hold on ourselves, mm?"

"Time we did."

Roused by two corded arms thrust beneath her slack body, Mercedes found herself turned, bent, and spread. Two hands cupped the breasts touching her lover's chest, even as a still-rock-hard, slick shaft drove into her rear passage. A gasp escaped her as Nikos thrust with greater force than Julian had ever employed, but no pain, no tearing, no discomfort even, marred the pleasure those thrusts engendered.

Drawn downward by strong hands, as well as impelled by the force of those vigorous penetrations, she felt herself impaled on Julian's rigid organ. Flattened by Nikos' weight, she lay prone on the man beneath her, her loins again worked by two hard, invading members driving into her alternately, rhythmically. Having climaxed so recently, she experienced no rapid rise to a new peak. Moaning with pleasure, she lay sandwiched between two thrusting, hard-muscled bodies.

After a seeming eon, the neophyte surrendered to the intensely erotic dual stimuli, and gave herself up to the delicious slow onset of shivers, contractions, and heat. The pounding of her heart transmitted itself to the man against whose chest her bosom pressed. Her pulse throbbed in her throat. Again lifted to ecstasy as her climax stretched into seeming infinity, she heard as if from far off, a groan, and then another: low, hoarse, long-drawn-out sounds signifying that both men ejected the essence of their passion.

Dimly conscious of being possessed, filled, satiated on carnal delight, Mercedes sighed as she slid over an intangible mental boundary into an iridescent realm of formless light, her torso enveloped by the muscular bodies of her two satiated partners.

The entranced female partner never knew when the man above her slid sideways, pulling her off Julian. She likewise failed to notice when her master thrust an arm under her head, and drew her close, nor did she realize that Nikos sprawled prone against her left side, his cheek pillowed on her breast. Three entwined hedonists lay motionless: one wrapped in luminous light, and two in half-trance, dimly aware of the ebbing tide of rapture draining inexorably away.

When at last the guest sat up, prompting his host to do likewise, the two masters pulled the woman gone so limp as to seem boneless, to a sitting position between them. Resisting any return to full consciousness, she sought to collapse anew, to no avail. Encircled by Julian's scarred arm, which held her pressed against his shoulder, she sighed resignedly.

The classic face of the guest lit with mischievous vivacity as her eyes opened, focused on himself, and smiled with beatific warmth. "You're a treasure, little initiate," he commended her in a seductive drawl, consciously exerting the full force of his persona to pierce the final wisps of now-dissipating fog induced by rapturous fulfillment. "If you ever find yourself without a master, think of me. It's easy to reach me—just call one-eight-hundred-oh-six-six-six, and leave a message. That number's easy to remember, eh?"

Jolted back to reality by that bold advance made in the hearing of her lover, Mercedes retorted ironically, "Devilishly easy." Leaning back against Julian's erect frame, belatedly sensible of the compliment implied in the impudent invitation, she laughed, her response a rippling effusion of friendly warmth, lacking any trace either of derision or sarcasm. "I'll wager your phone bill's astronomical, Nikos, as marvelous a lover as you are," she observed sagely.

"One call from you is all I'd need to render me oblivious to the rest," came the swift, patently sincere retort. Addressing the peer managing to maintain perfect mastery of his face, he expressed graceful thanks for an evening that afforded him exquisite pleasure. Insisting that neither host nor hostess rise to assist him to dress or see him out, he donned shirt and pants, smiled one last time on the pair in the bed, and departed.

Drawing his cherished companion into the hollow of his shoulder as he lay back against the pillows, acutely aware that his gut felt as if crimped by barbed wire, Julian rigorously controlled the nascent anger which his peer's invitation ignited, well aware that Mercedes had in no way invited it.

When she turned, settled herself comfortably in the circle of her lover's arm, and raised a quizzical face to his, he divined that she half expected an angry outburst. His hand idly caressed her breast, but his expression the anxious observer saw to be more than a little bleak. "You seem to have shed the inhibitions causing you that initial shock," he opined guardedly—a shade tartly.

Green eyes widened, only to narrow ominously. "I gave you my word, never expecting you'd share me. Never once, by word or look, did I offer Nikos the least encouragement. He admitted as much! *You* initiated this joining of three partners—and now *you're* jealous?"

The overtly sardonic tone of that final query aroused regal wrath that the man flayed by jealousy swiftly suppressed. Acknowledging the justice of his lover's retort, he took a few seconds in which to regain his composure.

The hot ire briefly igniting died to ashes. When he spoke, his melodic voice conveyed no overtone of annoyance, let alone anger. "Of course I'm jealous," he admitted equably. "Nikos is a decade younger than I am, far more handsome, and possessed of a rakehell charm which few women can resist. You seem to be one of the few. I'm glad of that, Mercedes."

Mollified by that candid summation, the widow let the tension drain out of the body gone taut. Raising herself so as to face her lover squarely, she judged accurately that no suppressed anger simmered below the surface. Reassured, she melted against him, tired by the long day full of new experiences punctuated by fierce assaults on her sense of propriety.

"Will you be calling him next week?" came the studiously nonchalant query.

Certain when she relaxed that the minor tiff lay behind them, Mercedes reared upright, and fixed questioning eyes on her interrogator. "Will I find myself without a master, next week?" she inquired levelly, allowing no asperity to color her tone.

"Not unless you yourself sever the tie," came the low, hoarse answer. Strong arms crushed her against a hard-muscled chest. "If that decision rested solely with me, I'd never let you go. But it's in your hands, Mercedes. Damned if I don't hate the thought that you possess the power to leave me!"

Startled by the intensity of that fiercely impassioned admission, held so tightly that her breasts hurt, Mercedes gasped audibly. "Julian, I'm not one whit tempted to call Nikos next week!" she managed to articulate.

As the arms loosened their iron grip in response to that vigorous rejoinder, she affirmed with passionate vehemence, "Nikos strikes me as being twice as dangerous as you are! So are all these men! If I found myself alone here—if you left without me—I'd be scared spitless! I trust you—I told you that! I want to belong—but only while knowing that you stand between me and them like an impervious shield!"

Shock coursed through the hearer. "You want to be a part of this society solely on *my* account?"

"Yes! It's part of you: the universe that defines you—makes you what you are. If I remain an outsider, catching only tantalizing glimpses of what lies beneath its surface, I'll never understand you. And I want to, Julian. You're utterly unlike any man I've ever known—dangerous, but irresistibly fascinating; cruel, yet uncannily skilled at understanding me; possessive to a degree that ought to terrify me, yet able to make me feel giddily free of every crippling inhibition my society instilled in me."

The striking face of the man riveting his eyes to the flushed, guileless countenance of the woman offering that candid assessment of her impressions of him, mirrored shock which swiftly transmuted into savage elation. Certain now that this unique partner would prove as impervious to the sexual appeal of any or all of his peers as she just did to one of the most formidable of his potential rivals, he debated with himself as to just how far he could go with regard to allowing her to participate in certain activities which he knew would severely test the resolve she just expressed so emphatically.

"You might be overestimating the extent of your liberation from your cultural inhibitions," he observed trenchantly, tucking the perennially errant strand of hair over his partner's ear, the better to read the subtle changes crossing her open, fluidly expressive face.

"Perhaps," came the candid reply, "but I passed my word, and I trust yours—know with perfect certainty that you won't cause me any significant injury."

That serene declaration of faith in his honor touched the man contemplating a move which he knew he could only risk if he placed perfect trust in the word of this woman whose will remained unfettered by the conditioning which would have subjugated it to his. Frustration galled him, as he again wished that he could have completed her initiation before bringing her here.

Thrusting that profitless thought aside, he scanned her ingenuous face even as he resolved to run the risk he meditated. "And I place perfect trust in your word," he assured her, smiling mischievously. "As you'll discover tomorrow." His mouth closed over hers in an intimate, erotic kiss consciously designed to convey possessiveness.

Held against her demanding master, her tongue absorbed into his mouth, her heart fibrillating, her loins quickening, Mercedes congealed against him, possessed, mastered, content to be his. When he freed her mouth, settled her against him, and said no more, she sought to compose herself for sleep. To her annoyance, she failed to order the questing mind that perversely tended to reason the more clearly for verging on slipping through the dark portal separating awareness from oblivion.

Musingly, the stranger to this society reviewed the events of the day. Frowning, she sought to imagine how these other men conditioned their partners into agreeing blithely, even eagerly, to engage in sexual coupling of the sort in which she had indulged on this night. Still buoyed by a euphoric glow, she pondered that enigma.

At length, exhausted emotionally as well as physically, she focused on the pleasure afforded by knowing herself potently desired by this autocratic, cruel, but marvelously skilled lover whose arms maintained their forceful grip even as he slipped into sleep. Relaxing, she imitated him.

Opening her eyes to find her bedmate propped on an elbow, regarding her out of half-lidded, pensive eyes, Mercedes smiled up at him, prompting him to kiss her lightly on the lips. Driven as usual to retire to the bathroom by the need inevitably assailing her on awaking, she returned to find him on his feet, stripping the bed.

A glance at her watch informed her of the hour: a few minutes before seven. Reflecting that time seemed of no especial importance in this antique warren of windowless rooms and porches shielded from the hot desert sun, she grew curious as to why he opted to rise so soon after waking. Aware that he unconsciously regarded her as his slave, she correctly surmised that he saw no need to explain himself on that or any score.

Bidden to shower, she did so, and emerged to find him holding out a fresh gown that he dropped over her head. His arms encircled her torso; his hands deftly pinned the strap.

The remark passed by Nikos rose to the mind of the woman glancing at the ornament. Insatiably curious as to just what the rite of passage to the rank of adept entailed, she yet refrained from asking. Smiling at the man who smiled back before retiring to the bathroom, she made the bed afresh with sheets and pillowslips removed from a shelf in the closet. The soiled linen her partner bundled, and placed outside the door as they departed for breakfast.

Few diners occupied the porch at this early hour, Mercedes discovered. When the newcomers advanced into the sitting area bearing trays, Alexander beckoned to them. He and his consort Irene, a slender, shapely woman of perhaps sixty, crowned by a mass of dark curls sparsely streaked with gray, which framed a face notable for strikingly luminous violet eyes, appeared to have just seated themselves.

Bending at the waist, Julian kissed the hand of the consort who flashed him a most vivid smile. Noting that Irene wore the ruby pin in the five-petaled flower, Mercedes experienced a twinge of what she realized with a start, constituted envy.

At the conclusion of the meal, Julian left his companion in the company of the pair discussing the switch to vegetarianism growing popular among certain facets of American society. Discovering that the couple deplored the trend, owing to the ignorance of many of the practitioners regarding what combinations of vegetables offered a balanced, nutritious diet—especially for the children whom the parents fed what they themselves ate—Mercedes vigorously agreed. "Of course, having once owned cattle, I'm prejudiced," she acknowledged with a wry smile, after extolling the benefits of grass-fed, lean beef. "But we enthusiastic consumers of our own product raised remarkably healthy sons and daughters."

As the talk turned onto the dangers to the health of children whose families never sat down to regular meals, but rather ate on the fly while running out to school, work, or recreational activities, Julian returned, bearing a pot of coffee from which he poured refills. Seating himself, he joined in the discussion. After a pleasant interlude, Alexander and his consort rose, and excused themselves.

Finding himself alone with his cherished companion, the man conscious of taking a calculated gamble remarked matter-of-factly, "At nine—fifteen minutes from now—I'm due to attend a business meeting of the Council, chaired by Lorenzo. Given that I'm one of only three Council members, I feel obliged to attend. It won't last much more than an hour, but I've made arrangements insuring that you won't find that time hanging heavily on your hands. So. I'll escort you to your destination now."

Observing the mischief dancing in the tawny eyes, Mercedes braced herself for some new assault on her modesty, but she asked no prying question.

Tucking her arm into his, Julian escorted her up the stairs to the hall leading to their bedroom. Striding by the door to their room without pausing, he proceeded to the far end of the hall, which Mercedes recalled as giving access to the stairs leading up to the squat building on the edge of the heliport. This time, however, she found herself being ushered down the circular stone stairwell.

Passing one landing featuring a closed door, the guide continued down the stairs to the third and last level. Emerging into a passage identical to that onto which the bedrooms opened, but featuring far fewer doors, Julian stopped before an entry designated only by the stylized flower-design used for the pins—here wrought in iron. Opening the door, he strode through.

The woman on his arm swept her eyes around a spacious chamber notable for a ceiling higher than those of either the bedrooms or the sitting area. Riveting her glance to the central feature, she failed to take conscious note that the air seemed surprisingly warm, despite this level's being below that of the ground. In the center of the expanse of stone floor, she beheld a huge black sculpture of the five-petaled flower.

Fascinated, Mercedes stared at the object dominating the space. The gleaming petals, three of which she saw to be spaced relatively close together on the far side, and two spaced equally close to each other on the near side, extended from a convex center. Two gaps appeared between the two groupings of petals curving outward and downward on their ends. The center of the flower, convex on top, but shaped like an inverted teardrop beneath, tapered to a blunt point which rested on a short, flared, massive base bolted to the stone floor.

Wrenching her eyes from that sight, the woman fixed them on the four youths who entered the chamber from a side door: young men whom she recognized as members of the group who served behind the buffet-counter. Naked now except for abbreviated coverings of their genitals, they drew up in a specific formation. The one of their number wearing purple briefs stood to the front of the three distinguished by blue codpieces.

Mercedes tried valiantly not to stare at those, but failed. Soft, profusely wrinkled fabric covered each youth's flaccid male organ like the skin on a banana gone too loose to lie flat on the fruit within. The remainder of the briefs she saw to be comprised of smooth, stretchy fabric seamlessly joined to a belt of stiff material fastened not by a buckle, but by a tiny brass padlock. Naked except for those oddly contrived coverings and the stretchy black slippers identical to those universally worn by men and women, the young men bowed deeply, in perfect unison, to the pair entering.

All of those impressions flashed into the woman's mind during the fraction of a second that elapsed before she fixed her full attention on the youth standing at the head of the group. That lad straightened with sinuous grace to stand erect, his eyes meeting those of Julian squarely. Shoulder-length hair the color of ripe yellow corn fell freely from a part in the center. Long lashes adorned eyes as limpidly hazel as the sky surrounding the setting sun at midwinter.

On studying his aspect, the intrigued viewer saw that his features fell short of the classic perfection of Nikos's face. A nose slightly hooked, eyebrows less perfectly arched, a wide, full mouth less delicately bowed, suffered in comparison to those distinguishing the Byronic master. Although the youth's countenance lacked the worldly sophistication characterizing that of the older man, its owner projected intense vitality.

The woman saw the cocksureness of youth reined in by adherence to a strict discipline. Discipline voluntarily embraced, or imposed from without? she wondered. On reflection, she concluded that the members who refrained from forcing women to accommodate their tastes would prove just as unlikely to coerce young aspirants desiring membership into following a strict training regimen.

Respectful without conveying the least hint of awe, shyness, or fear, the blonde lad simultaneously projected keen anticipation: boyish zest. The three other youths, a shade more abashed in the presence of the master raking them with a penetrating glance, exhibited equal respect.

Another split second sufficed for the woman to catalog these new impressions.

Julian spoke, his melodic voice carrying on the still, warm air. "This lady's Mercedes: my cherished companion. Mercedes, these young men will assure that the time doesn't hang heavily on your hands in my absence. Apprentices learning erotic art, they'll practice on your lovely body the techniques they've studied. They're not only forbidden to impregnate you, they're physically prevented from doing so, but you'll skim from peak to peak under their assiduous care. So."

Even as shock fogged her mind, the lone woman felt arms encircle her. Fingers drew out the pin, allowing the gown to fall to the stone floor. Exhibited by her master to these men in their early twenties, in a gesture as flamboyant as that with which he offered her to Nikos, she stood tautly still, and strove to control her face.

Even as she engaged in that struggle, she beheld the male organs of all four apprentices rise erect, that change startlingly obvious, given that the wrinkled sheaths now expanded to a diameter of about six inches in response to the stiffness of the organs they concealed.

Realizing that the erections must trigger inflation of the obviously featherweight coverings, rendering impregnation impossible, the badly disconcerted object of their scrutiny found that Julian afforded her no time in which to dwell on the phenomenon. Two corded arms lifted her, and laid her supine on the black flower.

As her head rested on the center of the three clustered petals, the youths, acting in concert with the master, each gripped either a wrist or an ankle. Four pairs of hands stretched those limbs on the four other petals, so that the startled woman lay spread-eagled, her back arched over the convex center of the sculpture, her legs spread almost painfully wide. The hands deftly fastened padded fetters to wrists and ankles, and secured those to strong elastic tethers that they pulled over the rounded lip of the petal, and fastened to rings on the underside.

Stretched almost to the limit of her muscles' ability to withstand the tension, Mercedes grew exquisitely aware of her total vulnerability.

His amber-flecked eyes brimming with mischief, Julian

smiled down at her. "You're free now of any need to fetter your body with your mind," he informed her airily. "Give yourself up to the pleasure that will overshadow any other stimulus. When I return, I'll deliver you the satisfaction which these young men are prohibited from offering." Bending, he kissed her lightly on the lips, and turned to the four youths. "You'll keep count of how many times she climaxes," he ordered. "I'll require that information of you."

The honey-haired youth who Mercedes judged to be the leader, asked a question, his voice musical, his unaccented English cultured. "May we offer your cherished companion the kiss of exploration, Master Julian?" he inquired.

"You each may do so once."

"Will you allow me to inflict pain enough to add spice to the pleasure we bestow?"

"You may employ the Mastiff, but only after she's climaxed three times, and only once."

Bowing as deeply as previously, the quartet of apprentices murmured their acquiescence with the terms. Julian strode out the door without a backward glance.

The senior apprentice now positioned himself between the thighs of the patently flustered woman gazing up at him. His mischievous, amused smile reassured her, despite her acute consciousness of lying so flagrantly exposed to four pairs of eyes belonging to total strangers. Two of the leader's cohorts stationed themselves on either side of her, one occupying the narrow gap between her head and her outstretched arm, the other standing in the wider gap between the two clusters of petals. The third, a dark-haired, black-eyed lad, occupied himself in rolling a round table on castors close to the sculpture.

"Relax, Mercedes," the leader commanded, his lilting voice bearing no overtone of savage, ill-restrained lust.

"You'll enjoy this hour—believe me." Reaching to the table, he picked up a pair of soft, smooth, flexible, cream-colored shafts about eight inches in length, fitted with handles. "Raise her legs," he directed the black-eyed youth, who held a remote in his hand.

The two petals on which the woman's legs were stretched, bent below her knee, even as they rose upwards, curving her torso, and offering her attendants easy access to her feminine orifice and the small brown opening in close proximity to it. Having lubricated a shaft, the leader slid it gently into her anus, leaving the handle protruding. A touch on a control initiated rhythmic pulsations, which throbbed relentlessly through the woman's entire groin.

The second device, he inserted in her cunt. That he set vibrating. Stepping back, the remote in his hand, he watched intently as the black-eyed youth who took his place waited until the petals again flattened, before sliding the two shafts in and out, alternately, rhythmically, relentlessly.

Satisfied, the leader nodded to the pair awaiting his signal. Each of them proceeded to tease a nipple. He himself advanced to the unoccupied gap between two clusters of petals. Dropping to one knee on a footstool, he bent his head, and closed his mouth over the woman's erect clit. He then proceeded to employ every teasing technique in which her older lovers had at one time or another indulged.

Stimulated in every site best suited to generate erotic arousal, Mercedes forgot her embarrassment, her outraged modesty, the tautness born of fear that these young men might unwittingly inflict injury out of ignorance, or too vigorous a use of the implements wielded. Their skill she discovered to be superb. Arousal—swift, sudden, potent—set her panting audibly.

The youth standing opposite the leader ceased tonguing

her nipple. Turning her face towards him, he kissed her on the mouth, erotically, intimately, but gently. When at length he freed her lips, he bent, and again closed his mouth over her breast, this time to suckle the erect nubbin.

Roused at this juncture to raw lust, the woman welcomed the onset of climax, moaning as it overtook her.

The other apprentices desisted, allowing her time to savor the shivers, the euphoria, the delicious pleasure centered in her loins. Smiling knowingly, the blonde youth caressed her with his voice. "Nice, mm?" he observed, his eyes dancing. "You come with such ease, you'll skim to a good many peaks before your master collects you, Mercedes. We'll see to that."

The petals again lifted, exposing her twin orifices to the maximum. The three blue-clad youths changed places, as the leader removed the inserts. A tall, slender lad possessed of liquid brown eyes and short brown hair now slipped a new, well-lubricated implement into her anus. That she saw as it appeared briefly in her view, to be identical in design to the last, but green in hue. He followed that insertion with one targeting her feminine depth.

When the petals again lowered her tautly stretched body to the horizontal position, the woman spread to the manipulator's view experienced potently erotic vibrations in her rear passage. The second device pulsated, its rounded tip swelling, and then deflating, with each throbbing pulse. Those the new wielder slid in and out as before, changing the angle every few thrusts, so as to target new sensitive sites. Two other attendants kissed, massaged, and otherwise teased her breasts, as the third licked, sucked, and tongued her clit.

Time stopped for the woman held utterly immobile on the slick, smooth, hard surface of the stylized flower. The flight of doomed seconds ceased to exist. Her world contracted to become this exotic chamber; her awareness narrowed to intense concentration on the delicious sensations threatening to short out her overloaded sensory system. To her surprise and delight, she achieved two more peaks in swift succession, patently elating the young men assiduously offering such potent stimulation.

Still rapt from the most recent rise to bliss, the object of their attentions grew aware of a hand laid flat on her abdomen. "You've missed one essential element, eh, lovely lady?" the leader crooned seductively. "Longed for the spice of pain that enhances and intensifies the pleasure . . . mmm? I'll give you now what you'll find renders your surrender complete. Ahhh . . . not a twitch; not a quiver. You crave the bite of the Mastiff . . . that's obvious. So. Come for us again, little initiate. Mmmm?"

Astonished to discover that she indeed craved the pain now radiating from the soft flesh of her mound, Mercedes grew exquisitely conscious that the pressure of the teeth produced a relaxation of sphincters, and a loosening of her loins that rendered the pleasure produced by the black-eyed youth's moist mouth and questing tongue even more arousing than it would otherwise have been. Yielding her will to her youthful attendants, the neophyte gave herself up to enjoyment of all the sensations combining to lift her again to fulfillment. The leader's mouth closed over her own. His tongue intruded, exploring the moist depths of the orifice of which he blithely made himself free.

Recalling that not once had Nikos kissed her, Mercedes intuitively divined that only the master of the woman shared by peers held the right to offer her that intimate salute. She guessed—accurately—that Julian willingly waived his privilege, so that these lads could practice even that skill.

Roused to a white heat of passion, the woman so relentlessly and thoroughly stimulated caught herself wishing that this vitally alive, vividly eager, beguilingly youthful man could slide his tool into the orifice stimulated by an inanimate object. Shame scalded her as she realized the degree to which she had cast her inhibitions into the void: shame that dissolved in the euphoria attending her latest rise to culmination.

No whit lax in performing their assigned task, the apprentices displaying unflagging enthusiasm raised their charge to rapture three more times before the instigator of the exercise appeared to judge the efficacy of their efforts. Finding his cherished companion limp, spent, enjoying the glow produced by their latest effort, he raised an eyebrow as he impaled the leader with a questioning glance.

"Seven peaks, Master Julian," came the prompt tally. "She buoyed our self-esteem, I'll frankly admit. I'll wager she craves the whip, mm?" That final question came accompanied by an impish grin.

A musical laugh greeted that sly rhetorical question. "She's learning," came the amused reply. "So, little hedonist," he announced, directing those words to Mercedes. "You need a hot cock, to top off your achievement, eh?"

"Mmmmmm." That all but inaudible murmur of assent wrenched out of the woman stripped of the last iota of her modesty, produced renewed hilarity in the master being freed of shirt and pants by four assistants. As the apprentices stood two to a side, Julian positioned himself between his lover's thighs. A touch on the remote caused the flower to tilt until the cunt oozing juice came within easy reach of his turgid organ. Driving into his partner's warm, wet cunt, he thrust deeply and repeatedly, while four pairs of hands and four moist tongues teased the moaning woman's breasts, navel, and clit.

Even as she cried in the privacy of her mind that her capacity to climax must surely be exhausted, the woman surfeited on sensual pleasure achieved a peak that sent her into half-trance. As she basked in that blissful state, the tall youth gently bathed her clit and pussy-lips with warm water and fragrant soap. As pliant as if molded of warm butter, the object of his attentions enjoyed the ministration without generating a single qualm originating in her temporarily suspended sense of propriety.

Awash in euphoria, Mercedes grew only dimly aware that hands freed her wrists and ankles, and strong arms lifted her slack body off the flower. Set on feet that failed to support her while gripped by iron hands that held her upright, she sagged as if intoxicated while the blonde youth pulled up her gown and pinned the shoulder.

Julian supported her as he smilingly commended the apprentices. "I'll report most favorably on your achievement," he promised them.

Cradled in strong arms, Mercedes riveted a fascinated glance on four grotesquely enlarged, rigidly erect, fabric-sheathed male members. That final impression shimmered within her misted inner vision as her master bore her to their bedroom.

Chapter Eight

Bearing his burden to the bed, Julian stripped off her gown, and laid her in the center. Dispensing with the garments only donned for the passage through the hall, he reclined next to the woman still caught in the ebbing wash of ecstasy. Melting against him, she closed her eyes, and let her mind drift.

A good thirty minutes later, the hedonist stirred, and opened her eyes. Shifting to prop his chin on the palm of a hand supported by a bent arm, her lover studied her expression. Relieved to spy no evidence of incipient anger, no painful blush or pursed lips indicative of outraged modesty, he smiled at his cherished companion, not troubling to hide his amusement.

Fixing ironic eyes on the man she knew to be assessing her reaction, his lover drawled, "I must say, time most surely didn't weigh heavily on my hands! I'll bet that blonde lad grows to be three times as dangerous as you or your friends."

Moved to laughter, Julian responded with perfect honesty, "I heartily agree. I expect you realize that you've developed marvelously efficient circuitry which enables you to come with gratifying ease?"

"I've developed a most unnerving lack of inhibition," came the wry rejoinder. "Do I owe that disconcertingly unique experience to some compulsory requirement of the Order, or was my participation optional?"

"It's an ancient custom, frequently followed, but not mandatory," her master informed her, smiling into her faintly reproachful face. "You benefited from the reinforcement given to your circuitry, and those apprentice masters obtained much-needed practice in their art, which they're only allowed to gain in that fashion."

"Wasn't your enjoying me in front of them a bit cruel—given that they're denied the privilege of fucking the woman they raise to such a height of bliss?"

"Cruel, perhaps, but necessary. They're learning to exert flawless self-mastery. They'll eventually be taught how to achieve mental ecstasy without ejaculating. They'll likewise learn to control to perfection not only their emotions, but also the course of their passion. They follow an ancient discipline—one far more demanding, far more rigorous, and far harder to complete successfully, than any regimen they'll ever require a woman to endure at their hands."

Intrigued, Mercedes digested that assertion for a time. At length she asked, "How long would it have taken you to initiate me—to condition me so thoroughly to subordinate my will to yours, that I'd willingly offer to become your slave?"

"That depends. Three days . . . or perhaps four, given the strength of your will. Once you formally consented to undergo initiation, I'd have sequestered you in a place devoid of any distractions, and devoted the entire time to the task at hand."

"Would you have deliberately employed devious psychological means to render me unable to do other than agree to live as your slave?"

His every delicate sensor shrieking danger, the man exquisitely aware of the combativeness mirrored in the green eyes of this woman he dreaded losing, unerringly judged that the slightest evasion would prove fatal. "I'd have employed pain, pleasure, and proven techniques approaching mind control, to subordinate your will to mine," he admitted levelly. "Extraordinarily effective techniques, perfected over many centuries by a long succession of masters of erotic art. I'd have reinforced your masochistic tendencies, and ended by bending you to my will without breaking your spirit."

"What if my will remained unbroken?"

"I'd have taken you home, and vanished out of your life."

"So . . . with you . . . it's all or nothing?"

"With me, and with any master who seeks a permanent companion—a consort."

Chilled by that ultimatum, the fiercely self-reliant widow assessed her reactions to that bald, direly troubling admission. When she spoke, her voice conveyed impassioned conviction. "Julian, I can be swayed by logic, and convinced by well-reasoned arguments. I can be beguiled into a dangerous liaison by shrewd appeals to my emotions, or even to my passions. I may place an unwarranted degree of faith in my intuition, and in my skill at judging character, but if that judgment turns out to be faulty, I assume the full blame for the consequences I suffer.

"I'm finding that I'm learning to crave the whip—that I'm losing my inhibitions. But if you'd employed subtle psychological techniques amounting to mind control—sought by such means to achieve a permanent suspension of my will—I'd have tumbled to what you were doing. You'd have roused the deep-seated, stubborn refusal to submit to coercion of any sort, that lies at my core.

"No amount of pain would have overcome that fundamental intransigence—not even pain accompanied by injury. I'm enough of a masochist that I can readily accept pain as a form of erotic foreplay, but I couldn't be brainwashed into offering myself as your slave. If I ever *do* so offer myself, it will be because I act freely, after concluding that I can only be happy living that way. I could never be conditioned or manipulated into making that choice."

Staring into the eyes gone hard as green agate, Julian perceived that this fiercely independent-minded descendant of hardy pioneers spoke the naked truth. Shock blended into overwhelming relief that blind chance prevented his making an egregious, irremediable, incomparably costly error.

Shaken by his perception of the narrowness of his escape from disaster, he struggled to regain his aplomb. He succeeded, but only after the shrewd observer caught an ephemeral flash of potent dismay. "Now that you know me capable of employing subtle psychological means to bend you to my will, do you regret accepting this invitation?" he queried in a tone studiously kept neutral.

The recipient of that deceptively matter-of-fact probe took a second to reflect, before shaking her head. "No," she responded firmly. "You told me that your code of ethics differed radically from that currently held in this day and age. I accepted that quirk of your character, given that you do live by a code. I knew you were dangerous, Julian. I merely underestimated both the nature and the magnitude of the danger."

Vast, unqualified relief suffused the man crushing his lover against his chest. "I'm no danger to you, Mercedes," he breathed in her ear. "Never to you."

Conscious that her feelings for this man unlike any she had ever known suffered no alteration in the aftermath of his disquieting admission, Mercedes wondered bleakly whether passion at this juncture might be fatally clouding her judgment. She yet found herself unable to do other than cling to him in relief, grateful that no unbridgeable chasm just opened between them.

Sensing that her relief matched his, Julian savored burgeoning satisfaction even as he grimly warned himself that she remained fully capable of breaking off the relationship if he violated some central tenet of the code of ethics rooted in deeply held philosophical beliefs, rather than merely offending the sense of propriety which she regarded as a social imposition, not a conviction.

Incipient wrath vied with frustration. A savage wish flayed him: that his affair with Mercedes might have proceeded as smoothly, and ended as satisfactorily, as that which his brother Michael not too long ago initiated with the potently attractive woman now supremely content with her life as his slave/consort.

Resolutely, he refused to dwell on a reality he found himself powerless to alter. You merely face a greater challenge than Michael did, he chided himself sardonically. Disaster isn't inevitable! This woman's daring equals both her stubbornness and her strength of will. She could learn to match what you feel for her, if you manage to avoid any new gross miscalculation.

Closing his mouth over that of the partner melting against him, he possessed himself of her tongue, and sucked until he regained his full sense of dominating her completely. The pounding of her heart transmitted itself to sensors extended to the utmost; set his pulse-rate racing in synchrony with it. When at long last he freed her lips, he asserted forcefully, "I love you, Mercedes. I desire you, yes, but what I feel for you far transcends mere lust. I love you for all that you are."

Shock melted swiftly into heady ebullience: joy so great that it almost hurt. Tears momentarily threatened to film the green eyes alight with elation. Hugging the man still holding her close, Mercedes buried her face on his shoulder as she fought down a most unaccountable urge to weep.

Holding her away, Julian tipped her chin upwards, forcing her to meet his glance. "Will the admission I just made interfere with your learning to love me?" he asked, his yearning to hear a negative answer showing nakedly, despite his keeping his tone commendably matter-of-fact.

"It's too late for that," came the unhesitating reply. "I think I've loved you from the first day we met . . . from the first night. Nothing that's happened since seems to have done other than deepen that love. I desire you, but that's only a part of the emotion you generate in me."

Fierce delight suffused the man dreading that he might hear an uncompromising affirmative. Again, he locked this woman for whom his heart hungered into an unbreakable embrace, but his kiss proved purely affectionate. "I'm glad, Mercedes," he murmured as his lips brushed her hair. "I can't change what I am, what I believe, or what I demand of a lover. You'll need to accept that."

Still a trifle shaken by his earlier admission, the woman weighing that plea remarked wistfully, "I expect that you've told numerous previous partners that you loved them . . . mmmm?"

"Only one, Mercedes. Long ago."

"And you . . . stopped loving her?"

"No. She died . . . young. Far too young. That wound healed, but it left an ineradicable scar."

The pain freighting the voice far huskier than its wont tore at the heart of the woman herself bereaved. Hugging the man whose debonair self-possession developed cracks at this juncture, she murmured an inarticulate phrase the tone of which, rather than the words, brought the hearer comfort.

His arms tightened around her. Defensive armor, worn so long that it seemed a part of his nature, suddenly metamorphosed into an iron restraint constricting Julian's breathing, and preventing free expression of his feelings. Unable to cast off the encumbrance, he merely held this woman unlike any he had ever known, savoring the sensation he feared to identify as happiness, lest it flow through his impotent fingers like water, and vanish in the arid desert earth.

For a span of minutes, two lovers who only now realized the magnitude of the loneliness each had combated vigorously but with only partial success, maintained a silence that had nothing in it of constraint. At length, Julian held his breathless companion away. Tucking the habitually delinquent strand of ruddy hair over her ear, he suggested lunch.

Smiling tremulously, Mercedes nodded. Rising, she helped him dress, as he did her. Her arm tucked possessively into that of her master, she accompanied him to the dining area, her heart suddenly as light as her step.

Passing through the line moving along the buffet, she discovered that the same four youthful apprentices who had practiced their art on her body presided behind the counter. Maintaining admirable control of her face, she ascertained to her relief that theirs matched hers. Only when she stood surveying a basket of assorted fruit, and pointed to a pear too far to the rear of the elaborate arrangement for her to reach, did she see the blonde youth wink conspiratorially as he placed the pear in her hand. For a millisecond, his eyes grew alight with mischief. Almost instantly, his face regained its initial blandness, and his gaze shifted to the food.

Warmed rather than flustered by that gesture gone unnoticed by anyone but herself, she smiled benignly on the youth before advancing down the line, reflecting once again that five or ten years hence, he would undoubtedly eclipse Nikos in rakehell charm.

An hour later, replete with a delicious lunch, emotionally drained by the events of the morning, Mercedes welcomed the chance to stroll on the arm of her lover down a tree-shaded walk, to a secluded spot where two rustic chairs woven of bog-willow stood in a small flagged circle off the main path. The air, clear, pure, warm, and heady with the scent of flowers strange to her, stirred only fitfully.

"At one, we're invited to join Lorenzo and Francesca and their guests, in their private bathing area," Julian informed her casually. "The Grand Master shares the bulk of his estate freely with his fellow members, but he reserves that one segment for the use of himself and those he gathers for conversation. He hates the impersonality and background noise integral to large groupings, preferring to visit with only a few friends at a time."

"How civilized." That remark came accompanied by a lilting laugh that fell on Julian's ears like the silvery cadence of wind chimes. "Who are the other two men on the Council?" Mercedes asked, emboldened by having noticed that questions regarding the organization or symbolism of the Order seemed not to annoy this man so reluctant to divulge the most innocuous revelation regarding his private life.

"Manuel and Raoul," came the equable, unhesitating reply. "But given that Raoul's currently living in seclusion, he delegated Alexander to serve as his proxy."

"I see." Aware now that rank must indeed combine with the forcefulness of Julian's personality to earn him that special deference on the part of the members, Mercedes experienced an upsurge of pride in the mature, masterful lover who enjoyed high status among his fellows.

Knitting her brow, she contemplated a possible outcome of the exercise in mutual understanding that had occurred earlier. Boldly, she resolved to address it. "Julian, nothing that you revealed earlier today makes me less willing to explore to the hilt the customs of the Order. Please don't feel that you need to shield me from seeing, or even experiencing, the customary rituals in which a cherished companion takes part, even if participation tests my ability to cast my inhibitions into the void. I want to belong—for your sake."

For a surreally stretched instant, a most enticing vision shimmered in the mental space of the man gripped with savage elation. Forcing the temptation out of his consciousness, he smiled on the lover regarding him with faint anxiety. "I won't conceal from you knowledge of any custom merely because I suspect that hearing about it will shock you, but I won't levy demands guaranteed to drive you to the brink of rebellion—or even push you over the edge. As I told you, you take delicate handling, Mercedes. A light touch." That affirmation came accompanied by an ironic smile, but the melodic voice conveyed a perceptible overtone of regret.

"I'm tougher than you assume," the ranchwoman averred musingly, her smile as close to being provocative as the man raking her with amber-flecked eyes had ever seen it come.

"Mmm. I judge you tough as five-ply laminate. Let me feel my way, Mercedes. I'm conducting an experiment new in the annals of the Order."

Wisely deciding to leave the matter so, the widow nodded, and said no more on that subject.

Ten minutes before the hour of one, Mercedes, clad in her gown, emerged onto the porch, escorted by the lover who chose to stroll through the park rather than around its perimeter, under the balcony. Noting that they seemed to be heading for the third of the park's circumference unbounded by porch or balcony—that part featuring the waterfall—she drank in the beauty of the wooded area only minimally impacted by alterations wrought by the hand of men. Recalling Julian's mention that the host and hostess entertained in their private bathing area, she wondered why they wore what she regarded as formal garb, rather than robes. On reflection, she decided that the Grand Master must stand on formality with his private guests.

Stopping before an openwork arch fashioned of iron, upon which a vigorous vine climbed, Julian opened the gate set within the arch, and proceeded through. Halting in the small flagged enclosure bounded by trees, he divested his companion of her gown, which he folded. Wrapping the ornament in the folds, he laid both her attire and his own over a stone bench upon which rested four stacks of other neatly folded garments. Stark naked, he led his equally nude companion down the path.

So much for formality! Mercedes reflected wryly.

Patches of mist obscured the sky above the trees, floating wraith-like amid the trunks. Tucking his companion's arm in his, the guide advanced down a flagged path that passed through thick vegetation. The woman studying her surroundings noted that only one side path wound away from the main thoroughfare. Dense growth surrounded them until they emerged upon a wide expanse of bare rock. A gently slanting sheet of stone, more or less smooth, stretched to the foot of the cliff. At the base of that sheer eminence, a mass of huge boulders broken off from the face lay in a jumbled pile.

Two-thirds of the way up the rugged, steeply ascending wall, a torrent of water issued from a roughly circular fissure to fall in a single smooth column towards the boulders. Upon striking those, it lost its uniformity, breaking into numerous secondary streams that plunged onto artfully designed, spoon-shaped artifacts affixed to the living rock. Those metallic objects directed the streams outward, and spread them into umbrella-like showers of sparkling droplets adorned by myriad shimmering rainbows. Those showers fell mostly on the flat rock, just beyond the mass of boulders.

"Oh—how lovely!" the woman breathed, awed by that lavish display of water spewing out of the bowels of the earth into the dry air of an arid desert. "It's almost too much so!"

"I know. It seems an extravagance, given the parched earth stretching away on top. The springs seem to be fed from conduits leading from that rock older than the layers surrounding it. Some subterranean watercourse must intersect far beneath, with rock heated by an upwelling of magma at some vast depth."

The closer Mercedes approached the sparkling showers, the more entranced she grew. Lorenzo and Francesca stepped out from an enclosure shielded from the view of those approaching, by the boulders ringing it. Both host and hostess Mercedes saw to be as nude as their guests.

Grown far more accepting now of the custom of bathing in the buff, she yet experienced a resurgence of embarrassment on finding herself expected to stroll about in the hot sun in the company of the Grand Master and his consort, while stark naked. Reminding herself acidly that she felt far less distressed on that score in the flower-chamber while enjoying the sensual pleasure conferred by four total strangers, than she did preparing to enjoy a dip in the springs, she got herself in hand, and smiled serenely on the pair offering warm greetings.

Manuel and his lissome courtesan now emerged from the shielded enclosure. Simultaneously, Jason and Shirley advanced at a swinging stride from the flagged path beneath the trees. All four newcomers Mercedes divined to revel in the freedom from confining fabric, as if warm air, smooth stone, and hot sun formed their natural element.

Slipping her arm through that of her master, Francesca suggested that they enjoy the shower first, given that Mercedes and Celeste beheld the waterfall for the first time.

Having graciously acceded, Lorenzo advanced to the edge of the terrain upon which the artificially generated rain splattered upon the rock, producing pleasing white noise. Eight bathers, seven utterly uninhibited, and one firmly controlling what visceral tension remained, stepped into the downpour of cold droplets through which rainbow light scintillated.

The brisk massage, the soothing patter, the invigorating coolness, the feeling of belonging: all combined to annihilate the last of the ranchwoman's qualms. Clasping her hands behind her head, she let the delicious force of the spray beat on breasts rosy from the impact, no whit troubled by the open admiration bestowed on her mature but commendably trim figure by the brawny mercenary. She grew aware that Lorenzo regarded her meditatively, his quizzical glance betraying faint amusement.

Jason she saw to be wholly engrossed in contemplation of Shirley's hard, lean, enticingly shapely body. Julian she divined to be concealing inner hilarity at the swiftness with which she shed her qualms. Smiling wryly at him, she laughed when he winked, being reminded forcibly of the irrepressible blonde apprentice.

Disporting herself beneath the forceful, invigorating spray, the widow again gained the sense of having slipped through an intangible boundary into a strange, intriguing realm where natural laws unlike those in her old reality operated. The thought crossed her mind that she loved a man whom she only knew from encountering him in this parallel world so different from her own. That notion troubled her, until she admitted to her quivering alter ego that she felt totally liberated here: free from the threats posed by the dreary sameness of her associations, the aridity which had developed in her sensual life owing to her bereavement, and the loneliness which she had so valiantly battled to ignore, but which had lain at the heart of the life she had striven hard to keep purposeful. Standing naked, gazed at by near-strangers, she felt free as the hawk circling high in the azure sky. That realization first startled her, and then elated her.

At length, the company emerged from the downpour, vastly refreshed. Lorenzo led them to the flat expanse bounded by huge boulders, which Mercedes discovered to form a natural antechamber to a cave in the upward-thrusting rock face. The guests followed him down a smooth, water-sculpted, downward-slanting dark passage about twenty feet in length, emerging in a spacious, dome-shaped, misty natural cavern dimly lighted by fissures in the top of the dome: cracks leading to the rock face. Except for a narrow band of bare stone floor at its perimeter, the lofty chamber the raptly gazing widow saw to be a warm pool.

In the center of the expanse of liquid rose an outcropping of rock, which the fascinated viewer saw to be roughly cone-shaped. Water flowing out of the top of the cone ran down the sloping sides of the natural feature, and drained away down a fissure in the far side of the cavern.

Warm mist swirled around the nude bodies of the entrants whose eyes slowly began to adjust to the dimness. Four wide, slightly sloping couches covered with waterproof vinyl extended outwards and slightly downwards, from points equidistant from each other, around the cone. On each of those, water flowed around two raised headrests, to pour down the length of the couch.

"We'll disport ourselves for a half-hour or so—enjoy the warmth and the closeness with our partners, before repairing to the house for drinks and conversation," Lorenzo announced serenely. "Meditate on the uncertainty of life, my friends, while enjoying the only true reality: the sensations we savor at this moment."

More intrigued by the comment than taken aback at the invitation, Mercedes allowed Julian to propel her into the water, which she discovered to be only a few inches deep at the edge, and waist-high at the perimeter of the cone. Bidden to recline on the water-covered couch, she obeyed, noting that the headrest kept the water cascading down her body away from her face. In her absorption with peering into the misty, cavernous expanse of space surrounding her, she failed to notice the vinyl hose, about a half-inch in diameter, tipped by a smooth shaft featuring holes through which water flowed, which lay between them, the head between their knees.

Slipping his scarred left arm beneath her upper back, Julian drew her closer to his side. Grasping the shaft in his right hand, he parted her pussy-lips, and inserted the implement into her cunt. Shocked to find that she now enjoyed a most unconventional douche, Mercedes felt the initial tension generated by surprise drain away. Relaxing, she lay in the curve of her lover's arm, laughing into his ear. "Do all the couches boast this highly personal feature?" she inquired.

"They do. Francesca designed and installed them. Nice, mmm? Massage my cock, little sensualist. Make me hard."

Taken severely aback, the startled woman whispered, "The others will hear us—perhaps even see us!"

"The others will be doing likewise, my love. The mist will veil us. Do as I ask, now."

Several minutes later, his shaft erect, throbbing, Julian withdrew the douche. "Get astride me, and work your lovely loins on my prick," he ordered.

Obeying despite her misgivings as to the degree to which the mist shrouded them, Mercedes employed all her considerable skill to lift to fulfillment the lover over whose body a transparent sheet of water flowed. Able to climax despite her awareness of the close proximity of three other couples, she heard the low, hoarse groans signifying that her master's culmination followed directly on hers.

Sliding off him to lie in his arms, her body now exotically caressed by the flow of warm water, she sighed in contentment as he slid the douche into the orifice awash in his juice. Lying bathed within and without, her mouth possessed by this wholly uninhibited sensualist, her feminine depth massaged by warm mineral water, she molded herself to him, consciously savoring the only reality: this precious, fleeting moment.

"I love you," her master murmured in her ear, when he freed her mouth.

"I love *you*," came the whispered response.

Two partners conscious now only of being cherished by the other, lost track of time. Their minds turned inward, etching this moment vividly into memory. Their abstraction caused them to fail to notice the others' rising, until they beheld Manuel standing at the foot of their couch, his arm around the willowy courtesan who stood gazing in patent admiration of this non-professional's ability to engross her worldly partner to the point of his losing all cognizance of the hour. Her long hair plastered to the rounded contours of wet, white shoulders, Celeste reminded Mercedes of a water nymph: lovely, desirable, ageless, immortal.

Flushing hotly as Julian withdrew the douche full in the view of the pair watching, Mercedes rose, and stepped into the waist-deep water. Her perturbation she managed to conceal from all but her manifestly amused lover.

Emerging into the antechamber open to the glare of the mid-afternoon sun, the bathers squinted. Quickly, they shaded eyes assaulted by the brightness, with hands held palm-down. Water dripping from their hair and bodies, they strode up the slope to the path, and turned off on the byway, which led to a structure standing among the trees: a building featuring rock walls, leaded-glass casement windows, a stout, iron-bossed wooden door, and a heavily beamed slate roof featuring an iron chimney-flue in the center. Muted, diffuse light streamed through the west-facing windows, warming the stone underfoot.

Entranced by the rustic beauty of the building, Mercedes gazed about her. The metal flue, flared at the bottom, descended to a point six feet above the flagging. A small but hot fire burned on the hearth only eighteen inches in diameter, which rose six inches higher than the floor. Four leather-covered hassocks, each flanked by a plump cushion on one side, and a small, rustic table on the other, reposed on the flags.

The items of furniture Mercedes saw to be arranged in a circle around the hearth from which fragrant wood-smoke rose to exit via the flue. Against one wall stood a table of carven hardwood, upon which rested cobweb-streaked bottles, silver bowls, linen napkins, goblets of delicate, hand-blown glass, handsome ceramic platters and plates, silver knives, hardwood cutting boards on which reposed a variety of cheeses, and baskets of intricate design, piled with fruit.

Having invited their guests to seat themselves, Lorenzo and Francesca sliced fruit and cheese, and poured wine, preparatory to serving their guests. Noting that the men settled onto the hassocks, and their partners dropped onto the plump cushions lower in height than the seats appropriated by the men, Mercedes sank onto a cushion, her weight on one cheek of her rear, her legs bent and tucked under her, her arm resting on Julian's upper leg. Gratefully, she savored the warmth of the blazing wood on her bare skin and still-wet hair. She noted that the heat of the fire, as well as its light, reflected cozily from the inner, rough-plastered walls, and the tan stone flags.

Francesca appeared in front of her, offering a goblet of pale wine, and a plate. Smiling up at the hostess, who informed her with manifest pride that the wine came from a vineyard located on the property, she again caught a glimpse of the delicate design etched into the graying hair of the consort's mound. Too well bred to stare, she kept her eyes glued to those of the woman now serving Julian, but as before, she found herself forcibly reminded of reading a brand on the hairy hide of a cow.

Manuel, who had added to the fire a few gnarled faggots taken from a stack by the door, reseated himself on Mercedes' right. His massive, tiger-supple torso she saw to bear a number of scars disturbingly similar to that marring Julian's arm and side.

Expecting that a mercenary soldier would carry the reminders of his adventures on his brawny body, she experienced no shock at the sight, but the thought crossed her mind that Manuel evinced none of that latent readiness to explode into action at a moment's notice which Julian had so plainly exhibited while visiting with her at her home.

Well . . . Julian's far more relaxed here, she reminded herself, and perhaps, so is Manuel. That supposition failed to allay her uneasiness. This professional warrior comes across as competent, decisive, tough, and formidable—a man who'd be no mean adversary in any violent encounter, she ruminated. Even so, Manuel doesn't radiate that aura of danger that struck me as soon as I met Julian.

Fear that had lain quiescent now stirred, but retreated to its lair as the man generating it murmured a soft injunction to open her mouth, and fed her a quarter of an apricot. "Francesca planted the orchard now producing an abundance of fruit," he remarked. "Superb, these."

While the guests sampled the fruit and cheeses, and sipped

wine guaranteed to tantalize the most discerning palate, Lorenzo swept shrewd, uncannily observant eyes from face to face, from body to nude body. Discovering no tension arising from outraged modesty in that of the cherished companion feeding Julian a sliver of cheese while extolling the flavor, her face alight with the contagious vivacity which made her appear to be far younger than her years, he savored satisfaction.

Reflecting that this uninitiated outsider seemed to take to the culture of the Order as naturally as would a hawk to the air, or a goose to water, he assured himself that no incendiary problem would disturb the tranquility of the week, or disgrace this valued Council-member running so formidable a risk to his standing among his peers by bringing a woman he had not totally subordinated to his will. As he drew that conclusion, the Grand Master let his eyes linger on Mercedes' mature but athletic body, admiring her as he might a fine painting, or a delicately evocative sculpture.

Once the guests finished sampling the fruit and the cheese, they began to cast about for an interesting topic of conversation. Sipping wine, they disposed themselves comfortably with no regard whatsoever for their nakedness.

These unabashed sensualists go about wrapped in the ceremonial robes of lofty, regal self-possession—clothe themselves in an abstract construction of the mind, the poet concluded, won to wry admiration of their serene ease in each other's company. I'm beginning to think I'll find clothing annoyingly confining, when I get home!

Glancing from Julian to Manuel, Jason tossed out a question. "Amazing, how one can forget all about world problems while enjoying a week-long respite from work and worry. How do you suppose the crisis in the Middle East will work out this time?"

The two men to whom that query seemed to be directed exchanged thoughtful glances. Manuel observed bluntly, "I imagine the administration in Washington will opt for air strikes, but they'll balk at deploying the requisite number of ground forces that would allow full resolution of the crisis. They'll shrink from taking the heat considerable numbers of casualties would produce—fear to face the political fallout.

"Fatal error, that. Air strikes called in by small numbers of special forces on the ground won't unseat this dictator whose mindset they consistently fail to understand, and whose propensities for atrocity they've either ignored at crucial junctures in the past, or used as a pretext for ineffectual action. They'll need an army prepared to crush his force, and to kill or capture him. Despite the stiffening of the national resolve produced by the recent tragedy playing out on its home soil, the world's only superpower still worries a bit too much about taking casualties." A rueful shake of the head accompanied that contention.

"Our government only acts when it perceives its national interests threatened—not out of altruism, I'm afraid," Mercedes contributed with a sigh. "Exactly as do our allies. Few Westerners knew the Bedouin as did T. E. Lawrence, but in his epic work, he chronicled his mental anguish at knowing, all during the Arab Revolt, that the promises England made so as to bring about that uprising against the Turks might well be repudiated later, because of a perception that the nation's welfare came before that of its smallest ally."

Two pairs of eyes riveted themselves to the vibrant face from which the woman now thrust back the offending lock of hair. "You've read *The Seven Pillars of Wisdom*?" Manuel inquired incredulously.

"Every word. Fascinating, I found it. Our leaders should read it, but I doubt that the decision-makers ever have. We

Americans seem fated grossly to misunderstand the philosophy governing Islamic peoples—especially Arabs. We can't fathom how they think, because their traditions, tribal organization, and culture differ so markedly from our own. T. E. Lawrence also remarked about Bedouins that each stranger makes his own poor bed among them. Ours seems to have been one of the poorest."

A broad smile now lit the rugged face of the professional soldier—a rare expression of approval that Mercedes rightly interpreted as an accolade. "This nation's leaders never really understood the Russians, for those same reasons," he vouchsafed, "but they did a bit better in that sphere than they have in the Middle East. Perhaps what America needs isn't a volunteer army made up of a relatively few professionals leading large numbers of green kids who join to receive a free education, and expect to get through the term of their enlistment without seeing combat.

"The American government ought to consider hiring a standing army of mercenaries led by experts entrusted with full charge of developing the plans for the type of campaign it would take to wipe this bastard—and then give those experts a free hand to launch, fight, and successfully conclude that campaign."

"A sort of modern-day French Foreign Legion?" Mercedes queried, intrigued by the idea.

"Exactly. But the leadership would never agree to give any mercenary commander the latitude he'd need to pull off total victory on the ground."

"That approach would never gain support, sensible as it sounds," Julian objected scathingly. "What would solve the problem for the populace living under the thumb of this mass murderer who preys savagely on his own people, is a successful political assassination both of the despot and the sons he's raised to be worse than himself."

"Do you mean a strike mounted by members of an opposition party—a rebel force? Or assassination by some agent paid by the United States to kill simply for money?" Mercedes asked, managing to avoid any overtone of repugnance.

"Either way would serve," Julian opined equably. "Of course, the latter method would be difficult to arrange, for the CIA at least. At this particular time in our history, they haven't yet recovered from the crippling constraints misguidedly placed on them before that error got rectified."

"An assassination could be arranged, if those making the decisions knew how to set about the task properly—knew whom to contact, and how, and where—but they'd undoubtedly jeopardize both the intermediaries and the assassins by leaking the news that such an attempt would soon be made. America has trouble keeping the most sensitive information secret," Manuel interjected.

"I'd purely hate to see the government go that route—view assassination of any leader, mass murderer or not, as being morally and politically acceptable," Mercedes objected, frowning. "Nor do I think that our officials ought to bring about such a solution covertly, and then deny any responsibility for doing so. Either way, they'd be casting a blot on America's honor. Tarnished as that's become, at times, some of us still wish that honor upheld."

"Mm. You'd prefer to see us bomb sites crammed full of women and children deluded into believing that their presence will deter an attack—wreak unspeakable agony on innocent, oppressed people lacking any decision-making power—and then send in an army—our own, or one we hired—to exterminate along with the hard-core members of the despot's bodyguard, the poor bastards swept off the streets and forced to man weak defenses, when that heavy loss of civilian life could be avoided by hiring a professional assassin?" Julian's voice held an edge.

Turning to scan the face he turned to her, Mercedes saw certain lines around the eyes and mouth leap into greater prominence, as the striking features changed expression: grew set, hard, grim.

No whit daunted, she yet took pains to argue dispassionately. "I'd prefer to see diplomacy work, I'll readily admit—though that approach seems fraught with the danger of simply giving the dictator time to stock up on weapons of mass destruction," she countered. "But ghastly as I find the notion of an invasion, I can't bring myself to condone political murder. It would be far too easy to go from that high moral ground—removal of a sadistic mass murderer fully as evil as Hitler—to condoning the assassination of *any* Middle Eastern leader who dares to think differently about what's best for his country and his people than do our leaders in Washington: men who so often pander to special interest groups like oil companies, rather than making decisions based solely on what's right."

"You're able to separate in your mind, your country's honor from that of your leaders—be critical, not cynical," Manuel remarked musingly. "I find that mental outlook refreshing, given the cynicism so prevalent among independent thinkers nowadays."

"Or naive," Julian interposed sardonically. "America's honor's no less sullied than that of any other industrial superpower. We're just more hypocritical than most. Mercedes, if you'd ever found yourself viewing the aftermath of a purge representing vengeance against those participating in an armed uprising—hideous murders of babies and pregnant women, for example—or if you'd ever witnessed the effects of diabolically gruesome torture inflicted on dissidents or political prisoners by a power-crazed despot, or discovered evidence of systematic genocide perpetrated on whole ethnic groups, you'd likely think an assassin's bullet too easy a death for a dictator guilty of committing similar atrocities."

"Such a man needs to be punished, I agree, but according to the rule of international law, as were those condemned at Nuremburg," came the calm but firm reply. "And few crimes the equal of those lie on America's national conscience."

"Native Americans like my grandfather could tell you differently," Shirley interjected, her eyes gone suddenly bitter.

Turning to meet the girl's glance, Mercedes nodded. "*Touché*," she acknowledged gracefully. "My great-grandfather was a trapper who lived for many years among the Shoshone, but he'd seen the devastation wrought among the Sioux. He deplored it, let me assure you."

"The Plains Indians employed torture, and massacred women and children at times, but their warriors lived by a rigorous code, and employed a mode of reasoning which seemed perfectly logical to them, if not to us," Julian remarked. "Those war-chiefs differed significantly from modern totalitarian dictators who commit massacres solely out of crafty self-interest—a lust for power so all-consuming as to render any atrocity acceptable in their thinking. No, I regard the assassination of such mass murderers as entirely justifiable, when weighed against the price their people would pay during a combination of air strikes and a bloody ground war aimed at crushing all resistance."

Manuel nodded in agreement, as did Jason. Lorenzo gave no hint of how he felt. Francesca boldly agreed with Mercedes; Shirley seemed intently interested, but undecided as to which argument she supported. Celeste merely stroked Manuel's thigh while remaining wholly neutral.

The talk now turned to another world crisis, this one purely economic. Riveting all eyes on himself, Lorenzo offered a shrewd, concise explanation for the course that potentially dangerous situation would likely take. Mercedes listened, but with a divided mind, her heart hammering as a supposition set ice crystallizing in her blood. Could *Julian* be a professional assassin? she asked herself in horror.

No. Impossible. You're letting your imagination run away with you. No! Any number of professions could have caused him to generate that aura of danger. Might he not be a foreign agent—a spy? No. He'd never work for any government agency. Never! Whatever he is, he's worked independently. He's suffered a gunshot wound. Shot by crmininals . . . rivals? Is he a gangster? A smuggler? My perishing soul—*a drug lord*? No. No! You're letting your imagination run amok! He could have been shot in some hunting accident! But no—not Julian. He's too careful—too coolly capable. Oh, my soul. How, then?

The guests now engaged in a lively debate turning on philosophical beliefs, but Mercedes silently struggled to banish a horde of direly unnerving suppositions, each worse than the last. Grown aware of Lorenzo's eyes raking her, she regained her grip on herself. Resolutely, she thrust those burgeoning fears to the back of her mind, and listened. When an opportunity arose, she passed a trenchant comment, once again joining the discussion.

Nonetheless, the uneasiness persisted: a time bomb awaiting the combination of factors that would initiate detonation. Certain that she concealed the danger perfectly, she failed to divine that both Lorenzo and Julian correctly deduced which facet of the conversation sparked her sudden lapse into silence following the latter's final argument. Neither did she dream that subtle, nonverbal cues betrayed the magnitude of her inner agitation to both uncannily perceptive observers.

Chapter Nine

As the supper hour approached, Lorenzo and Francesca walked with their guests back to the bench on which lay their folded clothing. The Grand Master and his consort dressed in full view of their fellows, before strolling in their company to the dining area. The group dispersed there, some to enter the line at the buffet, some to join people chatting as they waited for the line to thin out. Drawing Julian aside, Jason murmured a request that they sit down at a vacant nook.

Shirley, her face seeming to Mercedes to mirror a turbulent mixture of fierce pride and dire apprehension, sat down as well. Although the girl passed a polite, innocuous remark to the older woman, Mercedes divined that the bulk of her attention focused on the exchange between Jason and Julian.

As the latter cocked his head, and rested a quizzical glance on the master younger than most, Jason stated firmly, "Tonight, I'm demanding that Shirley undergo the rite of passage to the rank of adept. I've never requested a set of your brother's devices, figuring that he might consider my doing so an imposition, seeing as I scarcely know him. If you regard my mentioning that I wish to borrow a suitable portion of your set for one night as no less of an imposition, please say so frankly."

"Mm. Michael would readily oblige any member of the Order, so don't hesitate to contact him. You're a bit young yet to levy that exacting demand, Jason, but if you feel fully confident that your self-control will prove equal to the challenge you face, you're welcome to borrow what you select from my set. We'll leave the ladies here while we retire to my room, where I'll display the implements . . . mmm?"

The two men rose, and departed.

Relief suffused the tanned face of the girl whose apprehension Mercedes sensed to have grown considerably less severe, but that emotion failed to vanish. Shirley turned to study her companion, as if to weigh the effect of the electronic devices on someone whose master routinely employed them.

Encountering a warm, reassuring smile, she managed a wan smile in her turn, grateful for the wordless message of encouragement. Too proud to ask what she obviously wished to know, she sat erect, her chin up, her eyes resolute. As if to forestall the volunteering of any explanation by Julian's cherished companion, she expressed her admiration for Mercedes' skill at formulating cogent arguments. "I don't know enough about history or political science to dare to take on Manuel or Julian in debate," she acknowledged ruefully. "I majored at the University in animal husbandry."

"My major was English literature," came the reply that astonished the hearer. "With a minor in business. I read history for pleasure. That habit persisted, even when I took an active part in the ranching operation. Ever since I graduated, I've made a determined effort not to let my mind slip into a worn groove. I tried my best to stay mentally agile as well as physically fit. That rich mental life stood me in good stead, when my husband of three decades died suddenly of heart failure."

"I'm so sorry to hear that," the girl breathed, growing deeply moved as she beheld pain shadow the green eyes gone for a few seconds remote. "But . . . you're no longer lonely . . . are you?"

"No, not any longer, Shirley." Even as she voiced that vigorous affirmation, Mercedes grew conscious that the anxiety surfacing during the afternoon still lurked in the shadows of her mind, producing fear which no amount of logical analysis seemed able to banish.

The girl herself torn by direly conflicting emotions took the statement at face value. Smiling, she laid a hand in comradely fashion on that of the widow.

The two men's return ended any chance for the women to exchange further confidences.

Preceding Julian into their room after a leisurely meal followed by an interval of conversation with people they had not seen since yesterday, Mercedes again felt her gut tighten as she fought the devastating suspicion that no amount of self-castigation served to banish.

Purposefully, Julian undressed her, and laid her in the bed. Stripping with more haste than was his wont, he reclined beside her, and gathered her into his arms. "Now then," he announced in a tone that brooked no refusal, "you're going to tell me what's producing such acute mental distress."

Relief at the thought of getting the cause of her anxiety into the open overrode the widow's reluctance to ask this reclusive autocrat a direct, intensely personal question. "Julian . . . you're not a professional assassin yourself, are you?" she blurted, her fear showing nakedly in her eyes.

Taken sharply aback, the man fearing that this woman who lived by a code as rigorous as his own might consider the belief he had so vehemently expressed that afternoon so offensive that she contemplated wrecking the smooth progression of their relationship, perceived his error. Outrage contended with fervent relief; incipient anger dissolved in an onslaught of hilarity. None of those reactions did he let show. "And if I were—would that alter your feeling for me?" he asked evenly, his face expressionless.

Aghast, Mercedes took that question to be an affirmation of her fear. Her agony apparent to the man impaling her with a pitiless glance, she rasped, "Yes. It would."

Having proven to himself that this woman he loved would indeed refuse to compromise certain fundamental tenets of her personal code no matter what the cost, Julian relented. "I give you my word, Mercedes, that I'm not now, and never have been, a professional assassin. Will you believe that?"

Her relief so overwhelming as to render her faint, the distraught woman threw herself on her lover's chest as she fought back tears.

Having clasped her tightly for a few seconds, he held her away, and demanded sardonically, "You don't consider my admission that I believe assassination to be morally justifiable in certain situations an impediment to our relationship, but if I'd turned out to be implementing that belief, you'd stop loving me?"

The irony freighting that query nowise lost on her, Mercedes retorted heatedly, "That may sound illogical to you, but it isn't to me. People differ radically in their beliefs. I've got one friend who truly believes that abortion constitutes a woman's inalienable right, and another who believes just as passionately that abortion equates with murder of a baby. Both would unhesitatingly act according to those beliefs; they're a matter of deep conviction.

"If you chanced to be a downtrodden subject of a dictator guilty of heinous crimes, and you acted on the belief you hold—shot the bastard dead, out of perfect certainty that you were saving the lives of countless innocent people—I could condone your act as one performed by reason of deep conviction. But if you'd turned out to be a highly skilled, cold-blooded, stone-faced professional assassin who kills solely for profit—that I couldn't condone."

Outrage warred with potent amusement, but both strong emotions instantly succumbed to nascent admiration. "You actually believed it likely that I might be a professional assassin?" Julian inquired accusingly.

Flushing crimson, Mercedes yet held his eyes. "I thought it possible, yes. You project an aura of danger. Even Lorenzo, that day we met, remarked that he'd noticed your seeming readiness to explode into action at any moment. I misjudged you badly, today, without a shred of credible evidence. I apologize for that reprehensible lack of faith."

Mollified, won to admiration of both her principles and her frank admission, Julian drew her against his chest, and stroked her hair, awaiting the development he saw as inevitable. When she said no more, he again held her away. "Aren't you going to ask the next logical question?"

"No," came the prompt if abashed answer. "I fell in love with you not knowing what you did for a living. I can go on loving you, not knowing."

His admiration taking a quantum leap, Julian studied her for a time before resolving on a course. "I think it's time I told you," he vouchsafed wryly. "Before some new debate leads you to suspect that I'm a terrorist, or the head of an international drug cartel."

Her cheeks a flaming scarlet, Mercedes said nothing. Mutely, she awaited satisfaction of the curiosity that had plagued her.

Settling her against his shoulder, her autocratic lover smiled into patently embarrassed eyes. "If you'd asked, I'd have refused to answer," he admitted candidly. "But since you can stifle your curiosity to the extent of taking me on faith,

I'll tell you. I'm a pilot, Mercedes. I also speak seven languages besides English, well enough to express myself fluently in them, and understand those who speak them. I own a considerable number of aircraft, of various kinds. For more than a quarter-century, I've flown delicate, dangerous, private missions into the worst trouble spots in the world—for a price.

"My customers included entrepreneurs of varying nationalities wishful of doing business with rebel factions—mostly, selling war material: conventional arms, explosives, high-tech equipment, and such. I've acted as their agent as well as their pilot. I've supplied mercenaries like Manuel, for a price. I've routinely evacuated their wounded, and a few times, the remnants of their force, when they took on more than they could handle.

"I've also been hired by private medical relief organizations, refugees wishful of aiding other refugees, desperate political exiles seeking to incite a rebellion in their homeland, deposed members of one branch of a ruling family ousted by another, and the like.

"I've never hired out to openly avowed terrorist groups, or to drug traffickers, or to dictators richly deserving of being assassinated. Some of my customers I knew to be unsavory, but I viewed them as less so than the opponents against whom they struggled. I've mounted rescue missions to aid missionaries, scientists, researchers, businessmen, and even a few hippie globetrotters, when that sort of foreigner found himself trapped between two opposing factions noted for vicious war crimes.

"I routinely sought to avoid trouble, but it sometimes found me. I've been shot at, and on one occasion, hit two times in succession. I shot back when no other alternative offered. I've been targeted by assassins. At times, I barely escaped dying ambushed, bombed, strafed, wiped by land mines, or blown up in booby-trapped vehicles.

"I've killed men, Mercedes, but never any other way than in self-defense, or defense of noncombatant clients or people I rescued. I operated out of bases all over the world. I developed an intricate network of contacts, and avoided drawing the wrong kind of attention from intrusive, arrogant intelligence agencies. I gained a reputation for keeping my word, and delivering the goods. Nothing I did while flying those missions weighs on my conscience."

Profoundly relieved, Mercedes breathed, "I misjudged you badly . . . let my faith in you waver for no good reason."

"Mm. So you did. I nonetheless admire your staunch refusal to violate the code by which you live."

A new thought lanced out of the blue to set Mercedes' gut knotting. "And after you rest up—you'll be going back to that life?"

"No. Six months ago, I turned the entire operation over to my son. I bought that property next to you on impulse, because of the remoteness, the beauty of the area, and the penchant of the neighbors to mind their own business. I own several retreats, but I wanted one unostentatious address where I could live under my own name, quietly and openly. I was trying to relax, while casting about for some new venture that would engross me, when I met you—in the last place on Earth I ever expected to find a woman who'd suit me to perfection."

"The woman you loved bore you a son?"

"She died bearing me a son. Her death resulted from a complication the local medical practitioners on the remote base where I'd left her, failed to handle properly. Her death occurred while I was on a mission. He lived, and she died . . . at far too young an age."

"Oh . . . Julian . . . I'm sorry for your loss." That patently sincere commiseration emerged in a husky whisper.

"It happened a long time ago, but the scars still ache. I raised the boy. One-sided upbringing, he had, but it turned out far better than I expected when I took on the task."

Her affectionate regard for the dangerous stranger whom she had intuitively trusted from the start taking a quantum leap, Mercedes melted against him, vastly relieved. Her admiration for him having soared, she chided herself for having doubted him, even as she rejoiced at finally knowing what sort of life he had led.

Her curiosity on that score satisfied, she began pondering the question of how he had gained membership in the Order. Do they join, or are they born into it? she wondered, recalling its four-hundred-year history. Perhaps they *are* born into it, and train their sons to develop the singular tastes they all share. If that's so, do they encourage their daughters to submit to, and obey, some youthful master like Jason?

That conundrum inevitably led her mind back to the exchange between Jason and Julian. A chill crept down her spine as she recalled the girl's apprehension. Resolutely, she thrust from mind the questions that arose, judging that she had pried enough for one day.

As his patently relieved companion snuggled against him, Julian reviewed the present state of his unorthodox affair with this woman he loved more deeply with each passing hour. Frowning, he drew an inescapable conclusion. No whit less relieved than was Mercedes, he nonetheless decided that he needed to remedy a potentially dangerous situation: a side effect generated by the resolution of the problem. Thrusting his scarred left arm under his cherished companion's back, he held her immobile, as he so often did, raking her nude body with eyes gone both purposeful and cruel.

"Twice today, you set your will against mine," he observed equably. "And you prevailed. That hasn't angered me. On the contrary, I admire both your courage, and your adherence to an ethical code. But in doing what you did, you reinforced the strength of your will. Tonight, I'm going to put your submissiveness to a severe test. I intend to push you to the limit of your tolerance for bearing pain without flinching, and then raise that limit.

"I won't employ restraints. You'll be required to fetter your body with your mind: to exert perfect mastery over your urge to stiffen, to flinch, to writhe, to cry out, to struggle. You'll explore the pain I inflict—investigate it, welcome it, yield to it, and finally, enjoy it. You'll welcome it, because inflicting it gives your master pleasure; you'll yield to it, because at the close of the lesson you badly need, you'll achieve surrender so absolute that I'll find it easy to lift you to a dizzying height of ecstasy.

"If at any point you resist in the slightest degree, I'll finish conducting the lesson, but deny you the rapturous fulfillment you'll desperately crave at that point. So. Focus your full attention on the need to submit, to obey, to subordinate your will to mine."

Fear swirled up out of recesses emptied of that emotion earlier. Desire stirred, produced by the promise of final ecstasy. That emotion blended with lingering relief that no dark secret from his past barred her from loving this regally possessive, dangerous partner. Trembling half with fear, and half with poignant longing to please this cruel autocrat who demanded, and knew so well how to obtain, perfect submissiveness, Mercedes wondered just why she loved him—why she yearned to be united in transcendental ecstasy with so merciless a tormentor.

Her own body supplied a revealing clue. Even as he lifted

her pliant person in strong arms, she experienced a thrill of anticipation—a perverse, intense craving for the pain which triggered spontaneous relaxation, delicious anticipatory shudders, in loins, flesh, and nerves: organs which acted in concert upon the mind interconnected with them to produce the physical and mental surrender which this man alone of any she had ever known, demanded and invariably won from her.

Set upon her feet, facing the bench from which she noted that the case containing Michael's inventions had vanished, she obeyed the command that she spread her legs, bend at the waist, and place her palms flat on the polished surface. Forbidden to move, she awaited Julian's pleasure. A slight scraping noise apprised her that the panel slid back past the central pillars. Out of the corner of her eye, she saw her master disappear into the bathroom, and return with a basin and towel. Bearing those items, he passed through the wide portal into the inner chamber.

A few minutes later, she struggled not to go tense as a slender, ominously familiar, lavishly lubricated inanimate shaft slid into her anus, and the flange adhered to the skin of her buttocks. Braced to withstand the minor swelling experienced previously, she instead endured an ominous, relentless expansion of the intrusive device. Certain that it would split her open, she all but clutched at the affected orifice with her hands before the implement automatically stopped inflating. The familiar electronically generated pain now radiated from the site, accompanied by a faint echo of pleasure.

Suppressing a groan, Mercedes felt herself raised off the bench, and set erect, on her feet. "Face me, with your hands behind your head," came the imperious command issued by the man who stood assessing the reactions of the woman submissively obeying it. "You find that distention hard to bear, mm? But I require it of you. The device will stretch that all but virginal opening of your delectable rear passage. That precaution will render far less likely the chances of your being torn there owing to vigorous impregnation."

Lifting her, he held her, sweeping intent, appraising eyes over her inert form. "Submit mentally," he commanded. "Allow no single twinge of resentment, of anger, even of fear, to distract you from focusing your full attention on the pain I'll inflict. Let each new increment serve to deepen your perception of the intensified stimulus that will drive you to subjugate your will to mine, even as your spirit remains unbroken."

As he spoke, Julian laid his beloved on the support set as close to the floor as it would sink. Lying with her legs spread wide, and her arms flung back over her head, but with her back less severely arched than on prior occasions, she saw her master pull up a chair. Seating himself with his knees below the support, he gazed down at her exposed, naked, vulnerable person. His hands cupped soft flesh; his thumbs vibrated nipples that stiffened at his touch. "Lovely, your breasts," he opined judiciously, smiling down at the woman whose every taut nerve awaited new painful stimulation, in addition to that afflicting her anal area.

Reaching to the small table on which lay a few small items, Julian offered a device for his lover's consideration: a silver sculpture similar to the Mastiff. "This is the Wolf," he announced, his tone light, almost bantering. "Cousin to the Mastiff. His bite's more painful, though he won't break the skin." A hand laid flat on the taut abdomen sensed the relaxation of the muscles produced by a conscious effort of will. "Ahhh . . . that's right. Purge your mind of every emotion but acceptance. So."

As he spoke, teeth bit deeply into the flesh of Mercedes' mound.

"Hurts, the bite, mmm? The pain will increase a bit more, as the jaws finish tightening. There. You lie spread to my view like a lamb deposited on an altar, eh, little initiate? An offering designed to appease a powerful entity demanding tribute? But you're the suppliant, and the pain expanding to fill your awareness forms the offering: a metaphor for your willingness to submit, to meld your being, body and mind, with that of the master who accepts none but a complete sacrifice."

Those words couched in an irresistibly hypnotic voice, rich, musical, compelling, produced a shimmering mental image which increased the ineffable yearning suffusing the woman stretched on the pseudo-rack—yearning which the severe pain crowding out minor sensations evoked. Her loins quivered as she longed for the erotic stimulation that normally accompanied the infliction of pain.

Two fingers spread the pussy-lips guarding the orifice awash now in juice. Having assessed the wetness, they withdrew. One lingered, its tip slowly circling the smooth head of the swollen clit growing yet more rigidly erect under its touch. "I'll toy with you a trifle—tease you just enough to provide spice to the pain," the skilled tormentor averred, his melodic voice amused, lightly mocking. "Just the opposite of what you normally enjoy, mmm? Tonight the pain dominates: becomes your universe, little errant lover. Ahhh . . . that narrows your consciousness, eh?"

As he spoke, the fingers of the master's other hand worked the prongs of the device, weaving it back and forth, or sideways. Changing tactics, he pulled it upwards, and then pressed it flat against the skin of the mound from which intense pain now radiated. Even as those manipulations produced agony, the lone finger of the other hand continued to circle the wet tip of the woman's engorged organ of pleasure, producing a rabid desire for the seductive ministrations she had grown to expect while in the grip of pain that normally intensified the erotic pleasure conferred by expert genital massage. Frustration blended with the torment engendered by the worrying action of the metal jaws, producing fierce, unsatisfied desire.

At length the fingers ceased working the Wolf. “Hurts, my playing with the prongs, mmm? But after a time, the flesh thus pinched grows numb; the afflicted nerves short out. The pain lessens, and you accustom yourself to bearing it. You’re at that point now, but not for long. To offset that minor relief, I’ll reset the teeth. Ahhh. Pure agony, that new bite, eh? Tests your will to please, that sensation, mmmm?”

Finding the description apt, Mercedes stifled a groan. Valiantly, she fought an all but irresistible impulse to writhe. The mesmeric voice flowed through the cracks of her inner citadel of the self, invading the most private chamber of that edifice to take her will captive, and bend it to that of the man consciously employing that melodic instrument of coercion.

“You’re my possession, Mercedes—my belonging—my love-slave. I can welcome voluntary submission—bear with the need to exert a light touch on my cherished companion—but that submission must be unconditional: absolute. You exist for my pleasure, my love.”

The finger still circling the tip of her clit now moistened itself in the sticky fluid dribbling from her cunt. Quickly, it returned to massage the soft ring of ridged flesh encircling the tip. That sensation, teasing without promising fulfillment, accentuated the pain of the teeth gripping a new fold of skin still smarting from the prior bite. The other hand again manipulated the prongs; the lone finger idly under-stimulated the small organ swollen with need. “Tormented by a rabid desire for my cock filling your love-tunnel, mmm? Ahh . . . not yet, little love-slave. No. Your will’s too much your own, as yet.”

The teasing motions ceased, as did those causing waves of agony to course outwards from mound and distended, pain-racked anus. "Observe, now," the man savagely elated by the continued pliancy of the partner pushed ever closer to the limit of her ability to bear the pain designed to obliterate, slowly but inexorably, her consciousness of any reality save that pain. "This hollow shield forms a collar for the Wolf. It fits around him—thus. The collar governs these nipple-rings, which you'll experience as sharp-clawed paws.

"There, now. Your universe expands to accommodate the agony, eh, little wolf-prey? Your awareness of all else diminishes, as the claws impale tender flesh, and the collar enhances the pain of the bite. Concentrate on the augmented sensations, Mercedes. Yearn for my cock filling the rear passage widened to admit of freer love-play. Long for my mouth savoring the taste of your tongue. Let the pain loosen your loins, open you, spread you for my pleasure. Soon, now, that pleasure. Soon . . . but not yet."

The paper-thin hollow rings encircling nipples gone nut-hard, featured short, slender rods which fit the curve of the breasts: curved extensions tipped with teardrop-shaped knobs, the dull points of which pressed downward into the soft flesh. The sensation produced by the electronic stimulation mimicked that of claws piercing delicate skin. Held in the grip of pain so intense as to rival any other inflicted by this cruel, expert wielder of diabolically ingenious implements, Mercedes grew dimly aware that reality now receded.

Her desire to please put to a rigorous test, she floated in a haze of agony pierced only by the melodic, persuasive, cajoling voice which exerted potent hypnotic force. Her strength of will indeed eroded. The awareness contracted into needle-beamed focus on the pain and the promise of pleasure, now narrowed further, embodying itself in a single desire: to be possessed, no, absorbed into the persona of the master to whom Mercedes acknowledged bemusedly that she belonged. The pain seemed her destiny: the key that would open the door to the realm in which he and she would exist as one entity.

Tawny eyes riveted to the face of the woman lying spread to his scrutiny like a specimen on a glass slide, beheld the subtle cues signaling the crumbling of her innermost defenses. "You stand at the limit of your ability to bear pain without flinching," her master purred. "I now demand that you endure yet another incremental increase in that pain. You'll control your body, even as your will becomes merged with mine," came the merciless directive. "You'll bear the agony that will drown all other stimuli—surrender absolutely. So."

Unaware of what he intended, Mercedes all but started up as she experienced the frighteningly familiar intrusion of a whip-shaft into her moist feminine depth. Horror blended with the torment gripping her. Almost instantly, it faded, as her native stubbornness drove her to control her urge to clutch at the hands thrusting the instrument into the most private, the most sensitive part of her body. Her mind did indeed provide symbolic fetters, holding her passive, accepting, as a finger activated the device.

Torment so great as to render her faint, now possessed her, simultaneously with an intense pleasure-echo. Her fragmenting consciousness fastened on that latter sensation, forcing her pain-racked body to lie motionless, unresisting, while a hand rotated the handle in a slow, agonizing precessional movement that intensified both the pleasure-echo and the pain. "One more slow gyration, and your surrender will be complete," came the mesmeric, irresistibly compelling voice of her pitiless master. "So. You belong to me, Mercedes. Now and always."

The pain afflicting her cunt ceased. The distended anal orifice relaxed; the intrusive shaft withdrew. The claws rendered suddenly impotent, fell away from tortured breasts. The collar lifted; the jaws of the Wolf released the fold of ravaged flesh that remained hot and sore: a minor affliction. Strong arms lifted the inert body of the woman yearning to be possessed, longing for the ascent to ecstasy which would in retrospect make the sacrifice demanded of her seem a bout of pleasurable foreplay. Congealing against the hard torso of her master, her will suspended, her consciousness diminished, she awaited the fulfillment for which her soul hungered.

Julian laid her on the bed. Dropping to lie beside her, he kissed her breasts. His tongue circled her nipples, evoking a moan of pleasure from the woman whose forefinger and thumb closed into a ring around her lover's hard shaft preparatory to offering a brisk massage. When the hand grew tired, and she desisted, her lover changed position. His mouth closed over her erect organ of pleasure. He now offered the full range of intensely erotic stimuli he had denied her earlier, provoking soft cries of satisfaction.

The lingering pain of the wolf-bites served only to accentuate the pleasure delivered by expert hands, and mouth, and tongue. Thrusting into her lavishly moistened love-tunnel solely to lubricate his turgid manhood, Julian bade her kneel with her shoulders on the bed. Gripping her hips, he drove into the rear passage that he contentedly observed to be slightly less tight than on prior occasions. Maintaining his hold on one hip while encircling his partner's torso with the other hand, he worked her clit with such seductive skill as to drive her almost instantly into rapturous fulfillment.

As the woman drifting in a haze of euphoria lay inertly on the bed, her partner bathed his still-rigid organ, having achieved mental ecstasy without ejaculating. Reclining beside her, he crushed her against his chest. She flowed against him, the pleasurable tactile sensation merging with the mental rapture ebbing only slowly. "I love you," she murmured almost inaudibly.

The fierce arousal engendered by his cruel exercise in domination nowise diminished, Julian murmured with impassioned vehemence, "You belong to me, Mercedes—by free choice, by compelling need, and by the happy chance that sent you into my life when I most needed you."

The woman conscious that her exploration of that final totality of pain produced a subtle alteration in her relationship with this master of dark erotic arts, experienced a qualm of fear, even as she rejoiced in hearing him state that he needed her. "You said I'd grow to crave the whip," she murmured ruminatively. "I wonder, right now, why I love so cruelly demanding a master. Do you hypnotize me? Will I wake at some point aghast at having let you exert such power over my will?"

"No, little hedonist," came the equable, amused reply. "Like all strong-minded women, you've unconsciously yearned for a lover able to dominate you completely, and possess you fully. Few men know how to achieve that dominance without resorting to direly injurious, reprehensible brutality that we masters steeped in an ancient discipline abjure. You've learned the lesson all but forgotten in this age and place: for a woman, there can be no true ecstasy without surrender. Pain inflicted by a demanding master forms an irresistible inducement to achieve that surrender."

As if to punctuate that assertion, Julian closed his mouth over that of the satiated sensualist who bemusedly admitted to herself that his words caused some inner chord in her mind to resonate in harmony with them. As her lover sucked on her tongue as if to ingest it, Mercedes felt her loins quicken, and loosen.

Freeing her mouth, he gathered her into his arms. "You're to relax to the point of bonelessness," he commanded. Holding her in that firm clasp, he sat on the edge of the bed, and shifted her body so that she lay prone on his lap and outstretched legs, her head towards his feet. In a spectacular display of muscular strength, he raised the inverted torso obediently gone utterly limp, high against his chest, so that his lover's parted thighs passed by either side of his head. Maintaining that hold requiring prodigious strength, he stood erect, supporting the pliant body of the woman whose breasts pressed against his abdomen, whose breath now flowed over his rigid organ.

Shock blended with hot, primitive desire in the mind of the initiate held head-down against the hard body of this sadist she loved.

"Take my cock in your mouth, and use your every art to please me," came the imperious command.

As Mercedes obeyed, she felt a moist mouth engulf her clit. A tongue insinuated itself into the cunt quivering with delight. That dual focus of intense, supremely erotic, mutually satisfying stimulation, combined with the position requiring total relaxation on her part, and extreme physical exertion on the part of the man supporting the full weight of her inverted body as if it were negligible, produced an astonishing exhilaration: a lightness of being which acted on her senses like fine wine.

For a span of minutes seeming in the mind of the woman to last an hour, the partner thus uniquely positioned experienced ever-deepening, heady bliss.

Judging to perfection how close his beloved drew to fulfillment, Julian shifted her to his arms, and then to the bed. Stretching out supine, he bade the lover quivering with need to get astride him, and again take his cock in her mouth.

Grasping her hips as she bent to comply with his demand, he positioned her rear so that he could resume his oral caresses of her quivering loins. "When I come, you'll drink the essence of my passion," he commanded.

No whit loath to obey, being certain at this juncture that ingesting her lover's semen would lift her to climax, Mercedes moved her head so as to massage his stiff manhood with long, sweeping strokes, while sucking as if to milk him dry of juice. His tongue circled her swollen ornament before thrusting into her feminine depth. His seductive efforts brought on the quivers, the shivers, the contractions that signaled the onset of climax.

Even as she achieved full transcendental ecstasy, Mercedes swallowed the spurts of jism ejaculated by her lover. In her passion-befogged mind, that fluid equated with a sacramental draught bestowed by the powerful entity pleased by her earlier offering of pain willingly borne. Her mental exaltation combined with a surreally prolonged, ecstatic fulfillment, to drive her into trance.

His own consciousness all but suspended, Julian rolled on his side, tipping his rapt, limp partner off. Moving so as to enfold her in his arms, he relaxed, and let himself straddle the boundary of sleep and wakefulness. The state he now entered resembled an out-of-body experience. Floating at some ethereal, lofty vantage point, he savored his consciousness of ecstasy while warmed by the inert body of the woman he loved.

Chapter Ten

Awakened at six in the morning by an arm sliding under her to draw her close against the partner who closed his mouth over hers in a long, lazy, gently provocative kiss, Mercedes molded herself to the muscular torso of her lover. His hands moved over her body, slowly, sensuously, evoking incipient desire. When he freed her lips, he kissed her neck, her throat. Playfully, he nibbled on her earlobe. Shifting position, he licked her nipples. At length, he slid lower to tongue her navel. A rippling laugh, almost a giggle, fell on his ears like the seductive sound of water tumbling over rocks. His mouth found the clit gone erect, so as to offer the expert, infinitely erotic stimulation he so well knew how to give.

Sensing that the woman newly awakened now approached climax, he desisted. “Kneel,” he commanded. Having bent his partner’s upper body forward, so that her arms lay on the bed as her thighs spread, he drove into her cunt from behind. As her spine arched, allowing her to thrust against him with her buttocks, he reached around her and stimulated her stiff organ of pleasure.

The heel of Julian’s hand rotated the flesh still somewhat sore from the wolf-bites, as if to remind his lover that he claimed the right to inflict pain, but waived that prerogative on this particular morning. Even that minor stimulus served to loosen further the loins of the woman moaning softly with pleasure. No fleeting twinge of apprehension that she might fail to achieve a peak inhibited her rise to the all-absorbing, rapturously prolonged fulfillment that occurred simultaneously with that of her master.

Himself awash in euphoria, Julian remained slackly still, his arms enfolding the partner whom his shaft still penetrated. At length, he stirred. Turning the inert woman, he pressed her chest against his. She flowed against him like a viscous liquid, the racing of her heart perceptible to him. "You come now with gratifying ease, requiring no more foreplay than any experienced lover would offer," he murmured in her ear, his eyes brimming with amusement. "You're cured of those weaknesses in your mental circuitry, mmmm?"

"I am with *you*," Mercedes qualified his assertion.

"That's all that's necessary, eh, my love?" came the prompt, lightly mocking rejoinder.

"Absolutely all." Wondering what turn her life would take at the end of this five-day immersion in a culture still surpassingly strange to her, Mercedes consciously procrastinated: put off addressing any future concerns. Julian's reference to her ranking among his peers reminded her of Shirley's perturbation on the prior evening. Wondering a shade uneasily whether the girl's possessive, youthful master might possibly have alienated her by levying a harsh demand on a consort lacking maturity enough to handle the rigor, she launched an inquiry.

"Julian," she asked, her uneasiness manifesting itself to the man so practiced now in reading her body-language, "just what's required of the woman during the rite of passage to the rank of adept?"

Propping himself on an elbow, the better to study the oval

face which so clearly mirrored its owner's emotions, he replied equably, "Her master binds her loosely enough that she can move freely, but not flee. He then inflicts a degree of pain that exceeds the limit of her ability to bear it without flinching. For the first time during the course of their relationship, he indulges his desire to see her writhe, and twist, and struggle under the lash; to hear her plead and weep as he relentlessly forces her to an elevated level of surrender to his will. He takes her beyond the threshold never crossed until that moment, into a new plane of experience, thereby deepening her ability to subordinate her will to his. Relentlessly, he pushes her to the brink of a second boundary he's allowed to reach, but not cross.

"Although the rite doesn't require that the woman fetter her body with her mind, or exert any self-control whatsoever, it lays a rigorous demand on her master. He must know with exactitude where to stop. He's absolutely forbidden to continue past the point where his actions from there on would constitute the injurious brutality abjured by civilized sensualists. He's prohibited from conducting the rite, except in the presence of a peer who serves as a witness.

"If he goes the least shade too far, the witness calls a halt, and reports the dereliction to the Grand Master and his Council. The master who failed to exert perfect self-control suffers severe censure, and most generally forfeits the regard of the woman who, if she wishes, may then formally repudiate him, and request that the Grand Master inform the members that she desires a new partner. That outcome, of course, adds to the delinquent master's disgrace.

"If, however, the master succeeds in controlling himself to perfection, he gains elevated respect among his peers. The woman conscious that she gave her lover the most intoxicating sensual pleasure he can ever experience, discovers that surrender knows no limits, nor does the ecstasy which that surrender engenders. Her master thereafter cherishes his adept so ardently that she enjoys perfect security in her union with him, and gains the enhanced respect of his peers. She walks in pride, savoring her consciousness that in rising to an elevated limit of submissiveness, she conferred on him the ultimate gift."

Mercedes digested that unsettling summary for a full minute. Fear swirled out of the dim recess to which it had receded, flaying the woman who cried in disbelief, "You'd derive pleasure that intense from inflicting so ghastly a degree of pain on me?"

A hand tucked the rebellious lock of auburn hair over an ear. His striking face shadowed by the incipient lust engendered simply by describing the rite, Julian replied levelly, "I've derived heady pleasure from probing the upper level of your tolerance for pain, as you're well aware. I'm restricted by my code to stopping at that point.

"Of course I long to drive you beyond that threshold—to see you writhe under the lash, struggle impotently as you succumb to tears, and hear you plead as I inexorably exact a surrender more absolute than any in your prior experience. I yearn even more intensely to raise you to an ecstasy equally unprecedented.

"But I won't levy that demand on you, Mercedes. As I told you, you require delicate handling. I'd undoubtedly rouse that stubbornness you believe to exist at your core. I'd lose the cherished companion who willingly and admirably fills the role of initiate to perfection.

"A master's under no obligation ever to demand that his partner undergo the rite. I'm infinitely glad that a capricious fate sent you to me when I needed you most. I rest content to stay within the bounds of the promise I made you. As for the concern you harbor regarding Shirley, I suspect she'd run naked through the fires of the mythical hell if Jason laid that demand on *her*."

Even as relief suffused her inner being, the voluntary participant in this weeklong celebration of singular tastes in sensual pleasure paradoxically experienced a twinge of disappointment. Trusting absolutely that this cruel lover would never force her to submit to so frightening a prospect, she perversely found herself wishing to offer him the ultimate pleasure. Longing to know herself cherished even more highly suffused her. As those unaccountable regrets nagged at her, a new troubling notion rose to afflict her. "If a master doesn't possess a set of your brother's inventions, what does he use to inflict pain of that magnitude?"

"Leather whips—instruments specially created by highly skilled craftsmen to serve that purpose. A master's trained to employ a smooth, braided lash so expertly that he never raises a welt. He leaves only red stripes that fade quickly, as the marks of his favor. For the rite, he employs a heavier whip weighted at the handle, with which he raises welts without once breaking the skin. Those reminders leave no scar, but they cause the woman to be stiff and sore during the several days it takes for them to heal.

"Michael, even more than I, harbors scruples unique to himself, regarding inflicting such long-lasting, highly visible evidence of his passion—even though if you knew him well, you'd inevitably regard my older brother as far more autocratic, and far crueler than myself. His clever inventions I suspect will shortly constitute the norm, especially among younger masters."

Shivers coursed down the spine of the woman imagining a brawny, iron-thewed athlete like Manuel wielding what she pictured in her interior vision as a lead-weighted bullwhip.

"What if the woman passes out from the pain?" she asked accusingly.

"The masters who favor those implements unerringly read the cues which enable them to tell when their partner surrenders completely. They desist long before she reaches the point of fainting."

Reflecting that the women wearing the ruby-headed pin seemed those most devoted to their masters, Mercedes' initial horror subsided, but she determined on actively seeking to observe Shirley's demeanor on this morning.

As if he read her mind, Julian remarked mischievously, "Shall we seek out Jason and Shirley at breakfast, so you can judge how she fared, my love?"

"Let's do that," came the prompt, unabashed reply.

Arriving at the sitting/dining area earlier than most patrons of the buffet, Julian chose a nook that overlooked the entry leading from the stairwell from which he knew that Jason and his consort would emerge. When at length they entered, Mercedes to her relief perceived the girl's face to be suffused with both pride and joy. She noted as well, that Jason radiated intense satisfaction. His palm placed possessively on her back, he guided her to where he observed Julian to be sitting with Mercedes, Nikos, Alexander, and Irene.

Lorenzo intercepted the pair. Bending, he kissed the hand that Shirley breathlessly extended to the Grand Master. "I honor the fortitude you displayed while giving your master the ultimate gift," he announced, his eyes seeming to the new adept to search the most secret recesses of her soul.

"I thank you," she responded, her pride ballooning.

Rising when the couple neared the nook, Julian repeated the Grand Master's gesture, as did Nikos and Alexander. Irene laid a hand over that of the rosy-faced girl who glowed with pride.

Acutely conscious of his memory of Julian's candidly warning that he might be too young to run so dire a risk to his standing, Jason now privately agreed that the older man harbored a valid concern. Relief at what he admitted to be a frighteningly narrow escape from intolerable disgrace flooded his inner being. That emotion blended with fierce pride that he had withstood the temptation to continue past the point of his consort's complete surrender.

Even as those thoughts impinged, Jason's eyes met that of the Council-Member who had lent him the implements. Exhibiting no smugness, the youthful master expressed only the respectful deference that he habitually displayed to these men who enjoyed high standing in the Order, but nonetheless accepted him as a close friend.

Mercedes experienced a twinge of what she discovered with shock, resembled envy, even as she castigated herself harshly for affording too great an importance to status symbols. Relief that no disaster attended Jason's conduct on the prior night contended with a burgeoning wish to offer her lover the ultimate in satisfaction.

At that moment, Manuel strode into her field of vision, sparking a resurgence of the fevered images conjured by her master's description of the rite. Reminding her quivering alter ego that if Julian were to conduct it, he would employ his brother's inventions, not a pseudo-bullwhip, failed to allay the fear generated by those images, especially as she recalled his contention that the electronic implements used in certain combinations caused greater pain even than the leather whips which the mercenary soldier evidently preferred.

After the leisurely meal and the subsequent pleasant interlude of conversation, Jason conducted Shirley down the path leading into the park. As Julian and Nikos exchanged knowing smiles, the latter remarked lazily, "I doubt that we see them at lunch, eh, friend?"

"Most likely not." Both men chuckled before rising to go their separate ways.

Imperiously informed by her supremely athletic master that on this day he intended that they indulge in a bout of strenuous exercise to make up for missing their daily workouts, Mercedes wondered bemusedly whether so prosaic, so accustomed an activity, would mute her vivid sense that for six days now she had lived in a surreally distorted mirror-image of her normal reality. When Julian clasped her hand, rather than tucking her arm into his, and headed down the same path taken by Jason and Shirley, she matched the moderately swinging stride he adopted as sufficient to set her a stiff pace without stressing her unduly.

The route chosen by the guide wound through tree-shaded, narrow byways which led past picturesque springs frequented by a few nude couples who evidently liked to avoid the larger crowds typical of the afternoons. Emerging from the densely wooded area at a point directly across the bowl from the dining/sitting area, Mercedes halted to gaze at the waterfall far to her right.

Turning to view what lay ahead, she saw that a path led up the outcropping rising steeply before her. Its course consisted of a long series of U-shaped turns that in her local idiom were known as switchbacks. "This path and the destination to which it leads, lie outside Lorenzo's private preserve," her escort explained. "I've always wondered just why he didn't include it. Generosity, I expect. The climb will put your stamina to a rigorous test, my love."

Although the path proved to be smooth—easy to traverse in soft slippers—the steepness negotiated in the dry, rarefied air, added to the length tripled by the seemingly endless number of bends, did indeed provide a tough challenge to the guest who gamely exerted herself to the utmost. When the climbers reached an altitude that the panting woman accurately divined to be higher than the fissure from which the distant waterfall issued, Julian called a halt.

Entranced by the vista, Mercedes gazed out over the bowl. A few wisps of tenuous cloud floated across the azure sky. Far above, an eagle circled, borne on updrafts rising from the lushly wooded depression. Absorbed in the panoramic view seen from this new perspective, she focused her attention on that sight while neglecting to study the rocky face of the outcropping behind her.

At length Julian interrupted her reverie by reaching around her, and unfastening the pin from the ring. Her gown fell around her ankles. "Fold it, and lay it over your slippers, right here," he commanded. As she obeyed, he stripped to the buff and left his folded clothing next to that of his lover, but only after removing three small items from a pocket.

Perceiving that a weathered, ironbound, wooden chest reposed on the rock close by, Mercedes watched Julian open it, and remove two sizeable cans of tomato juice. Opening both with the implement dangling from a cord fastened to the handle, he offered her one. Draining it thirstily, the woman marveled at Lorenzo's thoughtfulness in providing this needed refresher to hikers who might otherwise grow dehydrated in the hot, dry desert air.

Dropping to sit on the flat-topped chest, while conscious of the puzzlement of the woman wondering whether he intended to enjoy her on this rocky ledge, he ordered, "Come here, Mercedes."

As she stood between his legs, facing him, Julian applied a shield to her mound. When the metal disc adhered as if it had grown there, he commanded, "Bend forward—so." Even as he spoke, he deftly slipped two nipple-rings into place, activated the shield, and bade the woman instantly gripped by substantial pain, to stand erect.

Rising, he conducted his partner, who asked no prying questions, to a site along the rock face where a narrow fissure, scarcely high enough to allow a man to stand upright, and barely wide enough to accommodate two people walking abreast, beckoned. Undaunted by the darkness ahead, Julian led his companion through the tunnel that sloped gradually downward ahead of them. The bright sunlight slanting at approximately the same angle as the slope of the floor allowed the fascinated guest to behold compelling evidence that water had once scoured the walls and floor—an ancient torrent that left ghostly reminders of its existence etched into the living rock.

The stranger to the premises perceived that the path passed through a portal allowing entry into a small chamber. By the dim light making its way through the doorway, Mercedes beheld an irregularly shaped pool in which floated what seemed to be a king-sized waterbed. That feature she saw to be tethered at its four corners to iron rings affixed to the flat rock forming a narrow pathway around the pool. A loop of cord hanging downward over the bed, she observed to lead via two pulleys to heavy black curtains that could be drawn across the entry.

Stepping into the pool, Julian lay supine on the waterbed. Reaching out, he grasped the loop of cord. "Lie next to me," he instructed. "Suck my prick until I'm hard."

The water the woman tested with a toe, she discovered to be almost too hot for comfort. Disposing herself rather gingerly on the warm, rubbery surface that rippled beneath her, Mercedes offered the exquisite stimulation that never failed to render her lover rock-hard.

"Impale yourself on my cock, with your chest against

mine," came the next directive. When his partner lay prone on him, so that both the nipple-rings and the shield pressed against his flesh, pain transmitted itself to his nerves as well as hers. When his partner set about working her loins against his, he bade her desist. Pulling on the loop, he caused the heavy curtains to slide across the entry.

Blackness akin to that of a tomb sealed for a thousand years engulfed the pair passively joined in physical union. Suppressing an irrational fear originating in mild claustrophobia, Mercedes lay still. Eyes opened unnaturally wide searched in vain for a stray gleam of light.

"Relax," Julian bade her, his melodic voice an aural caress. "This is the nearest you'll ever come to experiencing full sensory deprivation. No image impinges on your eyes; no sound except my voice falls on your ears. The only tactile sensation is the extensive contact of your skin with mine. The pain originating not in pinched flesh, but in your nerves and mind—pain that now afflicts us both—forms an interface between your flesh and mine, but that pain will focus our awareness on the physical union we enjoy, and meld us into one entity. Lay your legs on mine, and keep them so."

When his partner obeyed, Julian thrust his legs wide apart, thereby causing those of the woman penetrated by his erect organ to do likewise. She felt her lover's hands grip her wrists. Spreading his arms wide, Julian urged, "Lay your palms on mine." When he felt his partner's palms flatten themselves against his own, he smiled to himself in the Stygian blackness.

"You're now to lie silently, and meditate on the nature of the bond uniting us, my love—conscious only of warmth, the reassuring contact of my flesh with yours, and the pain afflicting us both. Let your mind open, even as your loins loosen. Seek insight, while remaining perfectly still."

The blackness so absolute as to defy belief, the warmth of

the moisture-saturated air, the uncanny silence, the exclusion of any tactile sensation but that of congealing against the flesh of her lover while gripped by the pain shared with the man whose turgid male organ filled her inner space: all combined to confer a sense of being suspended in a lightless, yawning void. Likening the effect to a return to the womb about to eject her, painfully and convulsively, into a world that she, the fetus, could not dimly imagine, Mercedes let her mind drift. A shade worriedly, she awaited the random rain of concepts that she suspected might fall like a shower of sharp-tipped arrows into the consciousness vulnerable to impalement.

Julian's heartbeat throbbed in the ear laid against his chest. No startling insight immediately illumined the darkness of the mind passively awaiting enlightenment. Instead, a sense of ineffable peace stole over the woman relaxed now to the point of bonelessness. Her consciousness narrowed to focus on this cruel, masterful lover so utterly different from any man she had ever known. The pain forming what he termed an interface between himself and her, shaded her perception of him, and served to remind her of his autocratic insistence on submissiveness and obedience. His words of that morning returned, producing a resurgence of regret.

Fear added lurid color to the fevered vision spreading itself across a mental screen blank until now. Julian's setting a limit on his demands both gratified and disappointed the woman wishful of experiencing this fascinating, frightening new culture in its entirety. Even as her flesh seemed to dissolve into that of the man beneath her, she knew herself fundamentally changed by her relationship with him. She realized that she had been subtly persuaded to embrace standards and customs foreign to those instilled by her rural community.

That insight deepened as the poet grew exquisitely aware

that in some respects, she had always walked as a stranger through that prosaic society into which she had been born: a culture which differed considerably from the inner realm into which she deliberately withdrew when she needed respite from the blatant practicality of men and women who lived entirely in the real world of grass, cows, machines, and challenging economic conditions.

Enfolded by silence and darkness, Mercedes pondered her longing for continued companionship with this demanding master with whom she lay physically joined. Musingly, she reviewed the vastly intensified, swiftly aroused carnal desires which she perceived at this juncture not as new, but as fully addressed, fully acknowledged, fully satisfied, for the first time in her life. The glimmer of insight beginning to appear slowly grew brighter. All at once, it expanded into a white-hot fireball of total certitude.

The impact of the dual insights searing themselves into her understanding produced an ethereal calm: a result of the cessation of nagging doubts which she had until now deliberately suppressed, so as not to be forced to address them. The decision just rendered left her feeling exhilarated. That ephemeral excitement swiftly transmuted into a state resembling coital trance. Deprived of visual and auditory stimulation, she melted against her lover, and dreamed while awake of being possessed, dominated, cherished, but most of all, understood.

As if some extrasensory message passed directly from her mind to that of the man himself contemplating the revelations gained through meditation, he moved. Arching upward, he drove deeper into his partner's cunt. When she remained passive, he began thrusting slowly, rhythmically, into the lushly lubricated passage enfolding his still-stiff prick.

That repetitive, languorous motion, uncannily matching

the beat of the woman's heart, stirred her not only to passion, but also to exaltation. Raptly, she rose and fell with those sensuous penetrations lacking urgency even as they conferred a sense of sailing through a vastly expanded universe on rolling billows of pure ether. No thought of offering caresses, let alone of thrusting in her turn, crossed her mind. Adrift in an unearthly medium, possessed by a leviathan of some trackless deep, she effortlessly achieved an otherworldly climax resembling a culmination experienced during a vividly erotic dream-sequence.

Julian's arms now enfolded her. In the absolute darkness, the humid warmth, the stillness unbroken even by the gurgle of water, the two lay entwined: one. His mouth found hers. Languorously, he explored its moist depths, toying with the tongue playing with his, before sucking on it as if to seal her mouth to his forever. At length, he desisted. Surrounded by primal night, he kissed her cheek, her eyes, her throat, finding them by instinct.

Rolling on his side, so that Mercedes slid off the body upon which she had lain for what seemed to her an endless minute, a swift-darting eon, a suspension of time, Julian crushed her against him, sending pain again radiating through his own body. Ripples gained seiche-like amplification within the waterbed, before abating. "Tell me what insights you gained," he commanded, his melodic voice adding a dimension that had been lacking, to the expanded, lightless universe.

"I belong to you," came the unhesitating reply uttered in a calmly judicious tone. "I can't imagine living apart from you, ever again. If, in the beginning, you'd tried to brainwash me into offering myself as your slave, I'd have resisted—fought you, and stubbornly clung to my independence. Because you set limits on your demands, I've mustered the courage to set none on my willingness to give you whatever pleasure your code allows you to enjoy.

"That being so, I consent to undergo the rite of passage to the rank of adept, purely because I wish to offer you that ultimate pleasure. I consent as well, to participate in any other ritual prescribed by your custom, which you'd follow if you'd originally conditioned me to submit without protest to any demand you laid on me. I love you, Julian. I always will."

Caught in an embrace that threatened to crack her ribs, Mercedes returned it with fierce ardor. When at last her lover slackened the force with which he held her, he declared with impassioned vehemence, "And I love you. I want you for my consort, Mercedes. I yearn to make you that promise formally, before my peers. I long to solemnize the vow that will bind me to you, and only to you, for so long as you live. I realize that the promise that will bind *you* to *me* is that of a legal marriage performed with your family and friends as witnesses. I give you my word: I'll marry you, when and where you wish, after we leave here.

"In making you my consort—in swearing to bed no other woman but you, for so long as you live—I'll be trusting implicitly to the word you'll give me, to marry me, to live with me, and to cleave to me for life. If you renege on that promise once you get home, or file for divorce at some later date, the formal, irrevocable vow I made in the presence of the Grand Master and my peers will still bind me. In repudiating your vow, you'll be condemning me to live womanless for the balance of your lifetime. So think well before passing that word, my love."

Divining intuitively that this adherent of a philosophy which differed radically in some of its tenets from her own, spoke bare truth, Mercedes reviewed her emotions. Lying in total blackness while surrounded by a brooding silence, spared any distraction arising from her environment, she found it easier to think clearly while projecting herself into a nebulous future. "Tell me what I can expect, being legally married to a demanding master," she urged, half fearing what she might hear.

"I'll reserve the right to order our life together as I wish, Mercedes, but I'll cherish you, support you, and actively seek to make you content with that life. We'll live at my main residence: the house where you first consented to engage in sexual relations with me. Occasionally, we'll travel, so as to visit members of the Order whom I count as my closest friends. I'll build you a greenhouse, a library, an office, or whatever else you need to keep you involved in the pursuits that currently absorb you. I'll indulge my tastes in sensual pleasure exactly as I've been doing, but never to excess.

"I intend to use the journal I've kept for a quarter of a century to write a scholarly analysis of the factors precipitating the world crises I've witnessed from an unusual vantage point. That endeavor will keep me from growing either restless, or obsessed with the pleasure you'll afford me. If I publish the finished work, I'll do so privately. I'll distribute copies only to close associates, so as to maintain the anonymity I so value.

"To your neighbors, I'll be a well-off, retired businessman who formerly owned a fleet of aircraft. I'll blend in, Mercedes. I'll seem unremarkable, if overly reclusive, to your family and friends, who'll judge me the ideal husband for a cultured, self-reliant loner like yourself."

Vastly relieved by that concise summation, the widow swiftly arrived at a momentous conclusion. In a ringing declaration, she voiced it. "I give you my word: I'll marry you, live with you, and cleave to you for life, when we get home. I keep my word, Julian."

"I trust that word, Mercedes." Relief suffused the man rejoicing in the outcome of his carefully calculated ploy: affording this woman for whom his heart hungered the chance to deliberate in a setting conducive to the gaining of deeper insights into her subliminal motivations. Joy surged through him as he reviewed her declaration. Almost absently, he sought and found the rough spot on the shield. The pain that seemed a part of this lightless universe ceased as if it had never been.

Experiencing a heady lightness of being, Mercedes beheld a shaft of light pierce the blackness, as her lover pulled on the loop of cord. Squinting against even that dim radiance, she obeyed Julian's command to rise, and wade to the perimeter of the pool. When the pair approached the entry, each shading his eyes with a hand, he halted. Drawing her close, he kissed her, his salute conveying fierce possessiveness. "I'll conduct the rite tonight," he informed her in a tone freighted with purposefulness. "I honor your courage, little staunch-heart."

Striding along in the bright sunshine, her hair blown about her face by a stiff breeze, Mercedes felt as if she just woke from a vivid dream. No whit wishful of taking back the dual promises made in that womb-like retreat so well suited to meditation, she yet shivered as she contemplated enduring so forbidding an ordeal. Forcing herself to think only of the ascent to ecstasy forming its culmination, she controlled burgeoning fear. Maintaining that control, she conversed with her usual vivacity over the dinner she ate with hearty appetite.

Intuitively sensing that underlying fear, her lover decided against leaving her alone in their room while he made certain arrangements. In a few minutes' worth of private conversation with Manuel, whom Julian accosted and drew aside as the new entrant conducted his courtesan to the buffet-line, he solved a minor problem. Together, the two close friends approached Nikos, and gained the blonde master's ready assent to escort both of their partners to the springs for a soak, an hour after dinner.

On hearing that latter exchange, Mercedes divined that any jealousy Julian initially harbored must have dissipated owing to his placing perfect trust in his soon-to-be consort. Cheered by the thought, she dwelled for a time on another observation scarcely less warming. These autocratic practitioners of an ancient discipline make no social distinction whatsoever between a courtesan and wives or lovers who wouldn't dream of accepting payment for sexual favors, she mused approvingly. Not only do they lack the least condescension to permanent partners in social situations, they exhibit none to *any* woman in their company—even one hired by a peer. I suppose they regard a professional partner like Celeste as an artist worthy of high admiration, given the value they place on skill at conferring sensual pleasure.

Nikos not only obliged, he exhibited delight at being asked. During the two hours during which the trio enjoyed languorous spans of immersion in various pools, he exhibited a gentlemanliness that elevated him in Mercedes' estimation. As boldly appraising as ever, he yet admired both of his charges equally, extending the same courteous attention to the lovely courtesan that he extended to the woman to whom he had so recently given his telephone number.

Secretly amused, but nonetheless impressed by the handsome master's making no distinction which might impinge on the notice of either herself or Celeste, the Westerner enjoyed the leisurely period of bathing, while firmly banishing from her mind the ordeal facing her later in the evening.

Strolling back towards the sitting area, wrapped in a robe of black silk, her auburn hair tossing in the brisk, warm breeze, Mercedes beheld Julian and Manuel approaching, clad in their shirts and pants. Having located their women, the pair invited Nikos to join them in a secluded nook among the trees, so as to enjoy a glass of wine from a bottle provided by the mercenary soldier. That aficionado, they discovered, brought along a half-dozen bottles besides those given as a gift to the Grand Master and his consort. The dark red wine brought and served by an apprentice whom Mercedes had seen only a few times behind the buffet flowed delicately over discerning palates.

Mercedes noticed that Manuel studied her musingly over his goblet of blown glass, but she ascribed that intent scrutiny to a desire to ascertain whether she appreciated the rare vintage. Smiling mischievously, she assured him that while no connoisseur, she knew right well that someone familiar with fine wines would bend a knee in homage before that bottle, prior to imbibing. That encomium earned her one of the brawny warrior's rare smiles.

Certain that Manuel's expression conveyed admiration as well as appreciation of her compliment, she idly wondered why. Uneasily, she hoped that the daring mercenary soldier would refrain from emulating Nikos' boldness—that Manuel would stop short of making some overt advance guaranteed to rouse Julian to jealousy.

The afternoon passed pleasantly, as did the dinner-hour. Julian escorted his cherished companion to their room directly after the meal, his every subtle sensor alert. Divining the magnitude of his lover's fear, he saw with pride that she maintained a rigorous control over that emotion. Slipping his arms around her from behind, he pulled the pin from the ring, and let the gown slide to the floor.

Lifting her, he seated himself on the side of the bed while cradling her in his arms. "I gave you my word not to cause you bodily harm," he reminded her, his eyes purposeful. "You'll need to cut me a further bit of slack, Mercedes, as you did when I employed the Mastiff and the Wolf. You'll smart afterwards, for a day, but suffer no lasting injury, or any stroke that could leave a scar. If you refuse to grant that minor concession, I'll employ combinations of the electronic devices which you'll find even harder to bear than the electronic whip I propose to employ."

Chilled, but resolute, Mercedes replied stoutly, "I set no limits, Julian. None."

Admiration blended with fierce satisfaction. "As I told you, little braveheart, a master's only permitted to conduct the rite in the presence of a witness. A member of the Council by custom asks a fellow Council-member, if the rite's conducted here. Manuel will fill that role. Since the witness invariably grows almost as aroused by observing as he would if he wielded the whip, it's customary also to allow him to satisfy that need in the body of the woman, once she achieves absolute surrender.

"But I've gone farther, Mercedes. I've invited Manuel to share with me the delight of raising you to a lofty height of rapture. That invitation represents a gift I give *you*, rather than the witness. You'll achieve a degree of ecstasy new to you, being pleasured at so critical a point in your evolution as a sensualist, by two highly experienced masters. That gift I regard as one well deserved by a cherished companion who freely consented to undergo the rite of passage, out of an unselfish wish to deny me no pleasure which my code allows."

The momentary shock produced by that announcement swiftly faded. In the fevered vision evoked by the revelation, Manuel's scarred, splendid physique assumed a new aura. Picturing him as a partner in sensual pleasure erased the far more forbidding visualization of the athlete as wielder of an implement resembling a bullwhip.

Desire surged up from some recess hidden below the plane of the initiate's consciousness, to set her loins quivering. Recalling the heady delight produced by the combined efforts of Julian and Nikos, she impulsively thrust her arms around the lover still cradling her in his arms, whispering, "I appreciate your gift. Don't imagine for a moment that I'll give you any cause for jealousy."

"Worried about that, eh?" came the amused response. "No need, my love. Manuel's my closest, most trusted friend, and you've proved yourself able to enjoy vastly enhanced pleasure while reserving your full affection for your master. Were I not certain of that, I'd not offer you the gift. My doing so serves as proof of my perfect trust in you. So. You'll don a robe, which you'll wear as I carry you to the chamber where the rite will take place."

Borne in the corded arms of the lover whose eyes she saw to reflect naked lust, Mercedes fought the terror suddenly assaulting her. For a few agonizing minutes, she regretted making the offer. That regret swiftly faded, as pride combined with ample courage to thrust that thought from mind. Recalling that she need not suffer the mental stress of striving to bear without flinching the agony now imminent, she developed a new and infinitely worse fear. Might Julian fail to stop at the threshold he must not cross? she cried to her quivering alter ego. Suffer disgrace—impair his friendship with the man forced by his code to report his best friend's reprehensible failure?

Oh, no—no. Julian exerts perfect control over himself. No. But might *I* develop fierce resentment—even hatred—of the man I vowed to marry? No! I brought this ordeal on myself! I'll not fight him—I'll willingly surrender! No!

Regaining her grip on herself, the initiate lay passively in the arms bearing her down the spiral stone stairs to the experience she dreaded even as her loins quivered with fierce desire.

Chapter Eleven

Despite her inner turmoil, Mercedes noticed that Julian bypassed the chamber designated by the emblem of the five-petaled flower, and advanced down the dimly lit, subterranean passage. Shivers coursed down her spine, despite the air's being warm. When he strode through an open portal, she beheld Manuel standing to one side. The witness closed the door, and advanced to where the man conducting the rite stood while holding his cherished companion in his arms.

At the center of the chamber—a high-ceilinged, square area fully as large as that housing the stylized flower—two chains suspended from the ceiling supported padded fetters. Identical restraints the woman staring out of dilated eyes saw to be attached to two short lengths of chain linked to iron rings affixed to the floor. A long, wide couch, one end indented in a V-shape, and the other featuring a bolster-like roll, reposed in the wide space between the chains and the far wall. That prominent feature the novice observing through a veil of fear saw to be upholstered in black leather.

To one side of the couch stood a bench upholstered to match. To the other, she spied a table on which rested a pitcher, basin, and folded towels. Flanking the central space, the initiate sweeping a fevered glance over the premises beheld a pedestal table on which lay the case containing the electronic implements. A three-legged wooden stool and a hardwood bench formed the only other furnishings. Closed, iron-bossed doors to her left and right—doors set into entries in walls constructed exactly like those of the hallways—impinged on her peripheral vision.

Julian now set her on her feet at a spot close to the center of the chamber. She stood erect, maintaining an admirable control of her face. As she reached to push back the errant lock of auburn hair partially obscuring her eye, her master stepped forward.

Having untied the belt of her robe, he thrust the garment off her shoulders. "Stand with your hands clasped behind your head," he ordered. "You'll submit without flinching to the preliminaries. Fetter your body with your mind until we bind you with restraints. At that point, the order will no longer remain in force."

Obeying instantly, the participant whose mind verged on terror watched as both her master and the peer serving as witness stripped off their shirts and pants, folded the garments, and laid them on the bench next to her robe. When they turned to confront her, she acted on impulse: lowered her eyes, so as to assess the magnitude of their arousal.

A swift but comprehensive glance apprised her that both men's pricks reared stiffly erect. Manuel's male member riveted her full attention for the few seconds it took her to ascertain that his engorged tool exceeded in size even that of the lover who she considered to be supremely well endowed. The fear engendered by the imminence of suffering blended seamlessly with that generated by the daunting thought of taking that massive cock in her ass.

As if he read her mind, Julian issued a brisk order to the peer raking the patently frightened woman with eyes that reminded her of polished obsidian. “Bend her forward, Manuel, so that her delectable rear’s well within my reach.”

Huge hands now exerted an unbreakable grip. Deftly, Manuel disposed her unresisting body in the ignominious position demanded by her master. The witness watched with intent interest as the principal in the proceedings inserted a soft, slender, well lubricated, flanged shaft into the anal passage only slightly less tight than it was in its virginal state. When the implement inexorably swelled, distending the orifice, the observer cocked his head. In a lazy drawl, he observed, “Now that’s an item I ought to acquire, old friend.”

Despite the agitation clouding her awareness, Mercedes found herself actually agreeing, counting the pain that now radiated from the site as more desirable than the tearing which this brawny athlete could so easily cause.

“Sit, and hold her supine across your thighs.”

Disposed thus, the woman mastering her urge to go tense, fixed eyes gone wide with fear on a shield new to her: one black, rather than golden. When the cold metal adhered to her mound, she discovered that the nipple-rings lacking any extensions matched the shield in hue. When with a touch of a finger her lover activated the device, she all but moaned aloud.

Pain exceeding any of this nature experienced prior to now racked her: agony accompanied by a matching increase in the attendant pleasure. Her fear mounted as she contemplated the probable consequences of rousing her cruel master to anger by failing to exert perfect self-control during what he termed the preliminaries. Set now upon her feet, and ordered to stand beneath the dangling chains, she mustered the courage she conceded to have flagged for a few seconds, and obeyed the ominous command to spread her legs wide.

The well-lubricated whip-shaft which Julian inserted into

her feminine depth, Mercedes saw with relief to be the type which generated the lesser degree of pain, but the cord she observed to have been replaced by a three-inch length of fine chain to which attached a small black metal sphere. That object he held in his hand until after he activated the shaft.

Managing to endure the torment produced by this new incremental increase in the electronic stimulus, the initiate watched her master set the ball swinging between her thighs. The mass she instantly judged to exceed that of the plumb bob. Agony ripped through her groin as the strong downward pull caused pain in addition to that produced when the shaft within her rocked in synchrony with the rapid swings of the dense ball. Dominating the effect of the multiple increments of electronically induced pain, she wondered in mounting desperation how she could possibly bear any further increase in the agony enveloping her.

Two pairs of hands now lifted her wrists, and snapped padded fetters around them. The hands next moved to her ankles, securing them. Through the fog of pain clouding her mind, Mercedes grew aware that she stood flat on the stone floor, and that the restraints binding her wrists offered her a limited ability to move.

A comforting thought impinged: she need not strive now to control any urge to stiffen, or squirm. Julian's words rang in her fevered consciousness. He wants me to writhe—to struggle, and cry out, she reminded herself. To plead; to weep. I might not be able to fight back tears, but I'll be damned if I'll plead with the man to whom I offered the ultimate gift, for any surcease of the pain. I'll suffer it willingly, and surrender swiftly. That will end my agony—hopefully, soon.

Julian now stood before her, naked, manifestly aroused, his eyes cruel as the grave. In his right hand, he held a whip the horrified viewer saw to bear a most disquieting resemblance to a bullwhip, even if it seemed lighter in bulk. A handgrip a foot in length, composed of four black-glass spheres, ended in a divider beyond which stretched four solid metal spheres serving to weight the handle.

Beyond a second divider, the affrighted woman beheld a round, tightly braided, smooth black lash six feet in length, and three-quarters of an inch in diameter where it attached to the weighted shaft. That evil appurtenance gradually diminished in thickness from its base to its free end. An extension she saw to be attached to the narrow extremity: a six-inch-long braided cord tipped by a cluster of feathery projections.

That seemingly harmless addition the ranchwoman instantly identified as a popper: a device enabling the wielder to crack the whip. As she stood with patently affrighted eyes riveted to the instrument that now assumed the blue aura, she quailed inwardly.

Her courage all but failed her. I can't bear the torment that whip will inflict! she shrieked in her mind. Why did I ever agree? Why?

Even as she savagely castigated her shrinking alter ego, Julian raised his right arm, and brought it down in a forceful, well-practiced movement. The lash described a sinuous curve in the air before shooting forwards malevolently towards the cringing victim. A swiftly executed backwards flip of the handle produced a crack that reverberated off the stone walls of the chamber, even as a two-foot-long section of the outer end struck quivering flesh, and clung. A stifled shriek escaped the woman whose entire front, from below her breasts to her thigh, felt as if afire.

Instinctively, she sought to pull away, only to find herself jerked forward by the electrostatic attraction stronger than the adrenaline-enhanced strength of her muscles. Agony enveloped her as the whip-stimulus tormented the flesh caught in so relentless a grip. When the snake-like implement finally lifted, the bulk of the pain died away along the thin red stripe promising to swell into a welt, but the torment within her cunt caused by the pull of the ball on the end of the short, wildly gyrating chain, intensified.

The whip cracked once more. The lash struck along a line parallel to the prior descent, searing the flesh with a combination of electronic stimulus and forceful application of the implement. Letting the black whip cling, Julian played the victim striving to twist away, like a trout on a line.

Pulled back around to face her tormentor while struggling in the grip of the tentacle, her vision obscured by the mass of ruddy hair falling forward over her face, Mercedes tossed her head back. Yielding to a sudden onslaught of rage, she ground her teeth. Her resolve to bear the whipping passively, while concentrating on surrendering swiftly, dissolved in a red haze of wrath.

Goaded by pain far too great to bear without flinching, the pinioned woman mounted an impotent but unflagging struggle to pull free of the bonds restraining her wrists and ankles. Frantically, she fought to avoid the next stroke of the lash unerringly targeting her abdomen, its tip striking just below her breast. Valiantly, she strove to stifle the screams threatening to tear from her throat.

Virulent anger contended with agony for dominance of the awareness narrowed to focus on those dual emotions. Refusing to give the cruel master wielding the whip the satisfaction of hearing her scream, she bit her lip until she tasted blood. Cracks resembling pistol-shots echoed off the walls—cracks that flayed the nerves of the sufferer unable to avoid the wicked stroke occurring almost simultaneously with that hated sound.

As the lash repeatedly fell, clung for a cruelly long span of time, and lifted, the agony mounted. Enveloped in a fog of pain-shot fury, Mercedes failed to blink back the tears that emerged to bedew her cheeks. She likewise lost the power to suppress the moans that inevitably escaped her, but she stubbornly refused to let a plea for mercy pass the lips she savaged with her teeth.

When he raised his arm to deliver the initial stroke of the whip, Julian savored the fierce elation blending with raw lust. The stifled scream tearing from the lips of the love-slave, who strove ineffectually to pull away, aroused him further, as did the sight of the thin red line commencing to swell into a perceptible welt that he knew would remain tender for some twenty-four hours.

Resolved to let the electronic stimulus inflict the bulk of the agony which would produce surrender, and keep to a minimum the raising of welts the pain of which would linger, he employed far fewer strokes than would a master wielding a whip crafted of leather. Purposefully, he let the lash cling to the flesh feeling flayed as it endured the prolonged electronic stimulus.

Pain became the universe of the woman still striving to twist aside while still fighting the restraints.

When his lover mounted so unexpectedly desperate a fight against both the lash and the bonds, Julian savored the pleasure engendered by the sight of her struggles. Aroused on an elemental level, stimulated to raw lust, he wielded the whip with a mastery that evoked unqualified admiration in the witness well able to pass expert judgment on that score. Special strokes allowing only the tip to land with moderate force on shrinking flesh left vivid red lines on the breasts thus cunningly tormented. In unhurried fashion, the conductor of the rite targeted the full range of sensitive sites on the body now striped in red.

At length, the whip-wielder frowned. Tawny eyes glittered as the untiring arm again descended. Awaiting an impassioned plea for a surcease to the agony the extent of which he well knew, Julian heard none. Raking the tear-streaked face of his pain-racked victim with an appraising glance, he determined with shock that fierce anger now gripped her.

That discovery sparked an answering ire, as the master driving his lover towards an elevated level of surrender instinctively interpreted that rage as a threat to his dominance. Aware of the necessity for retaining perfect control of his emotions, he strove to maintain a glacial calm, but succeeded only partially.

Hot wrath subsided into mere annoyance, but that lesser emotion insidiously altered Julian's strategy. He struck more often, letting the lash cling only briefly. When that tactic failed to wring screams, let alone pleas, from the woman whose rage intensified, he increased the force of the next stroke.

An angry red stripe now marred the white skin of the abdomen marked by an array of less pronounced marks. Not satisfied, the tormentor let the lash cling. His own anger flared, prompting him to jerk on the handle when the frantic victim convulsively sought to turn away.

Mercedes' face set like stone despite being bedewed with tears. A strangled sound, half cry, half growl, escaped her as the savage forward pull intensified the pain, but no high-pitched scream, no beseeching plea, passed her lips.

Damn this bastard! she shrieked within her mind. And damned if I'll give him the satisfaction of begging! I won't! This agony's too much to ask of me! Damn him!

A fresh impact set her teeth grinding anew.

The fury possessing her proved impossible to sustain, as the torment grew almost too great to be borne. All at once, she sagged in her bonds, and hung slackly, her face contorted, as the lash lifted off her flesh. She cringed as she awaited a new descent of the whip, too exhausted by her futile struggle to continue it. Her knees buckled. Blood trickling from her bitten lip reddened the corner of her mouth.

Even as his arm rose, Julian in a split-second burst of enlightenment perceived his danger. The next stroke fell with far less telling effect, and clung to the quivering hips encircled by the lash. With blinding force, the realization dawned on the man who had so savagely escalated his partner's torment, that this tough descendant of hardy frontiersmen did indeed possess an intractable stubbornness at her core. She *won't* plead! he acknowledged in a burst of luminous clarity. Not if you were to flay her raw!

Admiration contended with a new onslaught of wrath: regal rage that swiftly dissolved into shame. You damned fool! Julian castigated himself scathingly. You nearly let rabid anger goad you into escalating the force of the strokes until you crossed the line into brutal, forbidden excess. You're courting unbearable disgrace! This woman who voluntarily offered you the ultimate pleasure set no limits on her gift, and you determined on exacting a verbal response she's constitutionally unable to give!

Conscious only of agony, Mercedes hung passively in her bonds. All her anger dissolved in the flood of pain crowding out any other awareness. With that narrowing of focus came swift, total surrender. Hanging slackly, she suffered each ensuing stroke of the whip without so much as flinching, her mind a formless embodiment of torment.

I belong to this cruel master who delights in inflicting this degree of agony, she acknowledged within the core of her being. That single coherent thought penetrated the woman's befogged consciousness. I exist for his pleasure. Take me, she beseeched silently, inwardly. Fuck me. I can't bear any more!

Once again in perfect control of himself, Julian delivered three new strokes: light, quick impacts designed to force on a diminished awareness the inescapable necessity for surrender. When the subtle, telltale cues exhibited by the slack body grew apparent to both observers, he laid the whip aside. Striding forward, he set about freeing his cherished companion from the devices still sending waves of pain through loins and breasts.

Freed of the electronically induced stimuli, Mercedes grew conscious of the lesser but pervasive pain caused by a multitude of red wheals beginning to swell into raised welts. That lingering aftereffect sent shame surging through her bedimmed awareness, as she lay limply in the arms clasping her against their owner's chest.

You fought Julian! she chided herself. You succumbed to mindless anger! You offered the ultimate gift, and then sought to take it back! By forcing him to increase the severity of the whipping so as finally to encompass your surrender, you paradoxically deepened your own agony. Tears squeezed from under lids shut tightly. One by one, those drops rolled down cheeks gone pale as salt.

Fear swirled through the mind of the man wondering bleakly whether that brief, shameful loss of self-control cost him the love of this woman for whom his soul hungered. Seating himself, he cradled her in his arms. When she buried her face in his chest, and thrust her arms around him, relief so great as to render him lightheaded suffused him.

At length, when the tears ceased dampening his chest, he set her on her feet.

Manuel reached for her hand. Bending, he kissed it with all the fluid grace of a polished courtier. "I honor your courage," he informed her softly. "I've always derided the American government for training women to fight in combat. I've categorically refused to hire a female mercenary. But if I were ever to break that rule, it would be to take you on, little warrior."

Shocked to her core, Mercedes felt as a candidate for knighthood might, as a noble king's blade struck him on the shoulder. "I thank you," she breathed, wondering what aspect of the rite she perceived as marred by her hot, unreasoning rage, prompted that welcome accolade.

Slipping both arms around her, Julian kissed her on the neck. "Kneel, adept, and signify that you surrender your will absolutely to that of your master, by caressing my cock with your mouth."

Sinking to kneel erect, Mercedes took the hard shaft of her lover in her mouth. Eagerly, she offered the expert stimulation guaranteed to produce delight.

Awash in relief, Julian savored the erotic sensations even as he wondered uneasily whether that brief, reprehensible loss of self-mastery might have weakened the perfect control he normally maintained over the course of his passion. Bidding his lover to desist, he raised her.

Smiling into tawny eyes hot with lust, the newest adept asked gravely, her manner conveying no hint whatsoever of coyness, "Should I not signify that for this one night, I surrender my will to two masters?"

"But of course." Pride in her bearing now supplanted the relief engendered by what Julian still perceived as a frighteningly narrow escape from incalculable disaster.

Kneeling before the witness whose black eyes glittered with a combination of admiration and desire, she duplicated in ardor and duration the exquisite stimulation just offered her master. When she rose, Manuel lifted her, and clasped her against his black-thatched chest. "Tell me how you wish us to pleasure this treasure of yours," he demanded of the man conducting the rite.

"Lay her on the couch, and we'll both work to arouse her."

Her shame dissipated by the high compliment paid her by the brawny athlete bearing her in arms of iron to the oddly shaped couch, Mercedes now experienced a fierce yearning to be enjoyed by these two cruel masters simultaneously. No inhibition inculcated by her society tempered that longing; no fear that Julian might succumb to jealousy of his closest friend troubled her mind. Accepting the customs of the Order now as if born to the society practicing them, she sighed softly as she welcomed the quickening in her loins, and the gush of wetness lubricating her feminine depth.

The coolness of smooth black leather soothed the lingering pain of the stripes slowly swelling into red welts none of which had sufficed to break the skin. The witness gazing down at the new adept lying supine on the couch fully as wide as a king-sized bed took his cue from Julian. Both men reclined, positioning themselves on either side of her.

Rolling onto his side, Manuel thrust an arm across the woman's abdomen, and hooked his left elbow over the outside of her thigh. A huge left hand placed palm-down on her inner thigh pulled the leg bent at the knee, outwards, thereby spreading her thighs. A long finger slid into the orifice quivering with need; a moist mouth closed over the engorged clit protruding from its folds. The experienced master proceeded to demonstrate to the adept awash in bliss, not only his expert skill, but also his admirable control over his erection.

Even as waves of pleasure radiated from the site so expertly manipulated, Julian's scarred arm slid under his lover's shoulders, arching her back. Tipping his partner's head towards him, he closed his mouth over hers even as the fingers of his hands vibrated both nut-hard nipples.

The lingering pain of the welts now served to intensify the heady pleasure conferred by two avid devotees of erotic art. Aroused on a primal level, Mercedes rose effortlessly to a climax languorously prolonged owing to the two men's continuing to offer that expert stimulation while she enjoyed the fruit of their efforts. When at last they desisted, and smiled knowingly at each other over her supine, pliant body, she lay awash in euphoria, the memory of her ordeal thrust well below the plane of her consciousness.

Julian now lifted her, and disposed her body so that she lay with her legs spread along the arms of the V. "Make yourself free of our new adept's luscious love-tunnel, while maintaining your hardness, old friend," he bade the man rising to his feet with feline grace. When Manuel eagerly complied, driving his magnificent endowment into the dripping cunt spread to his view, Julian straddled his lover's chest, his weight resting partly on his knees, and partly on the buttocks resting on her bosom. "Take me in your mouth," he commanded of the woman who obeyed even as she wondered how she could accommodate him while so restricted in her ability to move. "Relax," he ordered. "Just enjoy what I do."

The man vastly relieved to find his ability to control the course of his passion undiminished, now thrust rhythmically into the moist mouth of the woman dually penetrated. As she raised her head, seeking to offer limited friction, he smiled into the green eyes gone dreamy, unfocused, as pleasure absorbed their owner. Placing his palms on her cheeks, Julian moved her head to and fro, pleasing himself. Kneeling astride her, he thrust until the head of his cock touched the back of her throat, won to admiration of her ability to control the reflex which almost inevitably caused an inexperienced woman to gag.

Bear-like hands thrust under the adept's buttocks, lifting her body, and changing the angle at which their owner's massive member drove repeatedly, forcefully, into the lavishly lubricated hole already feeling the gathering, the heat, the delicious shivers signaling the onset of climax. When it came, subtly intensified by the pain of the welts, the woman yielding herself with wanton abandon to two virile partners who achieved mental ecstasy without ejaculating, passed into a state of near-trance.

Both men stretched out next to the hedonist floating in a luminous opalescence that faded as Julian kissed her, passionately and possessively. Feeling his hard prick prod her thigh, Mercedes marveled at his self-control. The rapturous glow slowly abated. When he freed her lips, she murmured, "I belong to you, Julian. But now that you've driven home that absolute truth to your possession, would you permit Manuel to offer me the kiss of exploration?"

Moved to wry laughter, Julian bestowed an amused glance on the man whose shock—and suddenly deepened desire—he intuitively sensed. "You learned a few things from that blonde lad, damned if you didn't," he conceded, smiling into eyes gone soft, liquid, in the aftermath of bliss. "Manuel, pretend you're still an apprentice, and humor this voluptuary desirous of enlarging her experience of sensuality far beyond the norm. She's earned a dispensation which I'm not in the least reluctant to grant."

Enfolded in corded arms the color of oiled hardwood, Mercedes yielded to the questing tongue and moist mouth of the brawny athlete whose occupation, she strongly suspected, forced him to rely almost exclusively on courtesans for sexual pleasure. Aware that such women—at least, those of whom she occasionally heard of as providing their services to cowboys—regarded intimate kissing as presenting a danger to the emotional detachment necessary for their peace of mind, she concluded that he might seldom enjoy that delight. Untroubled by any such scruples, she responded with frank ardor to the brawny warrior's wantonly erotic kiss, knowing full well that neither he nor she would feel more than affectionate warmth for the other, afterwards.

Manuel took his time, savoring the unexpected but welcome gesture. Like Nikos before him, he perceived this mature companion of Julian's as radiating a most engaging ingenuousness: an illusion of innocence that stirred him to raw lust. Used to doing without affection in his relationships with the premier artists he hired, he found Mercedes' attempt to offer him pleasure equal to that which she gave her master, touching as well as arousing. Nonetheless, he knew as well as did she, that her intimate salute posed no danger either to his honor, or to his own peace.

Even so, he sighed as he freed her lips. "I envy you, old friend," he remarked to Julian with the candor habitual to him. "You needed what this lovely lady obviously gives you. I doubt that you'll grow restless, or regret that you no longer live on the edge, now that you possess so enchanting a partner."

"You don't need to live that way either, at this juncture," Julian observed ruminatively, unerringly gauging his best friend's reaction to the kiss he so readily sanctioned. "Why not retire?"

"I could, but I might spend the rest of my life searching, and not find a treasure to match yours," came the equable, frank reply. "And I'd rust, Julian. I'd miss the danger that's as addictive as a potent narcotic."

"You're unduly pessimistic, I'd say. You never know when a treasure will drop into your life by pure chance. The secret lies in recognizing the gift of capricious fate as such."

"I'll keep a sharp lookout, never fear. Shall we lift this netted bird to the final ecstasy?"

Borne in her master's arms, Mercedes melted against him as desire again stirred.

"Manuel, place the bench next to the couch, and fetch the lubricant," Julian instructed the peer who readily complied. Having positioned his burden so that she knelt erect on the bench, the lead player seated himself on the edge of the couch. "Bend her, so that she can take me in her mouth," he directed. "Then try the effect of the stretcher—but carefully, old friend."

Fear swirled up out of the recess where it lay quiescent in the mind of the woman striving not to let that emotion show. Manuel bent her forward, so that her shoulders rested on Julian's thighs. She took her lover fully, thrusting her arms around his torso while still kneeling on the bench, but positioned now so that her up-thrust rump offered easy access to the orifice about to be penetrated by a massive cock. Out of an instinctive sense of self-protection, she forced herself to relax so as to accept passively the entry she feared might tear her internally.

To her surprise, a long forefinger dripping with lubricant inserted itself deeply into her anus. When it withdrew, she found that the lavishly lubricated prick that followed in its wake slid into the slick passage without causing pain, let alone tearing.

Suffused with relief, she sucked her lover's engorged shaft as if to drain him of the essence of his passion. Expert fingers moistened by the lubricant massaged her clit, setting her loins quivering.

Julian now rose, lifting the body of the woman as he did so. As Manuel leaned back, his feet planted firmly on the floor, Julian thrust the torso of the woman still impaled in her rear by that massive shaft, upright. He then pressed her body back against Manuel's broad chest. As she knelt with her thighs spread, he thrust into her slippery cunt. That move accomplished, he gripped Manuel's upper arms for balance, and leaned back in his turn.

Manuel's hands now cupped Mercedes' breasts; his fingers vibrated her nipples. He thrust deeply, but not forcefully, into her rear, as Julian withdrew, and retreated as the other man's prick thrust into the love-tunnel she knowingly, deliberately squeezed repeatedly.

A slow, rhythmic dance began, as the two masters delighting in her response worked quivering loins, producing pleasure so intense as to border pain in the recipient of their efforts. Leaning forward, Julian fastened his mouth over that of his lover. Even as he continued the erotic love-play sending waves of delight radiating through her body, he sucked on her tongue.

Possessed wholly, penetrated in every orifice capable of taking a hard, erect organ, Mercedes yielded to both masters, her awareness narrowed to focus solely on the intense, indescribably erotic stimulation lifting her to a height of rapture new in her experience.

Heat suffused her loins, her thighs, her abdomen. Shivers cascaded up her torso, setting her heart racing. When through her befogged state of bliss she felt the contractions signifying orgasm begin within her, Julian freed her mouth. A groan escaped him as he ejected a voluminous stream of juice into the cunt he pleasured. A second later, Manuel's guttural utterance drowned out the shrill cry that tore from the throat of the woman whose body shuddered with the force of her climax. That long-drawn-out culmination drove her into full trance.

For a few seconds, the men themselves half in trance stood

like statues, savoring triumph. Manuel withdrew from the woman gone limp, as Julian did likewise. The latter partner lifted her, and laid her on the bed.

After bathing his slack member, Manuel collapsed prone on the couch next to the woman sprawled inertly supine. His arm paralleled that of the peer lying prone on the far side of her, his head pillowed on her arm. Each man hooked a leg over one of hers. Both masters let themselves slide into unconsciousness as deep as that of the satiated adept lying between their lithe, hard bodies.

Chapter Twelve

Mercedes fought her return to reality. Drifting down from the heights to find herself lying between her partners, she savored the warmth, the closeness. When the pair sat up, depriving her of both benefits, she opened her eyes only reluctantly.

Having stood her on her feet, Julian held his rubber-boned lover upright while Manuel thrust her slack arms into the silken robe, pulled it across her chest, and tied the sash. Her master again swept her into corded arms, and laid her on the couch while he dressed.

The adept enveloped in a haze of slowly ebbing euphoria heard him thank the witness who clapped his peer on the shoulder in comradely fashion. "I count myself privileged to have joined with you in raising your treasure to ecstasy," his fellow countered gracefully.

Moments later, borne in strong arms, Mercedes nestled against the chest of the lover striding towards their bedroom, dimly conscious of pain originating with the welts, but more aware of the lingering glow born of carnal pleasure. When Julian put her to bed, and slid in beside her, she congealed against him as she plunged precipitately into oblivion.

Upon awaking in the morning, the new adept grew instantly aware not only of pain, but of stiffness. When she rose, compelled by need, and headed for the bathroom, she shuddered as she envisioned how she would feel on this day, had Julian employed a conventional whip. While her movements served to limber taut muscles, pain stabbed her anew with every step.

Emerging to find her partner taking two clean sets of what Mercedes termed their formal clothing from the duffel, she discovered with relief that he chose not to engage her in strenuous lovemaking, but rather directed her to shower with him. Standing under the hot spray, enjoying the sensuous gliding of two well-lathered palms over her stiff, sore body, she harbored no regrets over consenting to undergo the rite. The memory of ecstasy exhilarated her.

As the newest adept advanced into the dining area, her gown fastened by a ruby-headed pin and a golden ring, Lorenzo accosted her. With regal grace, he bent and kissed her hand. When he rose, his piercing glance convinced the woman gifted with a high degree of intuition that he unerringly read her inmost thoughts. That belief grew even stronger as he averred softly, "Your daring matches that of the master to whom you come as a rare gift of capricious fate, Mercedes. He needs what you freely give him. I honor your amazing ability to adapt to our ways even more than I do your peerless courage."

Stunned by the implication of the compliment, the new adept recalled this uncannily perceptive leader's remarks on the day she first met him. He divined right then that Julian never subjected me to the customary regimen, she marveled. Lorenzo obliquely apprised his errant member that he knew, but the Grand Master offered no censure.

Breathlessly, Mercedes murmured a gracious reply even as her heart raced. I can't let any aspect of their culture—any ritual in which Julian demands that I participate—jar me into betraying shock, let alone drive me to rebel, no matter how deeply unnerved I may grow, she warned herself. I passed my word on that score! And surely, no rite could exceed that of last night in severity, now could it?

Having received similar marks of esteem from the members most closely acquainted with the master himself savoring fierce pride, Mercedes dined with hearty appetite, ignoring the twinges of pain that stabbed her with every move she made. The oval face framed in that shining fall of auburn hair—a face vibrant with eagerness, and alight with joy—seemed to Julian ageless: the face of an immortal wood nymph wooed out of seclusion by an ardent mortal lover, and beguiled into entering a passionate liaison.

Musingly, he recalled the promise she made him in the darkness of the meditation-chamber. An inaudible sigh escaped him as he contemplated the ironic circumstance that although she herself had set no limits, the word he had passed to her forced him to set a bound on himself: one he considered as necessary as it was regrettable.

After the leisurely meal and the conversation that continued for an hour after the conclusion of the repast, Julian rose, and escorted his cherished companion into the park. Curious on a minor score, Mercedes asked with deceptive lightness, "Did Celeste rate a well-earned rest, last night?"

That query produced a chuckle. "Hardly. Manuel arranged that she pleasure Nikos. I expect she earned twice what she'd net, otherwise, so I'm sure she welcomed the one-night switch."

"Mm. I simply can't imagine selling myself as she does."

"Yet you avoid displaying any hint of condescension, or frigid disapproval, in her company," came the lightly uttered reply conveying admiration.

"I don't disapprove," Mercedes stated with adamant force.

"If all women recoiled at the thought of selling sexual favors, men whose careers make a monogamous relationship impossible would inevitably be tempted to seduce girls whose passions turn out to be stronger than their judgment. Their lovers would get them pregnant, and leave, taking little or no responsibility for their offspring. My rural society quietly condones the existence of the age-old alternative to that far more reprehensible behavior. I merely can't picture *myself* choosing that career."

Thrusting an arm around the shoulders of this woman whose viewpoints the worldly ex-entrepreneur found refreshingly unconventional, Julian stopped his advance down the winding, tree-lined byway. Drawing her close, he kissed her gently on the mouth. "I can't picture you as anything but the delight you are," he murmured, as his lips caressed her cheek. "I love you, Mercedes."

"I love you."

When the slow progression of the pair resumed, Julian's arm still encircled his cherished companion's shoulders.

The destination the woman now perceived to be a stone edifice composed of two circular, capacious, slate-roofed mini-towers built side-by-side, connected by an enclosed archway. Small leaded-glass casement windows rimmed the towers below the overhanging roofs; an identical set flanked the entry. That portal, set into the archway, featured a heavy, iron-bossed wooden door resembling those in the main dwelling. Mist swirling up from vents in the slate roofing hung atop the twin towers.

Preceding her escort through the door he opened, Mercedes peered through dimness that slowly lightened as eyes used to the bright desert sunlight adjusted to the subdued radiance filtering through the narrow casements. Standing at Julian's side, she beheld a black-eyed, brown-skinned, slightly built, wiry master clad in a black silk robe. The long hair caught into a queue in back—hair once jet black—now sported streaks of gray.

Matsuo, she reminded herself, drawing on information stored in capacious mental files. Older than his physique would lead one to believe—they say he's eighty, at the very least.

Behind the aged master stood the same four apprentices who two days earlier had practiced their arts on her immobilized person. She saw their lean bodies to be clad in the same oddly-contrived briefs which she concluded they must wear in all situations except that of serving the buffet. Their youthful faces, grave as that of the authoritarian figure offering a sonorous greeting to the pair arriving, betrayed no hint of any emotion but respect.

Advancing, Matsuo bowed, and kissed the hand of the new adept. His seamed brown face creasing into a broad smile, he averred softly, "Your lady stands in need of my ministrations, eh, Julian? Although not nearly so direly in need as she might have, had you not employed your brother's unique inventions, I suspect. By the time I'm laid to rest, I won't require a successor, eh, lad?"

"We won't need to confront that sad eventuality for two decades at least, Matsuo . . . mmm?" Although the melodic voice held a jocular note, Mercedes caught the overtone of deep affection. "Today, old friend, I place my cherished companion and myself in your care, and that of your pupils."

"Bare her body, lad, that I may assess how best to proceed."

Arms thrust themselves around the torso of the woman warmed by the old man's smile: an expression worldly, wise, amused, benevolent. Fingers deftly pulled the pin, allowing the black gown to fall to the stone-flagged floor of the antechamber devoid of furniture but for a bench of carved wood.

Standing nude, palpably impacted by the keenly appraising glance of the piercing eyes riveted to her person, Mercedes to her astonishment grew conscious of a stirring in her loins paralleling that evoked by Nikos or Manuel. This old man projects no less masculine appeal than do his younger peers, she mused, a trifle disconcerted by her reaction. Is it his imperious, wholly authoritarian manner, as much as his maleness? Or am I growing obsessed with carnal pleasure?

"Ahhh . . . no daunting challenge to my skill, the welts marking your partner's lovely body," the master affirmed, smiling knowingly at the man still holding the upper arms of the cherished companion he exhibited to his peer. Turning to the blonde youth, Matsuo commanded, "Immerse this lady for three cycles, while I massage her master. Take care that I detect no deviation from the proscribed ritual when I return to observe. So. Julian, come with me."

As the two peers strolled off towards the door on the left of the entry leading to the second of the twin mini-towers, the four apprentices converged on the woman standing nude but for her slippers. As the tall lad swept up her gown, folded it, and laid the bundle on the bench, his dark-eyed, wiry fellow knelt, and removed their charge's footwear. With practiced ease, the four men lifted her unresisting body, and conveyed their burden through the door opposite that through which Julian and Matsuo vanished.

Borne into one of the two circular structures, Mercedes beheld two pools that seemed to have been left in their natural state. The surface of one she perceived to be so still as to resemble black glass; the other she saw to be wildly turbulent.

When her attendants stood her on her feet between the two roughly rectangular bathing sites, she noted that the chamber featured only two articles of furniture: a large, thick, rectangular mat reposing on the flags beyond the pools, and a cabinet fashioned of pleasingly carved hardwood standing midway between the two baths.

From that latter receptacle, the blonde youth withdrew a dipper. Thrusting the implement through the interface of air and still water, thereby sending concentric waves rippling outward across the glassy surface of the calm pool, he scooped up a dipperful of water, and poured the libation down the back of the woman whose arms remained gripped by two of his fellows.

A half-stifled yelp greeted the application, as icy fluid cascaded down skin expecting soothing warmth.

"Ahhh . . . arctic, the sensation, eh?" the blonde leader observed, his eyes twinkling. "But you need to be acclimated to the cold, little adept. You won't shame your master by resisting our ministrations, surely . . . mmmm?"

Warned by a somber note in that lightly uttered rhetorical question, Mercedes submitted meekly to three more applications of frigid water. Four pairs of hands now lifted her. The owners of the hands passed two to a side of the rectangular, glassy pool. Moving as one man, they deposited their protégée's shrinking body in the bath, thrusting her down until she lay covered to the chin in water colder than glacier-melt.

Her breath rattling in her throat, Mercedes grew aware of a muscled forearm sliding along the back of her neck. "Lay your head on my arm, and relax," the leader commanded in a fair imitation of Julian's imperious tone. "The cold will mute the swelling of those marks of your master's favor. He graciously allows you the benefit of our efforts to remedy the effects, rather than let the reminders of his mastery run their full painful course."

At the cost of giving me pneumonia! the recipient of the

treatment silently raged, feeling the cold penetrate to the marrow of her bones.

A few minutes later, as her teeth chattered audibly, four attendants obeyed a silent nod given by the leader. As one man, they lifted her, carried her to the space between the pools, and set her on her feet. Fetching thick Turkish towels from the cabinet, they rubbed her down with unflagging vigor, until her goose-bump-afflicted skin turned pink from the friction.

The brisk massage caused no undue worsening of the pain of the welts. On the contrary, the discomfort lessened. When the chill abated, the leader dipped up hot mineral water from the roiling bath, and acclimatized his charge's body to the impact of heat. At his silent signal, the four youths deposited their burden within the turbulence of the hot mineral spring.

Engulfed to the neck in churning water from which issued a faintly sulfurous odor, Mercedes needed no crisp command to rest her head on the arm of the tall lad notable for liquid eyes, short brown hair, and a seductive, British-accented voice. "Ahhh, my dear," he crooned softly, almost in her ear. "The warmth soothes the evidence of your master's favor, eh? Lie back now, and go limp. Just so."

Gone limp as unbaked dough, engulfed in welcome heat, Mercedes offered not the slightest resistance as the blonde leader's hands thrust her thighs apart beneath the surface. Fingers spread her pussy-lips, allowing hot mineral water access to the tender tissue of her cunt. Sitting on the edge, his hand immersed to the elbow, he held the flaps of flesh wide for the duration of the hot bath, allowing the roiling water to massage flesh a trifle chafed and sore from the dual penetrations of the prior evening.

When with flawless precision the team again lifted their charge and set her on her feet, he squeezed a generous ribbon of ointment from a tube, and anointed the orifice deep within its depth.

Marveling at the rapidity with which the medication alleviated the soreness, Mercedes stretched like a contented house-cat, only to give a slight start as the same long, deft finger inserted itself deeply into her anal opening, with similar beneficial effect. "There, now," the senior apprentice remarked airily, smiling up at her out of eyes alight with mischief. "Better, eh? When your master next avails himself of your luscious loins, he'll find you no less eager than himself."

The amused smile playing over the oval face of the beneficiary of those welcome ministrations vanished, as frigid water cascaded down her back, poured by the dark-eyed youth. Acclimatized by three more icy libations, Mercedes strove not to go tense as her four attendants again lowered her into the glacial bath. Groaning mentally, she recalled Matsuo's order. Three cycles! My perishing soul, I hope my heart doesn't quit on me.

At the end of six immersions, the last of which left white streaks of mineral salts on flesh which the new adept grudgingly acknowledged to be almost free of pain, the apprentices laved her with moist hands lathered with fragrant soap, before sponging her down with warm fresh water, and toweling her dry.

Standing in their midst, her tingling skin pink from the massage, the object of their ministrations noticed what she had failed to see earlier. Accompanied by Julian, Matsuo stood with arms folded, observing the finale to the bathing ritual. Both masters she saw to be stark naked. Unfazed now by anyone's nudity, she smiled a greeting even as the four youths lifted her, bore her to the mat, and bade her lie prone thereon.

Mercedes noted that Julian proceeded to the baths, where

he immersed himself in the icy water, seemingly with enjoyment.

The compactly built, gray-eyed, sandy-haired apprentice who the beneficiary of the lads' efforts had never heard speak, lifted a stoppered stone jug out of the hot pool. Pulling the cork, he poured quantities of floral-scented, viscous liquid into the cupped palms of his fellows, and then into his own. Four pairs of hands now applied the warm, fragrant, oily liquid to the body upon which the welts had subsided to faint red stripes. With assiduous care, the trainees massaged the lotion into the skin upon which the hot mineral water had acted as an astringent.

Sighs of satisfaction floated out on the ambient air as palms smoothed warm oil onto every square inch of the adept's afflicted flesh. One set of fingers insinuated themselves into the crack of the buttocks, and anointed the tender skin within the cleft. A forefinger slid into the anal opening, and massaged the passage no longer the least bit sore. Other fingers rubbed the well-oiled back, neck, arms, and legs of the woman reveling in the soothing treatment.

At length, the leader bade her turn onto her back. With no less painstaking care, the four attendants now applied warm oil to neck, breasts, rib cage, abdomen, arms, and legs. The blonde youth laved the loins of the woman who spread her thighs without being so directed, his fingers massaging her clit, her pussy-lips, and the tender skin of her inner thighs.

Given that the attendant lingered a bit longer than might be deemed absolutely necessary on the most sensitive areas of her groin, his efforts set the woman's loins quickening. She caught an ephemeral wink at a point in the proceedings when the master evaluating the efficacy of the apprentices' efforts saw only the youth's back. The lad's mobile, vibrant face swiftly regained its gravity, but not before Mercedes impulsively returned his wink, having made sure that his body interposed between her and the overseer.

Absorbed in the delicious sensations provided by the young men, the adept failed to notice that Julian rose from the hot bath, and toweled his body dry, contenting himself with the stimulation provided by only one cycle.

At length, the anointing complete, the four youths sat back on their heels, and bowed to the two observers who now walked forward. "Well done," came the grave commendation from the older man. "Kneel, Mercedes, and kiss your master's cock, to express your appreciation for his having cut short the lingering effects of the ritual."

Kneeling on the mat, the adept indeed free of pain took her lover's stiff prick in warm, moist mouth. Unfazed by the witnesses, she proceeded to demonstrate her skill at offering that exquisite pleasure. When at length Julian bade her rise, she again caught in her peripheral vision the sight of four grotesquely enlarged, fabric-sheathed, stiffly erect male members. Matsuo she perceived to be as hard as her master: a reaction that seemed to her perfectly natural, in this dream-dimension of the reality she normally inhabited.

The wiry masseur now directed, "Bear her into the other chamber, Julian, and I'll complete her treatment."

Lifted in the arms of her master, Mercedes nestled against him, savoring the fragrant aroma enveloping them both. Matsuo preceded them; the four youths brought up the rear. When Julian laid his burden on a padded, segmented table identical to that in the chamber adjoining their bedroom, the apprentices ranged themselves along both sides, being allowed, evidently, to observe their mentor's mastery of his ancient art.

Placed prone, flat on her stomach, but with her legs spread, and her arms stretched out beyond the head turned so as to press a cheek against the slick surface on which she lay, Mercedes beheld the small man position himself to one side of her supine body. His seamed brown face purposeful, he began to massage the flesh still marked by faint red wheals. Strong fingers probed, prodded, and vibrated, setting the nerve-endings below the skin tingling.

No square inch of skin escaped that intense, expert kneading. Stiff fingers stabbed nerve centers, producing instant relaxation amounting to paralysis in the surrounding musculature. Pain momentarily flared into being as the masseur relentlessly kneaded stripes no longer swollen. That pain swiftly abated, as the magically knowing fingers limbered the afflicted skin, and massaged the affected sites, banishing the ephemeral, spectral sensation. Back, buttocks, arms, thighs, calves, even the bare feet, came in their turn beneath those tireless, iron hands.

Sighs of pure pleasure escaped the woman relaxed now to the point of seeming boneless. When the youths, obeying a silent gesture of their mentor, turned her limp body so that she lay supine, they lifted dead weight. Green eyes, half-lidded, unfocused, widened only fleetingly as the attendants settled their charge so that she lay with her arms thrown back, and her legs spread wide.

To her delight, miraculously non-fatigued fingers repeated the massage on her entire front: neck, chest, breasts, rib cage, abdomen, arms, legs. Soft expulsions of breath reached the ears of the silent viewers absorbed in watching the exercise of premier skill.

In conclusion, Matsuo slid two fingers deep into the feminine orifice of the woman conscious of feeling no pain whatsoever in the stripes rapidly fading. The questing fingers targeting exquisitely sensitive sites relentlessly stimulated those areas. The fingers of the masseur's other hand now caressed the clit swollen with need. "She needs what you'll give her," the old man observed to the younger peer whose tool he saw to be rigidly erect, as was his own. "Complete her cure, lad."

Shaking his head, Julian instead slid an arm beneath Mercedes' back. As both of his hands cupped her breasts, he urged, "Make yourself free of her lovely loins, old friend. She owes you that pleasure—as do I."

Nodding, the aged master thus compellingly adjured raked the supine feminine figure with eyes filled at this juncture with hot desire. Standing between the woman's outthrust thighs, he drove his hard member into her lavishly lubricated depth, provoking a moan of pleasure. As the beneficiary of his superb skill at massage arched to meet him, he thrust again, and again, even as his fingers manipulated the small organ engorged to its fullest.

When Matsuo divined that his partner's climax neared, he slid both hands beneath her buttocks, lifting her so as to change the angle of penetration. Rising with supreme ease to a shuddering climax, unaware that she cried out, Mercedes achieved culmination simultaneously with the oldest member of the Order.

When his peer stood back, patently triumphant, the man who so imperiously offered the gift waited while the blonde apprentice strode forward to bathe the loins of the woman lying slackly upon the padded surface.

When the youth withdrew to stand once again in front of his fellow apprentices, Julian lifted his cherished companion, and smiled in open admiration at the aged but still virile master who cocked his head, and observed sagely, "Your lady will rise to an even greater height of bliss as she pleasures her master, Julian. She skims from peak to peak with effortless ease; I've no doubt whatsoever. Take her to the water-garden, and prove me right."

"I know you to be right, Matsuo."

Borne in strong arms through a door opposite the entry, Mercedes gazed in delight at the circular chamber roofed by a concave shield of burnished, silvery metal supported on four slender stone pillars. The walls, except for the small portion of the circular perimeter forming the stone-walled entry, she saw to be formed of a continuous sheet of water cascading off the roof: a shimmering veil of rainbow-shot liquid, undifferentiated into droplets. That sheer fall of water descended into a pool bordering the circular space featuring a stone-flagged floor. On that surface rested some dozen stone urns containing plantings of flowering vines, colorful blooms, and dark evergreen shrubs.

In the center of the space stood a couch upholstered in creamy leather. Opposite that, a matching hassock reposed on the flagging, flanked by a plump cushion, and a round table on which the admiring adept beheld a bottle, glasses, and a bowl of fruit.

Soothed by the white noise generated by the continual fall of water, charmed by the accents of vivid color impinging on her fevered vision, awash in the ebb-tide of sensual pleasure, Mercedes again gained the sense of existing in an exotic, supremely hedonistic version of her normal reality.

When Julian laid her on the couch, reclined next to her, and bade her pleasure him, the new adept reacted with wanton abandon. Kneeling astride his supine body, she kissed his throat, his chest, his nipples. Sliding downwards, she tongued his navel, and took his prick in her mouth. Having rendered him rigid, she mounted him. Kneeling erect, facing him, impaled by his cock, she worked her loins on his upraised member until his groans advised her that her efforts lifted him to rapture.

Dropping to lie prone with her legs between his, she thrust

against him with her pelvis while madly squeezing the organ invading her inner space. Her pendulous breasts massaged his chest as she murmured her intent to milk him of the essence of his passion. When the contractions within her became spontaneous, uncontrolled, her lover ejected a voluminous stream of juice into the feminine depth of the partner whose shuddering torso and rapt face told him that she achieved culmination moments after he did.

Lying spent, awash in euphoria, Julian stroked his beloved's back, content but for a single nagging dissatisfaction. Sternly reminding his alter ego of the need to accept that necessity gracefully, he sighed inaudibly, and resolutely reviewed his gains. Conceding those to be vastly greater than he dared to anticipate in his most optimistic projections, he fastened his mouth over that of his beloved, and kissed her with passionate fervor.

When at long last he rose, and bade his companion sit on the cushion while he poured her wine, Mercedes gratefully savored her pain-free state. Sipping sparkling rosé wine from a blown-glass goblet, she smiled at the lover whose thigh she caressed with her free hand. "I feel reborn," she acknowledged, her vibrant face alight with joy, and health, and the exhilaration deriving from carnal pleasure.

"Mmmm. I'll wager, so does Matsuo," came the amused, bantering reply. "That offer I made as a gift to him, my love, not to you—but you didn't suffer by it."

A rippling laugh fell on the man's ears like silver bells. "No," came the frank admission. "But those poor apprentices suffer daily, evidently."

"While their self-mastery strengthens, and their knowledge grows apace."

Resolved to voice a concern which rose to trouble her peace, Mercedes asked guardedly, "Julian . . . when you take me for your consort . . . will I face some new rite about which I know nothing, as yet?"

Impaled by tawny eyes gone dark with desire, Mercedes yet heard her lover affirm, "No. I'll merely make you the vow in the presence of my peers, after the supper-hour."

"I see. Odd, I find that. I rather expected that so definitive a moment ought to be rendered memorable by some ritual for which I might well need to prepare my mind to accept with serene grace."

"Normally, that moment would be rendered singularly memorable, but I can't conduct the rite which ought to follow my promise to engage in sexual intercourse with no woman other than yourself, for so long as you live. I passed you my word never to cause you bodily harm, Mercedes. And when I give my word, I keep it."

The green eyes widened in manifest astonishment. "The rite . . . entails *injury*?" she gasped, shocked to her core.

A sigh, audible this time, slid from between her lover's slash of a mouth. "Mercedes, when a master makes a consort that promise, by ancient custom he imprints the indelible mark of his favor on her nude body. In the presence of at least one peer serving as witness—or two peers, if he conducts the rite here—he immobilizes her on the black flower.

"He then heats in a flame the silver pin wrought in the design signifying the crest of his House. He presses the red-hot metal against her mound, searing her flesh deeply enough that the imprint becomes permanent. The mark's small, and the lines delicate, but the scar remains noticeable, given that the hair never again grows on the heat-scored skin. She carries that imprint to her grave."

Enlightenment struck, as to the origin of Francesca's scar. "You *brand* the consort to whom you make that promise!" the ranchwoman exclaimed as shivers ran down her spine.

"Exactly. The custom's ancient, my love. The pain's excruciating for a short span of seconds, but grows bearable quickly. The master inflicts no other pain before or after the ceremony, and the ritual confers on the consort the right to wear the ornament fashioned in the likeness signifying the Order. As I told you, a woman who wears the ruby pin the five-petaled flower, we honor above any other."

Used to assisting at brandings of calves, Mercedes felt none of the shuddering horror that the description of the rite would otherwise have evoked. Well aware that the practice universal in her rural society seemed more cruel to urban beholders than it actually was, she yet shivered again as she pictured in her vivid imagination the ritual described by the master seeming so unalterably resolved to forego the privilege of conducting it.

Even as those quivers assailed her, she grew conscious of disappointment that this lover who freely offered her that word, so as to insure her willingness to submit to him, now suffered an obviously galling consequence of his action.

"Surely, if you gave that word to me privately, I could release you from it . . . isn't that so?" she ventured, two creases furrowing her brow.

"No, my love," came the adamant reply. "A man's word has to be inviolable. If he made exceptions, his self-mastery would suffer. He'd grow more susceptible to the temptation to seek, and find, far less valid excuses during future, similar dilemmas. Never, at any point, at any time, will I inflict significant injury: cause any hurt that breaks the skin, leaves a scar, produces severe bruising, or causes any other long-lasting aftereffects."

Disappointment contended with admiration on the piquant face of the adept.

"Now, let's not dwell on what won't happen, but on what

will. It's customary, but not required, for a master who makes his consort the vow I'll make you, to announce that he'll never, while he lives, share her with any peer, ever again. I don't intend to make that stipulation.

"Sharing you on rare occasions with masters like Manuel or Nikos—or even our venerable Matsuo—will constitute a gift I'll give you, from time to time: a gift I feel you deserve, for submitting to me willingly, and entering so freely and completely into the spirit of our culture. You set no limits, Mercedes. I honor the courage and value the affection prompting that decision on your part."

That pronouncement provoked a radiant if bemused smile. "I'm honored by the trust you place in me," came the sincere response. "I must confess that I'm developing into a most uninhibited hedonist. But Julian . . . I wish I could give you what your sense of honor forbids you to take."

"So do I, my love. But you can't."

Hearing finality in the voice of the man so staunchly true to his word, Mercedes sighed in her turn, conscious that as on the prior day, Julian's refusal to levy a harsh demand without—or in this instance, even with—her consent, rendered her perversely wishful that she could freely accede to participating in the rite. Wondering at herself, she set her glass on the table, and stood up.

When he rose to face her, she congealed against him, her arms enfolding his torso. "I belong to you," she declared with adamant force. "Now, and for all time. Rite or no rite."

Fierce elation gripped the man crushing this woman he loved as he had loved no other, against his heaving chest. That tumultuous emotion continued to grip him during the interval when he and his soon-to-be-consort sipped wine, and enjoyed a light repast of sun-ripened fruit. The feeling persisted during the ensuing span of time, when they again made love on the couch, and lay entwined, whispering endearments each to the other.

Roused at last from the lethargy induced by sensual satiation, Julian decreed that they take a brisk walk through the park. Having dressed in the archway vacant now but for their own selves, the lovers emerged into the bright sunlight of mid-afternoon, and proceeded at a swinging stride down a narrow, winding path.

As they walked hand in hand, the woman musingly reflecting upon Julian's dilemma again felt that perverse, unaccountable sense of having been cheated of the right to give him what he obviously desired. Free now of the fog of euphoria that had enveloped her for most of the day, she pondered the problem.

An idea lanced out of the blue, to anchor itself firmly in her interior vision. The more she considered the concept, the more logical it seemed to her, although she reminded herself scathingly that she constituted no expert judge of what ideas these autocrats might deem acceptable, coming from a woman.

Shrugging, she strove to banish the notion, but the harder she tried to drive it out, the more tenaciously it clung. Abandoning the attempt, she let it shimmer on the fringe of her awareness throughout the remainder of the afternoon. She focused the bulk of her attention on enjoying the company of the man who in his own mind, she knew, considered this span of golden hours his wedding day.

Chapter Thirteen

At the end of the dinner-hour, Julian rose from his seat, and strode to a point at the center of the dining area, his cherished companion on his arm. Lorenzo took up a position facing the couple; Manuel and Alexander, Julian's fellow council members, flanked the Grand Master. The hum of conversation ceased, as Julian's melodic, incisive voice, pitched to carry, floated out over the assemblage.

"In the presence of these formal witnesses, Lorenzo, Manuel and Alexander, and in the company of the informal witnesses gathered here today, I take Mercedes to be my consort-for-life. I swear on the honor of my House never to engage in sexual intercourse with any woman but my beloved consort, for so long as she lives."

Lorenzo waited for an all but imperceptible span of time for the qualifier that by custom followed such a declaration. When he divined that it would not be forthcoming, he intoned gravely, "I, Lorenzo, Grand Master of the Order of the Black Lily, do formally state that this oath shall be recorded in the annals of the Order. I welcome Mercedes into the fellowship of women enjoying high honor in the perception of all of our members: those attending this gathering, and those who are with us only in spirit."

His piercing eyes, limpid as a pristine glacial lake, rested on the woman flushed with pride, and radiant with joy. Shifting his glance to her proud, eminently pleased master, he commanded, "Julian, confer the kiss of possession on your consort-for-life."

Swept into strong arms, Mercedes melted against the man whose mouth closed over hers in an intimate, erotic salute. When at length he freed her lips, and again faced the Grand Master, his arm encircled her. His striking face serene, he awaited the question he had steeled himself to answer in the negative.

"Will you, at this time, conduct the rite which solemnizes your vow?"

"No. Not now, or ever. I waive my right to imprint the indelible mark of my favor on the body of my consort."

The soft, hushed murmur that rippled through the assemblage as that unexpected response registered on their understanding died away to a breathless silence. Lorenzo's eyes seemed to Julian to read his naked soul, but the younger man bore that intense scrutiny with serene calm. When that compelling glance rested on Mercedes, the Grand Master perceived the conflict in the eyes green as emeralds. As he sought to read the nonverbal cues she unconsciously displayed, she spoke, startling the formal witnesses.

"Lorenzo, may I respectfully submit a request to the Grand Master, regarding my beloved master's irrevocable decision to waive his right?"

"You may," came the measured reply, which seemed to the hearers unhesitating.

Having launched on her course, Mercedes mustered all the force of her personality, all her admirable inability to be intimidated by any personage, no matter how imposing. "Early in our relationship, Julian freely and voluntarily gave me his word that he would refrain from inflicting any injury on me severe enough to break the skin, or cause permanent scarring. In that respect, he harbors the same private, personal scruples held by his brother Michael.

"Earlier today, wishful that my master might not be denied the right of conforming to ancient custom, I offered to release him from that word, but I discovered that I possess no power to do so. I therefore appeal to you to conduct the rite yourself, as Grand Master of the Order—that you imprint the indelible mark of Julian's favor on my body with your own hand. Since, as I see it, the rite would take place by your authority, rather than his, no stain would fall on his honor."

The shock nakedly visible on the striking face for once stripped of any guard, apprised Lorenzo that this wholly unorthodox appeal took Julian completely by surprise. Raking the oval face of the woman whose plea so shrewdly avoided giving any intimation that she sought to contravene the will of her master, or obtain a dispensation from ancient custom which would spare her pain, he divined her appeal to be genuine rather than a theatrical gesture made by an exhibitionist secure in the knowledge that the plea could not, or would not, be granted.

Frowning, he turned the full force of his compelling persona on the master struggling to compose his face. "When you passed your word, did you not foresee that this dilemma might well arise?"

"I did. But I counted the benefit which accrued to me at that time well worth the sacrifice I'd be forced to make at some future point."

Exquisitely aware of the deeper meaning underlying that statement which the members hanging on every speaker's words found enigmatic, Lorenzo weighed the appeal for a few seconds that stretched in the mind of the applicant like a millennium.

When at length he spoke, his resonant voice sent quivers coursing down nerves strung tautly as guitar-strings. "Whatever decision I render will set a precedent. Matters purely procedural lie in the province of the Council, but since Julian must abstain from acting with regard to a matter involving his personal life, and custom demands a two-thirds majority affirmative vote, I'll break a tie, should one occur.

"So. A master possesses the fundamental right to forbid any member, even the Grand Master, to inflict pain upon, or otherwise use, the body of his consort, without his consent. Julian, do you wish your consort to bear on her body the indelible mark of your favor?"

"Yes," came the hoarsely uttered but manifestly impassioned reply.

"Members of the Council: shall the Grand Master henceforth possess the power to conduct this ancient rite at the request of the consort of a master who desires the outcome, but is prevented by a prior vow from conducting the rite with his own hand? Alexander."

After a brief pause for deliberation, amid a silence so profound that individual breaths seemed to echo off the walls, Alexander replied firmly, "Yes."

"Manuel."

No hesitation attended the vigorous response given by the professional soldier. "Yes."

A soft sigh rippled through the company. Lorenzo turned a reflective glance on the vibrant face of the woman whose relief he saw to be absolutely genuine. Admiration suffused him: emotion he took no pains to conceal. "I honor your devotion to the master who trusts you to the hilt, Mercedes. Your daring equals his," he commended her softly, his words carrying only to the three Council members.

"I thank you," came the reply couched in a husky whisper.

Again projecting his voice so that it carried to the fringe of the assemblage, Lorenzo issued brisk commands. "Alexander and Manuel: you'll act as formal witnesses to the rite. Julian will take no part in the proceedings until after the imprint is made. Manuel, you'll bear your peer's consort to the flower-chamber.

"Francesca, you'll escort Irene and Celeste to the side chambers, where they'll serve their masters' pleasure at the conclusion of the rite. You'll await me in the Grand Master's chamber. So. Let us proceed without delay to implement the unanimous decision of the Council."

Lifted in the brawny arms of the man whose admiration for her courage he took no trouble to conceal, Mercedes lay limply in his embrace, her mind churning with a blend of tumultuous emotions. Relief dominated. Dread of the agony she knew to be imminent inevitably assailed her, but it paled before the exaltation gripping her. The long, languorous hours filled with sensual pleasure lacking the enhancement which moderate pain provided—a span of time during which her autocratic master drove home to her the intensity of the love he bore her—generated a fevered desire to give him what his fidelity to his word prevented his taking.

Julian's imagery of two nights back rose vividly to mind. Viewing the agony about to assail her as a sacrifice designed to please a powerful entity—a sacrifice offered by herself in the role of supplicant—she accepted that role as consonant with Julian's vowing to cleave to her alone for so long as she might live, while refraining from denying her the pleasure which his sharing her on rare occasions with a peer engendered.

Shame smote the adept as she recalled fighting her bonds, and succumbing to blind anger after making the last offering of this nature. No limits! she reminded herself. You promised.

This time, you'll bear the pain without flinching, however ghastly it might turn out to be, for the few seconds while the glowing metal sears your flesh. The aftermath you know will merely consist of soreness that passes after a day or so. This ordeal doesn't compare in severity to that which raised you to the rank of adept!

Fear nonetheless fogged her mind as Manuel, striding down the dimly lit corridor in Lorenzo's wake, bore her into the chamber dominated by the brooding presence of the huge, five-petaled flower. Fiercely, she battled the fear, and swiftly dominated it. When Manuel set her on her feet, she stood erect, her head high.

"Bare her body," came the imperious command, when Alexander took his place on Manuel's right, and Julian on his left.

Two corded arms encircled her torso; a bear-like hand pulled the ruby pin from the circular ring, and caught both halves of the golden ornament. The gown fell to the flags, encircling her ankles like soft, flat-black restraints.

In response to the Grand Master's next order, Manuel lifted her nude person, and disposed her as she had lain on the prior occasion: her head on the center of three petals, her arms laid back along the other two forming the cluster of three, and her legs spread wide apart, along the remaining two petals.

Knowing what to expect, Mercedes sought to relax as the two witnesses attached the padded fetters to her wrists and ankles, pulled the elastic tethers over the lips of the petals, and fastened them to the second of two pairs of rings affixed to the lower surface. Stretched even more tautly at this juncture than on the prior occasion, she grew exquisitely conscious of her total inability to writhe, much less to struggle.

That realization, far from terrifying her, served to calm her.

I can't resist, she acknowledged in relief. Can't fight Lorenzo. Can't disgrace myself. Her cognizance of lying utterly helpless, utterly vulnerable, spread to the view of four cruel, autocratic masters, uncannily aroused her. I exist for my beloved's pleasure, she adjured her alter self. I belong to him, but not so exclusively—not so completely—as he now belongs to me!

While those thoughts raced with the speed of light through the mind of the woman immobilized upon the black sculpture, the four men stripped, and laid their garments on the bench. Lorenzo took his proper place: stood at the gap between her legs. Alexander flanked him, bearing a tray upon which lay Julian's pin, a pair of tongs, a black cylinder pointed on one end, a friction-lighter, and a strange implement the purpose of which the woman failed to fathom. Julian stood in the gap between his consort's left leg and left arm.

Manuel took up a position in the narrow space between the woman's head and right arm. Lifting her head, he thrust beneath it a wedge-shaped block contoured to fit the curves of head and neck.

Finding her head not only immobilized, but thrust forward until her chin all but touched her chest, Mercedes heard him inform her equably, "Custom requires that you watch the glowing metal imprint the mark of your master's favor." His eyes, dark with lust, belied the lack of passion implied by the tone of his voice. At a touch of his finger on a remote, the flower tilted forward at an angle of some twenty degrees, bringing the loins of the woman stretched thereon well within the reach of the Grand Master's hands.

Having set the tray on a small table, Alexander lifted the black cylinder, and pressed a control. A hissing noise assaulted the ears of the consort denied the opportunity to look away. A spark from the friction-device caused a blue flame to flare at the narrow end of the torch the witness held upright:

a flame distinguished by an inner blue cone.

His face grave, his manner regal, Lorenzo employed the tongs to grip the silver pin by its fastening. Thrusting the pin into the flame, he took care to hold it just above the inner cone. Practiced at the task that faced him, he waited until the delicate tracery grew incandescent. Raising the implement out of the fire, he advanced full in the sight of the woman unable to tear her eyes from the glowing metal drawing ever nearer to the targeted site. Deftly, unhesitatingly, the Grand Master pressed the red-hot tracery against the flesh of her mound, and held it there.

Excruciating pain assaulted the senses of the woman whose breath rattled in her throat, but no scream, no moan, no cry of any sort passed her lips. Thick gray smoke curled up around the red-hot pin. The smell of burning hair assaulted the nostrils of victim and witnesses.

Those effects scarcely registered on the mind of the sensualist absorbed in the contemplation of the agony she viewed as a metaphor for her voluntary submission to the will of the man whose crest at this juncture burned into her flesh. In a moment of voluntary surrender so absolute as to eclipse any prior experience of that nature, Mercedes welcomed the torment that became, for ten endless seconds, her universe. Her loins loosened; her bowels melted. Heat suffused her thighs; moisture gushed into the cunt experiencing a rush of pleasure akin to that produced by a satisfying climax.

The Grand Master withdrew the still-glowing implement. Reaching out, he swept the palm of his hand firmly across the burned area so as to brush away the hair no longer joined to the seared flesh. The observers now beheld the pearly gray scar framed in ruddy, undamaged hair. Riveting their eyes to the imprint, the two formal witnesses judged their leader's skill at conducting the rite to be flawless.

His eyes fixed not on the scar, but on the consort's swollen clit, Lorenzo observed the trickle of moisture dribbling from the pussy-lips that he spread with two fingers. Shock melted into profound admiration as he unerringly interpreted the evidence. The woman's face he saw to be rapt, exalted.

"No need exists for you to arouse your consort by employing the traditional method," the Grand Master informed the man staring in disbelief at the same incontrovertible proofs. "Your lady lies near to fulfillment—aroused solely by her unqualified acceptance of the pain. Impregnate her, Julian. Her surrender at this moment you can see to be absolute."

Roused to raw lust by witnessing the rite, Julian at this juncture divined with lucid clarity that his beloved consort just experienced excruciating agony as a conscious act of total submission to his will. That certainty lifted him to an exaltation matching hers. Advancing to stand between her outthrust thighs, he drove his turgid organ into her feminine depth, consumed with a rabid desire to master her, to dominate her, but most of all, to lift her to transcendental ecstasy. Thrusting forcefully, rhythmically, he willed her to rise to a plane of cosmic union unprecedented in either his or her experience.

To the woman stretched immobile on the five-petaled flower, Lorenzo's words seemed to drift in from afar to impinge only marginally on her self-absorption. When the glowing metal rose off her seared flesh, she grew dimly conscious of the lessening of the pain. A momentary, perverse regret arising from that cognizance transmuted almost instantly into a fierce desire to be possessed by the man to whom she surrendered her will. When he drove into her, it seemed as if her entire prior life served merely as a prelude to this precious moment of transcendental union with a masterful lover whose engorged cock she perceived as completing her.

Rapture now elicited the moans which agony failed to force from her throat. Lifted to a plane of ecstasy unparalleled in her experience, Mercedes achieved a culmination that stretched surreally into endlessness. Passing into trance, she existed in an altered state in which severe pain blended seamlessly with the greatest pleasure ever to etch itself into her awareness.

Julian's climax matched hers in its intensity, its uniqueness, and its ability to drive him into full coital trance. His groans masked the cries of his beloved as he ejected the voluminous stream of his juice. He stood for a few seconds, erect, still, experiencing mental fulfillment that conferred exquisite satisfaction.

When at last he withdrew his tool, dimly aware that he must, he staggered, and all but fell. Manuel gripped one arm, Lorenzo the other. Together, they supported him, as Alexander obeyed an urgent command that he open the door to the Grand Master's Chamber. The two men half carried, half guided Julian to the oversized couch forming the central feature of this adjunct of the main hall housing the flower.

Francesca, lying stark naked on the furnishing, awaiting the advent of the conductor of the rite, whose passion she intended to satisfy, leaped to her feet in astonishment.

"Stand back, my love," Lorenzo directed, over his shoulder. Addressing Manuel, he instructed, "Lower him onto the couch. So. Now fetch his courageous lady, old friend, and lay her in his arms."

While Manuel and Alexander loosed the bonds, and conveyed the entranced consort of her equally entranced master to the chamber normally reserved for the use of the Grand Master, Lorenzo slipped his arm around the willowy woman who now divined what had transpired. Her arm encircled him as the two witnesses laid the slack form of the new consort-for-life in the arms of her master.

"Alexander—Manuel—retire to your respective chambers, and enjoy the ministrations of your partners," their leader directed.

The witnesses exchanged concerned glances. "Lorenzo, I can retire to my bedchamber," Manuel protested, reluctant to usurp a prerogative of the head of the Order.

"Do as I command, my friends," came the adjuration couched in a tone that admitted of no argument.

When the two men bowed in unison, exactly as if they were still apprentices, the Grand Master serenely accepted their homage. When each vanished through a side door that he closed behind him, Lorenzo soundlessly shut that leading to the chamber in which the rapt pair lay entwined on the couch. Smiling down at his consort, he observed musingly, "Julian came late in life to the ecstasy he enjoys at this moment. I thank whatever ineffable entities rule our destinies, that I found you in my youth, and recognized your potential to become the peerless partner I've loved so deeply all these years."

"As do I," came the breathless reply. "Lorenzo . . . lift me onto the flower, and take me as you did so long ago."

Sweeping his aged consort-for-life into arms not appreciably less strong than they were forty years earlier, the Grand Master laid Francesca on the sculpture, and fastened the restraints. Tilting the flower to the proper angle, he took his time lifting his beloved to a height of rapture all but matching that of the woman clasped in the strong arms of a man twenty years younger than himself.

Julian came back to reality slowly, and most reluctantly. Conscious only of the pressure of a slack, nude body pressing on his, he enfolded it in his arms without opening his eyes. The faint, pungent scent of semen mingled with the fainter, far more elusive fragrance emanating from the loins of his partner. That subtle aroma, which he unconsciously equated with her essential femininity, teased olfactory nerves never dulled by indulgence in tobacco.

Contentment suffused him. Unaware of just where he lay, he dismissed the question as irrelevant. What mattered was that he possessed this woman for whom his heart hungered to the fullest extent possible to a master of erotic art. Marveling at her reaction to the agony of the imprinting, he savored his memory of her voluntary offer.

Ignoring his surroundings, he dwelled in wonder on the irony he only now perceived. Had I let Mercedes persuade me that she possessed the power to release me from my word—had I conducted the rite with my own hand—she'd never have surrendered her will so absolutely as she did when she conceived her pain to be an offering freely made to a man in whom she now knows she can place perfect trust. What a treasure she is! How did I live so long without her?

Grown dimly aware of hands stroking her back, Mercedes stirred, confused as to what followed the agony she recalled as a spur to ecstasy, not as a horrifying ordeal. The pain throbbing in her mound contended with the warmth and the touch of her lover's hands, for prominence in her awareness. Those pleasurable sensations superseded the lingering hurt, and soothed her into lassitude.

Lips brushed her cheek; moist breath flowed along skin reveling in the sensation. "You're mine now, little sensualist," came the seductively melodic assurance. "Lover, partner, consort-for-life. I love you, Mercedes. I always will."

"I love you, Julian. More than I ever dreamed I could love any cruel, demanding master."

An amused laugh floated by the ear hidden by tousled auburn hair. "You crave the pain that loosens your loins, my submissive love-slave. You've grown to regard excruciating agony as a premier exercise in foreplay."

"I did tonight," came the bemused reply. "But I strongly doubt that I could bear that degree of torment on a daily basis!"

Arms tightened around her. "No master would ask that of you more than once, little hedonist. Not myself, certainly. You needn't fear that I'll grow obsessed with the heady delight of inflicting pain on you. I'll remain in perfect control of my urges, never doubt."

"I trust you, Julian. Fully."

That's the key to this woman's heart, the man crushing her to his chest exulted. She gave me all any consort ever offered a master, and did so without any need on my part to condition her . . . to break her will. She voluntarily submits, because I won her trust. Happiness so great that it bordered pain surged through him.

Only after twenty minutes spent savoring that happiness fled into oblivion did Julian grow cognizant of where he was, and how he got there. Recalling only dimly being half-carried here, he realized that Lorenzo had given up his prerogative to the man who by rights ought to have borne his satiated consort to his bedchamber. Admiration mingled with gratitude as he reflected upon the Grand Master's forbearance.

Did Lorenzo know with certainty how my unorthodox venture would end? Julian asked himself in wry amazement. He's perceptive to a degree bordering on the supernatural. Perhaps he did. Or if he didn't, perhaps he merely hoped it would end like this, and did what he could to help the process along.

What irony, this development. My bond with Mercedes rests on a premise that the cumulative wisdom of the ancient masters rejects. Ancient teaching holds that a woman can't voluntarily offer herself as a slave/consort to a demanding master without being expertly and relentlessly conditioned to surrender her will to his. Is my beloved the exception that proves the rule, or is the rule flawed? I'll be damned if I know. She's unique, and she's mine. I guess that's all I need to know.

Rousing himself from the torpor presaging a swift descent into sleep, Julian reluctantly rose. Lifting his partner in strong arms, he bore her to the flower-chamber, which proved to be vacant, and set her on her feet.

Sweeping up his folded garments and hers from the bench, he thrust them into her arms. "Hold these," he bade her. Lifting her, he bore her nude body into the corridor, and strode, himself stark naked, up the stair and down the hall leading to his bedchamber. Given the hour, he encountered no one—not that he cared one whit whether he did. Having deposited his burden in the bed, and relieved her of the bundle, he shut the door. Collapsing beside her, he fell almost instantly asleep.

Awaking early, Julian stretched like a sun-warmed tiger before rousing his consort with an intimate, erotic kiss. Having demonstrated possessiveness, he bade her shower and dress while he shaved at the sink in the alcove. When she emerged, he inspected the scar, noting that it seemed to be healing without any complication.

Used to the sight of fresh brands, Mercedes expected none. The pain she found to be significant, but bearable.

Strolling into the dining area on the arm of her master, her gown fastened with the ruby pin in the five-petaled flower, the newest consort-for-life graciously responded to a myriad expressions of respect from the peers of the man taking no pains to conceal fierce pride. Lorenzo kissed her hand, his admiration evident to the beholders. Manuel did likewise, followed by Jason, Nikos, and Alexander.

As Shirley gave her a hearty hug, she whispered softly, "You'll never be lonely while Julian lives, Mercedes. I'm so glad for you!"

Seated in the midst of Julian's closest friends among his peers, Mercedes savored the sensation of belonging: of being an integral part of this strange but fascinating society. Aware that this meal would be her final one here, she enjoyed every minute of the conversation in which she took a spirited part. When her master rose to leave, she noted that he leaned down, and murmured an invitation to Manuel, who was still seated, to join him in his bedchamber.

Five minutes later, Julian, smiling the wicked smile, presented to his closest friend the case containing his brother's inventions. "I'm making you a gift of this set," he informed the mercenary soldier. "I know . . . you favor the older methods. But at some juncture, you might find these the key to unlocking the heart of a treasure you've yet to meet. They served that purpose for me, and I wouldn't be surprised but what they might for you. But whether or not you believe that, take them as a mark of my high regard."

Touched by the unexpected gesture, Manuel gripped the hand of his most valued friend. On the prior evening, enlightenment had struck him with instantaneous, blinding force, as to the meaning hidden beneath the enigmatic verbal exchange between Julian and Lorenzo. The reason for Julian's passing his word, and thereby necessitating Mercedes' request, grew exquisitely clear as he weighed the implications in the statements, and then observed her reaction to the imprinting.

Stunned by his cognizance that she had voluntarily submitted to the most rigorous rites in use among his peers without having been conditioned to surrender her will to her master, he marveled that Julian had trusted her enough to bring her to this place. As he contemplated his friend's success, he felt the fundament of his universe crack, until he reflected that this lovely sensualist impervious to the masculine appeal of any man but her master had to be totally unique in the experience of any member of the Order, even Lorenzo.

"I'll not lose hope, old friend," he assured his peer. "But I'll not hold my breath until a treasure drops into my lap, either. Mercedes, I honor your courage above that of any woman I've ever encountered. I'm leaving in ten minutes, given that I'm accepting a new assignment two days hence, but I'll drop by at some point in time—pay you both a visit."

"Do that, Manuel." Julian embraced his oldest friend. Sensible of having gained a high place in this bluff soldier's esteem, Mercedes impulsively hugged him. Warmed by both gestures, Manuel took his departure, and proceeded straight to the heliport.

When he left, Mercedes asked in puzzlement, "Isn't he taking Celeste with him?"

That query produced a chuckle. "No. He obligingly passed her on to Nikos, who developed a profound respect for her skill on the night you rose to the rank of adept. Celeste welcomed the opportunity to change clients with no profitless interval occurring. Nikos now knows with exquisite certainty that you won't be calling his number, my love."

A rippling laugh greeted that sally.

Borne homewards through a sky presaging storms to come, dressed in the conventional clothing she indeed found annoyingly confining, Mercedes marveled at the momentous changes wrought in her life in the span of a week. The pain of the imprint blended with the ebullient joy suffusing her, reminding her that she now belonged for life to a most demanding master. Frowning, she sought to assess whether the dark arts he practiced might pall, after a time, but she swiftly decided in the negative.

The very act of reflecting on those propensities set her loins quivering, and her pulse-rate quickening. In a burst of self-knowledge, she admitted that just as she had once assured him, she felt liberated, not confined, while existing in a universe defined by the circle of his arms. A vivid smile that seemed to her companion to take ten years off her age replaced the pensive expression that had persisted for five minutes. That expression mirrored the joy arising from the thought of adjusting to a life now forever imperviously fortified against the twin menaces which she had battled ever since her bereavement: loneliness and boredom.

Stealing a glance at her vibrantly alive, appealingly open face, Julian felt a fleeting surge of envy evaporate into the ether: envy sparked when Manuel's return to action served to remind him of the drawbacks inherent in his own withdrawal from life on the edge. Contentment expanded into the vacuum left by the departure of that momentary jealousy. Happiness enveloped him as he dwelled on the pleasure he intended to take upon arriving home with this woman who made retirement in a remote backwater seem high adventure.

Aboard a helicopter piloted by an employee of his corporation, Manuel lapsed into reverie. Bleakly, he wondered whether he would recognize a treasure if he stumbled over one. The unnerving notion struck him that had he met Mercedes at some innocuous social function at the home of an acquaintance who knew nothing regarding the Order, he might never have dreamed that she could metamorphose into a wanton hedonist who craved the whip and considered agony a spur to passion.

How did Julian guess? he asked himself in bemused wonder. Recalling his old friend's parting gift, he savored the warmth engendered by the gesture. I'll trust to luck, he decided. Keep a wary eye out, and use Michael's inventions.

Modernize in my sensual life, the same as I routinely do in the professional sphere. Having decided on a course, the mercenary soldier relaxed, and stared into the sky as clouded with uncertainty as was his future. As he consciously made that comparison, his rugged face creased into one of his rare but singularly engaging smiles.

ABOUT THE AUTHOR

An admirer of classical erotica, Alexandra Adams most emphatically believes that no social stigma ought to attach to the reading, writing, or publication of well-crafted literary works that celebrate sensual pleasure. Her erotic novels target mature, sophisticated, uninhibited readers who frankly enjoy character-driven narratives featuring explicitly sensual scenes. An author who writes passionately and evocatively of adventurous lovers, she consistently strives to fire the imagination and liberate the sensualist living within each of her readers.